Advance Praise for *Love by the Book*

"HUGELY enjoyable! Great fun, a gripping read, and very touching."
　　　　—*New York Times* bestselling author Marian Keyes

"*Love by the Book* feels like a no-holds-barred girls' night. I found myself laughing out loud at every turn. Melissa Pimentel is a great new voice. She'll go far!"
　　　　—Cara Lockwood, *USA Today*
　　　　　bestselling author of *I Do (But I Don't)*

"Melissa Pimentel's voice is wickedly funny and entirely appealing. Reading *Love by the Book* is like taking a tour of London on the arm of an audacious and hilarious new friend—in other words, a whole lot of fun!"
　　　　—Meg Donohue, *USA Today*
　　　　　bestselling author of *All the Summer Girls*

"Wincingly honest and hilariously perceptive, *Love by the Book* is a fresh, funny, clever take on dating, relating, and finding love."
　　　　—Anna Maxted, bestselling author of
　　　　　Getting Over It and *Running in Heels*

"A fun romantic comedy (or tragedy, depending on the day). If you love *The Mindy Project*, imagine Mindy in London surrounded by British hotties, fabulous friends, and way too much bad dating advice. A wonderful debut by Melissa Pimental. Can't wait to dive into her next novel."
　　　　—Kim Gruenenfelder, author of *A Total Waste of Makeup*

"I loved this book! So smart and sassy but with a great big heart, too. It sends up the whole game of modern romance by applying Harvard Business School techniques, Victorian dating rules, and Flapper ideology to the Tinder age. You'll go through this book as quickly as Lauren "swipes left" on her iPhone. *Love by the Book* will delight anyone who has ever tried looking for love."

—Naomi Wood, author of *Mrs. Hemingway*

"Who hasn't wondered whether if they just hit on the precise formula, they'd find the right man? In *Love by the Book*, Pimentel's protagonist, Lauren, explores this idea full-tilt by adopting an advice-book-of-the-month approach to the problem. I often found myself laughing out loud and quickly turning the pages to find out what that month's dictum would have Lauren doing. A fun, fast-paced read."

—Catherine McKenzie,
    bestselling author of *Hidden* and *Arranged*

"*Love by the Book* hits its humor beats in all the right places, and I love when someone comes up with an idea that prompts me to say 'I wish I had thought of that.' Pimentel's 'experiment' proves that the best book on love is the one you write yourself along the way."

—Elisa Lorello,
    bestselling author of *Faking It* and *She Has Your Eyes*

PENGUIN BOOKS

LOVE BY THE BOOK

Melissa Pimentel grew up in a small town in Massachusetts in a house without cable, and therefore much of her childhood was spent watching 1970s British comedy on public television. At twenty-two, she made the move to London to do an MA in modern literature at University College London. She has lived there happily for ten years, though she still adamantly refuses to eat a Scotch egg. Before meeting her fiancé, she spent her time trawling the London dating scene for clean, nonsociopathic men and blogging about it, which became the inspiration for her first novel. These days, she spends much of her time reading in the various pubs of Stoke Newington and engaging in a long-standing emotional feud with her disgruntled cat, Welles. She works in publishing.

LOVE BY THE BOOK

Melissa Pimentel

PENGUIN BOOKS

PENGUIN BOOKS
Published by the Penguin Group

Penguin Group (USA) LLC
375 Hudson Street
New York, New York 10014

USA | Canada | UK | Ireland | Australia | New Zealand | India | South Africa | China
penguin.com
A Penguin Random House Company

Published simultaneously in Great Britain (under the title *Age, Sex, Location*)
and the United States of America in Penguin Books 2015

LIBRARY OF CONGRESS CATALOGING-IN-PUBLICATION DATA

Pimentel, Melissa.
Love by the book / Melissa Pimentel.
pages cm
ISBN 978-0-14-312728-4
I. Title.
PS3616.148L68 2015
813'.6—dc23   2014032891

Printed in the United States of America
3   5   7   9   10   8   6   4   2

Set in Dante MT Std   •   Designed by Elke Sigal

To Katie and Simon, my two better halves

LOVE BY THE BOOK

March

This project was born, like so many things, from an egg. Two, to be exact.

Adrian walked in just in time to see me crack two eggs on the side of the pan and pour them into the sizzling butter. I leaned into him when he wrapped his arms around me and peered over my shoulder at the stove.

"You making eggs?" he said, voice still gravelly with sleep.

"How did you guess?" I said, turning to give him a quick kiss. "I remembered you saying you liked them, so I thought I'd make them for you." I gave the eggs a quick flip and slid them out of the pan onto the waiting buttered toast.

"You made these for me?" Adrian said, eyes widening.

"Yep," I said, placing the plate on the table before grabbing my bowl of granola and yogurt off the counter. I pulled the yellow terrycloth robe around me and looked at him.

"You're not having any?" he said, looking at his own plate with even more suspicion.

"Nope. I'm not a big egg fan."

"I see. You made these eggs just for me." I watched his pupils dilate out of fear. "Right."

"Christ, they're only eggs. Calm down. Do you want some pepper?"

I could see the wheels turning in his head. Eggs led to Sunday afternoons in antique shops, dinner parties with other couples, meetings with the parents, a marriage proposal, an elaborate wedding, three screaming children, a wife with fat ankles and, eventually, the sweet release of death. In his mind, eggs led to stuff. Scary stuff.

Within minutes of polishing off the plate, the man was up and out like a shot, pulling his shoes on and mumbling something about getting back in time to watch *Football Focus* with his roommate.

I had scared a man with eggs. I'd scared him so badly that he had chosen *Football Focus* over having sex with me. It wasn't looking good for me or for my vagina.

It had all started so promisingly. Last summer, I had moved into my room in Old Street with a heart filled with hope: that this move from Portland to London would be a fresh start for me, that I would wipe clean the traces of a relationship with the strong-jawed, kind-eyed man I'd left behind, that the job I had nabbed as the events coordinator at the Science Museum would lead to even bigger and better things and, possibly most pressingly, that I would have lots of great sex with attractive Englishmen who were as un-interested in commitment as I was.

I'd seen the apartment advertised on Gumtree just before I'd left Maine and had immediately sent through a request. It looked amazing in the pictures—the bedroom was painted a pale yellow and the furniture was all weathered white wood—and according to Google maps, the location was perfect. The woman renting out the room, Lucy, agreed to reserve it for me until I arrived in London the following week after I sent several pleading emails and the promise of a jar of Marshmallow Fluff.

When I arrived at the address, I was a little surprised to find a towering council estate rather than the little Victorian conversion I'd expected, but I took a deep breath and pressed the buzzer, images of the bedroom still dancing in my head. I was furry-mouthed with jet lag and essentially homeless; I couldn't afford to write the apartment off before seeing it.

Lucy met me at the door. "Hello! You must be Lauren. Come

on in, babe." I took in her wide smile, bright blue eyes and head of insane blond curls and felt immediately better about the situation. She led me into the cramped kitchen and put the kettle on.

The kitchen didn't quite match the design standards I'd seen in the photographs. Lucy had obviously made the best of things, filling the countertop with pots of fresh herbs and a bright pink set of scales, but the oven door was hanging at a precarious angle and there was a large hole gouged into the MDF floor. It wasn't exactly *Martha Stewart Living*.

Lucy flicked on the kettle. "Coffee?"

I nodded.

"How do you take yours?"

"Just black would be great, thanks."

"I don't know how you can drink it like that. I need about eight sugars and three pints of milk in mine. Especially today: I have such a hangover. Anyway, I'm glad you're here and seem normal—the last girl who lived here was a born-again Christian and didn't drink. Can you imagine? After the third time she tipped my bottle of rum down the sink, I said, good luck to you, love, but you're not staying here."

She handed me a mug and I took a sip.

"Let me show you the rest of the place." Lucy led me on a short but thorough tour of the apartment. "This is the lounge"—an enormous brown faux-leather couch marooned in the middle of four blood-red walls—"and there's a balcony, too"—a concrete slab slapped onto the side of the tower block with a strip of barbed wire running along the top—"here's the bathroom"—a microbe's paradise with one of those electric showers we Americans have nightmares about—"and this would be your room"—a bare mattress balanced atop a metal frame and a dilapidated IKEA wardrobe, the saving grace being a tiny window displaying an amazing view over London.

"Would you mind if I took a look at your room?" I asked. "Just to get an idea of the difference in size."

"Of course! Sorry, it's a bit of a mess at the moment." Lucy opened the door to her bedroom and—lo and behold—the fabled yellow room was revealed. It looked like Laura Ashley had spontaneously combusted in there—everything was pastel and floral and very, very neat.

"It's beautiful," I said. "It gives me hope that I might be able to do something decent with my room." I had a sudden vision of shabby-chic industrial interiors and reclaimed bookshelves made from old French wine crates, and made a mental note to sign up to Pinterest.

Lucy smoothed an imaginary crease on the pale pink duvet. "Thanks, love. Just takes a lick of paint and some elbow grease," she said. "Come on, let's sit in the lounge and have a chat."

I perched on the enormous couch and Lucy drew up a chair opposite.

"So, Lo," she said, taking a sip from her mug, "tell me how you ended up in London."

"I've always wanted to live here," I said with a shrug. That was an understatement: I'd dreamed of living in London ever since I was little. The childhood bedroom I'd shared with my sister had been covered with pictures of the London skyline, and I'd gorged myself on the Beatles and *Carry On* films from a young age. London was my fabled land and I'd managed to pull myself onto its shores like a shipwreck survivor.

Of course, I knew I had been at the helm of that ill-fated ship and had spent the past few months driving it straight into the rocks. I thought of the look on Dylan's face when I packed my bags, and the look on my father's face when he dropped me off at the airport, and pushed them both deep down to the dark recesses of my brain where I couldn't see them. I wasn't ready to admit to myself what I'd done, never mind a relative stranger.

I turned to Lucy with a bright smile. "Have you ever been to the States?"

Her eyes took on a misty quality. "No, never, but I've always wanted to go. One day!"

"Well, I'd be happy to give you some tips when the time comes."

"Thanks, babe. Now, what's happening on the man front? Have you got a boyfriend and, if you do, will he be staying often? Is he very loud and messy?"

I laughed. "Nope, no boyfriend and no plans to have one anytime soon. I just want to enjoy being single for a while."

"Thank God. I've just broken up with someone so I'm desperate to go out and let my hair down."

I grinned at her. "I'm completely on board with that. How's it going so far?" I asked. "Any exciting prospects?"

Lucy shook her head sadly. "Babe, it's been grim. I've started looking on Facebook to see if any of my old schoolmates are now attractive single men that I could get off with."

"That's not a good sign."

Lucy shook her head gravely. "It's not. What's it like in America? I just imagine lots of fit men called Brad or Tyson or whatever, wandering around being muscly and lovely. I bet you've had loads of gorgeous, hunky boyfriends."

The last thing I wanted to do was delve into my American dating history. "Not really," I said with a shrug. "The whole dating thing is super structured over there; it's all 'playing the field' and 'three-date rule' and relentless life scheduling. If you don't have a diamond the size of a grapefruit on your finger by the time you're twenty-nine, you're seen as some sort of leper."

"Grim."

I nodded. "It's pretty exhausting."

"Well, you're here now. I'm sure we can get up to some

mischief together. Two single girls in the big smoke." She scanned over my bedraggled reddish hair, oversized army jacket, ripped skinny jeans and trashed Converses. "First, we might need to take you to Westfield shopping center . . ."

And that was that. A couple of cigarettes on the balcony solidified us as partners in crime, and I moved in the following day. From there followed countless nights of shoe-borrowing, Jack Daniel's and Cokes (me), Bacardi and Diet Cokes (her), dancing in clubs reeking of sweat and stale cigarette smoke, 3 a.m. rants and morning-after catch-ups. It was unbelievably fun, and just what I'd hoped to get out of London.

She was right, though: the man situation wasn't quite as rosy as I'd hoped. It's not that they were assholes or anything. On the whole they were perfectly charming and, with me being relatively new to the country, their accents immediately bumped up their attractiveness quotient by several points. My new neighborhood, Hackney, was filled with slightly fey-looking guys wearing plaid shirts and smoking roll-ups, all theoretically ripe for the picking.

But there was a problem. As upfront as I was about not looking for anything serious, they refused to believe me. Deep down, they thought it was all an elaborate ruse on my part, a trap set to ensnare them into a life of suburban fidelity. One by one, they'd each fly off into the night after a few weeks, never to be seen again.

I was starting to think I was going about things all wrong: that by being upfront about what I was looking for (or, rather, what I wasn't looking for), I was somehow flicking the panic switch in every man in London. It was infuriating, and such a terrible waste of sexual promise.

And then I met Adrian.

It was at a Christmas party filled with people I didn't know. I was new to the British Christmas party tradition of getting blind drunk, flashing your underwear at everyone and making out with someone completely inappropriate, but I took to it like a duck to water and made it my mission to attend as many as possible. Which is how I ended up in the middle of Kensal Rise with a bunch of my colleague Cathryn's former schoolmates, who had gathered for their annual Christmas reunion. I had come prepared with a pack of Marlboro Lights and wearing a top that was masquerading as a dress.

I saw his excellent pompadour from across the room and nudged Cathryn.

"Who's he?" I said, topping up her drink.

"Who, him?" she said, putting her hand over the top of her glass and pointing incredulously to the bespectacled object of my attention.

"Yep, the Buddy Holly look-alike. Who is he?"

"With the glasses? That's Adrian."

"Adrian, eh? What's his deal?"

"Ugh. I couldn't stand him at school. So full of himself. Wanted to be a journalist, I think. Last I heard, he was working as a sub-editor in Sunderland. Ha."

"Well, he's here now and I like his glasses. I'm going to make eyes at him."

"Seriously? Adrian Dean?"

"Christ. Yes, Adrian Dean! I'm not asking *you* to make eyes at him!"

The eyes worked and soon he was bumming cigarettes off me as we smoked in the alley behind the bar, the condensation from our breath mingling with the smoke as we grinned at each other over our cigarettes. By midnight he had kissed me. By 2 a.m. we were in a cab on the way back to my place.

It was three great months of sex on tap with someone I didn't mind spending the before-and-after periods with—exactly what I wanted.

And then came that foolish morning when, in a rush of postcoital goodwill, I committed the grave error of making the man eggs.

Even Adrian, who I thought understood me, ended up convincing himself that I was trying to tie him down.

I thought that dating was meant to be easy; fun, even. Sure, I didn't have all that much experience playing the field, but I'd managed okay in college. Clearly my current seduction methods were failing me. I needed guidance.

And then a plan began to form.

I remembered all those "Ten Ways to Make Him Yours" articles in *YM* and *Seventeen* when I was a teenager. They were always depressingly similar, encouraging you to share his interests ("If he loves cars, why not take a mechanics course?"), flirt like a madwoman ("Pass him a note in PE asking if he's wearing boxers or briefs!") and generally change your entire personality and appearance around what a fifteen-year-old boy wants from a girlfriend. Tip number ten was always "Just be yourself!" though how you could manage that while flicking your hair around and brandishing a wrench, I could never figure out. Really, at the end of the day, a fifteen-year-old boy wants a girl with blond hair and large breasts, neither of which I have or will ever possess (which goes a long way to explaining my teenage dating record).

Surely, all those dating guides in the bookstores were the adult equivalent of teen magazine top-ten lists? They promised to get you your man, no matter the cost, but would their advice actually work? Or would I be left looking like a lunatic? Most importantly, would following these guides result in me having frequent sex with people who were not known psychopaths?

I started to get excited about the prospect. I'd follow a different guide every month and log the results in a journal (this very one!) for scientific posterity. It would be a sociological experiment. Jesus, after a few months of scientific study, I'd practically be Margaret

Mead! Maybe not quite, but at least it would be interesting. Much more interesting than scaring off men with eggs and being passed over for *Football* fucking *Focus*.

I immediately texted Lucy.

Me: Have you ever used a dating guide?

Lucy: Why?

Me: Just asking.

Lucy: Why are you asking?

Me: Just tell me!

Lucy: Maybe.

Me: Maybe?

Lucy: Maybe. Yes. Am I a saddo?

Me: Maybe.

Lucy: Fuck off.

Me: Which one?

Lucy: The Rules. Don't judge. Was at low point.

Me: No judgment. Have a new life plan. Tell you when I get back. Xx

I ran to my favorite bookstore, a little gem tucked behind the tube station at South Kensington. It was owned by a sweet, kindly, white-haired man with a Scottish accent so thick you could stick a fork in it. He'd become one of my favorite people in London, always pressing wonderful books into my hands and mumbling incomprehensibly about them. The bookstore itself was amazing: all tiny nooks and crannies, with a little attic space reserved for used books. I spent most of my lunch hours curled up there, searching for hidden treasure.

I got there ten minutes after closing, but the door was still open. I could see the owner tottering around inside, arranging a table of Seamus Heaney books and singing along to the radio.

He greeted me with a warm grin and a burble that I assumed was a hello.

"What can I do for you, love?" he said. "Come back for more Austen? Or perhaps some Thackeray?" He started pulling books from the shelves into a pile for me, as usual.

"No thanks, Hamish. I'm actually looking for something a little different today. Do you have any self-help?"

"Ah, love, you don't seem to need any help! What's it for, DIY? You should get yourself a strapping fella to do that!"

"No, it's not that." Christ, this was embarrassing. "It's . . . dating. I need dating help."

He straightened himself up on his cane and gave me a kind smile. "I'm sure that isn't true. You're a lovely lass! I bet the boys are falling over themselves to take you out on the town!"

"Not quite," I mumbled. "Anyway, it's for research. Scientific research." I tried to say it with more conviction than I currently felt.

"Ah, I should have known! You working at the Science Museum and all. I think I've got some of those books tucked away in the attic. Give us a shout if you can't find them and I'll go on the hunt."

I thanked him and ran up the steps to the attic room, which was filled to the rafters with perilous towers of used books. I found the right corner, blew off the dust and sifted through the titles: *Men Are from Mars*, *He's Just Not That Into You*, *Why Men Love Bitches* . . . lovely old Hamish had a great selection.

I heard him clear his throat and call up the stairs. "Sorry, love, but my seat in the Chandos is getting cold . . ."

"Be right there!" I yelled.

Found it! I pulled it from the stack and ran down the stairs, brandishing it and a ten-pound note triumphantly.

I returned to the apartment, my copy of *The Rules* in hand, and explained the plan to Lucy.

She was silent for a moment, clearly overwhelmed by my shrewd scientific mind.

"Babe, are you bonkers?" she said. "You're going to use your love life as an experiment?"

"That's right!"

"But . . . that's mental! What happens if you end up seeing someone for more than a month?"

"I can't really see that happening, but if it does, I'll have to change tactics and follow the new guide! So suddenly my behavior will TOTALLY CHANGE and I'll document how that affects them!"

"What happens if the book tells you to do something really weird? What if it says you have to let them pee on you during sex? Or do lots of Japanese bondage or something?"

"Lucy, it's a dating guide, not fringe porn."

She clutched my arm. "Lo, I've heard some of those guides tell you to"—her eyes widened—"*stop having sex.*"

I arranged my face into a Zen-like expression. "I'll just have to draw on my reserves of inner strength."

"Hmm." I could tell she was wavering. Her eyes brightened suddenly. "What happens if you fall in love with one of your test subjects? What then?"

I rolled my eyes. "I've had enough of that love shit to last me a lifetime. This, my friend, is for the advancement of single women everywhere!"

"In that case, I'm all for it!" she cried, and we raised our glasses to toast.

"To science!"

BOOK ONE
THE RULES

April 1

Written in 1995, after both the first and second waves of feminism had crashed on our shores and in the middle of the post-structuralist tidal pool of the third, *The Rules* preaches a message that could be described as old-fashioned. Victorian, even. Chapter headings include "Don't Talk to a Man First (or Ask Him to Dance)" and "Don't Stare at Men or Talk Too Much," which sounds like the advice a fictional grandmother would give her young granddaughter in a made-for-TV movie about the Amish.

Most worrying is this: "Don't Discuss *The Rules* with Your Therapist." Surely it's a red flag if a book is encouraging you to behave in a way that you should hide from your therapist?

The main concept behind the book is that you're meant to make him chase you. Forever. Apparently, by seeming like an elusive creature unlike any other, who never looks a man in the eye, only speaks when spoken to and with no discernible thoughts or opinions, you'll be the sexiest damn thing on legs. Stick that in your post-structuralist pipe and smoke it.

The idea seems to be that you repress your entire personality in order to become some sort of mysterious feminine ideal. "Be feminine," the book advises. "Don't tell sarcastic jokes. Don't be a loud, knee-slapping, hysterically funny girl . . . be quiet and act mysterious, act ladylike, cross your legs and smile." As I tended to feel more like smiling when opening my legs than when closing them, I was a bit worried about how suited I was for this challenge. *The Rules* had some comfort on that front: "You may feel that you won't be able to be yourself, but men will love it!"

I was daunted, but at the same time I could see there was a method to the madness. Here's the working ratio:

Seventy percent total and complete horseshit that goes against all I believe in to thirty percent total genius.

The more I read, the more I wondered if it was actually . . . well, empowering in a way. *Rules* girls don't date men who don't want them, the book proclaims, and if a man really wants you, he'll chase after you. He'll make the effort. I thought briefly about Adrian and *Football Focus* and the distinct lack of effort that had come from him in recent months. Hmm.

I tried to distill the essence of it to Lucy after work that night.

"So, you're not meant to call him, ask him out, talk very much, return calls or look at him?"

I nodded.

"That sounds grim." Lucy took a drag on her cigarette, looking pensive. "How are you meant to flirt?"

"That's the thing! You're not. Or at least you're not supposed to flirt in the way we flirt. You're meant to be all shy and bashful." I heard a keening sound below and leaned over the balcony. "Are those guys fighting their dogs down there?"

Lucy looked over my shoulder. "I think it's a drug deal, actually."

"Anyway, according to this, we're meant to be intangible. Like some kind of wood nymph. Men are never supposed to be completely comfortable or sure that they've won us over; they're meant to constantly work to win our affection."

"Well, I suppose that would make a change. I can't remember the last time a man worked for anything."

Later that night, we went out to see Lucy's latest possibility doing his best Ed Sheeran impersonation in the dank basement of a Soho bar. Max was a slightly aloof sports-car-driving martial arts aficionado who, we were now witnessing, had a penchant for singing songs about butterfly kisses.

He was also extremely good at playing hot and cold, and would go through the whole wine-and-dine rigmarole with Lucy one night and then disappear for three weeks, only to resurface by calling her on a random Tuesday at 11 p.m. and asking her to come around to his flat. This had been going on for weeks now.

Lucy and I both thought he was kind of an asshole but unfortunately, as is so often the case, he was an asshole who was good in bed and also capable of wielding that all-powerful form of female kryptonite: the acoustic guitar. Personally, I would have rather licked the bottom of my flip-flop after a backpacking trip around India than sit on the edge of a bed while a man sang a song to me, but Lucy was a different animal. She loved it. She actually sang along with him. I shuddered at the thought.

As Max rounded out his set and stepped off the stage to a smattering of applause, he glanced over at Lucy, flashed a killer smile and gave her a wave. I felt my heart flutter a bit on her behalf: he was pretty hot.

"Okay, here's the deal," I hissed. "When he comes over here, you keep it to five minutes maximum and then tell him you have other plans."

"Are you mad? I would like him to take me home tonight. I would *like* to have sex."

"I know, but *The Rules* says—"

"I'm not the one following the bloody *Rules*! You are!"

"I know, I know! But you shouldn't be waiting around for him—he should be chasing you!"

"Are you forgetting that I would like to have sex?"

"YOU ARE A CREATURE UNLIKE ANY OTHER!"

"Be *quiet*! He's coming over!"

Max appeared at our table, holding a pint and looking pretty pleased with himself.

"Hello! And how are you lovely ladies? Did you enjoy the set?"

Lucy and I murmured approval noises.

He turned to Lucy. "Baby, I've got to go over and see my mates and my brother for a while. Are you sticking around?"

I threw a sharp glance Lucy's way. She scowled back, rolled her eyes and then said, "No, we've got to get going actually. We've got other plans."

"Yep, other plans!" I cried. "Big plans." It sounded more menacing than I'd intended, but I wanted to be supportive.

Max furrowed his brow. "Oh. That's a shame but . . . well, let's get together soon. It was great to see you."

I could sense Lucy crumbling beneath the weight of his brow so I jumped up and got our coats.

"We'll be late!" I trilled.

After a quick kiss on each of Max's cheeks, we stumbled out of the bar and onto a bus on our way back to Old Street for a nightcap. Lucy's phone chirped within minutes. It was Max.

You looked gorgeous tonight. Sorry you had to go . . . Dinner
next week? Xx

I felt a strange mix of triumph and horror. So this crap actually worked? It was time for me to try it out for myself.

April 2

As soon as I took on the project, I knew that I was seriously lacking in one thing: test subjects. And while I love going out and trying to pick up dudes as much as the next girl, experience indicated that technique alone wouldn't provide enough source material.

Cathryn and I had formed a pretty tight friendship over the time we had been working side-by-side, despite being in many ways the physical embodiment of the transatlantic divide. She was sleek and posh and stealthfully wealthy. She lived in a gorgeous terraced house in Notting Hill with her equally gorgeous fiancé, Michael, and she had glossy chestnut hair that she could sweep up into a perfect, perky ponytail without using a hairbrush. Enough to make me hate her, and usually in these scenarios we would embark on some bitter rivalry—probably over our dashingly-handsome-but-ultimately-callous boss. But Cathryn was also wickedly funny and very generous, and our boss was sweet and happily married and had an ever-thickening middle, so instead we became friends. I now hoped her generosity would extend to her extensive network of attractive male friends.

I walked into work the next day and dropped my bag on the floor next to my desk.

"I need your help."

I explained the situation to her; I wouldn't want her to unwittingly put one of her friends up as a test subject (though she obviously couldn't let them in on what was happening). Cathryn's perfect brow furrowed slightly and she looked at me with concern in her eyes.

"I'm not sure about this. Have you considered the ethics of the project?"

"What ethics? It's harmless! Women follow these rules ALL the time—that's why these books sell! The only difference is that I'm pursuing it from a scientific point of view. Come on, you like science—you should appreciate what I'm doing in the name of research!" I tried to look lofty and academic. "I'm actually being noble, if you think about it. Sacrificing myself in the pursuit of knowledge."

She rolled her eyes. "You're a modern-day Marie Curie."

"You know what they say: some of us are born for greatness . . ."

"Are you quite sure you're up for this? Your psyche aside, we've got so much on at the moment. The summer late openings are starting in less than two weeks and you've got to iron out the guest list."

"Oh, please. I'm American—you know how efficient we are. We love working! Not as much as the Germans or the Chinese, but pretty close."

"Well, then, what *about* your psyche?"

"I appreciate your concern, but I'll be fine. It's meant to be fun! And informative, of course."

I saw her vacillate and knew I had her. "It does sound interesting. I've been with Michael for so long I've forgotten all about various dating etiquettes, so I'd quite like to see what happens."

"Excellent. So, who've you got for me?"

Cathryn proceeded to tell me all about one of Michael's co-workers who was apparently good-looking, well-mannered and, importantly, single. Like Michael, he did something in finance that I didn't understand but suspected was destroying our economy while making him a shit-ton of money. I'd never gone out with a banker before but time was of the essence, so I put aside my concerns about capitalism and agreed.

Let's call him Top Hat, as it reminds me of Monopoly. I filled his details into my notebook.

Name: Top Hat
Age: 31
Occupation: Investment Banker

Nationality: Irish
Method: *The Rules*

"This is fantastic. Thanks! Can you try to set something up for this Friday? I need to get cracking."

"I'll talk to Michael tonight."

And just like that, I had my first test subject.

April 4

I hadn't spoken to my sister in over two weeks, which was unheard of for us, so when Meghan's number flashed up on my cell phone during my lunch break, I dropped my sandwich and picked up the phone.

"I have come up with a new life plan," I said breathlessly. We'd never been much for saying hello.

"Oh Lord. You haven't found God or anything, have you?"

"No, nothing that serious." I filled her in on my plans for the dating project, ignoring her frequent snorts of disbelief. I knew convincing Meg would be tough, but I wasn't quite prepared for her ire.

"I thought you called yourself a feminist," she scoffed.

"I do! And actually, if you think about it, this is an act of feminist rebellion."

"In what way is following a bunch of bullshit, probably misogynist dating guides a feminist act?"

I had to think quickly. While I do consider myself a feminist, I had to admit that I didn't put much thought into the mechanics of it. "By . . . um . . . infiltrating the enemy! Getting behind enemy lines! By using my archetypal feminine wiles to penetrate the male psyche for the betterment of women everywhere!"

Meghan laughed. "Kid, it's okay. Just admit you're doing it to forget Dylan."

I felt indignant. "Dylan has nothing to do with it! Dylan is the past, Meg. This project is my future!"

I heard her sigh on the other end of the line. "Whatever you say. Just look after yourself. The last thing I want is for you to go changing yourself for a bunch of pale English guys."

"Don't worry about me. I'm in complete control of the situation."

"I'm not sure if that makes me feel better or worse . . ."

I walked back to my desk and picked up my sandwich and my dog-eared copy of The Rules, brushing aside Meghan's words of caution.

April 5

Date night arrived surprisingly quickly. I'd been boning up on The Rules all week but I was still nervous about a couple of points. Rules girls aren't allowed to pay for anything on dates, as apparently being financially independent might undermine their creature-unlike-any-otherness. I am a big believer in splitting the bill, so I knew that letting him pay for everything was going to make me uncomfortable.

I was also supposed to end the date quickly, after just two drinks. I have a penchant for nights out that last way longer than advisable, so I suspected this would be tricky, too.

I wasn't allowed to suggest anything about the date, so I left him to choose the place. I was secretly grateful for that particular rule as I hate choosing dating venues and activities; all the venues I know are old-man pubs, dive bars and my bedroom, and the only activities I think are suitable for dating are drinking, smoking and having sex. I'm not even sure about dinner.

He chose a swanky-looking prohibition-style bar in Soho. *The Rules* encourages you to, and I quote, "wear sheer black stockings and hike up your skirt to entice the opposite sex." As it was a Friday-night date and I hadn't wanted to turn up to the office looking like I was moonlighting in a Mayfair brothel, I ran home after work, chucked on the nearest and smallest dress I could find, had a ciga-rette on the balcony and then ran out to meet Top Hat.

The bar was hidden away from the road and pleasingly secret-looking, with a discreet little doorway demarcated only by a lantern outside. Those places usually make me intensely nervous because I worry that I won't find the door and will wander around like Moses in the desert or, worse, I will find the door but be turned away for not being cool and interesting enough.

Thankfully, Top Hat had allayed both fears ahead of the date by giving me explicit directions via email and by assuring me that my name was at the door. Two points for him.

Despite all of these assurances, I was still a wreck when I walked up to the maître d' and explained I was meeting a blind date; he looked at me knowingly and guided me down the stairs.

"Thank Christ," I thought. "This man knows who Top Hat is! He must have told the maître d' when he came in. That's kind of sexy . . ."

He proceeded to lead me over to the bar, where a classic tall, dark and handsome was seated with what looked like an old-fashioned.

"BINGO!" I thought.

The maître d' left me there with a wink.

"Top Hat?" I said. (Of course, I didn't really call him Top Hat, but for the sake of my test subject's anonymity, I'll refer to him as such.)

"No," the tall, dark and handsome said.

"Oh," I said. "Sorry. I'm meeting someone and the maître d' led me over here."

He took a long look at my very short dress. "My wife will be here any minute and she won't be very pleased if she sees me talking to someone like you." He took a business card out of his pocket. "I work away from home a few nights a week, though, so have your boss get in touch with me about the details."

"I think we've got our wires crossed. My boss works at the Science Museum."

He looked vaguely annoyed. "Sorry, I'm not familiar with the lingo."

"Hey, buddy, I'll have you know—"

"Lauren?" called a voice behind me.

I turned around. At a small, tucked-away table sat a slim red-headed guy waving at me cautiously.

What a relief. I gave the man at the bar a dark look, tugged down the hem of my dress and weaved my way over to Top Hat.

We awkwardly kissed on the cheek and I carefully maneuvered myself into the chair next to him. He was cute. Not tall, dark and handsome cute, but boyish and kind-looking. I made a mental note to bring Cathryn a bar of chocolate on Monday.

"Grand!" he said. "Here we are! What would you like to drink?"

We ordered martinis and he told me a bit about himself. He'd moved over from Ireland six years ago for work and was now living in Hammersmith with his brother and cousin.

". . . and that's how I ended up over here! Sorry, I've been yarking on for donkeys' years." He took a sip of his drink and nodded toward me. "And how did you end up on this glorious isle? Did you come for the weather or the customer service? It's usually one of the two."

I let a loud laugh escape before catching myself and arranging my features in a way I hoped would look demure. "I came over for work."

"That's right, you work with Cathryn at the Science Museum! Lovely Cathryn. She's a cracking girl. What are you lasses working on at the moment? Anything of great import?"

Actually, we were about to launch a series of after-hours,

adults-only events that Cathryn and I had been working on relent-lessly for the past six months. But that would have been giving away too much, so instead I shrugged and said, "Not really," and took another sip of my martini.

"Right, just ticking along then?"

I smiled and looked down at the table. I felt like I was doing a Helen Keller impersonation.

Top Hat looked momentarily deflated, then threw himself back into the conversation with renewed gusto.

"I'm working on a big to-do with Michael at the moment. We're off to Tokyo next week—did Cathryn mention that?"

I shook my head.

"Well, we're off on Tuesday for a fortnight and I plan on eating as much Wagyu beef as I can fit down my gullet. It ought to be a laugh. Have you been to Tokyo?"

"Yes, once." In fact, I'd spent six months teaching English there after I graduated from college. I loved it.

"It's a fantastic place, isn't it? It's mad! Just totally mad! But in the most brilliant way. When did you go?"

"A few years ago."

"And what was your favorite bit?"

"Eating blowfish!" I wanted to say. "The one that kills one in every hundred people who eat it! I ate it and stayed up all night waiting to see if I was going to die. But I didn't and it was awesome!" Instead, I just shrugged again. "I couldn't really say."

"Did you see anything completely crackers? I'm desperate to see one of those robot bartenders they have in some of the flash places. Did you see one of them?"

"Yes! And I saw one of those vending machines that sell girls' used underwear!" I wanted to scream. "It was so amazing and so weird and so gross and I took a billion photos of it so I could show everyone!" Instead I said, "No, just the usual."

Top Hat smiled wanly and stared into his drink. I was losing him, I could feel it, but there was nothing I could do about it.

Unsurprisingly, the conversation dried up after that. I couldn't do anything to fill the long silences, as the book forbade me from introducing any new topics of conversation. So we sat there and sipped our drinks, Top Hat occasionally offering up a few questions and me murmuring monosyllabic responses. It was excruciating.

Thankfully, the end of the night came fairly quickly, as I had to leave after the second drink. After my last sip, I glanced at my watch and said what I'd been dreading having to say: "Well, this was really great, but I've got a big day tomorrow."

Top Hat looked both confused—it was only 9:35 on a Friday night—and relieved. "Oh, right then," he said. "I'll just get the bill."

The bill arrived and I had to sit on my hands to stop myself from reaching for my bag. I felt the least I could do was pay my fair share for this disaster, but instead I had ruined some poor guy's night and now he was going to have to pay for it.

Thankfully, Top Hat pulled out his credit card without so much as batting an eyelid. He probably just wanted to get out of there as fast as humanly possible.

We left the bar (with me pausing surreptitiously by the door so he was forced to open it for me) and Top Hat gallantly walked me to the nearest tube station.

"Thank you for a lovely evening!" I trilled.

"It was great craic. Sorry you've got to scarper."

"Well, like I said, big day tomorrow!" I cried. "Goodnight!"

I made a mad dash into the station and then snuck out the other exit to have a calming cigarette.

"Christ, that was hard," I muttered to myself as I took another drag. I pulled my coat around me, suddenly conscious of the fact I was standing on a street corner in Soho dressed in sheer black stockings and a tiny black dress. I ground out my cigarette beneath my heel: I'd already been mistaken for a prostitute once tonight and I didn't want to stick around for another invitation.

I turned to walk into the tube, perking up at the realization that I'd be home in time to watch *Curb Your Enthusiasm* on Channel 4. At least *Rules*-style dating wouldn't interfere with my TV-watching schedule.

"Lauren?"

I turned around to see Top Hat leaning out of the window of a cab.

"Oh, hello again!" I said, struggling to regain my air of elegant demureness.

"Do you want a lift? I'm going to listen to the deedley-deets with some mates in Shoreditch. I could drop you on the way?"

Deedley-deets? I couldn't help myself: I had to ask a question. "What's a deedley-deet?"

"Irish music! You know, it's all deedley-deets and that. Come along if you like!"

"No thanks."

"Oh, right—you've got that big day and all. Well, can I at least give you a ride home?"

I pondered this for a moment, thinking about what *The Rules* would do. I suspected they would frown upon it, but the April chill was currently blowing through my sheer stockings and a couple of older guys were leering at me from the doorway of a porn shop, so I nodded and jumped in the back.

"Thank you. That's very kind."

"No problem at all." Top Hat looked at me for a moment and then said, "Do you mind if I ask if you're feeling yourself tonight?"

Argh. It was too grim. He thought I was terrible. I forced myself to smile politely. "Yes, I'm feeling fine, thank you."

"It's just that you seem very . . . quiet. I hope I've not said anything to offend you? I can be a mouthy bugger so just give us a slap if I have!"

"Of course not!" I said. "You've been a perfect gentleman." I crossed my ankles and gazed at his left earlobe, determined not to make eye contact. He was being really nice, and he was so boyishly handsome in that slightly fey Irish way I loved so much . . . I was sure I would lunge if I looked at him straight on.

We fell into an uncomfortable silence. I stared out the window, watching the streets whiz past me and willing the cab to beam me directly into my living room.

"This is me!" I said as the taxi pulled up to the curb off Old Street roundabout. "Thank you again for a lovely evening!" I leaped out of the taxi and ran (well, wobbled—I am the worst at wearing heels) into the entrance of my building. I didn't look back.

As I turned the key to the front door of the apartment, an icy chill ran down my spine. "Oh God," I thought, "I didn't even offer him money for the cab!" Of course, I wasn't supposed to, according to *The Rules*, but I still felt a rush of shame. "He must think I'm the biggest bitch on the planet."

I poured myself a large glass of wine and took it out onto the balcony. The apartment was empty; presumably Lucy was off having fun somewhere, drinking and making out with boys and staying out past 10 p.m., unencumbered by the confines of *Rules* life. How I envied her.

If I'd been left to my own devices tonight, two martinis would have led to a couple of bourbons, and the night would have ended with us grappling in a drunken make-out session in a dark corner of a dive bar on Hanbury Street.

That's what I loved about being single: going on little adventures with a relative stranger to whom you're suddenly desperately attracted; bizarre, off-track conversations about your favorite breed of dog, or who would win in a fight between New Kids on the Block and One Direction, or whether or not Michael McIntyre makes the world a worse place; mad hunts for booze and cigarettes; the feeling that the night is slipping away from you and trying to grasp on to it and haul the cover of dark over you for as long as possible. I loved the giddy feeling of waking up in bed the next morning, fuzzy and headachy but mainly really, really happy, still high on the sense of possibility from the night before.

Instead, I was home at an absurdly reasonable hour, having forced a perfectly nice man to spend a brief evening in my extremely boring company and not offering a penny of my own money as compensation. I felt deflated and kind of gross.

This was going to be harder than I'd thought.

April 13

A week had gone by without any word from Top Hat. It had taken all of my willpower not to send him a text thanking him for the drinks and apologizing for not offering any money for the cab, but if I had done that, I'd be going against several rules in the book.

Michael had left for Tokyo with Top Hat and Cathryn hadn't heard any feedback about the date. I cringed to think what Top Hat would say about me; he was probably berating Michael for sending him on a date with such a frigid bitch. It was pretty humiliating, but I guessed I was going to have to prepare myself for that kind of thing now that I'd handed my love life to the experts.

Lucy and I had gone for our Saturday-morning run and our weekly shopping trip to Superdrug afterward, wandering around the aisles like a couple of zombies who were really interested in nail polish. I was standing at the checkout, paying for an electric blue liquid eyeliner I was very excited about, when I felt my phone buzz.

I pulled it out of my bag and looked at the screen. I had a missed call. Six, to be exact. All from Adrian.

It had been a while since I'd heard from him. Six weeks, maybe

longer. I'd given up and assumed he had retreated to the Island of
Lost Men, where he was playing *Championship Manager* with all the
other guys who had suddenly evaporated from women's lives.

But apparently he was off the island. And now, as I stood in the
middle of the shop and stared down at the little blinking cursor on
my phone, I was faced with a conundrum: to *Rules* or not to *Rules?*

"Adrian called," I said, grabbing Lucy's arm as we walked out
of the store. "Like, six times. What should I do?"

"Ooh! Ring him back! He's probably calling to say he's realized
he's madly in love with you."

"But the book says I can't call him back!"

Rules girls treat the telephone as though it's a one-way system: men
can call you but you definitely cannot call them. The reasoning behind
this is that if a guy really wanted to talk to you, he'd call you again and
again until he reached you. It's a very sensible edict, though it does re-
quire a breed of persistent, besotted man I have yet to encounter.

"I thought the book said that you couldn't return his first phone
call. Surely you can return his *sixth* phone call!"

"Right! I mean, what if he's hurt? What if he's been in an accident or something?"

Lucy's eyes widened. "Lo, it could actually be dangerous if you
don't call him back. You might be held liable or something."

"Oh my God. You're right. I'm sure I saw something like that
happen on *Law and Order.* Okay, I'm calling him when we get back
to the apartment."

Lucy nodded decisively. "You're doing the right thing, babe."

We hurried home, speculating on what crisis might have be-
fallen Adrian. Joblessness? Homelessness? Freak combine harvester
accident? Spurred on by the thought that I was only doing what any
responsible citizen would do, I pressed the call button as soon as we
walked through the door. He picked up on the third ring.

"Hello?" he said.

God, his voice was hot.

"Hi! It's Lauren. I saw that you called so I'm just calling you back. Is everything okay? You're not in the hospital, are you? Which hospital are you in? Should I come?"

"What are you on about? I'm not in the hospital, you mad-woman. I'm in the pub, about to watch Liverpool get spanked by Man City."

"Oh. So why did you call me all those times?"

"I didn't."

"Yes, you did. You called me six times, according to my phone. I figured it was an emergency or something."

"Shit. I must have sat on it and it dialed you. Sorry about that."

"Oh." I swallowed the bile that had risen in my gorge. "Okay. No problem."

"How are you, Cunningham? You well?"

"Yep! Yep! All good here! Been crazy busy with, you know, lots of activities and projects and work and dates and stuff! Especially dates!" Oh Lord, oh Lord, MAKE IT STOP. "Anyway! I've got to go. Busy busy!"

"Right, well, I wouldn't want to keep you when you're clearly so . . . busy. Sorry about ringing you." Adrian managed to sound both bemused and indifferent. He was infuriating. I was starting to wish that he *had* been involved in some kind of combine harvester incident.

"No problem! Bye!" I hung up and sat on the couch. Well. That hadn't gone according to plan.

Lucy was lurking outside the door and pounced on me as soon as I came out.

"So?" she said. "Is he all right? Was there an accident?"

"No."

"Oh my God, he wants to get back together, doesn't he? I knew it!"

"No," I said again.

"So what was it?"

"It was his ass. His ass called me, not him."

Lucy looked confused. "What do you mean, his arse?"

"I mean he sat on his phone and it dialed me by accident, apparently."

She looked crestfallen. I think she was more disappointed than I was. "Oh. Bugger."

"Tell me about it."

Preventative measures were needed. I looked up Adrian's number in my phone and changed his name to "Are You Drunk?" so that if I was ever again tempted to call him, I would be immediately rebuffed.

I went into my room and grabbed my copy of *The Rules*.

I lay down on my bed and flipped to the chapter entitled "Next! And Other Rules for Dealing with Rejection." I'd had my fair share over the past few weeks so was keen to see what wisdom they had in store for me. I read on.

"*Rules* girls don't get hung up on men who reject them. They say, 'His loss' or 'Next!' They carry on."

Say what you like about the *Rules* authors—I've been saying that they're shrill harridans set against me ever having sex again, for example—but I like the fact that there's no room for self-pity.

There was more: "*The Rules* recipe for rejection is to wear a great dress and flattering make-up and go to the *very next* party or singles dance." Seemed pretty sensible to me. I had never done that whole sit-around-crying-into-a-pint-of-ice-cream cliché that seems to have been thrust upon womankind through rom-coms and chick lit.

Luckily, I had a work event that night that could be rife with possibilities. We were launching the late-night series: the museum would be open until 2 a.m. on Saturdays and there'd be DJs, special exhibitions and cocktails. It wasn't easy enticing grown-ups into a science museum; sometimes you had to cajole them with liquor.

Obviously tonight would be all about me being the ultimate professional (at least for the first twenty minutes) but after I'd kissed the cheeks of all the important people I was planning on enjoying the open bar and hopefully bagging myself at least one new test subject.

In preparation for the big night, I flipped over to the section on *Rules* party skills. My heart sank: the evening might not be that fun after all.

Daunted but undeterred, I did my best to spruce myself up. I put on my favorite little red dress and, after finally managing to apply liquid eyeliner without poking myself in the eye, I ran into the living room to get Lucy's approval.

"Ooh!" she said, looking up from the latest issue of *Grazia*. "Where are you off to? You're looking very glam."

"Do you really think it's okay? I've got to go to the Nights at the Museum launch. Is this too *Pretty Woman* for a work event? I keep getting mistaken for a prostitute."

"Absolutely not. It's all very sexy secretary."

"Thanks. Now I've got to go roam around a room for several hours and not look at anyone. I'll call you from the bathroom."

"What?"

"I'll fill you in later. Bye!"

I left a confused-looking Lucy on the couch and made a dash for the tube. As usual, I was late.

I managed to squeeze on to the train just before the doors shut. Once on, I realized my mistake. It was, as always, fifteen degrees the wrong temperature—in this case, fifteen degrees too hot—and the run to the station hadn't done me any favors. I struggled to loosen the buttons of my coat but realized with rising panic that it had already begun: the tube sweats.

Within minutes, my dress was stuck to the small of my back and there were tiny rivulets of sweat making their way down my neck. Gross.

When I finally disembarked a half-hour later, my make-up had made a run for south of the border and my dress was clinging to me like cellophane. I ducked past the front entrance in case I was spied by a colleague/client/possible test subject and ran into my office, which was tucked neatly beneath the museum in an area I liked to call the Cellar of Despair. There was lots of gray and lots of dank.

I pulled out my emergency make-up stash and frantically reapplied while fanning myself down with a sheaf of museum leaflets.

At that moment, Cathryn walked in, looking regal in a blue maxi dress and heels that I would have to describe as sensible. If I wore them, I'd look about forty-seven. On her, they looked French and expensive.

"Are you all right?" she asked, taking one look at my beet-red face and assuming that I was about to stroke out.

"Fine! That goddamn tube was so hot and now I can't stop sweating, mainly because I'm thinking about sweating."

"For heaven's sake, stop thinking about sweating."

"I'm trying!" I cried as I fanned myself faster. "How's the turnout looking? Any cancellations?"

Cathryn flipped through the papers on her clipboard. "A few people have dropped out but it looks like we'll be at full capacity by eight."

"Amazing!" I kicked off my flats and slipped into my heels. They'd cripple me by ten, but hopefully that was long enough to make an impression. "We've only got half an hour before the doors open so let's do a quick sweep of the area and make sure the planetarium is ready to go."

The sweating had just about subsided and I gave my hair a final brush before following Cathryn to the front of the museum. The planetarium looked amazing. The DJ would be stationed up in the rafters and the crowd would be dancing beneath the stars. There was a bar being set up right outside the door so people could slip out and get another gin and tonic without spilling booze on any expensive science equipment. The powers that be had stressed that no expensive science equipment should be damaged in the name of a good time.

I was really proud. Sure, there wouldn't be a whole lot of learning happening, but at least it would introduce the museum to a new demographic and, hopefully, bring in some money from ticket sales. Mainly, though, I had set the whole thing up to realize my thirteen-year-old self's dream of having a party in the planetarium. Blame the Pink Floyd laser show I saw in junior high, I guess.

I smiled at Cathryn. "It all looks great."

"It does, doesn't it? I'm quite pleased."

"Seriously, we've outdone ourselves. If we don't get a promotion out of this, I'll eat my hat."

"That's probably going a bit far, but I do think it looks lovely."

I nodded. "I'm going to run outside for a cigarette and then I'll take my post at the door."

"Don't get lost!" she called as I ducked out the side door.

Cathryn and I had agreed to rotate the painfully boring job of standing guard over the door and checking people off on the guest list. I usually hated door duty and tried to get out of it any way I could, but tonight I was looking forward to it. It was like a sneak preview: I could take a look at the merchandise before it went on the shop floor.

I snuck into a back alley and lit up, thinking about the best way to tackle the evening without breaking any rules. No eye contact. No lingering. No approaching a man I was interested in. No giving out my number unsolicited.

I sighed and flicked my cigarette butt into the corner. I sensed this was going to be a long night.

Doors opened at 7 p.m. so I took my place with a clipboard and a smile on my face. At first, there was just a trickle of people filtering through but thankfully by 8 o'clock that trickle had become a steady stream.

So far, the talent was looking good. As with any event like this, it was kind of a mixed bag. Maybe one too many hooting preppy guys with popped collars for my liking, and I was pretty sure I got the hairy eyeball from a couple of graying sixty-something men who really should have known better, but I definitely noticed a few wan-looking hipsters slide past me. Underfed men with too much hair and brooding eyes are like catnip to me. My ideal man is one-third history professor, one-third guitarist in a struggling neo-folk band and one-third deranged hobo.

Finally, 9:30 rolled around and I passed door duty over to a slightly frazzled-looking Cathryn.

"How's it going in there? You all right?"

"Yes, all going well, though if one more trustee member gropes me, I can't promise what I'll do."

"They're like octopi, those guys! They should be heading off soon, though. I'm sure their wives will be calling them home."

"Or their mistresses. Right, hand me the clipboard and get yourself in there. There are some good-looking men and you need a new test subject."

"I know. Too bad I can't look at any of them."

Cathryn shot me a quizzical look as I ducked through the door.

I made my way through the throngs of people at the bar and then slipped behind it and helped myself to a well-deserved Jack and Coke, showing the bartender my free booze pass. I peered into the planetarium; it was full to capacity with loads of twenty- and thirty-somethings dancing maniacally to nineties hip-hop (my idea, thankyouverymuch). The trustees were pressed against the walls watching, like they had stumbled into a postmodern immersive theater experience.

I downed my drink and made my way into the furor. I wasn't sure how to approach this new style of partying. Usually I would just get drunk, make eyes with a guy, hope he reciprocated and then sidle over to him. But with the *Rules*, I realized my place was more with the trustees on the sidelines.

I squeezed myself next to a man in a suit who was old enough to be my father, hoping I could melt into the background. He smiled benignly at me and I quickly returned the smile before looking out at the dancing crowd.

"Bit loud in here, isn't it?" the father-figure said.

"Yep, but that's how they like it!" I had to shout over the music to be heard.

"Well, it's a bit much for our lot, don't you think?" He nudged me gently in the ribs. "You look like you'd much rather be home with a nice cup of tea and a good book, like me."

I smiled and shrugged, then slowly realized that he was lumping me in with his generation. He apparently thought I was in my sixties because I wasn't jumping around on the dance floor like a lunatic.

I felt old and lame. I had to get into the fray.

I decided to try out *Rules*-style mingling. I couldn't make eye contact, but I could move around. I excused myself, then started circling the room like a restless buzzard, pushing my way through the crowd before eventually getting pinned against the wall by a couple of guys hooraying themselves a bit too enthusiastically to Kid 'n Play. Things weren't going according to plan.

I decided to try another *Rules*-approved tack: act removed and vaguely entitled. With the "dance like no one's watching" mantra quoted so much on Facebook posts running through my head, I staked out a spot in the middle of the dance floor, closed my eyes and went nuts to "Jump Around." I mean, I really got into it. By the end of the song, the people around me had cleared away, leaving me in the middle of an empty circle. I'm not sure how refined I looked, but no one could say I was on the prowl for a man.

I stayed the course, doing a low-key, interpretive dance-style performance to "Gin and Juice" before throwing everything I had at Missy Elliott. It was strangely liberating, this whole dancing-like-no-one-was-watching thing. Just as I was about to get to the finale of "Hot Boyz," I felt a tap on my shoulder.

I cautiously opened my eyes, willing it to be one of the rumpled hipster types and not Cathryn asking me to go back on door duty. Instead, I found myself staring at the face of a chiseled blond man.

"Hello," he said. "I'd like to buy you a drink."

He wasn't my usual type (he looked far too healthy for that) but he was very handsome. He looked like a poster child for the Aryan nation and I could see the outline of some impressively muscled arms underneath his neatly pressed button-down shirt. I decided to give it a shot.

"Sure," I said. "I need some air."

He smiled a white, even-toothed smile. "I'm not surprised, after that performance."

I tried to look demure. "I was just feeling the music."

We squeezed our way to the bar and he clicked his fingers at an annoyed-looking bartender and ordered two vodka tonics. He hadn't asked what I wanted, but as it was free, I accepted without complaint.

I was acutely aware of the fact that I had only a few minutes with him before the *Rules* pulled me back into the room to mingle. I had to work fast if I wanted to see those arms in more detail. We exchanged names. Let's call him Popeye (post-spinach, of course). Drinks procured, he looked at me politely but expectantly, as though waiting for a surprise to pop out of me like a jack-in-the-box. I remained staunchly silent for a few minutes before finally cracking under the pressure.

"How are you enjoying the museum?" I asked. "First time here?" Argh. What kind of a *Rules* girl was I if I couldn't go five minutes without asking a question? I put my most uninterested face on as penance.

"No, I'm an old museum pro. I brought my nephew a few weeks ago."

"Aw, that's sweet."

"Yeah, he's four. He loved it. Couldn't get enough of the Launchpad bit, and I had to drag him out of the planetarium. He just wanted to look up at the stars for ages."

"Yeah, that's always a little-boy pleaser. So, are you having fun tonight?"

"It's great. Though I've got to say, it's a bit of a different vibe tonight than when I was here with my nephew."

"Yes, more drunken." I concentrated on looking aloof.

"My father is one of the museum's patrons, so I've spent a lot of time here. What brought you here tonight?"

"Your father pays my salary. I'm one of the events coordinators here."

"So this is your event? I'm impressed! It's fantastic."

"Well, I wouldn't go that far. But thanks." I pulled my eyes away from his and settled on his left bicep. Surely that counted as avoiding eye contact? God, he was hot. I wondered what he looked like without a shirt. Maybe doing some carpentry.

I could sense I was getting into dangerous territory. My *Rules* fairy godmothers pulled me away. "Anyway, I should get back. Circulate or whatever. It was really nice to meet you, though, and thanks for the drink."

For a second, he looked surprised—he obviously wasn't used to being rebuffed—but his chivalric side recovered quickly. "Of course. Here, let me get the door for you."

I walked through, trying to look elegant and graceful. "You are a creature unlike any other," I thought to myself. "A creature unlike any other."

The mingling began anew, with me bouncing from wall to wall like a well-played game of Pong. I danced to a couple more songs but, despite DMX's best efforts, my heart wasn't in it. When it reached midnight, I decided to call it a night. Being out and surrounded by attractive men but unable to do anything other than look aloof and dance by myself was boring, and my shoes were officially two hours past the bearable mark. It was time to turn back into a pumpkin.

I grabbed my coat from the office, slipped my blistered feet into my flats, checked that no one had broken any important science equipment, said goodnight to Cathryn at the door and set off down the front steps.

Halfway down the street, I heard footsteps approaching rapidly behind me and then a hand grabbed my shoulder.

"Fuck you, fucker! I have mace!" I yelled as I spun around, grabbing a tiny bottle of hairspray from my bag. I tried to remember if I was supposed to head-butt a rapist in the nose or knee him in the balls first.

It was Popeye.

"Oh," I said, slipping the hairspray back into my bag. "Sorry about that. I thought you were a rapist."

He looked mortified. "God, no. I'm sorry I startled you. Are you all right?"

"Yes, I'm fine, and don't be sorry. I'm very relieved you're not a rapist."

"I saw you go and just had to run after you. I was watching you all night and I just think you're . . . I don't know . . . rather extraordinary. I'd like to see you again. Could I take you to dinner?"

"Oh, um. God. Sure."

"Great. I know a wonderful little place. My treat, of course."

"Sounds good." *Look demure look demure look demure*, I chanted to myself.

"Lovely. Could I take your number?"

He took out a gleaming iPhone and I tapped my number in.

"I'll give you a call during the week," he said. "Now, let me put you in a cab. I don't want you to have another fright tonight."

This guy was unbelievable. I was sure that one of the *Rules* authors had put him on to me to convince me of the merits of their ways. I glanced at his arms and decided I didn't give a shit.

And so it happened that I had my first glimpse of *Rules* success. He hailed a taxi, kissed me on the cheek and stared longingly after the car as it sped away (I know this because I watched him in the reflection of my phone). I was sure he would call.

Regardless, it was out of my control, which actually felt kind of good.

April 14

"So let me get this right: a gorgeous man reaches into his pocket with these apparently amazing arms of his and buys you a drink, and you leave him after five minutes in order to wander around a room by yourself. He then runs down the street after you and tells you you're amazing."

"Yep," I said, spreading peanut butter onto a cracker as I lay on the couch in my bathrobe. Lucy and I were enjoying our Sunday-morning debriefing over instant coffee and nail polishing. "That's what happened. Can you pass me that raspberry-colored one?"

She slid the little bottle across the table. "And he's already rung you this morning?"

I nodded. "We're going out on Wednesday. He actually wanted to see me tonight but the book forbids me from accepting a date less than two days in advance."

"So *The Rules* works?"

I painted a single stripe down my thumbnail and watched as it immediately bled into my cuticle. I looked up at Lucy. "I mean, I wouldn't go that far. That banker friend of Michael's didn't exactly fall at my feet. But, yeah, it seems to have worked on this guy, at least for now."

"Why do you sound gutted? Shouldn't you be pleased to have cracked the secret?"

I squinted as I tackled my pinky nail. "I don't really want to go around acting like some feminine zombie for the next sixty years, so I'm kind of rooting for it to fail."

"Well, I think it sounds brilliant. I might need to give it a try after all. Max has gone quiet on me again and I have zero prospects on the horizon."

"No!" I cried. "You have to have a normal life and bring me back stories from the real world! Speaking of which, how was your night?"

Lucy let out a long sigh and took a sip of her coffee. "Hayley and I went to the Electricity Showrooms for the eighties night, which was decent, but full of bridge and tunnel types. So of course we ended up in the Horse and Groom until three in the morning."

My eyes widened. "I am so jealous. How was it in there? Man, I miss that place."

"Same as always. I was harassed for an hour by a man called Boomer who was wearing a woolen hat and kept talking about his ex-wife's dog. He was a good kisser, though. Asked for my number at the end of the night so I gave him Amy's."

Amy was the evangelical, teetotal former roommate of Lucy's who was an obsessive tidier of shelves and alphabetizer of spices. Lucy had never forgiven her for dumping her rum and had taken to giving out her number to Shoreditch's weirder male inhabitants. Lesson learned: don't mess with a girl's liquor.

"See? That's so much more fun than being all demure and elusive and shit. I circled a room like a neutered piranha for hours while you were out enjoying your youth and making out with crazies. Science sucks."

Lucy rolled her eyes. "Um, excuse me? You were told you were amazing by some incredible mystery man with great arms who is now probably going to buy you dinner. So fuck off."

"Okay, okay," I said, taking a sip of now-tepid coffee. "But if Popeye turns out to be a psychopath and cuts me up into pieces and stores me in a meat locker, you won't think I've got it so good."

"Oh! I forgot!" Lucy suddenly jumped up from the couch and ran into the kitchen. She returned holding a postcard covered in tiny sailboats. "This came for you."

I flipped it over.

"You can never cross the ocean until you have the courage to lose sight of the shore"—Christopher Columbus

Good luck on your scientific adventure—just make sure you don't capsize!

Love, Meg

I smiled and tucked it into the pages of my journal. She always knew just what to say to make me feel brave.

April 19

The first date with Popeye was a resounding success, and I didn't end up in a meat locker at the end of it. I had to work late that night so we blew off dinner and went to the pub instead for a drink.

He chose a cozy little pub in St. James's that dated back to the seventeenth century. I'm a sucker for that kind of thing, and when I asked him about it, he shrugged and said he was a traditionalist.

He really wasn't kidding about that. It seemed like he was on a one-man mission to bring back the Arthurian age.

I walked in and he stood up immediately, took my coat, hung it up, pulled my chair out for me and went to the bar to buy me a drink. It was like being in the eye of a chivalry tornado.

He was polite, considerate, attentive. He asked questions, he complimented me, he bought drinks without awkwardness or hesitation. I don't know where this guy had come from but I definitely wasn't complaining.

After his allotted two hours were up, I sweetly told him that I had a big day ahead of me (a slightly more probable excuse on a Wednesday night) and said goodnight. Polite kiss on the cheek and one last yearning look at his truly excellent ass as he walked away, and I was back home to gush to Lucy about how eerily perfect he seemed.

This was confirmed when he called the next day to ask me to dinner on Saturday. Annoyingly, *Rules* girls aren't allowed to accept weekend dates past Wednesday because we are just Too Damn Busy and our time, like everything else about us, is precious. So we made a date for the following Saturday, which gave me an extra week to fantasize about him picking me up and tossing me around in exciting sexual positions.

April 27

I had prepared notes ahead of tonight's date with Popeye:

Name: Popeye
Age: 26 (A younger guy! In your face, gender stereotypes!)
Occupation: Consultant (A fake job if there ever was one, but never mind)
Nationality: English

Description: Really, really hot. Have I mentioned the arms?
Method: *The Rules*

We arranged to meet at a little Italian place in Soho, so after an action-packed day of exercising, painting my nails and eating cheese and crackers while watching a Food Network *Cake Wars* marathon, I made my way to the West End. I found the place pretty quickly, so I hid around the corner and smoked cigarettes until I was five minutes late. I'm a modern woman and very happy to sit on my own in a bar most days (maybe that just makes me a modern alcoholic?) but I hate being the first person to turn up on a date. I want the guy to be early, preferably with a drink waiting for me.

I walked into the dimly lit restaurant. There was Popeye, lifting some kind of manly, brown-colored drink to his lips with a massive forearm. He was definitely an alpha male: the type who not only had a firm handshake but who also did that thing where he put his hand on top of yours, just to emphasize his genetic dominance. This was a man with Darwin on his side. In spite of myself, I found this kind of thing hot. My stomach did a very, very small flip.

Once again, he stood up immediately when he saw me, kissed me on the cheek, slipped off my jacket, pulled out my chair and pushed me into the table in one fluid movement. It was like being mugged by gentlemanliness.

He sat down and pushed a cocktail across the table to me. "I've ordered this for you. I hope you like it—house specialty. How are you? You look gorgeous."

"Thank you." I took a sip of my drink, which was shocking pink and sickeningly sweet. Not my kind of thing at all, but I necked it nonetheless and tried my best to look demure while doing so. "Great place. I've never been here before."

"It's one of my old favorites. Went to school with the owner."

At that moment, a well-dressed man with impressively slick hair magically appeared holding several dishes of delicious-looking Italian tapas. Normally I hate tapas as it involves sharing, but I could make an exception for this.

"Hello, old chap! Always a pleasure to have you in my humble establishment, especially when you bring a gorgeous creature like this with you." The slick-haired man smiled and kissed my hand.

Popeye made the introductions. "Joff, this is Lauren. Lauren, this is my dear friend Joff. He's as much of a wizard in the kitchen as he was on the rugby field!"

"I was nothing compared to our man here. He used to eat up the turf like nothing else. Still got that cauliflower ear of yours, you ugly bugger, you?" Joff enveloped Popeye in a bear hug from behind. It was still the most macho thing I'd seen since the log-rolling competition at the Maine state fair.

Popeye shrugged him off. "You're one to talk, mate! You lost about eight teeth in the scrum."

"All in the name of glory. Anyway, I do apologize: I'm keeping your guest waiting." He turned toward me. "Would you like some champagne? Of course you would. A woman like you should be bathing in champagne. I'll send the waiter straight over." With that, he evaporated in a puff of smoke.

"Great bloke, Joff," Popeye said. "And he obviously has great taste." He reached across the table and touched my hand.

The waiter suddenly appeared at my elbow and began pouring champagne into glasses. I don't like champagne—always gives me a headache and I can never fit my nose into the champagne glass— but I was forbidden from turning my nose up at any of Popeye's date decisions, so I had to live with it. Tough life, I know.

He raised his glass in a toast. "To you. The most beautiful woman in the room."

We clinked glasses. He smiled. I narrowed my eyes. Where the hell did he come from?

"I feel I did the talking for both of us last time," he said. "I want to know everything about you."

"Oh, there's not much to tell," I said, trying to exude quiet mystery.

"Okay, well, let's start with the simple things. Where are you from originally?"

"Maine. A little city called Portland."

"What's it like there?"

"Oh, you know. Small-town America. Lots of land, lots of sea, lots of coffee shops. The usual."

"Sounds like heaven. What brought you over here?"

"Work, mainly. And the weather, of course." Shit, I'd made a joke. That was definitely against the rules.

Popeye laughed more heartily than the comment deserved. "Ah, yes, the great British weather. Beautiful, isn't it? Although I do think there's something to be said for taking a bracing walk in the countryside and then hiding in a pub when it pisses down."

"Yeah, that's true."

"Personally, that's the sort of thing I love to do with a girl-friend. Book a really gorgeous B&B someplace and whisk her up the M4 to the Cotswolds for a weekend away."

"That sounds . . . nice," I said. I wasn't sure what to make of this.

"That said, I love quiet nights in, too. Whipping up a cozy meal for two and opening a bottle of Châteauneuf-du-Pape."

"Just one bottle?"

He gave me a slightly disapproving look, then laughed. "Oh, Lauren. You're a gem."

"Thanks," I said, shifting uncomfortably in my seat.

The waiter reappeared with two menus, but Popeye took them both.

"We'll start with the *insalata di polpo* and move on to the *pollo alla cacciatora*." He gazed over the menu at me. "You eat meat, right, darling?"

"Yes," I said. Though usually I like to know what type before I eat it, I thought silently, but the book forbade me from saying anything. In the eyes of *The Rules*, Popeye was being a gentleman and protecting my delicate female brain from making any decisions— and I should just shut up and be grateful.

"I hope you don't mind me ordering," he said as the waiter whisked away the menus and glided off to the kitchen. "I've eaten here a thousand times so I know the best things on the menu." He reached his hand across the table and intertwined our fingers. "And you deserve only the best."

The evening went on as it had begun. It was as though I was a prospective employer and Popeye was trying very hard to get the position of My Boyfriend, even though I hadn't realized I'd been advertising. He fed me food off his plate. He told me that he was good with people but also enjoyed his own time. He mentioned that he wanted to go to Paris with someone special one day.

Honestly, if I'd produced a written test and asked him for a urine sample, I'm pretty sure he would have happily agreed to both and would have passed with flying colors.

I couldn't help wondering why on earth this gorgeous man was trying so hard to win me over. What sort of deep, fetid secret must he be hiding? Because, surely, someone this attractive and successful and charming had swathes of women falling at his feet and didn't need to try so hard to win my approval? Unless he had something seriously, horribly wrong with him . . . images of meat lockers started flashing before my eyes again, but I swiftly swept them aside and took another sip of champagne.

The food came, was eaten and plates were discreetly taken away. The champagne turned to wine and flowed like there was no tomorrow. He continued to ride around the room on his white steed, asking if there were any damsels in distress who needed rescuing. At one point, a man started coughing loudly and Popeye leaped to his feet and asked if he needed the Heimlich maneuver. Turned out he was just getting over a chest cold.

I couldn't decide how I felt about this charm offensive. It was so entirely different from what I was used to, and maybe that wasn't such a bad thing. It was a little weird being the focus of so much attention, but it beat sitting on Adrian's couch watching him play *Championship Manager* on his laptop and occasionally being asked if I wanted some more potato chips. And Dylan and I were together for so long, our idea of romance was taking out the trash so the other person didn't have to. All this chivalry was a nice change.

And so, at the end of the night, when the taxi pulled up in front of my building and he asked if he could come up for a cup of coffee, I said yes.

So it was entirely possible that this whole gentleman act was just a clever ruse to get me into bed. But you know what? I was fine with that. Really, aren't most people being polite to one another in the hope that it could lead to them getting laid? Even when I'm doing something charitable for someone outside of my sexual demographic (an old homeless woman, for instance), I'm secretly hoping that there's some really hot guy who's watching me be charitable and thinking, "God, look at that girl being charitable—how incredibly attractive. I must fly her to Fiji on my private jet." I'm pretty sure Doctors Without Borders runs almost entirely on doctors looking to impress the opposite sex with their selflessness.

Besides, it had been a while since I'd had sex—we're talking at least a month here—and it was basically our third date, so *Rules*-approved. (I was counting the night we met, yes, so sue me. *Months*, people!) We went up to my apartment and I made him a cup of Tesco's finest instant coffee granules, which was inevitably left to cool on the counter as we got down to business.

And down to business we got. If I thought I'd seen an audition in the restaurant, I was mistaken. That was only a warm-up.

He picked me up. He spun me around. He put me down briefly so that he could undress me with his teeth (I was worried about the dress, but he was surprisingly deft with his incisors), then picked me back up and spun me around again. He stood in front of me and peeled off his own clothes like a former Chippendale and, I have to admit, the show was spectacular. The arms were just the beginning: the man was Michelangelo's wet dream.

In spite of the display, there was something slightly . . . off about the whole thing. He choreographed sex in the same way he had choreographed dinner. He had a vision in mind, and I was just another actor on his stage. And not a principal character, either: I felt like the Greek chorus in *The Bacchae*. At one point, during a particularly complicated set of moves, I caught him watching himself in the mirror. Not me. Himself. He was basically starring in his own porn film.

That's not to say I didn't enjoy myself, because I did. He was great in bed, probably because he put so much effort into perfecting his starring role. Nevertheless, I felt unsettled when it was over, particularly when he got up and started to put his clothes back on.

"Where are you going?" I was trying to rearrange my hair into something not resembling a bird's nest, but gave up when I saw my reflection in the window.

"Sorry, darling. I've got an early start tomorrow so I'm going to shoot off home."

I'm not sure if it was the champagne, the wine or the images of meat lockers, but the last vestiges of the demure *Rules* goddess were lost and a mad harridan stood in her place.

I pulled the covers up to my chin. "Oh, okay. Fine." I tried not to pout but felt the corners of my mouth drift southward.

He came and sat on the edge of the bed. "Don't be upset, lovely girl. You told me yourself that you need a good night's sleep tonight for your run tomorrow."

"But that doesn't mean you couldn't sleep here, does it? It feels weird that you're just racing out the door."

He looked irritated for a second, then rearranged his face into an expression of paternal patience. "Shh. You just go to sleep, sweetheart."

I felt a stab of anger. "If this is just going to be a one-time thing, that's totally fine but don't bullshit me and say otherwise."

"Darling, of course I want to see you again! What happened tonight makes me want to see you even more so."

"Whatever. I mean, don't put on this whole Mr. Perfect show for my benefit."

"It's not a show! I want to treat you like the princess you are. I'll call you later, all right?" He bent down and kissed the top of my head.

"FINE."

As soon as I heard a door click shut, I leapt out of bed, suddenly convinced that he had stolen my wallet. So *that* was his motive: he was a thief! A common thief! Okay, sure, he'd seen the inside of my admittedly shabby apartment, and I vaguely remembered him mentioning his parents sitting on a pile of money somewhere in Hampshire, but that made it even more sick!

I pulled on my furry yellow bathrobe and ran into the living room to check the contents of my bag.

Once I'd confirmed that all £2.35 was still accounted for, I scurried back to my room, bag clutched to my chest, and ran smack into him as he came out of the bathroom.

"Hello," he said, surprised.

"Hello," I mumbled.

I walked him to the door.

"Okay, well, bye."

"I'll see you soon, darling."

"Whatever."

The door clicked shut and I stumbled back to bed, muttering about thieves and sexual bandits.

April 28

I woke up with an unpleasantly fizzing brain and had a moment of peace before remembering the purse-clutching incident.

Ack.

But the weekend had yet more trauma in store for me. I had a terrible shock in the afternoon when, in my hung-over and vulnerable state, I tried to call Meghan and accidentally dialed Dylan's sister, Molly, instead. I'm not sure what was to blame—the iPhone or my shaky, apparently enormous fingers—but when I heard Molly's incredulous "Lauren? Is that you? You've got one hell of a nerve, calling here . . .," I wanted to travel back in time and throttle Alexander Graham Bell for his cursed invention. I mumbled my apologies and got off the phone, swiftly pouring myself a whisky to calm my nerves.

I couldn't get the hurt and anger I'd heard in Molly's voice out of my head. I knew Meghan had been sugar-coating her dispatches from home, but now I'd heard the truth for myself. I was Public Enemy Number One back in Portland. I lit a cigarette and contemplated throwing myself off the balcony.

When Lucy got home from her trip to Westfield, she took one look at my ashen, clammy face and dropped her Topshop bags.

"Babe, what happened? You look like you've seen a ghost!"

"I have, sort of."

"What the hell are you talking about? And did I hear you bring a boy home last night? I thought I'd come home to find you and Mister Perfect wrapped in each other's arms!"

"Oh, Luce, it's all gone horribly wrong!" I was shocked to find myself on the verge of tears. Crying is usually an event reserved for extremely bad toe-stubs—certainly not for accidental phone calls or morning-after blues.

"Right, that's it. Up you get!" Lucy pulled me off the couch and directed me toward my room with a firm pat on the ass. "Get dressed and put some make-up on. We're going to the pub!"

And so, after a month of fastidious *Rules* following, booze and paranoia had blown all of my careful research. I had no idea if I'd hear from Popeye again or if my burst of lunacy had put him off for good. Regardless, *The Rules* was done and it was time to assess.

The main thing I learned from *The Rules* was that I'm really not very good at following *The Rules*. My natural instinct with men is to try to force things to a head (ahem) because I don't like not knowing how things will turn out. Hence the big old freak-out on poor Popeye.

So, in a way, it had been good for me to be forced to be more reserved. I should probably leave the ball in the other person's court more often. I get so caught up in the drama of a new assignation that I don't stop to think if it's something I actually want to get involved in, and then I end up driving it over a cliff.

And it had been strangely refreshing to let the guy make all the effort and I'd realized that, most of the time, they prefer it that way. Sometimes it's nice to have a man make a fuss over you.

The Rules in Conclusion

Works best on . . .

Alpha males who are used to getting what they want and who love a challenge. They tend to be happy to make a big song and dance out of things and to spend money in order to get what they want, especially if it's particularly hard to get. They're the ultimate capitalists.

To be used by . . .

Women who don't need instant gratification and who are looking
for commitment (though how you could keep up the Princess and
the Pea act for forty years of marriage, I have no idea). And it's
probably preferable if you're a teetotaler, as following *The Rules*
when drunk is pretty much impossible.

So it was with sadness tinged with relief that I put *The Rules* aside.
The only way forward was through a new book, this one fittingly
called *The Technique of the Love Affair.* I obviously needed some help
fine-tuning my technique.

BOOK TWO

THE TECHNIQUE
OF THE LOVE AFFAIR

May 1

Shockingly, I heard from Popeye again. He texted during my epic pub debrief with Lucy on Sunday night to say he was going to be away for a week on business and would be in touch when he got back. I'm not holding my breath.

I am, however, holding the new book in one hand and a cigarette in the other and thoroughly enjoying both.

The Technique of the Love Affair: By a Gentlewoman was first published in 1928 and caused quite a stir at the time, with Dorothy Parker (beloved wit, glorious alcoholic and devoted divorcée) saying that if she had read the book earlier in life she may have been "successful rather than just successive." It was out of print for years but is happily back in circulation, complete with helpful editorial notes.

Let me tell you, my friends: it is fucking awesome.

It was written in the time of the Bright Young Things and conjures up the frothy, tongue-in-cheek attitude that epitomized the post-WWI era (see also: Noël Coward, Evelyn Waugh and the aforementioned Ms. Parker). It was a time of bootleg gin, sharp wit and romantic dalliances. The author, Doris Langley Moore, was only twenty-three when she wrote the book. (She was married at the time but later went on to divorce her husband. After reading some of her advice, I can't say I'm surprised.)

The basic principle revolves around the idea that the "love affair" is an art form and should be viewed as a diverting hobby rather than a necessity. The author advises her readers to garner as many suitors as possible; you're meant to be light, charming and flirtatious with everyone and invest in no one. It's all about building and maintaining your "prestige" (which is essentially what we now refer to as the upper hand). By showing a man that you care more for him than he cares for you, or by investing in one man to the exclusion of others, you lose your prestige and therefore your appeal.

Swept up in the excitement, I made a list in my notebook of things I thought would come in handy over the coming month:

cigarette holder
kohl eyeliner
very short flapper-esque dress
bathtub gin distillery (?)

I was chomping at the bit to get started but while enjoying a homemade highball after work (in the name of research, of course), I realized that, once again, I had an alarming lack of test subjects. With Popeye AWOL, possibly never to be seen again, the cupboard was bare, and I needed someone to experiment on. And the nature of the book dictated that I didn't need just one someone—I needed several. There was no way I could summon up an army of men to be flirted and trifled with just by batting my eyelashes on the tube (though I'd certainly be giving that a shot). I needed help. Modern, forward-thinking help.

I needed the Internet.

So, on my lunch hour and after doing a quick sweep of the area to make sure no one was around to catch me, I signed up for Castaways.

Castaways is based on the idea that one person's trash is another one's treasure. People nominate friends who've recently been dumped but who deserve to meet Prince/Princess Charming. The Dumper can also nominate the Dumpee if they feel their ex is a wonderful person but couldn't quite get over the way they pronounced the word "prosciutto" or whatever.

I wasn't entirely convinced that the people doing the nominating were genuine, but I'd heard that it was filled with decent, non-disgusting men and I didn't have to take a psychological test to join, so I was sold.

The catch was that I had to ask someone to write a testimonial saying how unbelievably gorgeous, talented, brilliant, hilarious, sexy I was and how they just COULDN'T BELIEVE that I was still single and it must be because men are intimidated by me because of my incredible beauty and searing intellect. At least that's what most of the testimonials I scrolled through seemed to say, always accompanied by a very arty black-and-white photo of a pouty mouth or half a hooded eye.

I asked Meghan, as I figured she knew me better than anyone and was bound by blood to say nice things about me. She doesn't have all that much experience in the dating world herself, having married her soul mate, Sue, after they met at a Lilith Fair revival back in college.

They live in a converted barn and spend their weekends blissfully making jam and knitting each other scarves. Meg owns a successful gardening center and Sue's a surgeon at Mercy Hospital. That's right, my sister is married to a doctor. Meanwhile, I'm conducting my love life as a science experiment, accidentally phoning my ex's irate sister and joining a dating site presumably filled with

lunatics and weirdos. Obviously luck is one thing that does not run
in the family.

Anyway, I asked her to write something that would entice the
menfolk and she came up with the following:

> Lauren is an American expat who's been in London for a
> while now. She reads, drinks and smokes a lot. She excels
> at the following activities: having fun, making sure her
> companions are having fun, eating baguettes, being clever.
>
> As a child, she rode a very fat horse named Jason, played
> defense in football, kick-boxed on a regular basis and got in
> trouble at her Catholic high school for reading *Candide* in
> church. When you meet her, none of this will surprise you.

Now. First of all, let me say that all of the above is true. But more
important to the cause at hand, it makes me sound like Ignatius J.
Reilly out of *A Confederacy of Dunces*. And yes, I know that reference
just reinforced her description of me, but I'm trying to hide my
true, hideous self from prospective suitors (at least for a little while).

So Meghan's description just wasn't going to cut the mustard. In
the end, I confessed to Cathryn that I'd signed up to Castaways and
begged her to write my description, hoping that her relatively scant
knowledge of my adolescence would work in my favor. I was right,
and Cathryn wrote a great, slightly fabricated couple of paragraphs
that made me sound eminently more attractive than Meghan had.

It went online today along with a full-color photograph of my
entire smiling face and from then on it was in the hands of the Internet dating gods.

Soon, messages from Castaways started pinging into my inbox.
I was retrospectively pleased that I'd used my hotmail account
rather than the work email as, by the afternoon, I'd clocked up over

fifty emails from various online suitors vying for my attention. My head had swollen to the size of a watermelon.

When I got home from work, I mixed myself a sidecar (more research) and started clicking excitedly through the replies. I soon realized that the number of emails wasn't at all a reflection on my good self. The guys on this site were playing a numbers game, as there were lots of generic one-line emails from men who were just spamming all of the female Castaways out there, hoping one of them would bite.

In fact, after a little bit of scrolling, it became clear that quality merchandise was thin on the ground. It was kind of like being a kid in a really shit candy store, one that was mainly filled with slightly stale licorice sticks with the occasional peanut butter cup shining through.

After I deleted all the spammers, I weeded out anyone with a tag name like "Rocstarz" or "ChocolateBum." These men have qualities of their own, I'm sure, but they are not to be sampled by me.

Here's the thing that I quickly discovered about online dating: it enables shamelessly shallow behavior. All of these codenamed, speechless photos blinking up at me . . . it was impossible not to judge fairly heavily on the photo. So out went the hideously ugly, the morbidly obese, the wearers of wraparound sunglasses. Off you go, Oakleys! Back in the sea!

Finally, and most crucially, I got rid of all the dudes who used text-speak in their emails or, worse, emoticons. What self-respecting man uses a winking smiley face in a pick-up line? I ask you.

I assessed my lot after the cull and was pleasantly surprised to find half a dozen decent-looking, sane-sounding, proper-grammar-using guys still in my inbox. I fired off what I hoped were reasonably witty replies while eating an avocado in my old gym shorts. If this was any indication of online dating, I was hooked. Not having to wear heels in some sweaty meat-market bar was incentive enough.

May 8

My first Castaways date! Hooray! Eeek.

His online name was inoffensive enough, and after a few fairly promising email exchanges, he suggested we meet up for a drink. Whoop! How easy was that? I immediately agreed and a date was set for this evening.

Here's what I knew about him. He photographed well (if a little moodily). He had dark curlyish hair and brown eyes and appeared to spend a fair amount of time leaning up against slightly grimy walls in East London. A female friend recommended him to the site, which made me slightly suspicious because if he's so great, why wasn't she dating him herself? But his profile made him seem funny and clever and interesting, so what the hell. Plus, I needed to start testing out my technique and he was as good a candidate as any.

One interesting little curve ball: he was a fashion photographer. This was both alluring and terrifying. On the one hand, I quite liked the idea of someone a bit artsy and right-brained but, on the other, I hated the idea of going on a date with someone who spent lots of time in close proximity to models. I could already feel a hot kernel of jealousy ready to pop inside of me and I hadn't even met the guy yet. Not good.

I got ready in the bathroom at work, Cathryn looking on in fascination as I applied eyeliner.

"I don't know how you manage to get it in a straight line. I've tried it a few times and I've always got it in my eye," she said, blinking at me with her irritatingly long-and-mascaraless eyelashes.

"Practice. My sister and I used to give each other makeovers all the time when I was a kid. I've been an eyeliner expert since I was seven."

"You were allowed to wear make-up when you were *seven?*" Cathryn touched her peachy cheek with her hand, horrified.

"Christ, no. Not out of the house. It was just for fun! What kind of a nut do you think I am?"

"Thank God," she said, gently exhaling.

I swiped some red lipstick on, knowing I would end up eating it off before I even got to the bar, and cuffed the hems of my jeans so my new yellow heels were on show.

"All right, I'm off. Wish me luck!"

"Be careful! Remember to call if you need to make your excuses! And for goodness' sake don't follow him down any back alleys!"

"Thanks, Mom. See you tomorrow!"

I stood outside the pub in South Kensington, took a couple of drags on my cigarette and then gave a piece of Trident a couple of chews to cover the smell. As much as I'd brushed off Cathryn's warnings, I was a little nervous myself. The Photographer could be anyone. He could be a sociopath. He could be a drug addict. He could slip me a mickey and sell me into the sex trade.

Within five minutes of meeting him, I knew my evening wasn't going to be anywhere near as exciting as all that. The Photographer was a dud.

He stood up nervously when I approached him and gave me a slightly damp handshake.

We ordered our drinks (separately, with no movement to order/pay for/carry mine from him—suddenly I missed *The Rules*) and sat down at the bar so that I could begin to dazzle him with my sparkling conversation.

Within fifteen minutes, I had resorted to talking about the weather. He was a nice-enough guy but, Jesus, it was like getting blood out of a stone.

I referred to the book's advice:

> You must always seem attentive to his conversation;
> conceal the signs of flagging interest at any cost, but yet
> don't look too eagerly engrossed, or he will soon feel his
> talk is so delightful to you that he does you rather a favour
> by talking at all. Equally elementary, but highly effective,
> is the well-known policy of drawing a man out to speak
> about himself.

I put on my most engaged-yet-slightly-disengaged face (remaining careful not to go cross-eyed in the process) and played a fine game of twenty questions.

Throughout the Q&A, I was the perfect 1920s flirt. I nodded enthusiastically. I laughed merrily. I opened my eyes wide in fascination. To an outside observer, I'm fairly sure I looked like I had snorted speed earlier in the evening.

The Photographer remained impressively stone-faced throughout the performance, answering only in haiku:

Q: Where do you live?

A: Leyton, by the station.

Q: Where did you grow up?

A: Stoke. It was shit.

Q: How did you get interested in photography?

A: My uncle. Also, porn.

It got to the point where I was asking him about childhood pets and his favorite color. Except for the mention of porn, it was like interviewing a shy five-year-old.

The only moment of fun (and the only time the book seemed to work) came when he went to the bathroom. Two attractive guys walked in and sat down at the table across from me and immediately started an entertaining discussion about the decor of the pub (which was, bizarrely, Sherlock Holmes–themed).

"Banter!" I thought. "God, how I've missed you. TAKE ME WITH YOU."

One of them looked over at me sitting at a table on my own with two full drinks in front of me and two empty glasses to one side.

"Drowning your sorrows, I see? And two different types of drink as well! Must have been a rough day."

"Man, you have no idea. This is just a warm-up. It's bourbon next."

"Why not go straight for the absinthe? That always sorts me out." He smiled at me and I noticed that he was very handsome indeed. I raised what I hoped was a flirtatious eyebrow and was about to say something suggestive when the Photographer returned to his seat, which prompted the handsome man to raise an eyebrow of his own. I gave him a little shoulder shrug and the Photographer and I resumed our slow death march to the end of the date. After our second drink, the Photographer asked if I was hungry.

"No, I'm fine, thanks. Actually, I should get going. It is a school night, after all!" I looked down at my watch and realized it was only seven o'clock. Oof.

As we walked out, we went past the other table and the fellow I'd chatted with gave me a long, brooding look. Ah, frisson. The Photographer picked up on the frisson and gave the handsome man a dark glance before putting his hand protectively on the small of my back. It was the most action I'd had all night.

The book goes into detail about the benefit—nay, necessity!—of encouraging male competition and inciting jealousy. Morally, flirting with one man while on a date with another isn't exactly a high point for me but there is something strangely thrilling and Discovery Channel–ish about pitting two guys against each other. It's evolution, guys! And didn't I say I was in this for science?

For the notebook:

Name: The Photographer
Age: 29
Occupation: See above
Nationality: English
Method: The Technique of the Love Affair
Description: Dark hair, brown eyes, possibly the victim of one of those
    brain traumas from an Oliver Sacks book in which his personality
    was wiped out
Result: Flirting makes even the most painful social occasions more
    diverting

May 12

Popeye was back in town but his ardor seemed to have waned. He sent me an innocuous text at a suspiciously late hour on Friday asking what I was up to, which I ignored. It was possibly the first time I've chosen having the upper hand over having sex. Victory doesn't taste all that sweet.

I waited until this morning, Sunday, to reply as breezily and coquettishly as possible. The book encourages you to play suitors off one another and to make it seem as though you constantly have men clamoring for your attention. Thus:

Hello! Sorry I haven't got back to you—my weekend has been crazy! Have literally just got in from the night before and about to go to a BBQ now. How are you?

It wasn't strictly truthful: I'd stayed up late drinking wine on the couch with Lucy, yes, but it hadn't exactly been a wild night.

And the BBQ was actually just me taking a book and a croissant to the park. But, hey, my prestige was at stake here.

The response was almost immediate:

> My weekend has been much quieter than yours by the sound of things! What a popular girl you are . . . Would love to see you again soon . . . xx

So far, so good. I didn't respond and didn't have plans to—in order to maintain my prestige, I had to hold out on him as much as possible, especially since he had been kind of useless recently.

Incredibly, I also received a text from the Photographer saying he'd had a great time the other night and asking if he could take me to dinner next week. Maybe he was having an out-of-body experience during our date? Maybe he was a masochist? I wasn't compelled to dig any deeper, so I sent a polite decline. I know I needed test subjects, but I couldn't face another Q&A evening.

May 13

Today, a shock.

I was sitting at my desk putting together the costs for our new children's after-school program when my phone rang. I looked down to find my cell phone judging me.

Are You Drunk?

"Of course not," I muttered to myself, "it's three forty-five in the afternoon!" The penny dropped. "Oh shit."

I answered as I ran into the corridor.

"Hello?" I said, trying to sound breezy while catching my breath (now proven to be a physical impossibility).

"Hey, Cunningham. It's me."

"Yeah, I know it's you. What's up, Adrian?"

"Why didn't you say so straightaway? And where are you? You sound like you're training in a wind tunnel."

"I'm at work, jackass. Some of us have actual jobs. In offices. With computers and shit."

"Hey, I worked today! I wrote for an hour and a half. Now I'm in the park, doing research."

"The park can go fuck itself."

"That's no way to speak of our city's green spaces."

"What have they done for me lately?" I was now making for street level at full speed. I suspected I was going to need a cigarette for this. "What do you want?"

I heard a long sigh on the other end of the phone. "Look, I think I was a bit of a shit."

I pushed open the emergency exit door and lit my cigarette—which was now a cigarette of triumph. "Yep, I can confirm that. Anything else?"

"I just wanted to explain what happened between us, because you're a nice girl and I'm—"

"A douchebag?"

"Now, that's not very nice, but yes, fine. A douchebag. I just felt like we were heading into relationship territory and I wasn't ready for relationship territory."

I took a long drag. "First of all, stop talking like a pioneer. Second of all, I told you all along that I didn't want a relationship! I just made you eggs! And sometimes eggs are just eggs."

Adrian laughed. "Yeah, I suppose. But you didn't eat them yourself! You made them just for me."

"That's called being a nice person, asshole. It's not entrapment."

"Well, anyway. I just wanted to apologize for disappearing like that."

"Apology accepted."

I took another drag and held it in, waiting for him to say something. Something like, "Can we go for a drink tomorrow and then have lots of filthy sex?" "Can we pretend these past two months didn't happen?" "Can we resume a twice-weekly almost-platonic sexual relationship?"

But it was Adrian, so instead he said, "Right, Cunningham. I'm off: research calls."

"Yep. Bye, chief."

And then he was gone. I stubbed out my cigarette, walked back to my desk and spent the rest of the afternoon in a daze.

Lucy and I dissected the phone call at length in the evening over wasabi corn cakes at the new Peruvian-Japanese fusion place that had opened up in Hoxton Square.

"Well, I suppose it's something that he apologized," she said as she took a long drink from her pisco sour.

"I guess. Though what am I meant to do with an apology?" I nudged a bit of sashimi onto a tortilla chip and crunched. "Do you think I'll hear from him again?"

"I wouldn't be surprised, lovely. That one is like a recurring case of thrush. Just when you thought you were rid of it, the itching starts again. Anyway, enough about that knob. Let's plan our party!"

I had convinced Lucy to throw a house party in the name of science. While researching this month's book, I had come across a flapper's dictionary and in that dictionary, shining up at me like a little diamond, was the term "petting party." And, from there, a dream was born.

Apparently, a petting party was a "social event devoted to hugging"—I think it was sort of like a rave, but without the ketamine (or whatever the kids are doing these days). How could I resist? I was hoping it would be like the game of seven minutes in

heaven I played at my thirteenth birthday, only this time hopefully
Joey Richardson's braces wouldn't get caught in my hair.

"Okay. I think we should keep it small. Why don't you invite
Hayley and Georgie and I'll invite Cathryn? And then lots and lots
of dudes."

"Cathryn won't come, will she? It's too far east for her. Didn't
she once confuse Hackney with Harlem?"

It was true, she had.

"Yes, but I should ask just in case and, besides, maybe Michael
will have some cute single friends lurking around."

A waifish waitress wearing a baby-doll dress and knee-high
athletic socks appeared at our table, having been summoned by
Lucy's frantic waves. "Yeah?" she asked, boredom etched artfully
across her face.

Lucy acknowledged her with an eye roll before turning to me.
"Do you want another sake, babe?"

"Yes, please!" I said brightly, beaming at the waitress. Ever
since my bartending days back in college I'd made an effort to be
nice to wait-staff, however incompetent or surly. I turned back to
Lucy. "Okay, Saturday night, as many prospective men as we can
handle. I'll invite Popeye to see if I can stir up some jealousy
in him."

"I'll invite Max. He's gone all quiet again so he might need a bit
of a kick up the arse as well."

"Perfect. Now. One question. Should I invite Adrian?"

"Lauren . . ."

I took a long sip from my fresh sake and tried to look innocent.
"Well, he did call and apologize . . . maybe we could be friends!"

"Friends? You can't be in the same postcode without wanting to
shag him." She took a ponderous sip from her drink. "Though I
suppose he would get to see you with Popeye."

"Exactly! I could incite jealousy all over the place!"

"Fine. But I'm hiding the breakables."

"You're a wise woman, Lucy."

May 15

Inviting Popeye involved a certain amount of finesse. When I first broached the subject, he wasn't available because he had to go to the birthday party of a family friend. Regardless of whether or not this was true, I was getting tired of him not being around. If I'd been following *The Rules*, I would have never contacted him again. But *The Technique* had a different approach, offering up this little gem of advice: "Let your relations with men leave memories of seething fury and hatred rather than embarrassment."

I've had enough embarrassing assignations in my time, the memory of some of which still have the power to stop me dead in my tracks and bathe me in the white heat of shame. Rage and fury, however, were largely uncharted territory.

I was never one for confrontation, but this time I was pissed off. After all of that knight-in-shining-armor shit I felt like he should just be a bit . . . better! Did the man not understand that it had now been several weeks since we'd had sex? It felt like I was slipping into another Adrian situation: ambiguous, lackluster and mildly infuriating.

So to get the rageball rolling, I sent this *Technique*-approved text message to him:

Well, I have been as pleasant as I could, but you are apparently determined to be dull, so I shall go and spend my time in more responsive company. Let me know when you are feeling more amiable!

His response was swift: five minutes later, a text flashed up on my cell phone.

> Sorry, darling! I know, I've been a bore. I'll try to come to your party, I promise. Xxxx

He texted again the next day to say he'd canceled on the family friend and was coming to the petting party. Ha. Screw you, old family friend! I've got more prestige than you!

Adrian, on the other hand, accepted the invitation immediately, no finessing needed. Maybe it was a full moon.

May 18

Petting party time!

Lucy and I spent most of Sunday pawing through the rails at a vintage store on Holloway Road, looking for suitably flapper-ish outfits. I settled for a black, high-waisted, obscenely short playsuit and a feathered hairband and Lucy ended up with a cleavage-enhancing drop-waist dress and approximately three hundred strands of fake pearls.

We put bowls of cigarettes out for guests and filled the bathtub with ice and bottles of gin. Hair done and make-up applied, we started helping ourselves to the Tanqueray before the guests arrived.

Cathryn had gracefully bowed out of the evening, citing yet another family dinner. Being posh seemed to involve a lot of family dinners. But a couple of other colleagues had agreed to come, and Lucy had a bunch of her friends coming along (thankfully some of them male).

The doorbell rang at 8 p.m. sharp and from then on a steady stream of people flowed into the apartment. Some of them even looked vaguely familiar. Max turned up wearing a flat cap and holding his guitar. Popeye came with a bottle of Scotch and a guy wearing two polo shirts called Henry.

"How many of these people do you actually know?" I asked Lucy as I poured drinks for Popeye and Co.

"Hmm. About sixty percent?"

"Okay, that's reassuring. I know about ten percent. Thirty percent is a manageable unknown variable."

At that moment, the opening strains of "Waterfalls" blared out over the speakers.

"I've got to go find Popeye," I said, making a dash for the balcony.

It was a petting party, so hugging had to be a part of the evening. I couldn't figure out a seamless way to weave it in, so in the end I had made it a house rule that every time TLC's "Waterfalls" came on (which was surprisingly often due to my dubious iPod DJ-ing skills), everyone had to find a partner and hug through the chorus.

"Hello!" I said brightly. "It's hugging time!" I grabbed Popeye and Henry, and the three of us swayed gently to the chorus while I tried unsuccessfully to keep from burning myself with my cigarette.

Popeye obviously felt a little sheepish about the hugging and poor Henry looked like he was seriously considering hurling himself off the balcony. I suspected that when Popeye asked Henry if he wanted to go to a petting party, he'd slightly mis-sold the idea.

But after a couple of hours, the Jägermeister had made its appearance and everyone was hugging like it was going out of style. Henry in particular was clinging on to two of Lucy's more buxom friends like he was a shipwreck survivor and they were flotation devices.

"I have to confess, I've not been to many house parties. Well, not this sort of house party." Popeye eyed the cement balcony, now full to the brim with drunk youths.

"There's booze in the bathtub and nineties hip-hop on shuffle. Whose kind of party *isn't* this?"

He smiled wanly. It definitely wasn't Popeye's kind of party.

At that moment, a pilled-up young man whose name I think was Felix sidled up to us and started stroking the hair on my left arm.

"Would you like to hear a poem I just wrote?" he asked.

"Sure!" I said. Popeye nodded imperceptibly.

He proceeded to regale us with several (surprisingly pretty good) poems. And then a Billy Connolly impersonation. And then a couple of tricks with his trilby.

Forty-five minutes passed.

Something strange occurred during this time (other than the obvious). It's fair to say that it was extremely obvious to anyone not on a massive amount of drugs that pilled-up Felix would make a pretty poor challenger in the suitor department, but the more he talked to me, the more proprietary Popeye became. At one point, he leaned over and, nodding toward pilled-up Felix, said, "It looks like this fellow is sweet on you, darling. Is he bothering you? Shall I have a word?"

I assured him that an intervention wasn't necessary as the pilled-up man certainly wasn't making any overtures toward me; he was too busy gurning his face off.

Regardless, the chivalrous, complimentary Popeye from last month suddenly returned with a vengeance. There was hand holding and admiring glances and more compliments than I could shake a stick at. Eventually, Felix drifted off, probably because I was too busy saying thank you and being distracted by the hand on my ass to listen to any more of his poems.

I hadn't seen this side of Popeye before: the competitive, possessive side. It was hot. I looked around the room to see if there were any other patsies who could help me incite jealousy in him.

Like a gift from God, the buzzer rang.

By this point, I'd given Adrian up as a lost cause but then, at a quarter to midnight, a full three hours after he promised to show

up, there he was with a marshmallow bunny on a stick and a mate
called James about whom I'd heard only filthy, deviant things. I immediately introduced him to Lucy, who was looking increasingly
worn out by Max's insistence on playing the acoustic version of
Jay-Z's "Can I Get A. . . ."

I took Adrian's proffered bunny and, with something approaching glee, introduced him to Popeye.

The two shook hands, Popeye puffing himself up considerably
in his button-down while Adrian looked on shiftily, a little grin on
his face.

"Hello! How are you, Cunningham? I've not seen you in ages!"

"I know! I don't know why it's been so long . . ." I smiled at Adrian
while trying to burn a hole through his forehead with my eyes.

"We mustn't leave it so long next time." He turned his attention
toward Popeye. "And you must be Lauren's beau. At last, to finally
meet you! I've heard so much. How long have you two been together now? A year? Two? Any nuptial plans on the horizon? She's
not getting any younger, you know!"

Popeye dropped my hand like it was on fire.

"Perhaps you're thinking of someone else. Lauren and I have
only been out a few times, though she is an amazing lady." Popeye
gave me an alligator grin and I heard Adrian stifle a laugh.

"Hmm. Yes, maybe I'm thinking about the bloke she used to go
out with. Very good-looking, him. Such an artistic air about him.
Wasn't he a writer, Cunningham? What was his name again?"

"Go fuck yourself," I hissed.

"I remember you saying how good he was in bed, too. Whatever
happened to him?"

Popeye took a sharp intake of breath. "Lauren hasn't told me
much about her love life."

"Well, there's lots to learn! Lots to learn." And he didn't know
the half of it.

"I can't think of anything worth recalling in recent months, actually," I said as I pulled Popeye away. "Help yourself to the gin in the bathtub, Adrian. Careful you don't drown."

"Don't worry about me!" Adrian said as he made a beeline for the bathroom door. "I'm known for my buoyancy."

"What an asshole," I said. "Sorry about that. Do you want another drink?"

"No, I'm fine. So who's this chap he was talking about?"

"Oh, no one. Just some idiot I used to date. Old news."

"Good," he said, and then he kissed me for the first time that night. "I don't like competition."

The evidence indicated otherwise.

May 20

"Oh God, what happened last night?" Lucy was standing in front of me in last night's dress and a pair of slippers.

"I think you made out with Adrian's friend. Coffee?"

"James? Oh no. Yes to coffee, though."

I flicked the kettle on and got out an extra mug. "Don't worry, you just kissed. He whispered something into your ear and you flew into a rage and threw him out. I think it may have been something about a threesome."

"Ugh. Why are men always asking for threesomes? If I want to have one, they'll bloody well know about it."

"I know. It's like kids begging for chocolate before dinnertime. You just want to slap their hand and say 'Not now!'"

"Did Adrian go with him?"

An image of him staggering out the door holding a bottle of gin and bellowing the words to "Engine Engine Number 9" flashed through my head.

"Yeah, I think so. He was such a jackass last night in front of Popeye."

"That's hardly a surprise. What happened with Popeye? I saw you two snogging on the sofa."

"He left a couple of hours ago." I handed her a cup of coffee and a cigarette.

"Ooh. So? How was it this time? Still a one-man show?"

"It was . . . vigorous. Lots of lifting up and putting down and spinning around."

"Ooh!"

"I knew I was on to a winner with those arms. Although it did feel like he was trying to prove something. You know when it's like you're having sex with a dude who's performing for the camera even if there's no camera there?"

"Mmm-hmm."

"I mean, he was calling out directions at one point. It was all 'arch this' and 'bend that.' I was Debbie, and we were definitely in Dallas."

Lucy wrinkled her nose. "Sounds a bit much."

"Honestly, I blame the Internet. Every guy now seems to think he's auditioning for YouPorn." My eyes widened. "Oh my God, you don't think he'd put us on YouPorn, do you? My parents just learned how to use Google—what if they find it?"

"I think you're getting ahead of yourself, love. I'm sure you would have noticed if he'd been filming you."

"That's true. I don't think he would have managed all of the acrobatics if he was juggling a phone in one hand."

"Well, at least you had a decent shag. Max was nowhere to be found this morning." A shadow of dread suddenly passed over Lucy's face. "Wait . . . what exactly happened to Max?"

"I'm pretty sure you threw his guitar out the door."

"Oh God." A pause. "Oh fuck." A second pause. "I remember now. He kept insisting on playing the acoustic version of everything, and when I tried to lure him into my bedroom, he said he'd be disappointing his audience if he left."

"Musicians, eh?"

"Fuck it, I'm glad I tossed his guitar out."

"There's always James," I trilled.

Lucy buried her face in a sofa cushion. "Don't remind me."

I slunk away to the balcony to check my emails. There were a couple of promising Castaway candidates so I tried to set up dates with them for the following week. I needed to get a coterie together by the end of the month and time was seriously running out.

After my third email, my phone flashed with that familiar phrase: **Are You Drunk?** I picked up on the fourth ring.

"What the fuck do you want, Adrian?"

"Is that any way to talk to an old friend?"

"When that friend is an asshole, yes."

"Come on, Cunningham! I brought you a marshmallow last night! No one who brings confectionery can be a *complete* arsehole."

"You also pissed off the guy I'm seeing for no apparent reason and tried to convince him that I'm a giant slut. So yeah, you're an asshole. Marshmallow or not."

"Ah, I was only joking. Besides, that bloke seems like he has a rod up his arse."

"He's a gentleman, actually. *And* he has great arms."

"Mmph. So you're, like, seeing him?"

"I dunno. I guess so. Sort of."

"Sounds exciting. Him and his big arms."

"It is, actually."

"Look, let me get you dinner. To make up for the eggs thing, and for being a knob last night, and for being a twat in general."

Dinner. I had never had dinner with Adrian. We weren't had a dinner-having sort of relationship. At the very most, we'd had a meet-in-the-pub-for-a-chat-beforehand relationship.

"Dinner, eh? Okay . . . though I'm not paying for it, if that's what you're thinking. I'm not into supporting starving artists."

"Give me some credit. Jesus. I'll cook and everything."

I had lost the power of speech by this point, so I grunted my consent and then hung up. What. The. Fuck.

I guess this jealousy thing works on more than just Popeye.

May 24

The flirting project had gotten slightly out of control; I couldn't seem to stop making eyes with everyone.

Cathryn and I went to our favorite lunch place after a meeting at Imperial College about a potential lecture series. I realized that she was watching me with hawkeyed suspicion.

"Don't think I didn't notice what you were doing to that poor defenseless man at the counter," she said as we walked back to the office.

"What?" I said, clutching my overflowing salad box. He *had* been more generous than usual, and I suppose it *may* have had something to do with the fact I told him that he was looking particularly dashing . . .

Later, when waiting for the elevator at work, a couple of moving men pushed past us carrying a large desk.

"You're incorrigible," Cathryn said, shaking her head.

"What?! I didn't even look at them!"

"Well, it seemed like you were flirting with the burly one. At least, I think he thought you were flirting."

"You're being paranoid," I said, flicking a quick wink at the burly mover.

But she was right: it's like I've got flirting Tourette's.

Case in point: I went for a run tonight along the Embankment and while waiting at a traffic light and doing that annoying little hoppity run-on-the-spot jog that all runners pointlessly insist on doing, I made eye contact with a fellow runner and actually smiled. This isn't something I would normally do. I tend to have a look of grim determination on my face when running and try to avoid eye contact with other humans as much as possible.

But this time I was so swept up by my flirting addiction that I forgot to put my running face on and instead had my game face on.

He smiled back. He was actually surprisingly handsome, a fact made more pronounced by the way he was all flushed and sweaty and post-coital-looking from the run.

"Nice pace," he said.

"Thanks," I said, grateful that my face was already bright red from exertion so he couldn't see my furious blushing. "I have a lot of pent-up rage, so this helps."

"Oh, really?"

"Totally. If it weren't for running, I'd probably be a mercenary in Angola."

The light changed. I smiled, turned on my iPod and took off. I realized in retrospect that I had come across as a lunatic, but the beauty of running is that it doesn't matter what you look like or what you say to strangers waiting at lights, because you can always make a quick exit.

A few minutes in, I glanced behind me to see that Running Man had tucked himself behind my left shoulder and was matching my stride. He gave me a smile.

"I wanted to see the rage in action," he yelled.

"You sure about that?" I said as I sped up.

"I think I can handle it." He passed me within minutes and gave a little wave of encouragement for me to keep up. I was spurred on by the sight of his thighs and upped my pace.

Twenty minutes later, Running Man and I were huddled around a water fountain, taking turns gulping down water.

I bent over double and tried to catch my breath. "Christ, my lungs feel like a couple of punctured tires."

"Judging from that performance, you have some serious anger issues to work on. Good run, though. I think we've earned a drink or two. What do you say?" Annoyingly, he was way less of an out-of-breath, tomato-faced mess than I was.

I looked down at my sweat-soaked top. "I would love to, but I don't think I can stand being in these disgusting clothes for much longer."

"Fair point. Rain check then?"

I agreed and he tapped my number into his phone before taking off at a blistering speed. I limped home thinking about Running Man's lovely thighs, a smug grin having replaced the look of grim determination. God, I loved flirting. I was going to miss living in the 1920s.

May 31

The last day of living a flapper's existence and I'm proud to say that I've accomplished the main aim of the book: "There should be at least two men desiring you at one time—more if you are very skilful or fortunate."

This had proved trickier than one would hope, but I'd finally managed to collect a coterie of men (annoyingly, just at the point when I had to switch books).

There was Popeye, of course. There was Running Man, who texted straight after our death-match run and who I'm meant to see in a couple of weeks. And then there's this mystery dinner with Adrian coming up. It was pretty much a full house. So, after a month of shameless flirting, I think the author of the book would be quite proud of me; I'd turned into a fairly decent coquette (drawing on my own natural inclinations, of course).

But here's the thing: having a veritable harem wasn't giving me the glow of satisfaction I thought it might. Instead, I was growing increasingly bored. It was the dating equivalent of eating cotton candy: delicious at first, but soon you start feeling a little sluggish and sick.

I totally get the point of having as many men in your life as possible. When there are lots of different possibilities on the horizon, you don't get too invested in any one person. God knows I'd been too invested in one person in the past, so you'd think this would be a good thing. All those months ago, when I decided I couldn't stay in Portland a minute longer, the prospect of an endless array of men to choose from felt like Narnia. But now that I'm here, I sort of just want to crawl back through the wardrobe and go to sleep. It's overload—I don't have the time or brain space to get attached to any of them, and I'm starting to resent each one's tug on my attention. In a way, this is good, because if one falls off the radar or blows me off or turns out to be a massive Meatloaf fan, I can easily forget about him and move on. But on the other hand, I don't feel great about seeing a cache of men whose names I could easily forget tomorrow. (Adrian being the obvious exception, mainly because he was around preexperiment so was the subject of a whole Google-stalking campaign. I could probably lead a guerilla warfare–style ambush in his neighborhood considering how well I studied those streets.)

It sounds odd, but I find myself wanting to blow ALL of them off. Popeye's text messages are too banal, the Running Man will probably want to discuss protein shakes and energy gels, Adrian will probably cancel . . . Faced with the prospect of dating three men at once, I want to cancel all upcoming dates and devote myself to reading every book I never get the chance to read and finally giving myself a proper facial.

Of course, in terms of the experiment, the month has been a resounding success. I absolutely loved this book—the author was sharp, witty and completely uncompromising about what women should expect (and what they must demand) from men. Women aren't encouraged to pander to men or make them the central focus of their lives. The point of having a love affair isn't to find a husband; it's to have fun and test out your powers of persuasion. It was all strangely empowering, if exhausting.

The Technique of the Love Affair in Conclusion

Works best on . . .

As with *The Rules*, alpha males are probably the most susceptible: the relentless flirtation will fuel their competitive streak. But, really, most of us are susceptible to jealousy, so showing that you're sought after is likely to pique anyone's interest.

To be used by . . .

All women! Or, at least, all women who are looking to have a grand old time and flirt and feel desirable. Probably not a good idea to use this if you're looking for something long term and serious though, as all the jealous-making and suitor-balancing could backfire pretty easily. But the bottom line is that everyone could use a bit more flirtation in their lives.

BOOK THREE
NOT TONIGHT, MR. RIGHT

(or, as I like to call it, *Close Your Legs, Open Your Heart*)

June 1

Ah, a book on abstinence! Fantastic. I'd been looking forward to this one *so* much. That said, I felt I'd been involuntarily following some sort of abstinence guide for some weeks now, so I might as well do it officially. As having sex was pretty integral to my seduction strategy, I figured I had to try out a method that actively eschewed sex . . . but that didn't mean I had to like it.

I wasn't in the best of spirits when I walked into the bookshop to pick this one up, so you can imagine my displeasure when I was greeted not by the crinkly-eyed smile of the sweet, elderly bookseller, but by the inhospitable grumble of a youngish man sporting a shock of curly auburn hair and a tattered old cardigan. He would have been cute if it wasn't for the scowl deeply embedded on his face.

"We're shut," he barked as I walked through the door.

"Evidently not," I said. "Where's Hamish?"

He gave me a dark look. "He's gone."

I stopped in my tracks. Hamish, gone? But I only saw him the other day, and he looked like he was in rude health! Surely he wasn't . . .

"Gone?"

"Yes, gone! Retired to Tuscany, the lucky bugger."

Well, at least he wasn't dead. Still, I wasn't sure I liked this new situation. "Uh . . . and who are you?"

"I'm his grandson. I've taken over the place," he said, gesturing toward the dusty shelves and the precarious spiral staircase that led to the attic. "Now, what can I do for you? You've got five minutes before I lock the door. It's your choice which side you end up on, though I warn you that this place does get a bit cold at night."

"I'm Lauren Cunningham," I said, smiling what I hoped was a charming smile. "I think your grandfather had a book on hold for me?"

"Oh," he said, pushing an unruly lock of hair out of his eyes and looking at me more closely now. "You're the American." He didn't say this in an encouraging way.

"That's me!"

"Right. Hang on a sec. I'll get your little . . . romance book out of the cupboard." He cast a critical green eye over me, shook his head and walked into the back room, returning with my copy of *Not Tonight, Mr. Right*.

"What a load of old cock," he muttered to himself. He sat down at the desk and set about studying the cover with unbridled disgust. The guy had a lot to learn about customer service.

"Look, just tell me how much I owe you and I'll get out of your hair."

"Why do you want to read this pile of shite?" he said, tossing the book across the desk. He bent down and started rummaging beneath the desk, surfacing with the collected works of John Dos Passos. "Read this instead," he said, handing the tattered paperback to me.

I looked at the cover. "Already have," I said, handing it back to him. "How much do I owe you?" I put on my most haughty face.

He leaned back in his chair, put his feet on the desk and sighed. "Oh, fuck it, I don't know. Three quid?"

I pushed the change across to him and slipped the book in my bag, pausing on my way out to admire the antiquarian section. It was the only clean part of the shop and there, inside the freshly polished glass case, was a beautiful first edition of *Black Beauty*.

It had been my favorite book as a kid—my mom used to read it to Meg and me before bed, and I read it to myself as I got older. I'd been obsessed with horses until I was ten, and Black Beauty embodied everything I loved about them: the freedom, the spirit, the sense of wildness. My edition had been an old cheap hardback, but this one was gorgeous: thick brown leather with purple embossed lettering. I coveted it, hard.

I turned back to the bookseller, who was now in the process of pulling a thread from his cardigan that appeared to threaten the structural integrity of the whole thing, and said, "How much is this copy of *Black Beauty*?"

He let out a little harrumph but didn't bother looking up. "It's not for sale."

"Are you sure?" I said, leaning closer to the glass to get a better look. "It's gorgeous."

He got up from the desk with a bang and hurried over to the case. "Well, don't breathe all over it!" he said, shooing me away.

"All right! All right!" I said. "You don't have to get all angry about it. Sheesh."

"It's quite valuable, actually," he snapped. "It was mine when I was a boy." His voice softened and for a minute he looked . . . sweet. He shook himself out of it and looked at me with renewed annoyance. "Now, if there's nothing else you need, it would be marvelous if you would bugger off so I can finally shut."

I made a swift exit, already dreading the next time I needed a book. The new guy was easier on the eyes, but he was definitely lacking his grandfather's charm.

I made my way to the nearest pub, ordered myself a glass of

wine and cracked open my new guide, eager to learn the apparently myriad benefits of chastity. I guessed the first one would be the money I'd save on condoms.

Close Your Legs, Open Your Heart is meant to be a modern take on abstinence. You choose chastity not because of religious beliefs or moral codes; you choose it because of science. That's right! Apparently sex triggers some sort of neediness love chemical called oxytocin (not to be confused with hillbilly heroin, though apparently it's just as addictive). As yet another example of Nature's little ironies, the more orgasms you have, the more this chemical invades your brain and tells you that the man giving you those orgasms should be clung to like the last remaining life preserver in a cruise ship disaster. (Not that I can really blame my brain for this. There are worse things to cling on to than a man who can produce orgasms.)

So sex is bad because sex leads women to act like slavering, love-drunk possums. Of course, the author purports that this bonding drug is only released in women; men can sleep with a different woman every hour on the hour and never feel the need to plan a four-course meal for them on a Tuesday, "just because." In fact, the book's premise stems from the idea that somehow men only fall in love with women they are NOT having sex with, thus casting aside hundreds of years of reproductive science.

So it seems women aren't built to have casual sex. We just love *too much*! Sure, personal experience suggested otherwise. I'm fairly certain that every woman I know can name at least one man with whom they've slept where Cupid's arrow didn't strike. In fact, I'd be reluctant to share a croissant with at least three of the men I've had sex with, never mind a life. But the book insists that we're delicate creatures who can't handle sex without having our brains reprogrammed, so for the next month I was determined to be as pure as the driven snow.

Apparently, abstinence can have some profitable side effects.

For instance, I would be more assertive in the workplace because I wouldn't be having sex on my desk. Cathryn would certainly be relieved. I would also be more clear-eyed, goal oriented and self-confident. At least there were a few silver linings.

I thought the best way to tackle the prospect of a month without sex was to prepare myself as best I could, so I went shopping. First stop was Holland and Barrett for some valerian root. As I wasn't even allowed to, uh, take care of business myself (as masturbation fuels the sex drive, and my sex drive was now Public Enemy Number One), the author recommends taking valerian root as an alternative way to unwind. I bought a jumbo bottle, plus three bottles of wine from the liquor store next door. I had a lot of unwinding to do.

Second stop was Cos, where I picked up several high-necked white button-downs and a long, light-blue dress. If I was meant to act like the Virgin Mary, I might as well dress like the Virgin Mary.

Last but not least was an M&S bumper pack of extremely ugly underwear. I know it's a cliché of Bridget Jones proportions but I suspected that when push came to shove, I'd be a bit more virginal knowing that any man traveling south would be faced by acres and acres of high-waisted cotton.

I also canceled my Brazilian appointment and hid my box of Durex.

I was ready.

June 2

As sex wasn't an attainable goal this month, I decided to give myself a different type of physical challenge: I signed up for Tough Mudder.

For the uninitiated, Tough Mudder is a thirteen-mile assault course that includes scaling walls, crawling underneath barbed wire and, as a special treat, being electrocuted in a mud bath. I figured I could capitalize on all the clear-eyed assertiveness I was about to develop.

Now, I considered myself to be in pretty good shape: I ran a couple of times a week and I always ate my vegetables. But when I watched the promo video for Tough Mudder, which was filled with brawny men grimacing as they pulled tractor wheels up an enormous hill and chucking themselves off precipices into dubious bodies of water, I realized I might need to do a little bit of extra training. Especially as the race was at the end of the month.

I decided to start with a few push-ups. I hadn't done them since high school, but I thought I could easily knock out a quick set of twenty. By the third, my arms were shaking like a shitting dog and sweat had started to pool in new, alarming places.

There was definitely work to be done.

So, aside from abstinence, the new additional goal for the month was to be able to do twenty push-ups and at least one pull-up. I'd never managed more than a dangle in the pull-up department, so I knew this would be a challenge. Thankfully, I was going to have lots of time on my hands and energy to burn.

June 4

Push-up update: three and three-quarters before collapse

Pull-up update: dangling

Popeye and I went on our final date tonight.

The effects of the petting party had lingered on; over the past two weeks or so, Popeye had bombarded me with texts asking what I was doing, where I was going, who I was with, what I was wearing . . . the works.

At first, it was kind of sexy. The "what are you wearing" question led to me describing a gorgeous Coco de Mer lingerie set I'd seen in the shop window recently. In reality, I was wearing a pair of eighties basketball shorts and a T-shirt so full of holes it was essentially just a loose collection of atoms: such is the magic of our digital age.

But soon, it all started to get a little heavy. One night, when I told him I was having a night in with Lucy, he asked if I was sure no one else was in the flat with us, as though we had men stashed away in closets or under the floorboards. And when I canceled our dinner plans because of a crisis at work, he turned up outside my office with a takeout. I know that sounds sweet, but I had the feeling he was there to check up on my story rather than offer moral support.

Anyway, it started to freak me out. I worried that the petting party and Adrian had broken his brain and that his true nature as a possessive psychopath was about to be revealed.

Still, he did have great arms and I don't like to miss out on a potentially entertaining date story, so I kept our plans. Anyway, under the constraints of the new book I could only gaze at him demurely from across a dinner table.

We met at a sushi restaurant in Notting Hill, best known as a good place to spot Elizabeth Hurley sucking painfully on an edamame bean. I was wearing a long black dress that was so concealing I had an English Defence League member spit at me on the street.

Popeye was already there when I arrived, drink in hand and staring pointedly at the door. He looked relieved when I walked through it, and then annoyed.

"You're late," he said as he kissed my cheek. "Where were you?"

"Sorry!" I said, instantly chastised. I glanced at my watch. "Actually, I'm only six minutes late."

"I was worried. I was beginning to think you wouldn't come."

"Well, that's just nuts," I said. "What are you drinking and can I have one?"

"Gin and tonic. I'll get the waiter."

Drinks firmly in hand, we settled into our booth and started discussing the week's events. I was knee-deep into a story about Lucy and me going to the Horse and Groom and ending up in a long discussion about German expressionism with a Russian man and his two mistresses.

". . . and the two of them even went to get waxed together! Can you believe that? It was like something from the Playboy mansion."

Popeye didn't seem to be enjoying hearing about the mistresses' beauty regimes. He rolled his eyes and said, "I don't understand how you and Lucy end up in these conversations."

"Everyone's off their faces in that place. It's like shooting ducks in a barrel."

"Fish. Shooting fish in a barrel."

"Well, ducks seem like they'd be easier to hit, and you get my drift. Anyway, the guy said I could come take a look at his Kirchner collection whenever I wanted."

His eyes darkened. "I'll bet he did."

"Oh, please. He has not one but *two* freshly waxed twenty-one-year-old Eastern Europeans at his service! I don't think his intentions were untoward. I think he was just happy to talk to someone about his art collection who wasn't mentally adding it to his net worth."

"You must be more careful, darling. More sensible."

"I'm afraid you're barking up the wrong tree if that's what you're after."

He sighed a long, disappointed sigh. "Lauren, I'm just a little concerned about you. You're nearly thirty—"

"Uh, hang on a second, buster—"

"And you're out running around with Lucy talking to all of these strange men! Like that fellow Adrian who was at your party the other week. And that man who kept reciting those terrible poems."

"Some of them weren't bad. I thought the one about the tractor was decent."

"That's not the point! The point is, I like you. I want to look after you." He reached across the table, covered my hand with his big manly one and smiled. "I just want you all to myself. When I first met you, you were a quiet, demure little dove. Now all I seem to hear about are other men and mad drunken nights out. I want you to settle down. With me."

I know that in many of the romantic comedies at the start of this millennium, a speech like that would have triggered a tear of happiness to bead up in the heroine's eye as she realized that she had the love and protection of a strong-armed, strong-jawed man who wanted her all to himself. She would throw out her cigarettes, pour all of the whisky in her cupboard down the drain and start tagging meat-heavy recipes on Pinterest.

But as I mentioned at the beginning of this experiment, I wasn't looking for a knight on a noble steed, or Gerard Butler on a motorcycle, or even Ryan Gosling in a boat in the rain. I'd had enough of that back in Maine and the experience taught me that these things end in tears. I felt a pang of guilt. Popeye was a decent guy, even if he could be a little territorial. I couldn't lead him on.

I slowly extricated my hand and smiled.

"You're a great guy, but I'm just not looking for a relationship right now."

His smile faltered. "What do you mean? I thought this was going somewhere."

"I thought we were just having fun," I said, knowing that wasn't exactly the truth.

"But surely that has to lead somewhere? At some point, Lauren, you're going to have to grow up. Time isn't kind to women over a certain age. You don't want to wake up one day and find out the party's over, do you?"

I swallowed my feminist outrage: there was no point in getting into a heated debate about gender ethics. "You're a great guy, and you have fantastic arms, and I'm sure there are loads of girls who are desperate to meet someone like you. Look at you—you're a total stud!"

He perked up a bit at this. "Mmm. But I thought we were on to something."

"We had a good time. Isn't that enough?"

"I'm afraid not, and I'm afraid you're not the woman I thought you were. If it's all right with you, I'd like us to say our good-byes now."

"Of course. I don't feel much like sushi at the moment, either."

Popeye got the bill (a gentleman to the last) and we parted ways outside. I smoked a cigarette on my way back to the tube, thinking how odd it was that I'd never see him again. I realized I felt fine about it. Really, I felt nothing. He was a nice guy, if a little chauvinistic, but we'd both been playing roles that didn't suit us. It was for the best that the curtains had closed.

I sent Lucy a text telling her I was on my way home before stubbing out my cigarette and walking down the steps to the tube, careful not to trip on my skirt.

June 8

Push-up report: five (better!)

Pull-up report: still dangling. I might try doing one backward tomorrow and see if that helps.

Abstinence is boring and the valerian root is giving me a stomachache. So far, I hate this month.

Meghan called from Maine to check in on me this afternoon.

"Hey, kiddo. How's it going?"

"It's going. Thanks for the postcard." It had arrived last week: a

picture of an old clapboard mansion in Portland, days before it had
been demolished. The front yard was covered in rusted-out car
parts and green vines had nearly consumed the front porch. On the
back, she'd written:

> *"Everything has beauty, but not everyone can see"* —*Confucius*
> *Love you, M*

I had tucked it in the pages of my journal along with the last one.
"Just a little reminder of home," she said. "So how's the experiment? Any conclusions yet?"

"Well, Popeye and I parted ways last night."

"What happened? I thought he was a good egg." I heard the
sound of a dog whimpering in the background. "Hang on a sec, I've
got to let Harold out." I heard a screen door creak open. "There you
go, buddy! Where's Maud? Huh? Go find Maud!"

Maud was their new kitten, bought to catch mice in the farm-
house kitchen.

"Are you sure Maud really wants to be found?"

Meghan laughed. "Are you kidding me? She rides on Harold's
back like he's a horse! They love each other. Now, tell me what happened with Popeye."

"He wanted me to be Maud to his Harold."

"Oh. Well, I guess that proves that at least one of the books
works, right?"

"I guess so. I'm still not getting what I want, though."

"I know, sweetie. No strings attached, no lovey stuff, no feelings,
no emotions . . ."

"Exactly."

"People aren't robots, kid. People fall for other people, emotions get in the way, irrational decisions are made. You know that
better than most. You can't keep yourself away from that forever.
You'll have to let some light in there at some point."

"No, I don't. Why does love have to be the ultimate goal, the end result? I give zero fucks about love. I'm happier on my own."

There was a sigh on the end of the line, and then I heard an almighty crash in the background.

"Maud! Get down from there! Kid, I'm sorry but I've got to go: the cat has just scaled the china cabinet. Look, I'm sorry. I just worry about you."

"I'm fine! You don't need to worry. I've got everything under control."

"You've been saying that since you learned how to talk. 'I'm fine' were practically your first words. That's what I worry about."

"Yeah, yeah. Love to you, love to Sue."

"Love to you, too."

I hung up and threw my cell phone onto my bed. I glanced down and saw the small cardboard box peeking out from under the bed. I thought about opening it and picking through the old photographs and letters like week-old scabs. Instead, I grabbed my trainers and headed out for a run. Reminiscing wasn't going to get me anywhere: I had an obstacle course to train for.

June 9

Push-ups: five and a half (steady if slow progress)

Pull-ups: half a backward one with the help of a chair

Today the sun shone for the first time in a fortnight and I woke up feeling renewed. I decided to face this month's challenge with as much aplomb as I could muster. So what if I couldn't have sex? I was soon to be a lean, mean, Tough Muddering machine.

Speaking of which, I've got my date with Running Man next Saturday.

And, even more excitingly, or possibly disastrously, tomorrow is my dinner with Adrian.

I have no idea what to expect but I do know what NOT to expect, and that is sex. I can't believe I'm actually writing these words, but tomorrow I am going to see Adrian at his house (which is WHERE HIS BED LIVES) and I am not going to have sex. I feel like I've fallen into Bizarro World (which may explain the sunshine in London today).

Wish me luck.

June 11

Push-ups and pull-ups: none—too annoyed

Adrian canceled yesterday. Of course he did. Apparently there was a massive warehouse fire in Slough and he had to go cover it for the paper. I hope he got a fireman's hose stuck up his ass.

And to add insult to injury, Running Man canceled our date for Saturday too. Apparently his grandmother is ill or something. Selfish bitch.

On the bright side, a month of abstinence isn't going to be all that difficult to achieve if no one wants to have sex with me.

I've also noticed that all of last month's flirting has ceased abruptly. I don't know if it's all the demure clothes, or if I'm emanating some kind of anti-pheromone, but I haven't had a single glance thrown my way so far this month. On the tube, in shops, in bars: it's like I'm invisible. My light has definitely gone off.

June 13

Push-ups: two to three billion, all under duress

Pull-ups: none, though I can barely pull my pants up at this point so it's not surprising

Lucy and I went to boot-camp training in Victoria Park tonight after work. I thought it would make a nice change from our usual run and it was a glorious evening: still warm and bright with only the slightest of gentle breezes.

Before I knew it, that gentle breeze was whizzing past as I galloped up and down a hill while an enormous former Marine sergeant shouted insults at me. We were being forced around a gigantic circuit, each station bringing its own special blend of blinding pain and bullying from the instructors.

I caught Lucy's eye as she dove to the ground to do yet another burpee while a sadistic-looking blond man towered over her. Her pupils were dilated with fear.

At the end of the hour, we were both covered in dirt and brambles. Lucy's normally bouncy ponytail was hanging limply and I was convinced I'd dislocated my thumb in an overzealous forward roll. We went to the pub for a pint and a bowl of chips (carbohydrates being an important recovery food).

"Jesus," I said, taking a long sip from my pint. It tasted like cold, liquid heaven. "Those guys were a little . . . intense, don't you think?"

"Never again, babe." Lucy swiped a chip through the pot of mayonnaise and popped it in her mouth. "Those instructors might have been super fit, but I stopped thinking about shagging them when the blond man called me 'dumpling,' and I don't think he meant it affectionately."

I clinked glasses with her. "Here's to abstinence."

June 14/15

Push-ups: eight (amazing progress!)

Pull-ups: a quarter (again, progress!)

I had already changed into sweatpants and was folding laundry when my cell phone rang. The time was 11:03 on Friday night. It was Adrian.

I stared at the phone for a minute, wondering if I should pick up. That's a lie. Who am I kidding? Of course I was going to pick up.

"Are you calling to cancel non-existent plans just for shits and giggles? Cat up a tree this time? Bomb threat in Tesco?"

"Cunningham, are you still dwelling on that? You know what Billy Joel says: I didn't start the fire."

"Go to hell. What do you want?"

"I'm just by your flat and wondered if you wanted to get a nightcap."

"I'm in my pajamas."

"Even better. Shall I come up?"

My eyes darted around the room, which was currently covered in piles of socks. It wasn't exactly inviting. Plus, Adrian in close proximity to a bed was asking for trouble.

"No!" I blurted. "Do not come up here."

"Why? Have you got a suitor around? Dirty girl."

"No. I just don't want you coming up here."

"Fine, then come down here. Meet me in the Eagle in ten."

I made a noise like a trapped cat.

"Come on, Cunningham. Just for one. I'm buying."

Three hours later and dressed in torn skinny jeans and an oversized sweatshirt (my painstakingly assembled "I just threw this on and came down to meet you" outfit), I found myself pressed up against Adrian in the Horse and Groom as a drunk man in a bear costume stumbled past.

I had consumed more bourbon than I could recall, and Adrian had his hand on my inner thigh.

"Do you want another one?" His breath was warm and vodka-tinged and impossibly alluring.

"Sure. Can we go outside first? I need a cigarette."

"You and your nicotine . . ."

I followed him out and leaned against the wall of the pub. As I lit my cigarette, I glanced over at Adrian. His hair had fallen over his left eye and his white T-shirt had a huge rip down one side.

"What happened to your shirt?"

He glanced down at the tear. "Dunno. Been like that for months."

"Did you ever think about throwing it out?"

"Why would I do that? It's still functional."

"I don't know that I'd call it functional. I think you'll find the purpose of a shirt is to cover your torso, and that, my friend, ain't cutting the mustard. Where the hell did that phrase come from anyw—"

He lunged forward and kissed me, pinning me against the wall.

"Do you ever shut up, Cunningham?" he whispered.

"Hrrrmmmmmmgh," I mumbled.

"Let's get out of here. Back to yours?"

I nodded weakly as he placed his hand on the small of my back, guiding me through the crowd of smokers. I was powerless in the face of his voodoo magic. Where the fuck was my valerian root when I needed it? He stopped at the intersection to kiss me again, then slipped his hand under my sweatshirt to my bare back. (I was suddenly grateful for all the push-up work.)

We were a block from my apartment when I saw it: an enormous billboard featuring a neon-lit pint of Guinness and the words "The Best Things Come to Those Who Wait."

It was like a bolt of lightning sent by Zeus, or the angel Gabriel blowing his little trumpet right in my face.

I stopped short and dropped Adrian's hand like it was on fire.

"I can't do this."

Adrian looked startled. "Do we need to make a condom stop?"

"No. Ugh. NO! I can't have sex with you."

He gave me a lopsided, quizzical grin. "Of course you can. It's very simple, Cunningham. I believe you've done it before, though I'm happy to provide a refresher course. I can assure you that you'll have a lovely time."

"I'm sure I would but I just . . . can't. I'm sorry."

I gave his hand a quick squeeze and then ran across the road, narrowly avoiding being mowed down by a minicab in the process. I heard someone cursing me, but didn't want to turn around to see if it was the driver or Adrian.

June 15 Continued

Push-ups and pull-ups: none (all energy sapped from amazing display of willpower)

Lucy was perched on the edge of my bed, the hour hideously early for a hung-over Saturday. I was lacing up my sneakers while she poured black coffee in my mouth and pumped me for details.

"So? Did you sleep with him?"

"Lucy Hunter! What kind of girl do you think I am?"

"I know exactly the type of girl you are, so don't play coy with me. You reek of whisky and you look like the cat that got the cream. Give it over!"

I took a gulp of coffee and grimaced as it burned my tongue. "I am pure as the driven snow."

Her blue eyes widened. "Fuck off!"

"It's true! My honor is intact. Chastity belt still firmly locked. Are you ready to go?"

Lucy tucked her iPhone into her sports bra and tutted. "This bloody thing never stays put. Right, let's go. You can explain on the stairs how you managed to spend time with Adrian without shagging his brains out."

"It was a feat of enormous self-discipline. I almost caved, but then I ran away at the last minute."

"What do you mean, ran away?"

"I mean I physically ran away from him. It was the only way to save my pure soul."

"How did he react?"

"I didn't turn around to see."

"How do you feel?"

"Disgruntled, mainly, but also kind of smug? It's weird. Obviously I wanted to sleep with him, but there was something kind of liberating about waking up alone. I feel like I have the upper hand back or something. Of course, I'm sure he'll never speak to me again considering the ungodly case of blue balls I must have given him."

"I suspect Adrian's cock will survive."

"Mmm. It's resilient, I'll give it that."

"Anyway, I'm proud of you."

"Thanks, man. Me too. C'mon, help me sweat all this booze out."

When we got back to the apartment, I found a text message waiting for me.

> I've been very distracted this morning thinking about you, you
> little tease. A xx

And that, my friends, was the exact moment my brain exploded. Somehow, it had worked. After months of trying to get

Adrian's attention by having increasingly imaginative and acrobatic sex, it turns out that the best way to turn him on was by not sleeping with him. Go figure.

I spent the rest of the day highlighting passages from *Close Your Legs* and rereading the text from Adrian (to which, being of a sexual nature, I naturally did not reply).

Tonight, I broke out in a rash; the result of a valerian root overdose.

June 18

Push-ups: thirteen (huge burst of strength)

Pull-ups: two-fifths (better)

Three days have passed without a word from Adrian and without so much as a whiff of sex. I've spent much of my time doing laundry, rewashing the several white high-necked shirts I've been wearing all month. I've also reorganized the cupboard under the sink, painted one wall of my bedroom purple and embarked on an ill-advised curtain-sewing project using some Liberty print scarves I found at a vintage shop. My bedroom now looks like a 1970s bordello.

I have done so much exercise I nearly passed out from dehydration at work yesterday. Cathryn took one look at me and told me to go lie down on the sofa in our office, but we're working on a huge new exhibition on microbes and I had to finish drafting the press release. I've been working more hours than God gives us and my desk has never been more organized.

In short, going for this long without sex has made me a more productive, fitter, neater and more diligent person. It has also made me really, really fucking boring.

Thank God for cigarettes and booze, and for the light at the end of this very long tunnel.

June 26

A breakthrough: managed three-quarters of a pull-up before my hands slipped off the bar and I fell to the floor. I also did fifteen push-ups. I am basically bionic.

June 27

After weeks of arranging and rearranging plans, Running Man and I finally went on a date today. Well, sort of a date. We went for a bike ride after work.

I know: people are actually doing this now! Instead of sitting in a nice cozy pub and guzzling attractiveness-enhancing alcohol down their necks, people are opting to sit on bicycles and stare at each other's spandexed asses for long stretches of possibly deadly road, reach the designated point, briefly discuss the scenery, share a Power Bar, turn around and go home again.

Normally I would balk at the suggestion of going on such a clearly ridiculous and un-fun date, but I figured that nothing dampened passion like cycling gear and the smell of bike oil, so when Running Man suggested cycling along the canal to Hackney Wick, I agreed. I was almost a month into celibacy and couldn't be trusted to keep my underwear on in almost any circumstance.

Unfortunately for me, Running Man happened to have a seri- ously excellent ass, so I spent much of the ride thinking about biting it. As a result, I nearly ran over several small children and one very irritated goose.

When we got there, it took us fifteen minutes to find somewhere to lock up our bikes because of a Hackney-wide cycle-polo tournament, by which point I was half-starved and—thanks to a freak heat wave—had a tongue like a dried sponge. I suggested we go to Crate Brewery for a beer and a slice of pizza.

He looked at me with surprise and—if I'm not mistaken—a tinge of disappointment in his eyes.

"Do you mind if we go somewhere else? I'm in training for an ultramarathon so I'm really trying to hold off on eating any processed carbs." He punctuated the statement by patting his admittedly slim torso. "There's a macrobiotic place around the corner that does an amazing quinoa salad. We could pop in there if you'd like?"

My heart sank. I like quinoa as much as the next woman (by which I mean that I have trained myself to like it over years of enforced consumption) but I wasn't so hot on a guy who shunned pizza and beer for whole grains and green tea. I know I'm being sexist, but it just seemed . . . prissy.

Nevertheless, I was going to pass out if I didn't eat something soon, so off we went to the macrobiotic cafe, where Running Man promptly had a shot of wheatgrass and asked for a grilled chicken salad (no dressing, no croutons). I had a piece of organic carrot cake with tofu frosting (just about as gross as it sounds).

"When's this ultramarathon of yours?" I asked as I speared a runaway raisin.

"Next month. I'm fired UP!"

"How long is an ultramarathon again?"

"Hundred K. Can't wait."

"Jesus. That's a long trot."

He nodded enthusiastically. "I think there's something almost spiritual about running that far, you know? It's like you're one with the gods."

"Mmm. The longest I've ever gone is a half marathon, and I didn't feel particularly spiritual toward the end of it." In actuality, I'd pissed myself on the last mile, but I thought I'd keep that to myself. (Hey, you try running 13.1 miles without a bathroom break and see how you fare.) "I'm doing Tough Mudder in a couple of days, though, so that should be a challenge."

He looked disgusted. "Tough Mudder is nothing. It's just a little mud and a few hills."

"And barbed wire."

He waved me away. "Those things are just distractions. What you want to do is distance. Pure distance. Just you and the road. Once you free this—" he leaned over and tapped the top of my head—"you can run forever. Did you know that there's a group of Japanese monks who run forty thousand kilometers over a thousand days?"

"Yeah, but they're monks. What else do they have to do?"

"Lauren, they're *spiritual beings*. They understand that pain is purely physical. To achieve true enlightenment, you have to transcend that pain barrier. I ran the Three Peaks marathon in Wales last summer, and within the first mile I tripped over a root and fell off the trail."

I bit my lip to stop myself laughing. The image of people falling over does it to me every time. "What happened?"

"There I was, lying in a ditch, my ankle twisted, watching all the other fellas tear down the course ahead of me. And then I heard this voice."

"A voice?"

"From above."

Here we go. "What did it say?"

"It said, 'Stay the path. Feel no pain. You are a warrior.' I got up and started running. The front of my trainer was torn, so I ripped it off and ran on without it."

"So you basically ran a marathon in a sandal with a sprained ankle because a voice in your head told you to?"

He nodded solemnly. "Yes. At the final mile, I collapsed. I had lost several toenails by that point, and what remained of the trainer was soaked in blood. People were shouting for me to stop and get help. A medic tried to pull me off the course and into a waiting ambulance."

"It sounds like you needed it. You could have really hurt yourself."

"That's a loser's attitude. I knew that if I just transcended the pain, I could finish."

There was a long dramatic pause as his gaze locked onto mine, his eyes burning.

"And so I finished. It was a new personal best. I still don't have feeling in the toes on my left foot, and it's taken a year for the toenails to grow back. But it was worth it."

"Fuck."

"Yes. You see? It's all in the mind."

"Maybe, but I'm still not sure I would want to lose toenails over it."

"You hardly miss them when they're gone." He took another swig of wheatgrass and looked determinedly into the middle distance.

We cycled back to Old Street and parted ways at the top of my street, him proclaiming that he was off to do a brief 50K cycle before going home. He asked if I wanted to come along to his running club meeting on Wednesday, but I demurred. I wasn't ready for transcendence.

I crossed the street and went into the liquor store for a bottle of wine and a Milky Way. As I thumbed through a copy of *Vogue*, I realized I'd already forgotten what Running Man looked like.

He was a nice guy, sure, and part of me was strangely attracted to his fitness zealotry. His ass was certainly a selling point (I actually can't think about it too much right now for fear of boiling over) but with the prospect of sex off the table, his ass was a moot point. At the end of the day, I had found him kind of boring. It wasn't his fault, and I was sure there was a pert female ultrarunner out there waiting for him, her blond ponytail swinging in the breeze, but in the immortal words of Bob Dylan, it ain't me, babe.

Name: Running Man
Age: 37
Occupation: HerbaLife Sales Rep
Nationality: Australian
Description: Can't remember concentrating so much on his face, but
       he does have an unbelievable body
Method: *Close Your Legs, Open Your Heart*
Result: If there's no chance of sinking your teeth into a banana cream
       pie, there's no point in going to the bakery

I thought about what Running Man had said about marathons, about hitting that point of clarity and everything else just falling away. That's how I felt coming to the end of this month. Don't get me wrong: I definitely missed sex, but at the same time, there was something liberating about not having to think about it. When I was sitting across from Running Man at that cafe, I wasn't wondering what he'd be like in bed or imagining that muscle right above the hip flexor, or wondering if I had any condoms back in the flat. I was thinking about how I was having a fairly dull time, and how I'd rather be at home with a bottle of wine, a Milky Way and a copy of *Vogue*.

This is going to sound a little corny, but I've really enjoyed concentrating all my energy on myself this month. I feel like a saner, stronger, more self-sufficient person. So while I wouldn't recommend abstinence full-time, I would say that there's something to be said for clearing the palate occasionally and just focusing on you. A little abstinence sorbet, if you like. And now that my mouth was all fresh and clean, I was ready to stuff my face again. Plus, as of this morning, I can do seventeen push-ups and seven-eighths of a pull-up: not bad for a month's work.

Not Tonight, Mr. Right in Conclusion

Works best on . . .

I didn't feel particularly more attractive to menfolk during this month, though I did end up feeling marginally more attractive to myself. And I guess to Adrian, though I don't think he can be considered an average test subject considering how deeply, deeply subnormal he is. So maybe it works best on yourself?

To be used by . . .

Anyone who enjoys feats of endurance, valerian root and their own company.

June 29

While I'd wrapped up the dating side of this month, I still had one more thing to cross off my list before I could officially move on to the next book: Tough Mudder, of course.

I turned up to a field in Sussex at an ungodly hour of the morning. I had two cups of coffee and a banana before I left the house, and I could feel both of them quietly curdling in my stomach as I lined up at the starting line. I was surrounded by groups of men wearing customized T-shirts heralding their local five-a-side club or their company name (almost entirely from the banking sector). I was one of the only women, and I was definitely the only woman on her own. There was so much testosterone in the air, I was worried I'd grow a beard.

And so, when the starting pistol fired, I wasn't feeling particularly confident.

But three hours and twenty-eight minutes later, covered in slime and with bruises blooming across every inch of my body, I crossed the finish line. I'd had some help up the walls from some of the banking bros, and one of my few fellow ladies gave me an energy gel when I was flagging post mud-mile, but I had done it. And that feeling of accomplishment, that rush of endorphins, that enormous surge of unfettered sisters-are-doing-it-for-themselves pride was better than any sex I'd ever had.

BOOK FOUR
THE RULES OF THE GAME

July 1

I got back late from work to find Lucy starfished on the couch. She hadn't come home at all over the weekend and had sent me several cryptic text messages about staying with a friend when I'd tried to track her down.

"Hey, stranger! Where the hell have you been? I was worried about you last night. Wait till I tell you about Tough Mudder."

"Lo, I have some big news."

"Hang on a sec—let me get an ice pack." One of my knees had swollen to the size of an eggplant since Saturday and I was trying to keep it under control. "Is the landlord finally going to fix the hole in the kitchen floor?" I called out to her from the kitchen. "I almost knocked myself unconscious on the countertop!"

"No! Much more important than that."

"Thanks for your concern," I muttered.

"Lauren! This is serious!"

"Okay! Okay! I'll open a bottle of wine."

I hobbled in from the kitchen with a bottle of red, two glasses, a jumbo bag of mini eggs I'd been hoarding since Easter and a pack of frozen peas for my knee. "Shoot."

Lucy sat up straight, tucked an errant blond curl behind her ear and said, "I'm in love!"

"Shit. What? Since when? With who?"

"Since Friday! I met him at work. He sat in on one of our strategy meetings and we couldn't stop staring at each other. I could barely make it through the quarter two derivatives."

Lucy's job involved something to do with accounting that I didn't really understand. I made a mental note to Google the word "derivative."

"Anyway, he pulled me aside after the meeting and asked me to have dinner with him that night. He took me to Dabbous—I have no *idea* how he managed to get a table at such short notice—and then for martinis at Dukes. We ended up going back to his—Lo, he lives in a *penthouse* off of *Hyde Park*!—and we spent the whole weekend in bed. I've only come home tonight because I've got that big meeting to-morrow and need to get some sleep. Oh, babe, he's just amazing. He's handsome and smart and clever and kind and rich . . . he's perfect!"

"That's very exciting! And what's this Mr. Perfect's name?"

"Tristan. Tristan Fraser-Clarke. God, even his name makes me swoon!"

"When are you going to see him again?"

"Tomorrow night! He's taking me to a private viewing at some gallery on Bond Street. You should see his art collection—you would just *die*."

"An art collector, too! This guy sounds incredible."

Lucy's eyes widened with excitement. "Oh, he is. He's like a proper Prince Charming. And fit! He has silvery-gray hair, and these amazing dark-green eyes with those sort of crinkly bits at the sides—"

"He has gray hair?"

"Yes. He's very distinguished." There was a defensive edge to her voice.

"Just how old is Prince Charming?"

She suddenly looked coy. "Well, he's a bit older than me. But with age comes wisdom, experience . . ."

"A penthouse . . . Come on, spill it. How old?"

"Fifty-seven, which is actually not *that* old, when you think about it. Not in the grand scheme of things. Besides, I've always had a thing for older men."

"That's a pretty big gap, Luce. Does he have kids?"

"No, he's been a confirmed bachelor his whole life . . . until he met me!"

"Well, God only knows guys our age aren't worth their weight in retro high-tops. You might as well date up." I still had my reservations about the age thing, but one look at Lucy's radiantly happy face told me I'd better keep them to myself.

"Exactly."

"Now, the important part: how was the sex?"

Lucy's eyes lost focus and glazed over. For a moment, I thought I'd lost her.

I snapped my fingers and topped up her drink. "Hello? Anyone home? Or did he *literally* fuck your brains out?"

"Sorry, sorry. Lo, the sex was incredible. We did things that I didn't know were possible. Dirty, filthy things."

I lost her again for a second.

"You really have hit the jackpot!"

"I know. I'm telling you, he's the one! This is it!"

I took a sip of my wine and smiled. "I'm happy for you. I really am. Come on, let's go have a cigarette."

"Okay, and then I'm off to bed. I'm shattered and my hips are killing me. I don't think I'll be able to sit down properly tomorrow."

I rolled my eyes. "Excuse me if I don't feel too bad for you. I think my hymen has grown back at this point."

Cigarettes extinguished and Lucy off to dream of silver-haired foxes, I ran myself a hot bath. As I sank into the steaming water, I thought about Lucy's news. I wanted her to be happy—of course I did!—but a tiny, mean part of me hoped that things with Tristan wouldn't work out. Lucy was my number-one partner in crime in London, and losing her to the world of relationships would be a serious blow. Why did everyone have to pair off in the end? What about the freedom—the joy!—that came from being single? Why was everyone so keen to get into something I had been so desperate to get out of?

I dunked my head under the water. It didn't matter what everyone else did. I had to focus on the project. Tomorrow was the start of the new book, and it looked like it was going to be a doozy.

July 2

I should preface this by saying that when I went into the bookshop to purchase this month's book, the new bookseller picked up the copy I'd found in the attic, threw it across the room and tried to force me to buy Simone de Beauvoir instead. I explained that I'd read all of her work years ago—and her complete correspondence with Sartre—and that I'd go buy my copy of *The Rules of the Game* from Waterstones, thankyouverymuch.

Anyway, you're probably familiar with the whole "pick-up artist" scene by now. There was a show on MTV about it featuring a guy who looked suspiciously like Kid Rock circa 2003 and who always wore a giant furry top hat. Apparently, this man has slept with thousands of women, a fact that makes me grieve for my gender.

The Game is probably the best-known of all the pick-up artist books, and *The Rules of the Game* is the author's thirty-day step-by-step guide to put you on the road to amateur porn stardom. Each day gives the reader a new mission with the ultimate objective being to secure a date with a woman. Like a really shitty James Bond.

The introduction begins by painting a world filled with su-perhot women who are behind some sort of locked partition. There are hot women everywhere! In *Maxim*, on TV, in porn . . . and yet most men are not having sex with these women! Something has gone terribly wrong. But never fear, because this book is going to provide the key that unlocks unlimited hot lady-goods!

I don't want to unlock any lady-goods (I have enough trouble unlocking my own), and I know men are from Mars and women are from Venus and all that, but can pick-up approaches really be that different based on gender? As you know, I am but the tool of science, so I decided to find out.

July 7

Day six of *The Game* and so far I've taken several self-assessment tests (results: worrying) and given myself a mission statement (which mirrors the mission statement of this entire project, i.e., to have frequent sex with people of sound mental and physical health).

I've also given myself a mini-makeover, as firmly encouraged by the book. This involved me approaching random guys on the street and asking them to recommend a good clothing store for women; this is one assignment that would presumably be more successful if gender roles were reversed, as I received two recommendations for Ann Summers and one for Isabel Marant. (I'm pretty sure the third fellow I asked wasn't playing for my team.) I ended up going to Zara and buying a couple of great little shift dresses that could double up for dates and work, as well as a pair of sequined short shorts that I was definitely at least eight years too old to be wearing but couldn't resist because they were shiny and on the sale rack.

The book also had me call random people in the phone book and ask for movie recommendations, compliment people I saw on the street, and generally pushed me into interacting with strangers far more than I was normally comfortable with.

I was beginning to see that the book worked on the law of averages: the more people you approach, the more likely it is that you'll end up having sex with one of them. It also forced you into a hyper-social space: you were putting yourself out there constantly. For someone who desperately avoided small talk and would walk up six flights of stairs rather than get in the elevator with another person, it was a challenge.

But nearly a week in, I was starting to acclimatize. Tonight was the night where I was meant to put all I'd learned into action. It was time to go to a bar.

As Lucy had fallen down the rabbit hole of new love, stopping into the flat only to collect fresh clothes and wander dazedly around the living room grinning to herself, I recruited a very reluctant Cathryn as my wingman.

We went to a bar on Dalston Lane that was marked only by an old pharmacy sign from the eighties. Inside, the requisite groups of hipsters congregated, admiring one another's ironic mullets and Hypercolor T-shirts, but there were also a few groups of normal-looking thirty-something guys.

Cathryn wasn't used to venturing farther east than Barnsbury, and inspected her surroundings with barely concealed fascination. I imagined it was what Richard Burton must have looked like on his first trip down the Congo.

"What do these people do all day?" she whispered, gesturing at a man wearing a bowler hat, cravat and knee-length shorts. "Do they have jobs?"

"Something based heavily in the theoretical, I imagine. What do you want to drink?"

We settled down at a table and I explained my mission for the evening: to approach several groups of guys and "open" with them by asking them for their expertise on a subject or situation I was curious about. As there were huge, yawning gaps in my general knowledge, I was spoiled for choice in terms of topics.

I picked out a group of guys, finished off my vodka tonic and told Cathryn to hang tight: I was going in.

I sauntered over to their table, trying my best to look nonchalant. This was a key element of the approach: to make it look as though the approach was an afterthought rather than a specific intention. The guys appeared to be in the middle of an in-depth discussion about the Bundesliga, but I forged on regardless.

I launched straight into my opener. "Hey, you guys look like experts. Can you help settle a bet between my friend and me?" I gestured over toward Cathryn, who did an embarrassed little wave.

The three of them looked up at me in confusion, but after a few seconds a scruffy blond wearing a Stone Roses T-shirt smiled and said, "Sure, we'll give it a try."

"Great," I said. "How were the pyramids built? I think it was through a pulley system, but my friend over there swears by the lever and fulcrum."

Silence fell on the table for several beats, until the stocky guy at the end of the table spoke. "Actually, I don't think either were used. Slaves just pulled everything by hand."

The blond man piped up. "Come on, there's no way people could have pulled those blocks by hand! How could they stack them on top of each other? They would have to have used pulleys."

"I think you're underestimating how many slaves there were in Egypt," the stocky one said.

"Can you even define those people as slaves, though?" the

bearded man chipped in from the corner. "At that point, Egypt didn't have a currency system, so there was no way to compensate the workers monetarily."

"Yes, you would most certainly call it slavery. Haven't you read the Old Testament? Moses didn't lead them through the desert for the hell of it." The stocky man looked angry.

The bearded man folded his arms in front of his chest. "Here we go again."

"Well, I'm sorry, but that sort of revisionist history is utter nonsense."

The bearded one and the stocky one seethed at each other across the table.

"Sooooo," I said, "you guys are thinking pulleys?"

The two men ignored me while the blond one looked up with a weary smile. "Sorry, it doesn't look like we're much use. You should probably just Google it."

"Yeah, good idea. Thanks anyway!" I said brightly as I made my way back to the table. When I sat down, I saw that the blond had gone out for a cigarette and the stocky one and the Beard were locked in an intense discussion.

"How did it go?" Cathryn asked, looking up from her book.

"Not really as I'd planned. I thought asking about ancient building techniques was noncontroversial, but apparently not."

"You asked them about ancient building techniques? What on earth were you thinking?"

"The book said I could open with any topic I was curious about, and I've always been curious about how the pyramids were built."

"Oh, Lauren," Cathryn muttered.

"Well, it did spark off a lively debate. Just not one that included me."

"Perhaps you should try something more general next time?"

"You're right. Okay, round two." I spied a group of men in their midthirties from across the room, all wearing expensive-looking cardigans and drinking expensive-looking bottles of wine, and started to get up from my seat.

Cathryn rolled her eyes. "You know, this isn't exactly a scream for me, reading my book alone in the middle of this strange bar."

"I know, I'm sorry and I promise I'll buy you dinner after this. But I've got to do my homework first."

"What's it this time? Asking about the Israeli-Palestinian conflict?"

"Nah, I'm going to ask a very guy-friendly pop culture question. Should be easy."

Cathryn picked her book up off the table. "*Bonne chance,*" she said. I don't think she meant it.

I walked up to the group of wine drinkers and picked out the best-looking of the bunch: rangy, dark-haired and green-eyed. "Hi!" I said brightly. "I need your help with something."

He looked up at me with an air of mild impatience while the rest of his friends continued their conversation, oblivious. "How can I help?"

"My friend and I were talking about eighties TV, and we were trying to remember the full cast of the *A-Team*. We can remember Mr. T as B. A. Baracus and Dirk Benedict as Face, but we're totally stuck on the other two."

His expression changed from impatient to bemused tolerance. He gestured at the other guys sitting around the table. "We all work in TV, so I'm sure we can help. Hey, lads, we've got a question here that needs answering."

The rest of the group fell silent and looked up at me in surprise, as though I had suddenly materialized out of a genie bottle.

"This woman was wondering about the cast of the *A-Team*."

A shortish man with glasses called out from the end of the table. "Film or television?"

The green-eyed man looked mildly disgusted. "Television, of course. She and her friend can remember Mr. T"—there was a snicker of derision from the sandy-haired man to his left—"and Dirk Benedict."

"So we're talking the series, not the pilot," the bespectacled man said. "Because obviously Tim Dunigan was the original Faceman."

The green-eyed man nodded. "Yes, that's right. So there's James Coburn as Hannibal, and—"

The bespectacled man looked like he was going to punch through the nearest window. "What are you on about, mate? Coburn wasn't in the *A-Team*! He was in the *Magnificent Seven*! Peppard was Hannibal!"

The green-eyed man looked calmly smug. "No, Brian, he was not. It was definitely Coburn."

The sandy-haired man sat back in his seat. "You're both wrong. It was Robert Vaughn."

The bespectacled man looked like he was going to spit nails. "Fuck off, the pair of you! It was Peppard!"

The sandy-haired man and the green-eyed man looked at each other and shrugged.

"Seriously, lads, I should know. I wrote a whole fucking thesis on the postmodernization of Peppard for my media studies course."

The green-eyed man nodded imperceptibly. "Fine, Peppard. So that's one."

"Thank you," I said, very quietly.

"So the real question is, who played Murdock?"

The table descended into chaos once again. I stood there awkwardly for a moment, occasionally trying to offer my own thoughts on the matter, but it quickly became apparent that I was effectively invisible; they were too immersed in shouting eighties TV star names. I was beginning to realize that guy-talk was a very different beast, in that it involved a lot more outward aggression (as opposed to the passive aggression often found in girl-talk).

I mumbled my thanks and they barely glanced up as I made my way back to Cathryn.

"That looked lively," she said as she folded down the page of her book.

"Apparently the *A-Team* is actually more controversial than the Egyptian slavery issue."

"Men will find any excuse for a debate. It's how they express affection to their friends—by berating them for their opinions."

I heard a loud noise erupt from across the room and glanced over to see the bespectacled man shaking the sandy-haired man by the shoulders. "Apparently so."

"Can we go now? I'm starving." Cathryn was in a perpetual state of self-proclaimed starvation, and yet she could pack away more food than anyone else I knew—and never seemed to gain a pound. I assumed it was something to do with genetics, like the whole flawless ponytail thing.

"Soon, I promise. I've got to approach one more table, and then we can go."

"Are you quite sure you want to risk another go?"

"A scientist's work is never done," I said.

I decided to try a scenario straight from the book (with slight tweaks to make it gender appropriate). It was called something like the "curious girlfriend" opener. Here's how it works: the guy approaches a group of women and asks for their opinion on a situation his buddy is currently going through. He and his girlfriend have been together for six months and everything's going great, but there's one snag: she just loooooooves making out with girls. Can't get enough of it. She doesn't see it as cheating, but her boyfriend does. The guy making the opener is then meant to canvas the opinions of the women in the group: is hot pseudo-lesbian action cheating or not?

This scenario sounds more like something in the "Letters to the Editor" section of *Penthouse* than a way to approach women, but what did I know. I was about to find out how a bunch of men would react.

I picked two hipster-types who were monopolizing the jukebox. There was one in particular I had my eye on: sleepy-eyed and slim with a mop of curly chocolate-brown hair and wearing an excellent pair of thin-whale cords. Last chance of the evening: I needed to make it count.

I made my way over to them, avoiding the eye of the bespectacled man as he poked furiously at the sandy-haired man while staring at his iPhone.

I put a smile on my face and tapped the sleepy-eyed hipster on the shoulder. "Can I trouble you guys for a quick opinion poll?"

He looked up at me and grinned, revealing a row of small, even teeth. "Sure."

It was going well already.

"Great, thanks. See my friend over there?" I gestured toward Cathryn, who had nearly finished her book and was gazing longingly at the door.

"The brunette? She's a fox," said the man next to him, who was wearing a seventies aviator jacket and jeans so tight I worried for his testicles.

"Yep, that's her. So she has this problem. She and her boyfriend have been seeing each other for a while now—about six months—and everything's going well"—the aviator's attention demonstrably waned—"except for this one issue. You see, she's kind of into women. She doesn't want a relationship with one, but she does like to make out with them sometimes."

The aviator perked up. "Man, that's some Girls Gone Wild shit."

"I know, right? Anyway, her fiancé hates it. He gets really jealous and feels like she's cheating on him"—the aviator scoffed loudly—"but she doesn't think it's cheating and she doesn't want to stop doing it because it's a side of her that she doesn't want to give up."

The sleepy-eyed guy nodded sagely.

"So what do you guys think? Is it cheating or not?"

The aviator rolled his eyes. "I have a more important question: why is she staying with a loser who doesn't appreciate how close he is to a threesome?"

"Yes, well, I guess that's a separate issue."

Sleepy Eyes shrugged. "I dunno. Seems like cheating to me."

The aviator slapped his forehead in disbelief. "Mate, what are you on about? His girlfriend is basically every man's fantasy, and he's acting like a wanker," he said, rising from his chair. "I'm going to have a word with your friend myself. You two are talking bollocks and she needs someone to lean on in her time of need."

I threw myself in front of him. "No! She'd be mortified. She's actually a very private person."

The aviator tried to move past me. "She doesn't sound all that private to me."

"Just leave it, mate," Sleepy Eyes said. He was a man of few words, but so far I liked all of them.

The aviator sat back down and started to pick the label off his bottle of beer, grumbling under his breath.

"Well, I'll get out of your hair. Thanks for your help!"

"No problem," Sleepy Eyes said. "Come back over here if you get bored."

"Will do!"

"Bring your friend!" the aviator called as I scurried back to the table.

Cathryn gave me a long-suffering look. "How did it go?"

"Better." I took a long sip from my drink. "Not great, but better."

"What was the opener this time?"

"Oh, just a theoretical question about a friend."

"Nothing controversial then?"

"Oh no," I said. "I kept it as vanilla as possible." I looked anxiously over at the aviator, who was openly leering at Cathryn. "Let's get out of here. Do you want to get dinner? We could go to the Turkish place around the corner?"

"Yes please—I'll eat anything at this point."

We collected our things and made our way to the door. I felt the eyes of several of the men I'd spoken with give me a quick glance, but most of them were too engrossed in their own conversations to notice.

Except for Sleepy Eyes, who nodded at me as I passed by.

"You leaving?" he drawled.

"Yep, we're off. Thanks again for the advice." I glanced nervously at Cathryn, who was just out of earshot. "I think it helped."

"Anytime. Hey, my band is playing this gig at the Old Blue Last next Thursday. You should check it out."

My stomach flipped but I tried to look nonchalant. "Sure, cool. That would be cool. Maybe. I'll check what I've got on. Busy schedule. Busy." I could feel my cheeks reddening.

His mouth curled into a slow, languorous grin. "Cool. See you around. Maybe."

I turned to see Cathryn being harangued by the aviator.

"I *told* you that I'm engaged!" she said, pulling her hand away and brushing it down the side of her pristine linen dress.

"But he doesn't understand you!" The aviator looked desperate. "I'm telling you, love, he's stifling you! I'd let you be free!"

"C'mon," I said, grabbing Cathryn's hand and pulling her toward the door. "Let's get out of here."

"Lauren, what on earth was that man talking about?" she said as we tumbled out onto Kingsland Road.

"Fucked if I know. I think he was on drugs. Lots of people around here are on drugs. Lots of drugs."

Cathryn looked at the group of steampunks across the street and recoiled slightly. "Mmm. Yes, that must have been it. What an odd place."

"It's sad, really. Now let's get some food into you."

After watching Cathryn suspiciously spear bits of kofte into her mouth ("Are you *sure* this is lamb?"), I went home and wrote up my notes from the night's experiment.

While it hadn't been a raging success, I had managed to make conversation with three groups of strangers. Sure, two of those groups descended quickly into argument, and I'd seriously tarnished Cathryn's gleaming reputation with the third, but it was progress nonetheless. I couldn't help thinking that what Cathryn said was true, though: men communicate with their friends in very different ways than women, and trying to apply the same rules to both doesn't always work out smoothly.

July 9

I decided to do a little bit of music research in advance of Sleepy Eyes's gig on Thursday.

I hadn't been to a gig in years (other than weird Max's, which obviously didn't count). The music scene in Portland had been, shall we say, niche; while I didn't object to the banjo, it wasn't necessarily enough to get me to change out of my pajamas on a Saturday night and hit the town.

I sat down with my laptop and put iTunes on shuffle as I made dinner, hoping that it would throw up some forgotten indie gem I could casually drop into conversation on Thursday night.

I'd been lulled into a false sense of security by an excellent run of early Justin Timberlake while chopping onions, so when the first strains of the song came on, it took me a second to register what it was. As soon as I realized, I threw the knife in the sink and leaped across the room to the laptop, mashing the keys with my damp fingers, but it was too late: Stevie Wonder's voice had been released into the air, and "Isn't She Lovely" was in my head. I sat down on the kitchen floor and put my head in my hands.

It had been our song. When we moved into our first apartment, the first thing we unpacked was our beat-up stereo. We'd put the volume up as loud as it would go and danced with each other in the kitchen, me in my dad's old overalls and him in faded jeans speckled with dried paint. He held me in his arms and sang the words softly into my ear, and I thought to myself, "This is what it means to be in love. This is what it means to be an adult."

We moved out a few months later—the bathtub leaked and the upstairs neighbor had a passion for salt cod, the smell of which had permeated all of our clothes—but the song stuck around. Well, for as long as I had.

I gathered myself up off the floor and called Meghan. When an iTunes ambush strikes, only a sister can help.

July 11

I'd spent my lunch hour locked in the toilet, staring at myself in a compact mirror and reciting the book's mantra: "You are perfection. You deserve only the very best. People feel privileged to speak with you. You are magnetic. You are irresistible."

When I emerged, Cathryn looked at me strangely.

"Were you talking to yourself in the toilet?" she asked.

"Just giving myself a little pep talk about tomorrow's meeting," I said. In truth, the pep talk had been more focused on Sleepy Eyes's gig, but I was too embarrassed to admit that to Cathryn, and we did have a big meeting coming up tomorrow.

"How very . . . American of you," she said, turning back to her spreadsheets.

With a little cajoling and the promise that I'd lead a group of six-year-olds on the museum tour tomorrow, Cathryn agreed to cover for me so I could slip out early in order to get ready for the gig tonight. I poured myself into my skinniest pair of black jeans, rimmed my eyes with an entire pot of kohl and, after a swift vodka or two, I was ready.

I had managed to lure Lucy out of her love cocoon to join me. I hadn't seen much of her in recent days, so I explained my next mission to her on the way to the bar.

"I've mastered opening, apparently, and now have to move on to disqualifying."

Lucy took a drag on her cigarette and checked her reflection in the window of a pop-up fried chicken joint. "What the hell is disqualifying?" she asked as she adjusted her cleavage.

"Basically, I have to get the guy to try to impress me rather than the other way around. It's some sort of power switcheroo."

"Right. And how are you meant to do that?"

"I'm supposed to figure out what I think his insecurities might be and then push his buttons."

"Hang on, is that what this book is telling men to do? Make women feel like shit about themselves?"

"Yeah, that's part of it. Though in my experience, a lot of men don't need to read a book to do that."

"There *is* something terribly familiar in all this. It's like smelling an awful, rancid smell, but not quite being able to trace it."

"I know what you mean. When I started reading the book, I was sure I recognized moves guys had pulled on me before, but I couldn't connect them with any one person."

"Thank God Tristan's nothing like that."

I looked at her dubiously. "What, he'd never pull this sort of stuff? An alpha male like him? Get real."

"I'm telling you, there's no way he would ever treat me badly. He says I'm his princess and he's just a serf living in my kingdom."

"He does not!"

"He does! He says he lives to serve me."

The whole thing creeped me out a little, but I did my best to hide it. I knew Lucy had had a rough time with a few dickheads in the past, so I was happy that she'd found someone who treated her well, even if I thought it was a little over the top. "That's great," I said. "He sounds like a keeper."

Lucy's eyes glazed over again. I was getting used to it. "He really is."

"Oh, brother. C'mon, let's get in there. They're on in fifteen minutes."

"What's his band called again?"

"Languid Brother Machine."

"What the fuck is that meant to mean?"

"Christ knows. I'll be sure to hit on that when I'm insulting him later on."

Watching Sleepy Eyes on the drums was a near-spiritual experience. He gave me a wink at one point and I almost had a stroke. I had a theory about drummers: if they had that sort of rhythm on stage, it only followed that they would have it in bed. Ever the science devotee, I was determined to test the hypothesis.

"Is that the one?" Lucy yelled in my ear.

I nodded.

"Fuck, Lo, he's hot!"

"I know!" I shouted back.

"Don't be mean to him! Have sex with him!"

"One thing is meant to lead to the other!"

The set ended and Sleepy Eyes climbed off the stage, sending that slow grin my way as he ambled over.

"Nice to see you," he said as he leaned in to kiss me on the cheek. He smelled like sweat and stale cigarettes. I fought off the urge to lick him.

Instead, I made a face and wiped my cheek with my palm. "Eugh, you're all sweaty!" I gave him what I hoped was the book's "playful swat." "This is Lucy, by the way."

He nodded toward her.

Lucy turned pink and showed him her dimples. "You were great," she said breathily.

"Cheers." He turned back to me. "I've got to go talk to the lads about the set. You around later?"

I looked at Lucy, who was nodding furiously.

"Maybe. We'll see."

"Cool." He reached out and brushed his hand up my arm.

"Hands off the merchandise!" I said. "Touching me doesn't come cheap. You owe me forty pounds."

He looked startled, then shook his head and smiled as he walked away.

Lucy grabbed my wrist. "What is WRONG with you?"

"I think you'll find it's called *flirting*," I said smugly.

"You're acting like an arse."

"That's the whole point! Think about how many douchebag guys we've fallen for in the past. There's got to be something in it."

We watched Sleepy Eyes lope off to the bar; his white T-shirt was translucent with sweat and clung to the muscles on his slim back.

Lucy grasped my arm, hard. "You *have* to sleep with him. It would be some sort of crime against womankind if you didn't. *Please* stop being mean to him."

"I'm not being mean! I'm doing the power switcheroo!"

She shook her head. "If you blow it because of this bloody experiment..."

"Hey, that's science you're talking about!"

We spent the next hour pressed against the back wall, listening to a band comprised entirely of banjo and ukulele players, while pouring as much alcohol down our necks as we could get our hands on. I spotted glimpses of Sleepy Eyes through the crowd, leaning against the side of the stage and talking to a man I quickly recognized as the aviator from the other night. Thank God Cathryn wasn't here.

"Speak to him!" Lucy said, giving me a little shove.

"No way. Not yet."

"I don't know how much more ukulele I can stand."

"We'll go soon, I promise. I'll buy you a cocktail at Happiness Forgets." I was doing a lot of friend-bribing this month.

Twenty minutes passed, and I was about to give up when Sleepy Eyes made his way across the room back to Lucy and me. He was so languid, he was practically a liquid.

"Sorry about that," he said, running his fingers through his dark curls and revealing a sliver of torso in the process. "Band stuff."

"Whatever," I said. "You're fired."

"Fair enough." He took a pack of Marlboro Reds out of his back pocket. "Smoke?"

I felt Lucy place her hand on my back and give me a firm shove.

We walked outside and sat down at an empty table around the corner. He pulled out two cigarettes, tapped them on the inside of his wrist and offered one to me. I hadn't smoked Reds since a brief stint with a Frenchman last October and I felt my lungs contract in protest on the first puff.

"I can't believe you smoke these things," I said, pleased to finally have a genuine criticism I could launch at him.

He shrugged.

"They're pure rat poison and arsenic."

He shrugged again.

"You *would* smoke them, though. You should just go whole-hog James Dean and roll the pack up in the sleeve of your T-shirt."

Another shrug. "They fall out."

"Whatever," I said, sulking visibly. I gave up. It was like trying to anger a turnip. I stubbed out my cigarette and stood up. "I'm going to get going."

He turned to me and gave me that slow smile, then stretched himself over the table, slid his fingers through my hair and kissed me. He bit my lip as he drew away, then smiled again. "Later," he said, and sat back down to finish his cigarette.

I went back inside, grabbed Lucy and pulled her out of the bar.

"Are you all right?" she asked. "You look as though you've been drugged."

"He kissed me," I whispered.

"Thank fuck for that! Why are we leaving?"

"Because I said I was going to leave right before he kissed me. I was trying the power switcheroo."

"So he kissed you and then you just walked away?"

"What else could I do? He didn't exactly beg me to stay! He just sat back down and smoked his stupid gross cigarette!"

Lucy stopped short. "Lo, you've got to go back there! A hot drummer just kissed you. Do you have his number?"

"No."

"Does he have yours?"

"No."

"For fuck's sake! How are you going to see him again?"

"I don't know, okay?! I have no idea. Maybe he'll track me down?"

"No offense, babe, but he doesn't seem inclined to track down his own pants, never mind a woman who just spent an evening telling him how shit he is."

"You're right," I mumbled.

"Now, we're going to go back there and you are going to get his number. Isn't this month meant to be about you being the man?"

"Kind of."

"And how long has it been since you had sex?"

"Too long."

"Well then, be a man! Go back there and get him!"

I knew when I was beaten. We turned around and trudged back to the bar to find Sleepy Eyes standing outside.

"Thought you'd left," he said as we bustled past.

"Lucy forgot her scarf," I said, ignoring the fact that it was a balmy July night.

Sleepy Eyes raised an eyebrow and the corner of his mouth.

"Yes, silly me!" Lucy sang. "I'll be right back—you stay here!" I owed her at least three drinks by that point.

I rocked back on my heels, looked up at the sky and tried to whistle. I could feel him watching me but couldn't bring myself to look at him. I thought I might explode in some sort of awkwardness immolation.

He leaned against the wall and started whistling, too.

After a few minutes, Lucy emerged empty-handed. "Couldn't find it," she said. "Someone must have got there first."

"Big demand for scarves these days," Sleepy Eyes drawled.

"You're so right," Lucy said. "Are we ready to go? Do you have everything, Lauren?" She gave me a significant look.

"Um, yep, I think so . . ." I started to walk away, then turned back to Sleepy Eyes as though just struck by a brilliant thought. "Actually, we're having a get-together in a couple of weeks. Just dinner with a few friends. You should come. Maybe. Whatever." I had just skipped ahead by several missions and was in unfamiliar territory.

"Cool," he said. "You got a pen?"

I pulled a Bic out of my bag and handed it to him. He took my wrist and wrote his number on the inside of my arm. I felt like I was back in high school (or what I imagined high school would have been like if I'd been popular).

"Cool," I said, hoping my face wasn't too bright a shade of magenta.

I linked my arm through Lucy's and we sauntered away as casually as we could manage until we knew we were out of his sightline, then dissolved into hysterics.

"I'm gonna get laid! I'm gonna get laid!" I sang while doing a little jig.

Lucy clapped her hands together. "He is soooo fit! Well done!"

"It's all down to you, my friend. You were like my spirit-guide back there."

"I hate to see a gorgeous man go to waste. Now what's all this about a dinner party?"

"Yeah, I was going to talk to you about that . . ."

The book's final mission was to throw a dinner party and invite a bunch of interesting people, including any people you'd managed to successfully game over the month.

"Sounds like a laugh," she said. "I'll invite Tristan. It'll be fun!"

"It'll be something," I muttered.

I got my trusty notebook out when I got home and jotted down what I knew about him:

Name: Sleepy Eyes
Age: I don't think I want to know. 23?
Occupation: Part-time drummer, full-time hipster
Nationality: English
Description: Slim, curly brown hair, dark-brown eyes, looks like he fell
     out of a dumpster (in the best possible way)
Method: *The Rules of the Game*

July 17

Today's mission was to note down interesting upcoming cultural events in a possible-date diary and to read a men's magazine in public and ask a male passerby for his opinion on one of the articles.

I went to the bookstore on my lunch hour, sneaking in past the new owner as he was busy debating Albert Camus's football career with an irate Frenchman wearing a trilby.

I thumbed through a copy of *Time Out* and jotted down notes in my notebook. This wasn't the first time I'd made notes of upcoming cultural events, but if I followed the book's guidelines, it *would* be the first time I actually attended aforementioned cultural events rather than brushing them off in favor of sitting in my living room and watching back-to-back episodes of *Biggest Loser USA* while drinking wine and eating stale seasonal chocolates.

When I first moved to London, I felt a constant low-level guilt about not spending every free moment gallery hopping and attending free experimental jazz concerts, but after a few months I realized that no one who lives in London actually does any of those things. *Time Out* is basically just a list of things you might have gone to if you hadn't been so busy getting drunk in your local pub or nursing your hangover in your living room. I felt infinitely comforted by the thought.

But this month was going to be different, or at least I was going to do a better job of pretending that it was going to be different. Events noted down included a food festival on Columbia Road, an art installation in Hanover Square and a debate on gender politics in Bloomsbury. I was already mentally preparing excuses as to why I hadn't gone to any of them.

First part of the homework done, I turned to the men's

magazine. The book encouraged readers to read *Cosmo* and then flag down a woman and ask her opinion on a particular article. I couldn't imagine any man doing this without expiring from embarrassment, as most *Cosmo* articles are about sex tips involving gelatin and nipple tassels.

I figured the male equivalent was *Maxim*. I flipped through the first few pages and realized there weren't all that many conversation-sparking articles in it. It was mainly photos of women in their underwear and guys with bloodied heads. I soldiered on.

"Excuse me," I asked a man in his early forties who was stationed firmly in front of a rack of computer magazines. "Would you say that this is accurate?" I pointed to a random article about something called "felching." I assumed it was some sort of muddy obstacle course invented by the Marines.

"Sorry?" he said, looking flushed.

"Felching," I repeated. "Apparently it's all the rage with guys at the minute?"

"I'm afraid I really couldn't comment on that," he said and hustled away.

"Christ, I'm sorry I asked," I muttered.

I looked back down at the article and started to read. I felt my ears begin to tingle, then burn. There was no mention of running or rope climbs, but there were some pretty disturbing pixelated photos accompanying the article.

"That poor man," I whispered.

I tried to slip out of the shop unnoticed, but the bookseller caught me just as I got to the door.

"What, you're not going to purchase any ridiculous nonsense pitted against your own gender today?"

"I've got everything I need, thank you," I said. "By the way, Camus wasn't a defensive midfielder, he was a goalkeeper. Everyone knows that."

He looked at me appraisingly. "How on earth do you know anything about football?"

I was incensed. "Um, how dare you impose your gender stereotypes on me? Just because I'm a woman doesn't mean I can't know about sports, you know."

He sighed. "Get off your high horse, Germaine Greer. I was referring to your nationality, not your gender. I have never met an American who knew anything about football. Real football, I mean. Not your . . . helmeted nonsense," he said witheringly.

"I'll have you know that I played *soccer* for ten years. My team won state three years in a row." I felt so smug I was practically levitating.

He had the momentary good grace to look suitably impressed. "Well, I'm not entirely sure what 'winning state' means but it sounds quite good."

"It is," I said, pulling myself up to my full height and slightly puffing out my chest. "We beat Mount Alvern in a penalty shoot-out for the title in my senior year."

"Nail-biting stuff."

I nodded sagely, ignoring his sarcasm. "It was."

And with that, I walked out of the shop, feeling enormously pleased with myself. There was nothing better than having the last word.

July 19

I arrived home and kicked aside a pile of recycling that had accumulated by the door.

"Lucy?" I called as I turned on the light. "Are you in?"

No reply. Presumably she was at Tristan's again. It was starting to feel like I had a two-bedroom apartment to myself—albeit a shitty, decrepit one. It was great in a way, as I could turn up Ani DiFranco very loud and dance around the living room without incurring any judgmental looks, but it was also kind of lame. I missed ranting with Lucy over the television, and my childhood fears of being murdered in my sleep had come back with a vengeance now that I was alone every night. I kept double-checking the locks and looking under the bed for serial killers. It was embarrassing.

I dug through the pile of mail on the kitchen counter and found another postcard from Meghan: a close-up photograph of an ear. I flipped it over and read the message scrawled on the back in bright purple ink.

"I would rather die of passion than of boredom"
  —Vincent van Gogh.
    Saw this and thought of you. Just don't go hacking off any
body parts in the process.
    Love, Meg

I sat down with a glass of wine and a salad I'd assembled from the fridge dregs and gave her a call.

The phone rang many, many times before she picked up.

"Hello?" she said, audibly panting.

"It's me. What the hell are you doing?"

"Hey, kid! Sorry, Maud was beating the shit out of Harold and I was trying to separate them."

"How does a kitten beat the shit out of an eighty-pound dog?"

"Trust me: where there's a will, there's a way. How are you?"

"Eh, I'm okay. Got your postcard. Don't worry, I'm still fully intact."

"Good to hear."

"Yeah, I guess." I let out a deep sigh.

"What's up with you? You sound like shit." Trust a sister to tell it like it is.

"I'm just a little lonely. A little homesick. Lucy's met this amazing new guy, so she's never around, and work's a little tough at the minute, and I'm following the dating advice of some douchebag . . . I'm a little filled with ennui, I guess."

"So come home already."

"I can't come home. You know that."

"Kid, you can always come home. The past isn't as scary as you think it is. It's not some monster living in the closet, waiting for you."

I glanced over at my bedroom door. "I'm not so sure of that."

She sighed. "Speaking of which, I saw Dylan the other day."

A little pocket of bile bloomed in my stomach. "You did? Where? Did you talk to him?"

"At Sangillo's. We talked for a second, but he was three sheets to the wind so it wasn't a very stimulating conversation."

The thought of him drunk at Sangillo's filled me with an inexplicable sadness. "Did you talk about me?"

There was a pause on the other end of the line. "No, but he wasn't exactly in a great frame of mind."

I felt a prick of guilt. It was my fault, I knew it. I took a sip of wine and changed the subject. There was nothing I could do to unknow it, but I could sure as hell ignore it.

I got off the phone soon after, promising that I'd think about what she'd said about coming back home. The thought of Portland swelled in front of me: the clapboard houses painted in blues and greeny-grays, the Eastern Promenade in the height of summer as the boats sail past, the quiet that descends on Old Town once fall settles in and the tourists clear out. I went onto the balcony and lit a cigarette, pushing the memory out of my head. I stared out across the London night. Portland wasn't home anymore. For better or worse, I'd made my choice.

July 23

After nearly a month of radio silence, Adrian turned up again like a bad but not entirely unwelcome penny.

I was at work, pretending to write a press release for an up-coming exhibition on electromagnetism ("It's hair-raising!"). Really, I was sketching out my "adding-value" story. The book asks you to think of personal anecdotes that convey your charm, sense of humor, bravery and general panache and then store them in your conversational armory for the right moment.

The only one I could come up with was when I spent a summer riding a pony on the farm near my house, culminating in a blue-ribbon win at a show-jumping competition, only to return the following summer to find that Jason had become too fat for anyone to ride and had been sent to that great big glue factory in the sky.

I was putting the final flourishes on Jason the pony when my phone flashed up with a text.

Adrian: Drink?

Me: It's 11:30 in the morning. I'm at work.

Adrian: Later?

Me: Maybe. What time?

Adrian: 7?

Me: Okay. Will meet you in Blue Posts on Berwick St.

Adrian: That place is gash.

Me: Then you'll fit right in.

I arrived at 7:30, factoring in Adrian's laissez-faire attitude toward timekeeping. He strolled in at 7:50, just as I was gathering my things to leave.

"Where are you off to, Cunningham? You wouldn't stand a man up, would you?"

"Do you think it's normal to be almost an hour late?"

He smiled infuriatingly. "Sorry, time escaped me."

"I'm pretty sure time has always escaped you, so you might as well call off the hunt."

He gave me a kiss on the cheek and then gestured toward the bar. "Want anything?"

I'd already necked my first glass of wine, so I nodded. "Get some peanuts, too."

He came back with the drinks and a packet of dry roasted and sat down. "So, what's new?"

"I was about to ask you the same thing. I figured there was some reason you wanted to have a drink with me."

His eyes widened in mock surprise. "Why would I need a reason to see my favorite American?"

I rolled my eyes.

"Now really, tell me what's happening in your world. Is all well in the land of science?"

I jumped slightly. How had he found out about the project? "What do you mean, science?"

"You do remember that you work at the Science Museum?"

Relief swept over me. "Oh! Right! Yep, science is good. I'm working on an electromagnetism exhibition at the minute."

"Sounds riveting."

"It is, actually. How about you? How's the paper?"

"Fucking awful. Everyone's getting sacked. Something called 'the Internet' seems to be interfering with our readership numbers."

"Is it really bad?"

Adrian smiled sadly. "They binned the whole of the arts and culture section today. Apparently they're going to rely on readers to send in their own reviews. They're rebranding it the 'YouView' section."

"That sort of shit drives me crazy. Every idiot with a blog thinks he's a writer or a critic these days, and no one's out there fact-checking or proofreading anything! I mean, people are professional critics for a reason—they actually know something about the thing they're critiquing. And now we'll have some jackass telling us that the new *Transformers* film is awesome because loads of shit blows up in it. We'll all be illiterate in ten years, mark my words."

"Yes, and more importantly, I'll be out of a job."

I decided this was the moment to test-drive one of my adding-value tales. "It kind of reminds me of this pony I used to ride as a kid."

Adrian raised an eyebrow.

"Well, you see, when I was a kid, I spent a whole summer riding this one pony at the farm down the street from me. His name was Jason. He was one of those brown and white splotchy ones— very handsome. I loved Jason and I was really good at riding him."

"I'll bet you were," Adrian said with a grin.

"Don't interrupt. Anyway, I went from trotting to cantering to galloping over a couple of months, and at the end of the summer we came in second place in the local show-jumping competition."

"Quite an achievement."

I ignored his tone. "It was, actually. Pretty soon after that, it got too cold to ride anymore and Jason and I had to part ways for the winter."

"How could you just abandon Jason like that? Heartless bitch."

"Shut up. Anyway, when summer came around again, I went down to the farm to see if I could take him for a ride, and they told me that over the winter, Jason had become depressed and fat—"

"Probably because you abandoned him."

I gave him a dark look and continued. "He'd gotten too fat to ride and they'd had to sell him. My mom told me that they sold him to a place upstate, but years later I found out that they actually sent him to Elmer's. As in the glue factory."

"Fuck, they made glue out of the poor chap?"

I nodded sadly. Inwardly, I was feeling pretty smug about my storytelling performance.

"So, how does this relate to me? Are you telling me that I've become too fat to ride and should be sent to the glue factory?"

"No, of course not! Can't you see? Print journalism is the fat pony!"

"That's not particularly encouraging, either."

"It was supposed to be an uplifting story of triumph over adversity . . . but I guess, on reflection, it's not all that uplifting. So what are you going to do?"

"That's actually what I wanted to talk to you about. I'm thinking of moving to the States."

My stomach lurched. "What? Why?"

"Well, because long-form journalism has more of a foothold there, so I could probably get a bit of work. I've been speaking with the *Huffington Post* and they seem keen—not that they'll pay me anything. Plus, chicks dig the accent over there."

"But what about a visa? Medical insurance? Crazy right-wing nut jobs?"

"It'll all sort itself out. I suppose if I really got into a jam, I could always marry an American . . . ?" He raised an eyebrow at me.

"Sorry, buddy, you'll have to look elsewhere for your visa bride. I'm sure you won't have trouble on that front."

I hated the thought of him in America. It was too weird, like some sort of freaky-Friday swap gone horribly awry. I pictured him surrounded by blond Texans cooing over him as he hammed up a Cockney accent.

"Ah, don't look so depressed, Cunningham! With time, the gaping hole left in your life by my absence will shrink."

"It's just strange thinking of you wandering around my homeland."

"Don't worry, with any luck I'll do something deviant and be deported immediately."

"I wouldn't put it past you. When are you thinking of going?"

"As soon as possible, really. No time like the present. I expect I'll be out of a job in the next couple of weeks, and I only need to give one month's notice on the flat."

"Fuck."

"So any helpful hints you could give me about that great country of yours would be much appreciated. You don't happen to know anyone in DC, do you? Ideally someone very influential and/ or devastatingly attractive?"

I thought for a moment. An old friend from college lived there, but I sure as hell wasn't going to introduce the two of them: she was way too pretty.

"Not that I can think of, but I'll ask around. More importantly, what are you going to do for your big send-off?"

He wrinkled his nose. "Dunno. Get massively pissed?"

"Well, let me know when you do so I can join you."

He gave me a kiss on the cheek. "I hope all Americans are as hospitable as you."

July 27/28

The night of the dinner was upon us.

"Lo, have you seen my black bra?" Lucy was standing in the hallway wearing black tights, high heels and an old Liverpool top.

"I think I saw it on the radiator in the bathroom," I said, struggling to zip up my dress.

"Fuck! It's still wet!"

"Just use the hairdryer." The dryer switched on for a few

minutes, and then Lucy emerged from her bedroom, resplendent in a black leather pencil skirt and a sheer black top. It was a big change from her usual floral tea dresses.

"Holy shit. You look amazing! Where did you get that skirt?"

Lucy blushed. "Tristan bought it for me."

"He's got a great eye. What do you think about this? Is it slutty enough?" I did a little twirl.

"Is it meant to be a top?"

"It's my party and I can wear what I want to. It's also my last chance to have sex this month, and Christ only knows what the next book will involve. I could have another month of celibacy thrust upon me. I can't leave anything to chance tonight."

"You're not leaving anything to the imagination, either."

"Yeah, yeah. Just because you're all saintly and monogamous with Tristan now doesn't mean you can go judging me."

"I'm hardly a saint, babe."

"True—you're wearing way too much black to have completely turned to the good side."

I heard her mumble something under her breath.

"What did you say?"

"Nothing!" she said brightly. "Now let's check on the lamb."

I am a terrible cook, but luckily for me, Lucy is a great one. She'd planned the whole menu, down to the delicate little raspberry tarts for dessert. She'd been poring through cookbooks and foodie sites for days, agonizing over canapés and cuts of meat: it was like some mania had been unleashed in her. I'd been sous chef and chief wine buyer, which suited me just fine.

The guys were meant to get there at eight, so we'd timed it so dinner would be on the table by nine. I busied myself by filling tiny vol-au-vents with smoked salmon and crème fraiche while Lucy trimmed the carrots into smaller, neater versions of carrots. We were a well-oiled machine. By the time the door rang at three minutes past eight, we were ready.

Tristan was the first in but, despite his relative punctuality and the bottle of more-than-decent champagne he'd brought, he was extremely contrite about his tardiness. He apologized to Lucy at least four times, which was odd enough, but even more surprising was the fact that Lucy just nodded sharply and said they'd discuss it later. I had no idea she was such a ball-buster.

It was my first time seeing him in the flesh and I had to hand it to her: he was dishy for an older guy. Close-cut salt and pepper hair, strong dimpled jaw, impeccable suit hiding only the slightest of paunches . . . he was the real deal. And, more importantly, they looked happy to see each other.

He opened the champagne and poured three glasses. "Here's to you two gorgeous creatures," he said, raising his glass. "Thank you so much for having me."

"All the thanks should go to Lucy. She's the one who cooked."

Tristan put his arm around Lucy's tiny waist. "I'm sure she's very commanding in the kitchen."

"Yep, she's been cracking the whip all day!" I said.

Lucy flushed bright red.

Tristan gave Lucy a significant look. "I don't doubt that for a moment," he said.

At ten past, Cathryn and Michael arrived with a bottle of dessert wine and a huge pavlova.

"I hope this is all right!" she said as she handed over the towering meringue, dripping artfully with cream and berries.

"Cathryn, it's amazing! It's a work of art!"

She looked at it critically. "It's slightly lopsided, I'm afraid. Sorry, I was in a bit of a rush when I put it together."

"Don't be ridiculous. It's amazing! You're too hard on yourself."

"I tell her that all the time," Michael said, handing me the wine and giving her a little squeeze. He was handsome in a very symmetrical way, all clean lines and polished angles. They suited each other perfectly.

"Stop it, both of you," she said. "My ego doesn't need any more inflating, thank you. That pavlova is a disgrace and I don't want to hear any more about it."

I rolled my eyes and poured them both a drink. "Come meet Lucy and Tristan," I said, pulling them into the living room.

Tristan stood up as soon as they walked into the room. I saw him blanch slightly as he took them in, but he recovered almost immediately. "Cathers? What a lovely surprise!"

"Uncle Tricky?" Cathryn said. "What on earth are you doing here?"

"You two know each other?" I asked.

Cathryn turned to me. "He's a great friend of my father." She turned back to him. "How are you? Lovely to see you. You remember Michael?"

The two men shook hands warmly. You have to hand it to posh people: they are amazing at acting unfazed in even the weirdest social occasions.

"Of course, of course. How are you, my boy? Cathryn, Michael, this is Lucy."

Lucy tottered out from behind Tristan, looking shell-shocked. "Hello!" she trilled.

"Lauren's told me so much about you!" Cathryn said. "Though obviously not everything," she added, looking archly at Tristan.

"Yes, let's all sit down and get acquainted," Tristan said, reaching for the champagne bottle, which contained just the dregs.

"I'll grab another bottle from the fridge," I said.

Lucy sprang to her feet. "I'll help!"

We huddled in the kitchen, whispering furiously.

Lucy was red. "Uncle Tricky?" she hissed. "I can't believe this. It's so grim! Do you think they're actually related? I know he's older than me, but I never thought of him being uncle age!"

"No, I think uncle is just something fancy people call family friends."

"Urrrgh. Even so. Cathryn must think I'm a tart! I can't bear it. How am I going to make it through the evening?"

"You're just going to have to suck it up. Besides, none of them seem bothered by it, so you shouldn't either. He's obviously crazy about you and that's all that counts."

Lucy took a deep breath and straightened her shoulders. "Right. Just make sure I'm never without a drink."

"Done."

At twenty-five past, Sleepy Eyes rolled in, offering monosyllabic greetings to everyone and giving me a very encouraging squeeze on the ass before sauntering out to the balcony for a cigarette.

I went out to join him.

"Thanks for coming," I said. I cupped my hands around the end of my cigarette as I lit it.

He nodded.

"How've you been?"

He did a sort of shrug-nod which I took to mean "I've been good, thank you. And yourself?"

"I've been really busy. Busy, busy! I went to, like, four gigs last week. And a gallery opening. And two wine tastings. And a food festival in Finchley." None of that was true, of course, but after a year in London, I'm well seasoned at talking about cultural events I haven't actually attended.

He nodded.

I took a long drag.

He tilted his head toward the living room. "That the girl from the other night? The one who's into chicks?"

Fuck. I'd forgotten all about that. As if the night wasn't complicated enough already.

"Uh . . . yep, that's Cathryn. But no need to mention any of that . . ."

"She here with her dude?"

"Michael. But they've sorted out that whole issue. All in the past! Definitely no need to bring that up."

He nodded wisely. "Cool."

"Come on, I'll get you a drink. Would you mind helping me with something in the kitchen?" One of *The Rules of the Game*'s dinner party tips is to encourage your intended target to be your "helper." Apparently it makes you seem in control, though at the moment I felt anything but.

"Sure. I'm just going to finish this."

I ducked back into the kitchen and found Lucy meticulously spooning jus over the lamb roasting in the oven.

I shooed her away. "I'll take care of that. Go play with Tristan and the gang!"

She looked worriedly at her lamb. "Are you sure? Make sure you keep an eye on it. It should be pink in the middle. It'll be ruined if it's overcooked."

"Don't worry, I'll watch it like a hawk. Now get out of here before Sleepy Eyes comes in! I've got to woo him with chores."

Lucy shot me a doubtful look before heading into the living room. Sleepy Eyes slid past her into the kitchen.

"You're here! Great. Would you mind chopping this up?" I handed him a bag of fresh mint and a paring knife, which he accepted with a shrug. "I've just got to do the potatoes."

"Cool," he said as he started chopping.

"Soooooo. How's the band?"

"Got another gig coming up."

"Really? That's great!" I realized I was being too positive and forced myself to slip in a neg. "I mean, at least you'll get some practice."

"Yeah, guess so." A curl had flopped over his left eye as he chopped and I reached over to push it back, casual contact very much encouraged by the book. He ignored me.

After much chopping and sautéing and panicking and cursing, dinner was served. Lucy and I had bought a couple of extra folding chairs and we all crowded around the IKEA dining table. Tristan,

Cathryn and Michael were doing their best to pretend that this was the height of sophistication. Sleepy Eyes straddled his chair backward and gazed at the ceiling, glassy-eyed but gorgeous.

"Is he stoned?" Cathryn whispered to me.

"I think he's just artistic."

Lucy asked Tristan to carve the lamb, a task he took to with impressive enthusiasm and care. Every time he moved to make a cut, he would look to Lucy for approval. She would nod and he would slice. It dragged on and on.

"Uncle Tricky, can you speed it up a bit?" Cathryn piped up from the end of the table. "At this rate, it'll be cold by the time we eat it."

"Or we will be," Michael muttered.

Tristan looked at Lucy, who nodded. He began carving like a man possessed.

After a short ice age, we started to eat. Lucy had outdone herself: the meal was a triumph. Even Sleepy Eyes managed a full sentence of approval.

"So," Cathryn said, looking at Sleepy Eyes, "Lauren tells me you're in a band. That must be awfully fun."

"Yes, what sort of music do you play?" Tristan asked. "Not that I'm very familiar with what you young people are listening to these days. I much prefer classical."

Sleepy Eyes nodded slowly and said, "I play the drums."

Cathryn smiled encouragingly. "That's nice."

"That must be very tiring on the old arms," Tristan said. "Do you play many shows?"

"Once a week," he drawled.

Tristan nodded. "Well, it's good that it's regular. What else do you do to fill your time?"

Sleepy Eyes looked mildly affronted. "Music's my life."

"Of course. Apologies."

Sleepy Eyes turned to Cathryn. "You should come to one of our gigs. We get a pretty mixed crowd at some of the venues. You might meet someone . . . you know . . . like-minded." He raised a languid eyebrow.

Cathryn now looked thoroughly baffled. "What do you mean, like-minded?"

I sprang up from the table. "More jus, anyone? I don't know about you, but I can't get enough of this jus."

Lucy nodded furiously. "Ooh, yes please!"

Cathryn was undeterred. "Sorry, but I'm curious. What do you mean by like-minded?"

Sleepy Eyes shrugged. "You know. Chicks and stuff."

"Excuse me?"

"Just a minute," Michael said from the end of the table. "What exactly are you saying about my fiancée?"

Sleepy Eyes raised his hands. "Forget it."

"I just don't understand what you're getting at," Cathryn said, shaking her head.

"I think we've all got our wires a little bit crossed," I said as I started to clear away plates. "Now, who wants dessert?" I looked pointedly at Sleepy Eyes. "Will you give me a hand in the kitchen?"

He got up slowly and started carrying the dinner plates through. "I didn't mean to piss anyone off," he whispered to me. "Why are they so uptight about it? I thought they were all open and shit."

"What was that?" Michael called from the living room.

"Nothing!" I sang back. "I told you to keep your mouth shut!" I hissed at Sleepy Eyes. I suppressed the urge to hit him upside the head.

The rest of the dinner passed without incident, thank God. Cathryn spent most of dessert criticizing her pavlova (which was, of course, delicious) while I quietly schemed to get Sleepy Eyes in bed. He might not be a man of many words, but conversation wasn't my first objective at this point. I needed to round out this month with a win.

The evening finally came to a close when Lucy stood up and said that she and Tristan had to leave. He jumped to attention and immediately phoned for a taxi.

Cathryn and Michael were the next to go. I washed and dried her cake stand and walked them to the door. "Thank you so much for coming, guys. And thanks for that amazing dessert."

"It was a disaster. Let's not speak of it."

"And sorry about all that weird talk at dinner."

"Yes, what was that all about? Why does he think I like women?"

"Must be the drugs. Probably fried his brain, poor guy. Anyway, get out of here—I'm trying to get laid."

"Good luck."

I slipped into the bathroom to ready myself for the final challenge. I'd come up with a master plan according to the book's advice: I'd ask him to stay behind to help clear up, during which we'd engage in some light banter and I would subtly neg him. I'd show my value using a sleight-of-hand card trick I'd been working on for weeks and would test out his receptivity to physical contact by punching him playfully on the shoulder and putting him into a playful headlock. Finally, if all that went well, I'd suggest we sit on my bed and watch a carefully selected comedic YouTube clip on my laptop. After that, well . . . it should all just unfold naturally.

I went into the kitchen to find Sleepy Eyes smoking a cigarette out of the window. "So," he said. "Wanna fuck?"

Sleepy Eyes wandered out around ten the next morning, tossing a "later" over his shoulder as he walked out the door.

I slunk over to the couch once he'd left and pulled out my notebook and pen.

The Rules of the Game in Conclusion

It's hard to tell if this book was effective, as I suspect that Sleepy Eyes succumbed to my charms not because of my elaborate plotting but because I happened to be directly in front of him at the time. Still, I wouldn't have met him if I hadn't been forced to make conversation with so many strangers. That's the real point of the book: behind all of the Jedi mind tricks and alpha-male stuff, it's about getting you out of your comfort zone and into circulation. It's mainly a numbers game, but playing the numbers can be effective.

I can also see why this works so well on women, because this sort of approach has worked on me so many times. Confident, slightly dickish men who are the center of attention are annoyingly attractive. Maybe it's some sort of evolutionary thing, like how the biggest, strongest lion in the pride is the one who does all the impregnating? And I've got to say, it was weirdly empowering being the biggest dick in the room for a month. Even though I found all the mantras and enforced socializing mortifying, I could feel its influence eventually sink in. The more I approached men, and the more I told myself that those men were lucky to be talking to me, the more I started to believe it. A clever confidence trick indeed.

Works best on . . .

Men with robust self-esteem and a high tolerance level. Also, guys who might be reluctant to make the first move—this takes all the work out of their hands.

To be used by . . .

Women who've always wondered what it would be like to wear the pants in a relationship . . . and who don't mind inflicting often-public humiliation on themselves.

BOOK FIVE
THE ART OF DATING

July 28 Continued

I was still wrapped up in my robe when Lucy walked in the door at noon.

"Hello, babe! Bit late for you to still be in your bathrobe isn't it?"

"Mmpf," I replied. "It's still before the *Come Dine with Me* marathon."

"How was Mr. Talkative after we left? Any progress?"

The memory of him pushing me against a wall and sliding his hand up my dress washed over me. "Mmm-hmm."

"Great! So did the plan work? Did you make your move over the washing-up?"

I glanced into the kitchen and saw a pile of dirty dishes stacked perilously on the countertop.

"Not exactly."

"Did you do one of those magic tricks from the book? The hand reading? The horoscope question?"

I was impressed with how much knowledge Lucy had absorbed over the month. If she and Tristan ever broke up, she was primed and ready to be an alpha gamer.

"No, it didn't come to that in the end . . ."

She sat down on the edge of the couch and gave me a hard look. "Out with it. What happened?"

"Well, after you guys left, he sort of just said, 'Wanna fuck?' So we did."

"That's it?"

"Yup."

"So you didn't need to do any of your fancy closing techniques?"

"Nope."

". . . which means you needn't have bothered with the whole dinner party."

"Probably not."

We were silent for a moment while Lucy considered this.

"That is so hot."

I sat bolt upright. "I know, right? It was sort of shocking how easy it was."

"Details, please."

"Well, my theory about drummers being preternaturally gifted in the sack was right."

"I knew it!" Lucy cried. "It's the rhythm, right?"

"And the strong forearms. Surprisingly useful."

"Lucky girl."

"There was one thing, though . . ."

Lucy propped her chin on her hands, her enormous blue eyes looking at me intently. "Go on."

"Well, he sort of . . . tried to sneak through the back door."

"Do you mean he left early this morning?"

"No, that's not what I mean." I raised a significant eyebrow. "I *mean* he tried to sneak *it* through the back door . . ."

Lucy gasped. "You mean he wanted to . . . he tried to . . ." She looked increasingly distressed. "Up the *bum*? On the first night?"

I nodded. "Without so much as a warning! He just decided to stoop and conquer."

"What did you do?"

"I redirected him."

"And what did he do?"

"Gave it another shot. I redirected him again, and he finally got the message. Or at least gave up."

"Do you think he may have just . . . got lost?"

I considered this for a moment. He wasn't the brightest bulb on the Christmas tree, that's for sure, but I suspected he was pretty well versed in the female anatomy—he was a hot drummer, after all. "I don't think so. I think he was just pushing his luck."

"What a bugger!" Lucy flushed. "No pun intended. Did he say anything afterward?"

"Nope, he just rolled over and went to sleep. I'm not exactly a prude, but to try to stroll through the back passage the first time we're in bed together feels like a bold move."

"Agreed. Are you going to see him again?"

"Who knows. Anyway, did you have fun last night? Tristan's great, by the way. A total silver fox. Was he really weirded out by the whole Cathryn thing?"

She shook her head. "He didn't seem to be. Didn't even mention it on the way home."

"Well, that's good. I mean, he's so obviously nuts about you that I can't imagine any amount of weirdness would put him off. It's like you have some sort of voodoo power over him."

Lucy shifted slightly in her seat. "I don't know if I'd say that."

"Seriously, Luce—he was hanging off your every word. I'm pretty sure that if you had told him to sit on the balcony in his underwear last night, he would have."

She looked slightly chagrined. "He's a doll. Anyway, enough about Tristan: more details about the drummer, please!"

"Only if you get me more coffee."

Eventually, after I'd given Lucy a complete blow-by-blow (in some instances, literally) account of my night with Sleepy Eyes, I poured myself into the shower and cleaned myself up. It was gray and misty out, so I wrapped up in my old college sweatshirt and settled into my next guide a little earlier than scheduled.

The Art of Dating by Evelyn Millis Duvall was written in 1958 as a guide to teenagers and college students just venturing out into the treacherous world of dating and, as a result, the book is pleasingly innocent. There are definitely sections that don't apply to me—I haven't had to ask my parents' permission to borrow the car since, well, the Christmas before last—but there's plenty of wisdom there.

The book describes dating as "grown-up, romantic and full of promise." Thirteen years of personal experience have taught me otherwise, but it's entirely possible I've been doing it wrong the whole time. I read on.

The basics were simple: be sociable, join lots of clubs (the author suggests church groups and the 4H, so I'll have to do some judicious substituting) and be nice. After months of being told to behave like a total asshole, it was refreshing to see kindness being encouraged.

Here are the book's three pillars of popularity:

1. Be careful of your appearance.
2. Be courteous to others.
3. Be fun to be with.

These qualities went completely against everything I'd learned about popularity in high school (unless being careful of your appearance involved owning stock in Abercrombie & Fitch and premium sportswear), but I was willing to give her the benefit of the doubt.

Flicking through the pages, I couldn't help but hope that the book would bring me back to a simpler time. A time before YouPorn and sexting and Craigslist. Sure, the 1950s were fucked up in their own unique way—McCarthyism wasn't great, and people were taking a lot of Vicodin—but chances were you didn't have to worry about running into your bisexual ex-boyfriend's new boyfriend.

I was eager to get started.

August 1

Cathryn and I had just sat back down at our desks after a client meeting when my phone bleeped with a text message. It was Sleepy Eyes.

"That's a surprise," I muttered as I slid the button on my iPhone.

Got a gig in Australia. Back in three months. Laters, sexy.

Yeah, that felt about right. He'd fit right in in the land down under.

Cathryn looked over at me. "Who was that, then? Mr. Chatty?"

"Yep. Gone to Australia apparently."

She looked momentarily confused. "What, for a visit?"

"For a gig. I think he's officially flown the coop."

"Well, I can't say I'm terribly disappointed. He was a bit odd, don't you think? He obviously had some sort of drug problem, and he said all those weird things about me meeting someone who was like-minded."

I cringed. "Yeah . . . that was definitely the drugs talking, I'm sure."

August 3

In order to get into the 1950s spirit, I needed to do some research. Thankfully, this weekend was the Goodwood Vintage Festival and I'd managed to convince Lucy to accompany me with the promise of lots of frilly dresses, pin curls and Victoria sponge cake.

I woke up to the sound of rain. The BBC had promised occasional bouts of sunshine for the day, but a year in this country had taught me that the BBC forecasters lie often and lie well, probably because if they told the truth about the weather, they would be run out of town like a pack of rabid dogs.

I went for a quick run in the morning to make room for all the Bakewell tarts I planned on eating. I got in, soaked, just as Lucy was emerging from her bedroom.

"Hey, love," she said sleepily. "You're dripping."

"I know. It's raining like hell out there. Coffee?"

"Yes please."

We sloped into the kitchen and I flicked on the kettle while she spooned coffee crystals into two mugs.

"Is Tristan still in bed?"

"He's not here."

This was weird. Since they'd met, Lucy and Tristan had spent every possible moment together, and definitely every weekend. His absence couldn't be a good thing.

"Everything okay?"

She shrugged. "We had a bit of an argument."

"Shit. What happened?"

"It was nothing, really. Just a silly little fight about this party we're meant to go to in a few weeks' time."

"What, some work thing of his?"

"Not exactly. Look, let's not talk about it. It's dull."

"If you need me, you know I'm here."

Lucy nodded and patted my hand. "I know. Thanks, lovely. Anyway, let's just focus on having fun today. What are you going to wear?"

"Well, the rain isn't helping that decision. I wanted to wear my peep-toe heels and that little playsuit I have, but a giant poncho is looking more likely."

She waved me away. "It always pisses it down at festivals—it's tradition! You shouldn't let that stop you from wearing the playsuit, though the peep toes might be a problem. Anyway, you'll get the real English experience this way! Do you have wellies?"

"No, I didn't bring them with me from Maine. I thought my climbing-around-in-mud days were behind me."

"Silly cow. Come on, I've got a spare pair."

Lucy charged off into her room and I heard the sound of her closet being disemboweled. She returned with a pair of electric pink rubber boots that were dotted with white polka dots.

"I know they're not your style," she said as she handed them to me, "but they'll keep your feet dry."

Dressed and be-wellied (Lucy looked amazing in a royal blue sailor-style dress with a cinched waist, though the look was slightly marred by her rainbow-colored wellies), we jumped on the first train to Chichester. By the time we arrived at the festival gates, the rain had cleared up and the sun was shining brightly on the mud. It was a festival miracle.

Inside, the field was lined with tents overflowing with gorgeous vintage dresses, dainty little tea sets from the 1940s and 1950s and more Battenberg cakes than you could shake a stick at. In the middle of the green, dozens of gleaming roadsters and hot rods were parked, their owners standing proudly next to them. The crowd was full of women with perfect beehives and cherry-red lips and men wearing immaculate three-piece suits. It was like stepping onto the set of an Audrey Hepburn film.

Lucy spotted a retro makeover tent and pulled me toward it, squealing with excitement. Forty-five minutes later, we both emerged in full vintage splendor, her with a head of shiny blond pin curls and a full red pout, and me with a Veronica Lake wave and ridiculously long fake eyelashes. Every time I blinked, they stuck together slightly. I was hoping it made me look sultry, but I suspected I looked like I was struggling to stay awake.

We wandered through the tents, Lucy buying a few vintage corsets (her interest in lingerie has skyrocketed since meeting Tristan) and me buying an amazing pair of Perspex cat's-eye sunglasses, which I immediately donned in the hope of hiding my increasingly gluey eyelashes.

After three hours and six Pimm's cocktails served in jam jars, I made a beeline for the portable toilets.

The queue was, of course, endless. I was eyeing a promising-looking bush when I felt a tap on my shoulder.

"Cunningham?"

Of course. It made total sense that he would turn up right now. "Adrian. What a surprise." He was wearing trousers, a button-down, suspenders and a bowler hat. And pulling it off, much to my annoyance.

"Having a nice day out?" He looked me up and down, taking in the playsuit and sunglasses. "You're looking very *La Dolce Vita* today."

I tried to flutter my eyelashes behind the glasses, but the left one stuck. "Thanks."

"It suits you. Though the boots jar a bit."

I looked down at my be-wellied feet and shrugged. "You can't have it all, I guess. What are you doing here, anyway?"

"What all these other beautiful young things are doing: feigning interest in a load of old crap while plotting who they'd like to fuck."

"Such a romantic."

"What about you? I didn't think you'd be into festivals."

"I'm here with Lucy. We've just been learning how to knit."

Adrian raised his eyebrows. "Is that right? You never struck me as the fifties-housewife type, Cunningham."

"I wouldn't go that far."

"Well, you can darn my socks anytime, my dear."

"You're a true gentleman." I'd finally reached the front of the line and was about to push open the porto-door when I blurted out, "Want to get a drink with me and Lucy? I can guarantee it will come in a jam jar." I was a glutton for punishment.

"How could I refuse?"

"Hang on a second while I pee."

"Not quite a lady yet, I see."

When I'd finished facing the horror of a festival toilet, I grabbed Adrian and pulled him over to Lucy, who was sitting at a picnic table trying to master purling. "Sorry I took so long. I ran into an old friend. You remember Adrian?"

Adrian emerged from behind me, grinning like an old goat. "Hello, darling! You're looking lovely as ever."

Lucy put down the enormous sleeve she'd knitted and smiled coldly. "Hello, Adrian. Full of shit as ever, I see."

He feigned indignance. "How could you say such a thing? I'm honest to a fault."

"One of many," I said. "Now, do you want a Pimm's or a lime rickey?"

"Lime rickey, please."

I returned with three more jam jars full of liquor (who was eating all this jam?) and sat down at the table, where Lucy was studiously ignoring Adrian and focusing on adding yet more rows to her sleeve.

Adrian sat down next to me and leaned in conspiratorially. "Not a fan apparently."

I shrugged. "She's just protective of me."

"I'm sure you don't need protecting from me."

I took a sip of Pimm's and changed the subject. "How are the moving plans going? Are you still set on invading America?"

"Afraid so. Plane ticket booked for next month."

I felt a stab of sadness in my gut. Even though he was a complete dick most of the time, I sort of hated the idea of not having him around.

He slung an arm across my shoulder. "Don't look so sad, Cunningham. We'll always have Clissold Park."

Last January, when we were dating (or whatever we were doing), he and I had spent an afternoon building a snowman in Clissold Park after a freak snowstorm hit London. I didn't know if I should feel touched that he remembered or annoyed that he was now teasing me about it.

I brushed his arm away. "I just feel bad for all my poor countrywomen. There should be a national health warning, like there was for bird flu. Women should be vaccinated to protect against you."

Adrian looked smug. "I've got an English accent: the women of New York will throw me a welcome parade. Anyway, I've got to run. There are huge swathes of twenty-two-year-old women here who I've not yet slept with, and I'd be doing them a disservice if I didn't give them the opportunity."

"Don't let me keep you from the lucky ladies."

He kissed me on the cheek, paused for a moment and leaned in again. "You look good a bit muddy, Cunningham," he whispered in my ear. "I always knew you were filthy. Let's have a proper good-bye before I go. I'm having a little soirée to see me off—you should come."

I swatted him away, trying to ignore the tingling between my thighs. "We'll see," I said, in what I hoped was a nonchalant manner. "Good-bye, Adrian."

"Good-bye, Cunningham." He turned to Lucy and gave her his most winning grin. "Good-bye, Lucy! A pleasure as always! And do take good care of this one for me, will you?"

"Better than you," she said, shooting daggers at him.

He bowed with a flourish and kissed both our hands before turning away. As much as I'd miss him, it would probably be a blessing to have him safely ensconced in New York City and far away from me.

August 5

With Sleepy Eyes off in the land of Oz, I needed a new 1950s dating partner. I revisited the section on suitable suitors.

One thing was for sure: this book was a big fan of homogeny. When posed with questions about dating people with differences in ethnicity, nationality, class or religion, the author's answer was always the same: it's probably best to stick with your own kind.

Brushing aside my intense discomfort with this level of xenophobia, I figured the best way to put the advice into practice was to do something I'd avoided for a long time and date a fellow American.

Don't get me wrong, I love Americans. Fondness for guns and crazy politics aside, they're some of the earth's best people: hospitable, funny and kind. There are moments when I'm at the checkout counter at a grocery store in London, being glared at by a sullen teenager as he whacks my eggs too hard into the bag (not a euphemism) and I would give my right eye for someone to tell me to have a nice day.

But dating them is another kettle of fish entirely. There are so many complicated, unspoken rules involved in American dating, and everyone is always trying to trade up on their original investment. It's like the sexual equivalent of *Homes Under the Hammer*. Not to mention the fact that most American men can't dress their way out of a paper bag. I don't know who this Docker guy was, but he has a lot to answer for.

Anyway, I didn't have all that much experience dating Americans. There were a few dalliances in college, but I don't think I'd describe making out with someone in the broom closet of a fraternity house a date. There was Dylan, of course, but we'd known each other since we were kids, so we never really went through the whole "dating" thing—it was more just hanging out with friends and then having a quick fumble on the car ride home. None of which had prepared me particularly well for the world of adult dating.

Still, I was starting to understand the appeal of dating a fellow American: a familiarity with the nineties *TGIF* line-up on TV and an appreciation for Kraft macaroni and cheese were things that no amount of properly fitted trousers or charming accents could replace. These were my people. It was time I gave them another shot.

Finding a dateable American in London was another matter. Apparently there were swarms of us here, but I didn't know one single American guy. As with so many other things in life, the answer was just a Google search away, which is how I ended up signing on to YoDate.

I know. YoDate. Doesn't sound promising, does it? But it's the biggest American ex-pat dating community in the world, and there are apparently almost ten thousand eligible American men in London signed up to it. Sorry, not men: bros. All of the guys on YoDate were categorized as "Bros."

I set up an account in the "Hoes" section (I don't think that needs clarification, does it?) and I was up and emailing Brads and Justins and Scotts like there was no tomorrow.

The next day, my inbox was flooded with messages. Sorry, not messages: sup'dates. That's what they called emails on YoDate. I almost unsubscribed when I saw it, but Cathryn dissuaded me.

"The name isn't a reflection on the men, Lauren, just the site they're on." She was loading paper into the printer with military precision as she said this. "And you're on it now, too, so you can't judge them too harshly." She shut the paper drawer with a decisive click.

As always, she had a point. I clicked on the first email and skimmed it, deleting it as soon as I got to the words "country music fan."

I screened out a few other candidates—a born-again Christian, a Fox news viewer, an NRA enthusiast—with Cathryn offering commentary over my shoulder.

"What on earth is wrong with that man?" she asked, pointing to a freshly scrubbed Ivy League type. "You've gone right past him!"

"His favorite book is *The Fountainhead.*"

"So? Isn't that quite popular? I'm sure I saw it in Daunt's the other day."

"Yeah, it basically means he's a fascist."

"I don't think Daunt's would be displaying fascist literature—"

"Next!" I yelled.

"Quiet!" Cathryn hissed, looking pointedly at our boss's door.

I kept scrolling until my eye caught on a pair of mischievous dark eyes.

"Him," I said, pointing to his photo icon.

Cathryn peered over my shoulder. "Yes, he's quite handsome."

I took in his close-cropped black hair and stubbly beard. His tag name was Frisco.

I gave Frisco a gentle virtual nudge—a "high five" in YoDate terminology—and hoped it would prompt him to get in touch.

August 7

It was the end of the day, and Cathryn and I were knee-deep in planning the sponsors' conference; it was all we were thinking about. Well, all *she* was thinking about. I had a few other things on my mind, particularly when the email pinged into my inbox.

"He's emailed!"

"The caterer? Has he signed the contract?"

"No, not him—Frisco! He just sup'dated me!"

"The one with the nice eyes? What does he have to say?"

"He wants to take me for dinner and cocktails."

"Dinner and cocktails! Is that how you Americans date? I don't think Michael took me for dinner during our first year together!"

"Yeah, dates tend to involve food in America. I guess it's the lack of pubs or something."

"Well, it all sounds very promising."

I sent off a quick email to Frisco suggesting some free evenings. Maybe dating an American again wouldn't be so bad after all.

August 9

Tomorrow is my dinner date with Frisco. In preparation, I spent my lunch hour Google-stalking him.

Don't act like you don't do it, too.

Actually, it's encouraged by the book! Well, sort of. The book recommends that, should a stranger ask you out, you should "ask around the neighborhood about his reputation" before going out with him. Surely, with the collapse of local communities and the rise of globalization, the contemporary equivalent of "asking around the neighborhood" is looking up someone on the Internet, right?

From his profile I knew his full name and his home state (California, obviously). I pride myself on being an excellent Googler— it's definitely in my core skill set—so within a few minutes I knew where he went to high school and college, his last three addresses, and had access to about a hundred photos of him through his (not privatized, the fool) Facebook page.

I spent ten minutes flicking through his Flickr (was that little blond woman an ex-girlfriend? What about the brunette? And, holy shit, was that his pug??). I forced myself to click away before I became overwhelmed with unwarranted pangs of intense jealousy and/or lust.

I scanned through the rest of the results and kept seeing references to something called Catify. I clicked on a link to Wired and started reading, coffee dribbling down my chin.

In 2011, he invented an app that could superimpose an adorable cat face onto any photo. I vaguely remember the frenzy it caused when it first came out. "Kitty me" became a popular catchphrase and celebrities everywhere released kittied photos of themselves on the red carpet and on film sets. Heads of state even got in on the act, kittying photos of their meet and greets. And then, at the height of the kitty-craze, Facebook bought the app for one point three billion dollars.

ONE POINT THREE BILLION DOLLARS, PEOPLE.

I clicked on another link: there was Frisco giving a TED talk about technology and self-expression.

Another: a photo of him shaking hands with Bill Gates.

I stood up from my desk and told Cathryn I was going out for a cigarette.

She eyed me suspiciously. "Are you all right? You've gone pale."

"I'm fine. I just found out that I'm going on a date with a billionaire."

Outside, I took a long drag and thought about my predicament. So Frisco was a billionaire, but I had to pretend that I didn't know that he was a billionaire when I met him tomorrow because if I mentioned it, he'd know that I was Google-stalking him and that would be gross. The first rule of Google-stalking is that you can never let on that you already know everything about the person you Google-stalked, even though everyone Google-stalks everyone these days.

I imagine things were much simpler in the fifties. Hearing some neighborhood gossip is substantially different to seeing a photograph of your date palling around with Bill goddamn Gates.

I was going to have to be on my A-game for this one. But how was I supposed to prepare myself for a date with someone psychotically rich? I had no experience with these sorts of things. What if there was a whole rich-people etiquette I knew nothing about? What if they somehow used their cutlery differently from me? What if he took me somewhere scary and fancy where they scraped the crumbs off the table with one of those silver things?

I needed someone who could guide me through this new rarefied world. I walked back into the office with a purposeful stride.

"Right," I said, perching myself on the edge of Cathryn's desk, "I need your help."

August 10

I was primed and ready for my date with a billionaire. Cathryn had taught me all about the correct order for silverware usage (work from the outside in, apparently) and the correct way to be seated at a table in a small fancy restaurant (wait for the maître d' to pull out the table, then sit down and allow him to shove the table back in place. Seems more complicated than just pulling out the chair . . .).

I was expecting Frisco to pick some extortionate two-Michelin-star restaurant that served only foams and essences, so I was a little confused when he sent over the address of a place in Kentish Town.

When I arrived, I was surprised to find a slightly grubby Ethiopian restaurant. I'd never had Ethiopian food before, but I remembered from an episode of No Reservations that you were meant to sit on cushions on the floor and eat with your hands. I suddenly regretted wearing the tasteful shift dress I'd borrowed from Cathryn.

I walked in to find Frisco waiting for me by the door. He looked just like his photograph: piercing eyes, deep dimples and stubble so perfect it looked Photoshopped. Instead of a well-cut suit, he was wearing a pair of board shorts and an old Pixies T-shirt.

I tried to sit on my cushion as elegantly as possible, though I was sure all of the restaurant had caught a glimpse of my Addis Ababa.

I launched straight in with flattering conversation, as per the book's instructions. "Wow, what a hidden gem! How did you find this place?"

Frisco shrugged. "I spent some time in Addis Ababa a few years ago, and a friend there told me about their cousin's place in London. I made it my first stop when I got here and I've been coming ever since."

No concierge service, then. In the end, he ordered for both of us, and a bunch of unpronounceable but delicious dishes started appearing on our mat. He showed me the best way to eat it, scooping up the spiced meat with pieces of flatbread, and didn't seem too horrified when I dropped a handful onto my (thankfully napkinned) lap.

I'd forgotten how nice it is to have the linguistic shorthand that comes with talking to another American. I was so used to explaining my cultural references to confused Brits who hadn't grown up with *Mister Rogers' Neighborhood* and hadn't seen the U.S. Dairy Lobby–sponsored commercials encouraging cheese consumption. I almost wept with relief when I made a joke about Bob Ross's happy little trees and he understood it.

I guess I'd underestimated how hard I'd been trying to make myself understood in London. This was just . . . simple. Maybe the book was right about sticking to one's own kind.

The flatbreads were cleared away and the honey wine was flowing like, well, wine.

"So," I said, "I'm assuming from your YoDate name that you're from San Francisco?"

He grinned. "Born and raised, though I spent some time in Mountain View before I moved over here."

Yikes. Even I knew that's where Google HQ is based. "What were you doing there?" I asked innocently. Presumably developing another billion-dollar app, or maybe a self-navigating hovercraft.

"Oh, you know. This and that. Do you want dessert?"

Several more glasses of honey wine later, Frisco walked me to my bus stop. It had been an amazing night, and Frisco had been the perfect gentleman . . . though knowing what I did, I was a little surprised when he let me split the bill with him. He was probably a feminist to boot and didn't want to seem like he was partaking in the traditional patriarchal fiscal system. Swoon.

"So, how are you getting home?" I asked. Private jet? I thought. Helicopter?

"I can jump on the bus from here, actually."

I didn't want the evening to end, but the 214 appeared almost immediately. For the first time in my life I rued a bus turning up quickly.

He put his hand on my shoulder and looked into my eyes. "I had a really great time, Lauren," he said.

"Me too." This was it. He was going in for the kiss. I met his gaze and steadied myself, licking my lips and hooding my eyes in what I hoped was an attractive way.

Frisco pulled me in for a hug, then jumped through the bus's open door. "See you soon!" he called.

August 11

Lucy had been at Tristan's when I got in from my date with Frisco, so tonight was the first night we were able to have a serious debrief. She was still working on her sleeve, which was now about six feet long.

"Don't you think you should start on the other sleeve soon?" I asked. "Or the body bit?"

"I'd love to, babe, but I don't know how to cast off, so I'm just going to keep going until I run out of yarn."

"It'll be a hell of a sleeve when you're finished."

Lucy was a rapt audience as I gave a detailed blow by blow of the date, only interrupting to suggest more wine or another cigarette. After almost an hour, we reached the point where he hugged me.

"Hang on, just a hug?"

I nodded.

"Not even a peck? A little cuddle?"

"A hug."

"Did you give him the eyes?"

"Oh yeah. He got all the eyes I could muster."

"What about the lips—did you plump?"

"They're not pillows, for Christ's sake."

"I'm being perfectly serious! Did you plump them? Like this?" Lucy made a face like a duck's ass.

"I fucking hope not," I muttered.

"Laugh all you like, but this pout has never let me down."

"Well, whoop-dee-doo for you. I guess I'm the only leper around here."

"Babe, you are not a leper! He did say that he wanted to see you again, so he must fancy you."

"Maybe he just wants an American buddy," I said, throwing myself back on the couch in despair.

"Don't be silly," she said, finishing another row on her giant sleeve. "Men don't want to be *friends* with women."

August 16

I'd heard from Frisco the morning after my debrief with Lucy, and we'd gone on a second date on Wednesday. He'd been just as dreamy and just as chaste as the first time.

But this morning, I woke up to a very exciting text from Frisco.

Frisco: Wanna hang out tonight?

I jumped out of bed and did a small dance of joy before responding.

Me: Sure. What did you have in mind?

Pleasesaysexpleasesaysexpleasesaysex . . .
My phone bleeped happily.

Frisco: Why don't you come over to my place? I'll make dinner
and we can watch a box set.

I let out a little whoop: dinner at his place—sex was pretty
much guaranteed.

Me: Sounds good. I'll bring the beer.

I spent the next twenty minutes agonizing over my choice of
underwear. As is always the way, all my good stuff was in the wash
so I had to hand wash my favorite Coco de Mer set (bought on sale
when drunk after a work event last year) and, despite my best efforts with the hair dryer, left the house in a slightly damp bra.

I couldn't concentrate on anything at work.

". . . so are you okay to compile the figures? Lauren? Hello,
Lauren?" I looked up to see Cathryn watching me with a mix of
concern and exasperation.

"What? Oh, sorry. I wasn't really listening."

"The figures, Lauren. For the sponsorship deal?"

"Oh, yeah. Sure, of course, I'll send them over." I started to pull
up the Excel spreadsheets, but was struck with a thought before I had
the chance to press send. "I mean, maybe he's just a gentleman, right?"

"Who? The client? I wouldn't say that, not after the way he
looked at my bum last week."

"No, Frisco! Maybe he's just old-fashioned, you know? Wanted
to wait until the third date before making a move. He probably just
respects me, right?"

Cathryn sighed. "Could be. I really don't know, Lauren."

I nodded decisively. "I'll bet that's what it is."

"I certainly hope so. I don't think I have the strength to deal with you like this much longer."

It took me eons to get to Peckham, so I was running seriously late by the time I staggered to his front door carrying two six-packs of Sierra Nevada and a lemon drizzle cake I'd impulse-bought from Gail's.

Dressing "appropriately" for hanging out and watching TV proved way more difficult than dressing "appropriately" for anything else; I'd settled on a pair of loose-fitting, faded jeans from my Portland days and an old Billy Idol T-shirt. I was hoping the effect was "effortlessly sexy" and not "effortlessly homeless." It had been sweltering on the bus and I was covered in a thin layer of sweat and grime.

I was greeted first by a scruffy, aproned Frisco followed by a waggy-tailed pug and a waft of delicious cooking smells, all in quick succession. It was like walking into a version of heaven created specifically by my vagina.

"Hey!" Frisco gave me a quick kiss on the cheek. "Come on in! You brought Sierra Nevada! Good call."

"I aim to please. Who's this little guy?" I knelt down and scratched his wrinkly little head. The dog responded by rolling over on his back and wiggling around on the floor. If only Frisco was as easily enticed.

"He's just showing off for the ladies, aren't you, Billy Budd?" Frisco scooped up the pug in one arm. I was overcome with the desire to be a dog so I could be scooped up in the other.

"Billy Budd?" I asked. "Like, as in Melville?"

He laughed. "Yeah. He's got this crazy squint when he gets excited, so I thought he looked like a sailor. Don't you, Budd?" He gave Billy a scratch behind the ears and his little face scrunched up. I had to admit, it was pretty accurate.

"So what's cooking?" I asked, following him down the corridor into the big, open-plan living space. "It smells amazing. Your place is great, by the way."

It really was. There was art on every wall in the living room— real, honest-to-God interesting art, not just a poster for *The Godfather* stuck on there with Blu-tack. There was a yoga mat rolled up in the corner of the room next to a photo of Bikram Choudhury and various knickknacks from around the globe, and there was a plant that was actually still alive on the windowsill.

He led me through to the kitchen, which was tiled navy and white and spotless, despite the fact that several pots and a casserole dish were quietly bubbling away on the stove.

The whole place felt like a sitcom set.

He gestured toward the casserole dish. "Are you okay with eating fish?"

"Love it." I didn't, not really, but I wasn't about to tell that to this dream man in an apron.

He opened a couple of beers and handed me one, and we talked while I watched him cook. Seeing him wield a wooden spoon was unbelievably arousing: it was like watching some sort of domestic striptease.

Billy danced between the two of us, begging for bits of food and presenting his belly for scratching. I wasn't sure which of the two I was more in love with.

I'd had a quick flick through the latest issue of *Wired* last night, so I was primed with what I hoped would be a few techy tidbits to drop into conversation.

"So," I said casually, "how about those bitcoins, eh?"

Frisco looked up from the stove. "What about them?"

"They're just . . . crazy, right?"

He frowned slightly and turned back to stirring. "Not really. It's just another form of currency. In five years' time, we'll all be using something similar. The concept of individualized national currencies is virtually dead."

Shit. I had no idea what he was talking about. Time to try another tack.

"You know, I tried Snapchat the other day," I said. "I sent a few photos to my sister, but they kept getting deleted after she'd looked at them."

"That's the point," he said over his shoulder. "They're meant to self-destruct so there's no incriminating evidence. That's why teenagers love it so much."

"Oh." Great, forty minutes trying to learn about the digital age for nothing. I gave up and concentrated on petting the pug.

We sat down to eat and he put a series of increasingly amazing-looking vegetable dishes on my plate, topped off with a steamed fillet of cod.

I took one bite and almost passed out. It was incredible.

"This is probably the best thing I've put in my mouth in a long time," I said, eyebrow raised suggestively. I waited for him to react to the innuendo, but he just serenely speared a piece of asparagus. "Where did you learn to cook like this?"

He shrugged and then bent down to feed Billy a scrap of fish. "I've always loved to mess around in the kitchen." I choked on a piece of roasted cauliflower before recovering myself. "It's actually why I decided to come to London."

"Really?"

"It's a long story, but I came here via Greenland."

"Greenland? What the hell were you doing in Greenland?"

"I went to a conservation forum in Greenland a few years ago. We ended up on a trawler with these fishermen who'd dedicated their lives to sustainable deep-sea fishing. These guys take it seriously—I mean, they're out there in blizzards and storms and all kinds of weather. Really inspiring stuff. But the best part was when this Icelandic guy on the boat gave me some hakari."

"What's hakari? Some kind of psychotropic drug?"

Frisco laughed a deep, dimpled laugh. "No, it's pickled shark."

"Why the fuck would you want to pickle a shark? Unless you're Damien Hirst, I guess."

He frowned. "It's actually a delicacy in Iceland. It was an honor for him to share it with me."

"Oh. Sorry."

"Don't be—I didn't know about it either. But as soon as I tasted it, I knew that hakari was my destiny. I went home, sold the business and moved to Iceland. I spent a year studying with some of the greatest hakari producers in the world, learning all the tricks of the trade. I'm now a level-three hakari master."

"Congratulations," I said, not knowing if that was the correct response. "How did that lead to London? I didn't know there was a great demand for pickled shark here."

"Yeah, but there's such an incredible food scene," he said. It was true: you couldn't sneeze in central London without spraying on someone selling pop-up artisanal hot dogs or snail gratins out of a truck. "There's no better place to bring hakari to the masses. I've been curing my own batch for the past four and a half months, and in two weeks I'm going to open my own hakari stall in Broadway market."

I nodded. So pickled shark was this guy's one true love. What chance did I have?

I remembered the book's advice: if you can't beat 'em, join 'em. "Can I try some?" I asked. I didn't think I liked the sound of pickled shark, but I was willing to try it for the sake of "sharing his interests."

He shook his head. "Sorry, it's still curing. You can't eat it until it's had its full pickling time."

"That's a shame," I said, feigning disappointment.

"I can show you where the strips of shark are hanging, though."

"I haven't had a better offer all year."

I followed him into the basement where, lo and behold, a truly ridiculous amount of shark pieces were hanging up, all emanating a special blend of moldy cheese, athlete's foot and death.

"Ohmygod," I said, resenting the exhalation because of the inhalation to follow.

"Amazing stuff, right? I mean, this is the smell of LIFE!" He took a deep breath and grinned.

I nodded maniacally and valiantly fought off my gag reflex.

"You should come down to Broadway market when I open the stall. Get a taste of the real thing."

I took a quick gasp. "Mmm-hmm!" I spluttered.

"So, now you've seen my baby. Ready for a cigarette and a DVD?"

I nodded again and ran up the stairs after him, getting a lungful of fresh air into me just before I started to black out.

Three episodes of *Justified* and nary a hand held or a thigh grazed later, I saw Frisco stifle a yawn. It was the moment of truth: could I stay or would I go?

I got up from my side of the couch and stretched in what I hoped was an alluring way. "Well, I guess I should get going . . . ?" I let the question dangle in the air for a minute, like so much pickled shark.

"Yeah, I'm pretty beat myself," he said, running his hand over his stubbly chin.

My heart sank, but I wasn't yet defeated. I leaned over his lap, ostensibly to give Billy a scratch but really to give Frisco the chance to look down my T-shirt.

He leaned away and gave Billy ample scratching room, which the dog appreciated and I did not. My little light of hope was flickering.

"Okay, well, thanks for dinner. It's my turn next time."

"No problem. I'll walk you to the door."

I shuffled down the hallway like a man on death row.

He opened the door and turned to let me out. "Thanks for coming all this way, Lauren. You're a great girl."

"And you're a great guy," I said. This was it. This was my chance: it was rape-kiss or nothing. I had to take it. I tilted my head and lunged for his face.

Frisco deftly caught my mouth with his cheek and pulled me in for a hug. "Be careful out there. Let me know when you get home. I'll see you in a couple of weeks at the market—you'll get a prime piece of hakari, I promise!!" he called before he shut the door.

"Whatever," I muttered. "Night."

I slunk away into the darkness, leaving the smell of pickled shark and defeat in my wake.

August 17

Lucy was away for the weekend with Tristan, so I had the flat to myself, and after last night's hug-and-run, I needed someone to talk to. I distracted myself by going to the gym for an hour or so (though not particularly successfully, as every time I picked up a weight or stepped onto a machine, I'd remember the hug and stop to mutter a few expletives under my breath).

Back at home, I sat on the couch and checked my watch obsessively until it was late enough that I knew Meghan would be awake in Maine. I stepped onto the balcony, lit a cigarette and dialed her number.

"Please pick up, please pick up, please pick up," I chanted into the phone.

"Hello?"

"Thank GOD! I have to talk to you about this American guy. He's a billionaire tech guy and I did loads of research on him to prepare for the date because the book told me to but I can't figure out what a bitcoin is and I hate pickled shark and he's super hot and smart but all he ever does is hug me."

"Whoa! Slow down there, cowboy—deep breaths. Now, what about bitcoin?"

I calmed myself enough to give Meghan a relatively coherent account of the situation with Frisco.

"What am I doing wrong? I'm following all of the book's advice, but it's just not working!"

Meghan sighed. "I hate to say it but . . . maybe he's just not that into you?"

"How am I supposed to know? I haven't read that book yet!"

"Not the book, numbskull, the concept. I don't want to harsh your buzz, but maybe he's not interested."

I felt a stabbing pain in my chest and tried my best to brush it aside. "But he asked me out again! And when we said good night last night, he said he'd see me soon!"

"Maybe he's gay."

"That's your answer for everything."

"Look, you're amazing. You're smart and beautiful and funny. This guy . . . if he doesn't see how great you are, he's not as perfect as you think he is."

I mumbled noncommittally.

I heard her take a deep breath down the phone. "So, I saw Dylan again."

My stomach contracted. "Oh yeah? How's he doing?"

A pause. "Look, I've got to tell you something, otherwise you're going to find out on Facebook or some shit."

I knew immediately that whatever it was, I didn't want to know. "Do you have to?"

A sigh. "Yeah, I think so."

"Better come right out with it."

"He's seeing Kelly Leibler."

"*That* Kelly Leibler?"

"The one and only."

"Oh." My stomach contracted further and I could taste a little bit of the morning's coffee in the back of my throat. Kelly had been the golden girl in high school: blond, tiny, permanently tanned, and mean as a box of snakes. I had spent my formative years skulking around in Doc Martens and black eyeliner, filling journals with stories imagining the demise of Kelly and the other golden girls. And now she had Dylan.

"They're shacked up together, apparently. I hear she moved into the house a few weeks ago."

I was silent for a minute.

"Sorry, maybe I shouldn't have told you, but I figured it was better to hear it from me. She looks like shit, if that makes you feel any better. Saw them together at Sangillo's—all those years on the tanning bed have started to catch up with her."

I tried for a minute to picture her as a wizened old crone, but it didn't do much to dent the feeling of free-falling emptiness. I took a deep breath. "I'm glad you told me. And I'm happy for him. He deserves to be happy."

"C'mon, it's me. You don't have to do this bullshit."

"I am! I'm very happy for him. I hope they have a long and fruitful life together and die in their sleep within seconds of each other, like that old couple in *The Notebook*."

I heard a long sigh. "Kid . . ."

"Okay, fine. I hate it, okay? He should be on the Island of Lost Men where he belongs! But here I am, getting fucking HUGS from a fucking YOGA ENTHUSIAST and he's living happily ever after with Kelly fucking Leibler."

"Feel better now?"

I sighed. "You know I have no right to say anything about what he does with his life."

"Yeah, I do. But I know that doesn't make it any easier to hear he's with someone else."

We said our good-byes and hung up. I knew it was none of my

business—I was the one who left him, after all—but the idea of another woman in the house we'd shared together, another woman taking my side of the bed . . . it was terrible. But more than that, I felt like I was watching one more person make the leap into adulthood while I regressed into extended adolescence.

I grabbed my laptop, already filled with self-loathing for what I was about to do.

You see, Facebook and I have an abusive relationship. No matter how many pictures of other people's holidays and babies I'm forced to slog through, I keep coming back for more. I'd log on with the intention of having a quick peek and find myself flicking through photographs of the cousin of someone I went to elementary school with. "Why? Why am I looking at these?" I would ask myself as I clicked through to the next reel.

But still, I came back. And now here I was, furtively searching for photographic evidence of Dylan and Kelly while feeling increasingly gross about myself.

It took some work as Dylan had unfriended me when I'd left and Kelly was using a nickname, but eventually I found it: a photo of the two of them sitting on my old front porch, blond and tanned and smiling, holding a couple of Budweisers out to the camera.

She still looked as mean as a scorpion behind that smile, and I was pleased to see that Meghan hadn't been lying about her overtanning: her face looked like a piece of untreated rawhide. And was she wearing a scrunchie? I leaned in for a closer inspection. Yep, definitely a scrunchie. I had to admit, I felt better. She was still super cute, and I was pretty sure her boobs had somehow grown even bigger, but . . . c'mon: a scrunchie? Who did she think she was, Kelly Kapowski?

I shut the laptop and spread out on the couch, determined to nap my way into oblivion. I figured if I could get a couple hours of sleep under my belt, when I woke up it would be a respectable time to start drinking.

I shifted slightly on the cushions and felt something sharp dig into my thigh.

"What the . . ." I felt around and found the culprit: a long chain with little clamps at either end. I figured it was a necklace of Lucy's and stuck it on the bookshelf.

I flopped back on the couch and drifted off, dreaming of an army of blond zombies intent on hugging me to death.

August 24

I had gone for my usual Saturday run and was sitting in the living room having my usual Saturday enormous wedge of cake when I heard a noise coming from Lucy's bedroom. I figured she'd slipped in when I was out running.

I hadn't seen her in days—she'd been working nonstop and had been sleeping at Tristan's most nights.

"Luce?" I called. "Is that you?"

More rustling, followed by an agonized cry.

"Lucy? Are you okay?"

No response. I got up and put my ear to her door. "Lucy?"

A whimper, and a bang.

"Luce, seriously, you're freaking me out. Can you come out here?"

There was a pause. The door suddenly flew open, revealing Lucy in a state of extremely high agitation. Her room, which is normally a bastion of yellow, floral-printed neatness, was a mess. Clothes were strewn across the bed, hanging from every edge of the wardrobe and covering most of the floor.

But that wasn't the weirdest thing. The weirdest thing was that all the clothes were black and seemingly made of leather or some sort of synthetic. I thought I saw some PVC in there, too.

"Oh, Lauren. You have to help me!"

"What the fuck is going on? It looks like the Addams Family blew up in here!"

"Oh, babe, I'm in trouble. I've got to find an outfit for this party Tristan's taking me to tonight and nothing looks right!"

"That doesn't sound like such a terrible emergency. What kind of party is it?"

Lucy looked coy. "It's a special sort of party."

"That's not helpful. Wait—is this the party you and he fought about the other week?"

"Yes, and I've agreed to go now and it's very important to Tristan and if I don't get the outfit right he'll be so disappointed!"

"Jesus, take a breath! What kind of outfit do you need? Is it, like, fancy? Black tie?"

"Not exactly, though there is an element of fancy dress involved . . ."

I rolled my eyes. "Can you just tell me what's going on so I can help you?"

"Fine, but you have to promise not to tell anyone. And you can't let on that you know anything when you see Tristan."

"Okay! Okay!"

Lucy led me to the couch and sat down across from me. "Tristan has . . . particular tastes in things."

I thought of Frisco and his hakari. "Rich people usually do."

"This is a bit different. It's sort of . . . sexual."

"Ooh! Exciting!"

"You see, Tristan has a very important and stressful job, so he likes to unwind when he's at home."

"Are you doing a magazine profile on the guy or are you telling me what he's into in bed?"

Lucy's eyes narrowed. "Fine. He's into . . . *spanking*," she whispered. "Whips and leather and all that."

"Kinky! The old guy has life in him yet."

"Babe, this is serious!"

"Sorry, sorry. I know it is." I put my hand over hers. "Are you okay with being spanked? Because if he's crossing a line and hurting you, I'll—"

She cut me off. "No, Lauren. I'm not the one being spanked."

The penny took a moment to drop, and then fell with a clang. "What, so *you* spank *him*? He's into *that*?"

Lucy looked mildly affronted. "He likes it when I'm in charge. He's the boss at work so he doesn't want to be the boss in the bedroom. Or something like that."

"Huh. So how into it is he? Is it, like, every time?"

Lucy hid her face behind her hands. "He has a room."

"What do you mean, he has a room?"

"A room! Filled with paddles and whips and things! There's a little box in there that he locks himself in when he feels he's been naughty. He calls it Aunt Dorothy's Cupboard."

I tried to suppress a snicker. "Why the fuck does he call it that?"

"I don't bloody know! I think it's to do with some mean old great aunt of his."

"Okay . . . so what happens in Aunt Dorothy's Cupboard?"

"I lock him in there and make him beg to get out. Admit that he was a very naughty boy and all that."

Suddenly, a lightbulb went on. I ran over to the bookshelf and started rummaging around until I found the chain I'd placed there weeks ago.

I turned and showed it to her. "This isn't a necklace, is it?"

She went a deep plum color. "Oh God."

It was a nipple clamp. I had accidentally sat on a nipple clamp in my own home.

"I thought it was a necklace! I thought you were getting all punk in your old age!"

I started to laugh and Lucy couldn't hold out for very long; soon we were both in a state of high hysterics.

"I can't believe you've been spanking him all along and you haven't told me!" I said between convulsions.

"I just couldn't bring myself to say it aloud! What was I meant to say: 'Lauren, the love of my life has turned me into a reluctant dominatrix?'"

"Oh my God, that's it! That's the name of your autobiography! *Reluctant Dominatrix: The Lucy Johnson Story.*"

That set us off again for a good five minutes.

"Seriously, though, are you okay with it?"

Lucy shrugged. "Sort of, I guess. It's kind of sexy being in control. Plus, if he gets on my tits, I can leave him in Aunt Dorothy's Cupboard for an hour or so and watch the telly. Anyway, enough of this—I still need your help with finding an outfit for this party."

"What is this party, anyway?"

"Are you familiar with the Torture Garden?"

August 31

In exchange for helping Lucy choose the perfect outfit for the Torture Garden party last weekend (we went with a classic black leather corset and pencil skirt with thigh-high PVC stiletto boots in the end—apparently it was a big hit), she agreed to come with me to Frisco's big shark reveal at Broadway market today.

We'd been texting all week, so I knew just how excited he was, but I wasn't prepared for what we saw when we got to his stall.

In truth, we smelled it way before we saw it. It was a blend of three-day-old diapers, teenage boy's bedroom and pure evil. It was like running an olfactory obstacle course.

There was Frisco wearing a fisherman's sweater, overalls and knitted hat (despite the fact that it was boiling out), presiding over a crowd of fifty or sixty hipsters all clamoring for a taste of his putrefied shark.

"Fucking hell," Lucy said, "I didn't know it would be such a bun fight."

"Neither did I," I said, watching a lithesome twenty-two-year-old with Rapunzel hair and the nation's smallest denim shorts attempt to choke back a bit of hakari. She swallowed—with some effort—before batting her eyelashes at Frisco and smiling appreciatively at him.

In fact, pretty much the entire line consisted of lithesome twenty-two-year-old women trying not to vomit while eating pickled shark.

Frisco spotted us and waved us over.

"Hey, bud! Glad you could make it! And you must be Lucy! Great to meet you." He kissed us both on the cheek and I felt fifty-three pairs of young, lithesome eyes glare at us.

"Look at you!" I said. "God, I had no idea it would be so popular!"

"Just wait till you try it," he said. "It'll knock you out."

"Possibly quite literally," Lucy whispered.

"Excuse me? Sorry, excuse me!" The three of us turned to see a Cara Delevingne–alike in a playsuit standing in front of the stall expectantly.

Frisco leaned over the counter, displaying a stretch of impressively muscular stomach. "Hey, babe," he said, "what can I do for you?"

"Sorry to interrupt, but I just had to tell you that that was the absolute *best* hakari I've ever had."

"You've had it before?" he asked.

Cara nodded emphatically. "I've been to Iceland loads on shoots. I did one for *Wallpaper* last winter and they did part of it on one of the trawlers. The fishermen were all desperate to feed it to me."

"I bet they were," I muttered.

"Yours is seriously the best, though. I just had to tell you."

Frisco smiled a smile I'd never seen before and leaned farther over the counter toward her. "That's so awesome of you to say. Hey, I'm swamped here but I'd love to talk more about Iceland. Can I give you a call sometime?"

Cara smiled back at him. "Tell you what, I'll come back around sixish and we can go for a drink once you've packed it in for the day."

"Sounds great. See you soon." Frisco watched her walk away, a wistful look on his face.

I tugged on his sleeve.

"Hey, sorry, Lauren! I'm being so rude—let me get you and Lucy some hakari. On the house."

I glanced at the tray of hakari and, beyond it, at the crowd of fawning young women clamoring to get a piece. It was then, over a pile of noxious, putrid shark flesh, that I knew Frisco was never going to have sex with me.

"Actually, I think I'm all set," I said, tugging at Lucy's arm. "I had a pretty big meal before this and I saw a whoopie pie with my name on it over there, so I wouldn't want to fill up on shark and spoil my appetite."

Frisco looked momentarily crestfallen. "You sure? You're missing out!"

"Yeah, I'm sure. Congratulations, though—looks like your dream is totally coming true."

He gazed at his surroundings and smiled. "I guess it is."

Lucy and I left him to his adoring fans and went and stuffed ourselves with baked goods before getting hugely and satisfyingly drunk on tequila.

"Thank God you didn't eat that rotten shark," Lucy said as we stumbled home. "It looked *vile*."

"Yeah, fuck that shark! And fuck him and his billion dollars!" I felt momentarily sobered. Just goes to show: you can give a guy a billion dollars, a perfect apartment and an adorable pug, but at the end of the day all he wants is someone who will appreciate his pickled shark.

The book cautions that there are several reasons why a boy might not be interested in dating a particular girl. It could be that he's shy, or that he hasn't noticed her, or that he has other, more pressing interests (like spending his billions on pickled shark, for instance).

This left me with the book's final explanation for a boy's lack of interest: he's too popular. If this is the case, the book advises the girl to seek out "some pleasant, shy, interested fellow rather than wistfully pine for an inaccessible man about town."

I guess I'll never know what Frisco's intentions toward me were. Maybe he was just lonely in a new city. Maybe he was looking for an ego stroke. One thing was for sure: my pining days were over.

I got home and jotted down my findings while nursing a large tumbler of bourbon.

Name: Frisco
Age: 32
Occupation: Billionaire, pickled-shark impresario, tech hero,
    heartbreaker
Nationality: American
Description: Stubbled, dimpled perfection
Method: *The Art of Dating*
Result: Nice girls (who don't look like Cara Delevingne) finish last

The Art of Dating in Conclusion

Being kind to my date (for once) had its good moments, and I wasn't as filled with self-loathing as I was following other guides, but all the research and relentless positivity about his interests (not to mention the time spent pin-curling my hair) wasn't all that rewarding. Plus, it didn't get me anywhere. In the end, guys don't necessarily want a girl to be their best friend (though what they do want still eludes me . . .).

Works best on . . .

Probably the pleasant, shy, interested fellow the book suggests you go out with. Definitely not one for the alpha males.

To be used by . . .

Women in the market for the boy-next-door. Thrill-seekers need not apply.

I wasn't quite ready to settle for the pleasant, shy fellow though. Which is why, next month, I'd be harnessing my inner sex goddess with *Belle de Jour's Guide to Men.*

BOOK SIX
BELLE DE JOUR'S GUIDE TO MEN

September 1

I charged into the bookstore with a new sense of purpose. Gone were the fifties, gone were the American billionaires who just wanted to be friends and gone was the nice-girl-next-door act. It was September and I was going to get laid this month if it killed me. And I knew just who to help me.

I crept past the bookseller, who was engrossed in a tattered copy of *Women in Love*, hand wrapped around a mug of tea and hair curling haphazardly across his eyes, and climbed into the attic, where I unearthed exactly what I was looking for: *Belle de Jour's Guide to Men*. For the uninitiated, Belle wrote several bestselling books about her sexual adventures as a high-end escort in London. She was later revealed as a research scientist who put herself through graduate school with her earnings as a call girl. So an expert in both sex *and* science: just what I needed.

I have to admit, I've never wanted to be a call girl. I've always wanted to be a stripper—just for a night—but never a call girl. I've also always wanted to drive (or is it conduct?) a train for a day and live in a lighthouse for twenty-four hours. Stripping, train-conducting and lighthouse-keeping are three things I would like to try. Prostitution: not so much.

First of all, moral and ethical problems with the sex trade aside, it feels like a lot of pressure. Sex can be stressful enough, never mind if someone's paying good money for it. Can you imagine how mortifying it would be if someone asked for a refund? I mean, I guess I could get my pimp to break the guy's kneecaps, but it would still dent my confidence.

Secondly, there's a lot of upkeep involved in high-end prostitution. A lot of grooming. Normally I work off the assumption that if I turn up, get naked and have sex with a man, he will be grateful regardless of the state of my bikini line. Not so if you're an escort: it seems you've got to be as plucked as a Christmas goose.

But desperate times called for desperate measures, and it was time to pull out the big guns in the form of Belle. If she couldn't get me laid, what chance did I have?

I clattered down the stairs with my prize, startling the bookseller in the process. He looked up from his book with a start and nearly knocked over his tea. "Oh, it's you," he said, turning his attention back to D. H. Lawrence.

"I'm here to make a purchase!" I said, presenting the book with a flourish.

He picked up the book and let out an enormous sigh. *"Belle de Jour's Guide to Men?"* he read with impressive incredulity. "For fuck's sake. What are you buying these awful books for? You seem like a sensible girl—"

"Woman," I said. "Girl is patronizing."

He rolled his eyes. "Fine, fine. You seem like a sensible *woman*. You know a bit about football. And yet here you are again, buying some load of old bollocks about dating."

I felt a little spark of anger flare up in me. "You see, this is exactly why people don't come into bookstores nowadays: because people like you stand around all day with your tweedy jackets and your old copies of Dickens and you judge people like me on our choice of books!"

"One of the only perks of owning a bookshop, apart from a lifetime of penury, is indulging in a level of curiosity and—yes—judgment about the literary preferences of our all-too-few customers. So I am well within my rights to tell you that this book is a fetid pile of shite and should be burned."

I let out a harrumph—an actual harrumph!—and said, "Well, not that it's any of your business, but it's actually for a research project I'm working on."

He raised a skeptical eyebrow.

I explained the project to him and, by the end of it, he was holding on to the desk for support as he was laughing so hard. I tried not to get too offended, but of course I did.

"Christ," he said between guffaws, "that is the biggest load of horse bollocks I've ever heard!"

"I'm glad you find it so funny!" I said. "I'll have you know that I've made some serious scientific inroads!"

He let out a fresh peal of laughter. "Have you indeed? I'd love to be enlightened about your findings."

I thought for a minute. "Well, everyone loves a chase."

"Jesus, woman, it took you five months of scientific study to figure that out? You should have just read that Wyatt poem. How does it go again?

'Yet may I by no means my wearied mind
Draw from the deer, but as she fleeth afore
Fainting I follow.'"

"Ah," I said, "but don't forget how it ends:
'Noli me tangere, for Caesar's I am,
And wild for to hold, though I seem tame.'"

I felt very smug.

"You see?" he said, looking suddenly furious. "What's a woman who can recite bloody Wyatt doing taking advice from a bunch of idiots like this?" He grabbed the guide from me and brandished it in the air like a sword.

I grabbed the book back from him. "I told you, it's for science!"

"I can't imagine you'll be appearing in the fucking *Lancet* anytime soon."

I shrugged. "I just find it interesting, okay?" I said, trying (and failing) not to sound defensive. "Isn't that why most people do things?"

"Most people don't go about selling their soul and acting like a twat just for interest's sake. It's self-sabotage." He looked at me evenly, and for a moment I felt myself fixed in place by his sharp green eyes like a wriggling little amoeba under a microscope. I looked away.

"Look, Dr. Ruth, thanks very much for the armchair analysis but I'm sure you'll understand my reluctance to take advice from a misanthropic, disheveled, clearly deranged manager of an unsuccessful bookshop, regardless of the number of cardigans you own. Now can I pay for this book or what?"

He smiled to himself, which was unnerving, and took my money without comment. As I was hurrying out the door, he called out to me: "Just don't let the bastards grind you down! And read a real book next time, for chrissakes!"

"Thanks for the wisdom, Yoda." I slammed the door behind me.

I took myself home via the liquor store, still muttering too-late comebacks for the bookseller on the way.

After a month of 1950s dating and celibacy, it was a relief (though not necessarily a surprise) to find that getting laid was one of Belle's top priorities. Unlike most of the guides I've followed so far, she doesn't assume everyone's in it for love: there's an entire section on navigating the murky waters of Friends with Benefits.

I was hoping that Belle would at last be able to unlock the key to successful casual sex for me. Turns out her strategy was pretty simple: have lots of sex, casually.

I was filled with righteous indignation. Wasn't that what I had been doing with Adrian all those months ago? Wasn't that exactly what I'd been trying to do all along? Thanks for nothing, Belle.

I went out on the balcony for a calming cigarette and started mulling things over. I guess things with Adrian hadn't been *that* casual. I thought of the texts asking how his day went, the prompts to make plans to see him, those godforsaken eggs . . . Belle's first point of advice when it came to Friends with Benefits was to avoid getting attached. The fact that I was still thinking about him months down the line proved that I'd fallen at the first hurdle.

His good-bye party was next weekend: it was my last chance to show him that I really *was* a goddess of casual sex, a no-strings-attached good-time girl. With Belle's help, I was going to fill that man with regret if it was the last thing I did.

I ground out my cigarette and marched back inside: I had some serious planning to do.

September 6

The party was tomorrow, so it was all about final preparations.

Over the past few days, Belle had become my own personal Maharishi. Where she led, I would happily follow.

I'd groomed and preened myself into oblivion: I'd gone to hot yoga every morning to maximize flexibility, had pretty much every hair waxed off of my body, finally used the body scrub Cathryn had bought me for Christmas last year and meticulously combed my wardrobe for the perfect Belle-approved outfit (not-too-short skirt, moderate heels). I spent an entire week's pay in Agent Provocateur despite breaking out in hives in the plush changing room (apparently I'm allergic to velour). I had my first-ever manicure and pedicure, enduring the horror on the poor Korean girl's face as she shaved the dead skin off my feet.

I took Belle's quiz to identify my man-hunting style and was pleased when I scored a seven, meaning I was a "Scary Bitch." I was officially deemed "not marriage material," a moniker I seriously considered getting tattooed somewhere on my person (and probably would have if I hadn't spent all of my money on a black lace thong and a push-up bra the day before).

There was one thing that worried me, though. According to Belle, if a Scary Bitch had a single thing left unticked on her sexual to-do list, it was her own fault.

I thought of Lucy putting Tristan in Aunt Dorothy's Cupboard, of the shock I felt when Sleepy Eyes tried to . . . defile me, of all the Torture Garden parties I'd never been to—or even heard of—until recently. For all my big talk, I was a prude.

There could be a veritable cornucopia of sexual predilections I'd missed out on all these years. Hell, I didn't even have cable television until I was twenty-three! I suddenly remembered my high school years, when all of my friends would discuss David Duchovny's infamous turn in the *Red Shoe Diaries* and I would just have to nod along, oblivious to what they were talking about.

God, I was so naive.

But no more! I had a reputation to live up to, and a brief window to seduce the man of my occasional dreams. I was a Scary Bitch and no one was going to tell me otherwise.

I pulled out my laptop and started Googling, hoping my firewall could withstand the inevitable pop-ups to come.

By the time Lucy arrived home, I'd smoked sixteen cigarettes and inadvertently learned the evolution of pornography over the past twenty years. The Duchovny *Red Shoe* YouTube clips led me to Jenna

Jameson's early work and to Sasha Grey, and then on to the murky world of YouPorn. (For the record, amateur porn is just as unsexy as you'd imagine. Some things are best left to the professionals.) And then I struck gold: Tumblr gifs of every single sexual peccadillo dreamed up by man or woman. From foot fetishes to granny porn to Furries ferreting away at each other in their giant animal costumes: I'd seen it all. And, unfortunately, I could never unsee it.

"Did you know about this?!" I shouted at Lucy as she dropped her keys on the side table.

"Know about what?"

I pointed to my laptop screen, where a man dressed as a giant baby was being paddled by three women in Bavarian costume.

"THIS!"

Lucy squinted at the screen and then looked at me with her big blue eyes. "Well, I did see something similar at a party last week, though I think the girls were wearing French maid costumes."

I let out a howl of agony. How was it that sweet, innocent-looking Lucy was more sexually enlightened than me?

Lucy wrinkled her nose and took a closer look at the screen. "Anyway, why on earth are you looking at that?" She grabbed hold of my laptop and started clicking through the twenty-some tabs I had open. Her cheeks turned pinker and pinker with each click. "Lo, what is—oh my GOD!" She had clicked on a particularly disturbing gif and shut the laptop decisively. "Babe, I know I should respect your privacy and all, but do you want to have a chat about all this? Are you having some sort of mental episode?"

I grabbed the laptop back from her. "No! I'm just trying to educate myself so I can be prepared for Adrian's party tomorrow night."

"Christ, what sort of party is he throwing?" She grasped my hand tightly. "You don't have to do anything you don't feel comfortable with, Lauren. Don't let that sick bastard pressure you into—" she gestured toward the laptop—"God knows what."

I shook off her hand. "It's just a normal party. It's at some ware-house in Tottenham. But it's my last chance to prove to him that he was a fool to break it off with me. And to do that, I need to be a sexual dynamo."

I explained Belle's approach and my worries about being a prude. "I mean, look at you! All into the S&M scene and every-thing! You even knew about men dressing up as babies and being paddled! It's like everyone took some sort of advanced course on kinkiness and I was sick that day and missed it!"

"You're being mental. Being good in bed doesn't mean you have to dress up in a weird polystyrene costume or be some type of contortionist. Being adventurous is fun, and obviously Tristan has his little preferences, but really the best sex we have is when it's just the two of us in bed on a lazy Sunday. Just normal, really."

I felt mildly soothed by Lucy's words, but I still Googled a few more things after she went to bed. I would be a sexual dynamo to-morrow if it killed me. Which, from the look of some of the posi-tions I'd discovered, it might.

September 7

This morning, I went for a run and spent the rest of the day meticu-lously constructing myself in Belle's image and fighting off occa-sional flashes of panic and self-doubt, managing to quell them by smoking at least thirty-eight cigarettes over the course of the af-ternoon.

And so it was that I started the night of Adrian's party the way I did most parties: by downing three vodkas at home while getting ready and then getting very lost on the way. Tottenham was unex-plored territory for me, and as I wandered around street after street of knock-off fried chicken places and discount tile emporiums, I felt secure in the knowledge that I hadn't missed much.

Three buses and a long walk later, I found the address Adrian had texted me, but I wasn't entirely sure I'd found the party. I walked around the shuttered warehouse for ten minutes trying to find an entrance before sending Adrian a nervous text asking if I was in the right place. The nights had started to get shorter and it was dark by 8:00 p.m., so the area was cloaked in darkness, presumably hiding all manner of scary people and things. I stood in the silent parking lot and felt a swell of panic rise. I smoked a cigarette and stared at the peeling Sedco Building Supplies sign to calm myself.

I'd give it five more minutes and then I'd forget the whole ridiculous seduction plan and go find Lucy in the pub back in Old Street. My eyes misted over briefly, thinking of a warm spot in the Eagle: civilization.

Suddenly, a rumbling mechanized noise ripped through the air and I watched in horror as an enormous chunk of the building appeared to rise up and disappear into itself, leaving a black hole in its place. I braced myself to run, quietly cursing Belle for her insistence that I wear moderate heels rather than Converse.

Out of the black hole, a monstrously tall figure appeared in silhouette.

"CUNNINGHAM! What the fuck are you doing just standing there? Come and give me a bon voyage kiss!"

I nearly collapsed with relief as Adrian, wearing a towering Uncle Sam hat, emerged from the shadows.

"You scared the fucking bejeezus out of me!"

"Well, why didn't you just come in rather than lurking around out here?" Adrian came over and put his arm around me. "Nice skirt, by the way. You look like a sexy estate agent."

I shoved him away, despite the fact that my stomach had somersaulted when he'd touched me. "I couldn't find the fucking door!

What the hell are we doing here, anyway?" We went through the gaping hole, which I now realized was a garage door.

"A friend of mine lives here. Converted the whole thing herself. Wait until you see the inside: it's mental."

He took my hand and led me down a dark corridor to an enormous corrugated iron door. "After you, my dear," he said, sweeping into a deep bow.

"Careful of your hat," I said as I pushed the door open.

He wasn't kidding when he said the place was mental. The door led to a cavernous living space, all exposed brickwork and vaulted ceilings. The space was divided by a series of stone archways, each being supported by a gaggle of artsy-looking hipsters sipping from old jam jars. The floor was covered with Pashtun rugs and minimalist furniture.

"Jesus," I mumbled.

"Amazing, right? She made the table and chairs herself," Adrian said, pointing to a gorgeous wooden table and leather-backed chairs. "And that sofa." He gestured toward a low couch covered in a stiff blue material. "That one's made entirely of reclaimed materials. The base is old milk crates and she wove the cover out of IKEA bags."

"Sounds like she's really something."

He nodded dreamily. "She's incredible."

My heart sank. Whoever this chick was, she'd obviously made quite the impression on Adrian. My only hope was that she was ugly.

"My pet, have you found her?" I heard the voice before I saw the face, but I knew immediately that I was fucked: she was French. And as every non-French woman knows, in the romantic game of Texas Hold'em, there is one hand that trumps them all: the French Woman.

And then she was in front of us, all coltish legs and kohl eyeliner. She looked like she'd just rolled out of bed after the best sex of her life. I glanced over at Adrian's adoring face: maybe she had.

Adrian clasped her wrist like she was the last lifesaver on the

Titanic. "Lauren, this is the amazing Emmanuelle." He presented
her to me like she was a finely wrapped gift. "Emmanuelle, this is
my friend Lauren."

She gave me a slow, lazy smile. "Lauren! The American! I've
heard so much about you." She enveloped me in the arms of her
enormous feathered coat.

I gave Adrian a suspicious sidelong look. "You have?"

"Of course! Adrian has been talking about you nonstop since
he arrived. You are very welcome here. Let me get you a drink—
would you prefer Aperol or Campari?"

"Um, do you have any bourbon?" I had a feeling I'd need something a little stronger to get through the evening.

"Ah, so very American! I do love that. I'll see what I can find for
you." She dashed off in a blur of feathers and tousled hair. Adrian
looked like he was going to be sick with longing as he watched her go.

So, this was my competition. I was clearly screwed. Or, more
accurately, I was clearly not going to be screwed.

Adrian started singing Emmanuelle's many praises as soon as
she was out of sight, and I did my best to tune them out. I tried to
look at him with clear eyes: why exactly was I trying so hard to get
this goon to want me? I took in his glasses and his ridiculous hat and
tried to conjure up disgust, or at least indifference. Just look at the
puppyish way he was gazing at the empty space Emmanuelle had
just occupied while telling me about her latest community art
project: pathetic! He was just some washed-up nerdy try-hard. She
could have him, I thought. He wasn't even good in bed.

An image of him pressing me against the wall of my balcony
flitted through my mind.

Okay, fine. He was good in bed. But he was still an asshole.
Good riddance.

Emmanuelle reappeared holding a tumbler full of promising-
looking brown liquid in one hand and balancing a ludicrously long

cigarette holder in the other. She handed me the glass and took a deep drag, blowing the smoke into perfect white rings.

I thanked her for the whisky and admitted that I'd never been able to manage a single smoke ring.

"It's simple. I'll teach you." She held out the cigarette holder so I could take a puff. I nearly choked when I inhaled: she was smoking Marlboro Reds. "Now," she said, "watch my mouth. Put your lips together and push your tongue against your teeth. Blow."

I coughed up an inelegant spurt of smoke and Adrian let out a snicker.

"Sorry. I guess I just don't have the touch."

"Nonsense. Try again."

She took another long drag on the cigarette and then offered it to me. A few more of these lessons and I'd be using an iron lung by the end of the night.

"Now blow." She shaped her mouth into a cupid's bow and blew another series of perfect rings. "Gently."

I tried again, and let out a yelp of delight when a little white circle emerged from my mouth and into the air.

"Perfect!" She put her arm around my waist and whispered in my ear, "I knew your mouth could do great things."

I glanced over at Adrian, who looked like he was about to spontaneously combust from this display. Suddenly, Belle's voice was in my head: if the guy you want takes a shine to another woman, there's an easy solution: take them both home.

And so it was that I decided to embark upon my first threesome.

I excused myself and went outside for a cigarette and a pep talk. "You can do this," I thought to myself. "You are a woman of the world! An extremely hot Frenchwoman is totally hitting on you! You can have sex with her! Or do whatever having sex with a woman entails! You can also have sex with Adrian! At the same time! . . . Somehow." I thought of the practical logistics and tried to remember what I'd seen on Tumblr the day before. I consoled myself with the thought that lots of people had threesomes all the time, and they all seemed to get along swimmingly. Besides, I was pretty good at Tetris; I'd probably excel at this.

I slipped back into the room and threaded my arm through Emmanuelle's. "So, will you give me a guided tour of this amazing apartment of yours?"

"Of course!" Emmanuelle took my hand and led on. Adrian followed behind us, eyebrow raised quizzically in my direction.

I had to give it to her, the apartment was incredible and she seemed to know exclusively extremely beautiful foreign people. Everywhere I looked, an exotic person was dripping off a perfectly formed design piece or an artfully reconditioned lighting fixture, having hushed conversations with each other about I could only imagine what. What did gorgeous foreign artsy people talk about? Monaco? Existentialism? And, as Adrian wouldn't stop pointing out as Emmanuelle led me around, she had made almost everything by hand. She kept demurring as she ran her fingers lightly across the small of my back.

I spent the next few hours being pawed at gently by Emmanuelle and pawing right back at her in turn. It turns out flirting with a woman is pretty similar to flirting with a man, but with more opportunities to share make-up tricks. It was fun! Weird, but fun.

Adrian's delight at the display was shading into annoyance: it was obvious he felt left out. When Emmanuelle disappeared to get me another drink, leaving a fug of Le Labo Ambrette behind her, he pulled me to one side.

"What's got into you, Cunningham? I didn't know you had Sapphic inclinations."

I tried my best to look mysterious and sexy. "There's a lot you don't know about me. I'm a woman of the world, you know."

"Well, you've certainly taken Emme's fancy, you lucky little slag."

I smiled beatifically at him. "I didn't mean to steal your girlfriend, A."

Adrian looked baffled for a moment before letting out a low

guffaw. "She's not my girlfriend, my sweet American friend. She went out with a friend of mine a few years ago and we've stayed mates, sort of. She heard I was moving stateside and kindly offered the use of her place for my farewell soirée."

"Oh. I just figured . . ."

"You know me, Cunningham: footloose and fancy free! Besides, why would I tie myself down when I'm about to be surrounded by gorgeous American women just dying to hear my lilting accent? Not that I'd kick her out of bed, mind. No man can resist a hot Frenchwoman."

This was my chance. I was about to go all Scary Bitch on his ass. But in a good way, I hoped.

I arranged my features into something I thought might resemble coy. "How about a hot American *and* a hot Frenchwoman?"

Adrian looked bemused. "Why, Miss Cunningham, you surprise me. Are you implying what I believe the French call a little *rouler dans le foin* with the two of you?"

"I don't speak French but I think I catch your drift. And yes, that's exactly what I'm suggesting. Do I shock you, Mr. Dean?" I tried to channel my inner Belle and smolder.

Adrian smiled. "You never cease to shock me, Miss Cunningham. But do you think our French friend will be game?"

I glimpsed Emmanuelle smiling at me as she weaved through the crowd, proudly holding another large whisky aloft. "I'll see what I can do," I said. "Think of it as your farewell present."

I felt Emmanuelle's hand on my back as she handed me a drink. "Here you go, darling. Drink up!"

I leaned over so I could whisper in her ear. "Shall we go someplace a little more private?" I was impressed by my own boldness. I was a total Scary Bitch when it came to the ladies.

She smiled and said, "I've been thinking that all evening. Follow me." She grabbed my left hand and I grabbed Adrian's with my right.

"Adrian too?" I asked sweetly.

Her eyes flickered over Adrian and her smile broadened. "Of course! What is it you say? The more the merrier?"

Adrian looked like a puppy who'd just been given a sirloin steak. "Precisely!" he said, before bowling down the hall to what I assumed was Emmanuelle's bedroom. She smiled at me, a little shyly this time, and tugged me along after her.

Her bedroom was in sharp contrast to the rest of her apartment: instead of plush fabrics and hand-hewn wood, it was extremely minimalist. Everything was done in shades of gray, and in the center of the room was an enormous bed. Seriously, the biggest bed I've ever seen. Emmanuelle placed her hand on my back and gave me a gentle shove toward it. Adrian had already made himself at home and was sprawled out on the comforter.

Emmanuelle slipped behind me and kissed the back of my neck while Adrian got to his knees and started unbuttoning my blouse. I froze. Oh fuck. Oh fuck oh fuck oh fuck oh FUCK.

I pulled away. "I'm going to run to the bathroom," I said. My voice sounded unnaturally high and strangled. "Be right back!"

Adrian gave me a slightly annoyed look as I slipped out of the room.

The party was still in full swing and someone had decided it was time to play German trance music. My head throbbed and I started to sweat. I ran into the bathroom, opened the window and lit a cigarette.

"Get a grip, champ," I said to myself. Suddenly, Madonna's "Like a Virgin" started up in my head. "Madonna wouldn't be hiding in a bathroom," I thought. "Madonna probably encounters this sort of shit every day. She's like, *Oh, is it a Tuesday? It must be Threesome Day!* Fucking Madonna." I tried to channel my inner Scary Bitch.

I tossed my cigarette out of the window and stared at my reflection in the mirror. "You, Lauren, are a sexual dynamo. Now go in there and get yourself some sexy French lady ass." I took a deep breath and pulled open the door: I was ready.

"Everything okay, Cunningham?" Adrian appeared in front of me. "You're not getting shy, are you?" He pulled me into him and pressed against me. "Because I have never been so hard in my life."

"No!" I trilled. "Not at all! Just, um, powdering my nose!" My voice was getting higher and higher; soon, only dogs would be able to hear me.

He leaned down and bit my collarbone slightly too hard. "Let's get this party started!" He took off his giant Uncle Sam hat and threw it down the hall, where it hit a Brazilian model and her coked-up art dealer. "Sorry, Ana!" he called as he pulled me toward the bedroom.

I took a deep breath, pushed open the door and silently thanked Belle for forcing me to buy nice underwear.

September 8

"Hello?" Meghan's voice was thick with sleep and I felt a momentary pang of regret at waking her up. But these were rare times, and Lucy hadn't been in when I got home. I needed to talk to someone.

"Meg? It's me."

"Kid?" I could hear the bed shift under her as she sat up. "Are you okay?"

"I'm fine! I just had to tell you something."

I heard a groan on the other end of the line. "It's two o'clock in the morning!"

"I know! I know! I haven't woken Sue up, have I?"

"No, don't worry. She's in the other room."

"At two o'clock in the morning?"

"I've got a cold and was snoring, so she slept on the couch." I heard a light click on. "What's this thing you're dying to tell me?"

I couldn't believe the words that were about to come out of my mouth. "I had a threesome."

"WHAT?" She was awake now, that was for sure. "With a chick and a dude or two dudes?"

"A French girl and Adrian."

"Jesus! I'm not sure you should be telling your big sister about this sort of thing."

"Hey, I had to hear all about your sexual awakening with Lindsey Wheeler when we were in high school, so it's only fair that you listen to this."

"Okay, okay: spill it."

I thought back to the night before. "You remember those old shows they used to air on public television at weird times of night? The Benny Hill ones? Well, it was like that, only much less organized." It was true: it had descended into farce pretty quickly, with me chasing Adrian, Adrian chasing Emmanuelle and Emmanuelle chasing me around the bed before any of us figured out what we were meant to be doing. "There was a lot more waiting around than I expected, too."

"What about the lady-sex? Were you into it? God, can you imagine if Mom ended up with two lesbian daughters? She'd never stop bragging about it." Our mom was a second-wave feminist and a bleeding-heart liberal; among her circle of friends, having a gay son or daughter was a point of pride.

"Well . . . I don't think I'm going back for seconds, let's put it that way." Kissing Emmanuelle had been like kissing a small, well-moisturized man. It hadn't been unpleasant, but it definitely didn't stir up any nascent longings in me. The rest of it had been frankly terrifying, and I had a newfound respect for men's attempts to navigate the female body. It was a wonderland, all right.

"Aw, man! I was hoping we'd have turned you." I heard her yawn and remembered what time it was there.

"I should let you get back to your snoring."

"Thanks a lot," she said. "Good night, kid."

I was about to hang up when I heard a tinny shriek on the other end of the line.

"Wait! I forgot to tell you something!"

"Nothing can top my news."

"It's Dylan."

I groaned. The last thing I wanted was an update on my ex. "What now?"

"He's cycling the length of the American-Canadian border."

Of course he was. It was just the sort of rugged, outdoorsy, communing-with-nature shit he loved—and I hated. I'd spent our whole relationship ducking out of plans to trek the Himalayas or hitchhike across Venezuela. But now that we weren't together, it made complete sense that he'd be embarking on some sort of cycling adventure. Prick.

"What about Kelly? Is she going, too?"

I could just picture it: Dylan's blond hair going almost white in the sun, his square jaw grimaced against the elements, his ass getting tighter by the day. And she would probably be cycling along next to him in a spandex onesie, ponytail swishing perfectly in the wind (probably held back in a scrunchie—ha!). Or following behind him in an old camper van, waving encouragement to him as he pedaled away and occasionally handing him Gatorade and energy gels while wearing denim hot pants and a selection of kerchiefs and vintage sunglasses. I could never pull off a kerchief.

"Nah, I think they broke up. I saw her throwing back tequilas at Sangillo's and hanging all over a bunch of guidos."

I felt a momentary swell of rage toward her for not telling me about this earlier, but brushed it aside. Theoretically, it was none of my business.

"Anyway, the reason I'm telling you about his Lance Armstrong moment is he asked for your address—apparently he wants to write to you along the way. You okay with me giving it to him?"

I worried about what he'd write, but I didn't want to put Meghan in an awkward position by saying no. Besides, it might not be that bad—maybe he just wanted to write me for sponsorship money. He'd probably be too tired to write, anyway. I'd probably never hear from him.

I told her to go ahead and hung up the phone. I was starting to turn the idea of Dylan contacting me around in my head when I heard Lucy's key in the door. Thank God. I ran to the kitchen and switched on the kettle.

"Come here and have a cup of coffee with me," I called. "Have I got a story for you!"

Name: Emmanuelle
Age: French women don't get old
Occupation: Artist and possible lesbian
Description: Beautiful and terrifying in equal measure
Method: *Belle de Jour's Guide to Men*
Result: I guess it cleared up a few latent questions

September 11

I hadn't heard from Adrian since I'd disentangled myself from him and Emmanuelle in the early hours of Sunday morning, and by this point I figured I wouldn't. His flight to America was scheduled for tomorrow and, to be honest, there wasn't much left to say. As my old soccer coach used to say, I'd left it all out on the field.

So you can imagine my surprise when my phone started playing a tinny version of the Carly Simon classic "You're so Vain" as we were finishing up our postconference debrief.

My boss looked around with his usual distracted air while Cathryn nudged me.

"Excuse me," I said. "I think it's my doctor." I slinked out of the room and picked up the call. "What do you want?" I whispered as I crept out into the hallway.

"Cunningham, you never cease to amaze me, you little minx. But why did you run off so soon?"

"Shhhh!" I hissed, rummaging through my bag for my lighter. I pushed through the emergency exit and immediately lit up. I was worried that my colleagues would somehow pick up on the general content of Adrian's thoughts and I'd be fired.

"Anyway, you have given this grateful Briton some very fond memories to take with him across the sea. Can I repay you with a cup of coffee in, say, ten minutes?"

"I'll ignore the fact that you think the two things are comparable and say no thanks. I'm in the middle of a meeting—which I really need to get back to, actually." I didn't think I could bear to see Adrian's face. I feared the image of him grinning up at me from between Emmanuelle's legs would be burned on my memory for the rest of my life.

"After, then. C'mon, Cunningham: I'm off tomorrow and I want to see you before I go."

It was tempting. I thought about Belle's advice about lost causes—i.e., don't fight them—and knew I shouldn't.

"Nah. I can't. Send me a postcard from New York. Don't forget to eat a lot of bagels."

"Ah, you disappoint me. Come visit whenever you're on the other side of the pond."

"Bye, Adrian."

I ended the call. I felt sad, sadder than I'd thought I would about him going. He was a jackass, sure, but over the past nine months he'd become *my* jackass. Aside from all the weird sex stuff (particularly recent events), he'd become my friend; they were few and far between in this country.

I finished my cigarette and pushed open the heavy metal door.

There wasn't time to dwell now and, besides, I'd finally accomplished what I'd set out to prove to Adrian. Right?

September 14

I gave myself a couple of days to get over the events of the past week before settling back down to the task at hand: channeling my inner Scary Bitch and experimenting on some new test subjects. I scanned through Belle's list of places to meet men, hoping that inspiration would strike.

> **Singles events.** Even Belle admitted that this was a cock-lite arena, with good-looking women far outweighing the men at these things. A last resort.

> **Work.** Surprisingly, working at a nonprofit museum meant that male colleagues were few and far between (probably because men like to, you know, earn actual money). The guys I did work with were all either weird, semi-autistic science types or married. And I wasn't about to go snatching some woman's husband, despite Belle's third suggestion . . .

> **Someone else's man.** She admits that this is a morally gray area and often more trouble than it's worth. I'm going to steer clear (unless I meet a particularly attractive man in a particularly unstable relationship).

> **Pubs and clubs.** Belle sums it up perfectly when she says "the odds are good, but the goods are odd." I don't know that I can face a sweaty Dalston basement bar at the minute. If in a pinch, I might try dragging Lucy to an area of town where the haircuts are less directional and try my luck in a pub there.

Somewhere mundane. You know how magazines are always saying that the grocery store produce aisle or in line at the post office are great places to meet men? When was the last time you met someone who met their boyfriend in the waiting room at the dentist? This is London: no one speaks to each other in those situations, and if they did, they would immediately be written off as a lunatic. And that would probably be correct.

Online. Oh God. I was only just beginning to recover from my YoDate experience. Could I really face another turn on the merry-go-round of the sexual interwebs? From what Belle said, it was my best bet. But no more American YoDate and no more boring Castaways. This time, I was taking a page out of the book of the two groups that seemed to be getting laid the most: The Gays and The Youths. I was going on Tinder.

It seemed a little weird and, I don't know, terrible to judge people solely on their picture, flinging those faces that disagree with you to the left, never to be seen again. It felt . . . harsh. It felt like something a dude with anger issues probably invented. But it also felt very much like something a Scary Bitch would be into, and besides, a friend of Lucy's went on it and swore that she got more ass than a donkey convention, so I signed up. (Also, it's free.)

It took me a long time to select my calling card (which is what was known as a profile picture in 2011). It was what people would judge me on, so it had to be good. You could load in a few other photos that could be viewed after you'd been picked, but let's face it: men have the attention span of a gnat. I needed to reel them in with the first hook.

I found a nice photo of me looking tanned and busty and (after several consultations with a beleaguered Cathryn, who was becoming more and more grateful to be affianced with every dating gimmick I thrust in front of her) I uploaded it and was off and running.

In the world of Tinder, left = bad and right = good. The first few attempts weren't particularly successful. Determining my left from my right has always been a struggle for me, so within five minutes I'd flung a bunch of weirdos into my "yes" pile and swiped a very promising-looking man into the ether, never to be seen again.

But I got the hang of it pretty quickly, and soon I was swiping with the best of them. "X! X! X! Maybe heart? X!" I sang to myself as I merrily swiped left and right (mainly left). "X! Sweet Jesus, what an X." It was addictive, this judging people thing. "X! X!" It was astonishing how many weird-looking people there were out there.

An hour passed. I had X'ed my way through at least half of London's male population, only hearting a handful of men. I decided to take a cigarette break before mounting my next attack.

When I picked up my phone again, I saw that one of the men I'd hearted had selected me, too. I had a match! How thrilling!

I clicked through to his other photos. He was sandy blond and baby-faced and potentially hyperactive: every photo featured him doing something extreme on a bicycle or a skateboard or—in one instance—one of those kite-surfboard things. I was just admiring his abs in one photo (where he appeared to be skateboarding down a volcano) when a message suddenly popped up.

Hey.

It was from him! There was his face, smiling blondly above the message. For a minute, I wondered if he could see me. What if the Tinder people had cruelly linked up with Facetime? I realized that no one would have sex again if that happened and stopped frantically brushing the cracker crumbs off my chest.

I wondered what I should write back. "Hey" wasn't giving me a lot to work with. I decided to fight fire with fire.

'Hey,'   I typed smugly.
Him: Nice pic. Want to meet?

Fuck! Was this the speed things moved here in Tinderland? No wonder all the kids were getting laid these days, and no wonder the gays loved Grindr so much. This truly is the future.

I considered what I knew about him: He was cute (plus). He was obviously fit (also a plus, unless he used his strength to murder me, in which case con). He was nearby (plus).

I then considered what I knew of myself: I had turned my love life into a sociological experiment; I had no immediate sexual prospects; I had little respect for my personal safety or emotional welfare; I was following the advice of a renowned escort.

My next move was clear.

Me: Sure. Where and when?

September 18

Tonight was my first date with the blond from Tinder. Considering it was the topic that made up 85 percent of his conversation, I'll call him the Bike Guy.

I had followed Belle's predate instructions to the T again, which meant I was dressed in yet another pencil skirt and medium-height heels. My bank balance couldn't face the purchase of another set of high-end underwear, so I was back in the lacy set I'd bought for Adrian's leaving party. Just slipping them on again had made me feel filthy—in a good way—so I was feeling very bullish as I set out.

On the way over, I inspected his photo again a few times and read through his little profile spiel. I was nervous that he had described himself as "adventurous" as, in Belle's words, this meant he would ask me to shit on his chest during sex. And while I had admittedly dedicated myself to expanding my sexual horizons this month, defecating on a man was a step too far.

I met him in a pub in Clapton, filled to the brim with sweaty bike messengers and fixies. Bike Guy was already there waiting for me with a pint in hand. I spotted his shock of blond hair when I walked through the door and made my way through a throng of men in tattered cargo shorts and Italian racing shirts to get to him, feeling conspicuously overdressed. In London's social hierarchy, the only people cooler than bike messengers were Peckham bartenders. I felt lame.

He was even cuter in person, his hair even blonder—almost white—and I could see his slim, muscled back through his T-shirt. I was into it. "Hey, there you are!" he said when I tapped him on the shoulder. He gestured toward the bar: "Pick your poison."

"Where are you from?" I asked as we waited for my pint to be poured. His accent was Australian, but somehow elongated and with more "ee's."

"I'm a Kiwi!" he said with a broad grin. "And how about you? I can tell you're not a Pom—you a Yank or a Canuck?"

"Yank!" I said proudly.

"Nice one! The States are choice!" He was grinning and nodding like one of those bobblehead dolls you see stuck on the dashboard of pickup trucks, but after months of dry British humor, it was a relief to talk to someone so . . . happy.

Nationalities established, the conversation moved on to bikes. Turns out Bike Guy runs a bicycle repair shop in Clapton. He'd had a successful career in marketing, but had a major epiphany a few years back and gave it all up to fix bikes for a living.

"So you just quit?" I asked, agog. I was always impressed by people who had started new lives for themselves like this. Sure, I'd moved halfway across the world, but that was the easy bit: breaking into a new career after twenty-two felt heroic. But more than that, I was fascinated by non-office people: those who were free to roam on weekdays, unshackled by the nine-to-five world.

Every time I took a sick day, I'd walk to the corner store for soup and be pushed off the sidewalk by freewheeling freelancers merrily going about their afternoons of leisure. They were everywhere: in coffee shops, buying artisanal espressos and tapping away at their Macbook Airs, or browsing leisurely through the racks of the exorbitant vintage store. I had to constantly resist the urge to quiz them on what exactly it was they did for a living and how I could get in on the action.

"Yeah, man!" Bike Guy's way of speaking was Kiwi-meets-California; I couldn't tell if it was an affectation, but it was weirdly sexy. "I was just like, fuck this! And I handed in my notice."

"Did everyone think you were nuts?"

"Yeah, my mates thought I was being a total weirdo. And my wife wasn't so keen, that's for sure!" He took a swig from his pint while I focused on not spitting mine out.

"Wife?" I tried to keep the incredulity out of my voice. I knew the whole Tinder thing was sketchy. Now I was inadvertently on a date with someone else's husband. Great.

"Ex-wife now," he said, still grinning merrily.

"I hope you don't mind me saying this, but no way do you look old enough to have been married, never mind divorced." It was true: in his old Clash T-shirt and low-slung skinny jeans, he didn't look more than twenty-five. I had actually been worrying about robbing the cradle.

"Ah, thanks, mate! People always tell me I've got a baby face. But yeah, we split up a couple of years ago. She wanted a house and a baby, blah blah blah: you know, typical stuff for a woman in her midthirties."

I studied his face more closely. There were a few lines, but nothing more than you'd get from being outside a lot. I still didn't peg him for more than twenty-eight.

"But I just wasn't into it, you know? All of my energy was going into the bike business, and the idea of a house and a baby was like—WHOA. You know? Just . . . heavy, man."

"Totally," I said, merrily sipping my pint. At least I didn't have to worry about this guy wanting to settle down any time soon.

"We're still friends, though. She's a cracker. She's got herself a new fella now—he's an accountant or something—and they're trying for a kid. So it's all good."

I was like a dog with a possibly ancient bone: I couldn't let it go. "Just out of curiosity—and you totally don't have to tell me, but—how old are you?"

"Forty-one!" he nearly shouted. "Mad, eh? I still can't believe that I'm, like, a proper fucking adult."

Forty-one? That made him, by some distance, the oldest guy I'd ever been on a date with. *And* he'd been married. What was I getting myself into? On the other hand, he was extremely cute and seemed genuinely nice, if a little nutty. I thought of Belle and my expanding horizons.

"Another one?" I asked, pointing at his pint.

That night, a little tipsy, I filled in my notebook.

Name: Bike Guy
Age: Physical, 41; Mental, 23
Occupation: Bike mechanic and overall dude
Nationality: New Zealander
Description: Blond, slim and forever young
Method: *Belle de Jour's Guide to Men*

September 24

"So do you think we could double date?" Lucy's enormous blue eyes looked up at me hopefully.

"I don't think so," I said. "I'm not really the double-dating kind."

"But he's basically Tristan's age! I'm sure they'd have loads in common." An image of Bike Guy waxing lyrical about the merits of Carrillos versus Bianchis while Tristan clutched the stem of his frosted martini glass flitted across my mind.

"First of all, nice try, but he is not Tristan's age. Second of all, I don't think they'd have all that much in common."

She abandoned the laundry she was folding and flopped down on the couch next to me. "So is it serious? Do you really fancy him?"

I shot her a sideways glance and shoved a handful of peanut M&Ms into my mouth. "Those are two very different questions," I said, careful to avoid candy shell flying everywhere.

She rolled her eyes and gave me a shove.

"I definitely think he's sexy. There's something sweet about him—it's like he's totally unjaded. I definitely wouldn't say it's serious, though. I've only gone on two dates with the guy!"

We'd gone on a cycling date around Hackney (I know, I thought never again, but he looked so cute on a bike). I'd somehow managed to get myself to the pub in one piece (thanks largely to Bike Guy carefully shepherding me through the streets and bellowing at any car/cyclist/cabbie who got near us) and we'd settled in for the evening and got pleasantly drunk on cider. Bike Guy regaled me with tales of when he traveled to Sweden on his own and accidentally found himself in an all-nude sauna with three blonds and a midget.

He was charming, all right. And very cute. I spent a good deal of the night imagining myself peeling his clothes off and, after the third pint of cider, was pretty determined to do so, but when I not-so-subtly suggested we go back to my place, he demurred, saying he had an early customer the next day.

The following morning he'd sent a text asking if I could come to his place for dinner on the weekend, so I had high hopes that I'd soon be ticking another thing off my sexual adventure list: the older man.

Lucy raised a lofty eyebrow. "Ah, but he's having you around for dinner on Saturday! That means love."

"No," I said, tossing an M&M at her head, "but hopefully that means sex." The month was running out.

September 28

After an epic journey to Stoke Newington (surely the least accessible place on earth, and yet somehow the most wanted postcode around), I arrived at the address Bike Guy had texted me.

I was impressed: it was one of those three-story Victorian jobs, complete with a little white cat sitting on the windowsill. Either the bike mechanic industry was booming or he'd made a killing in marketing before giving it all up. For a minute, I wondered about the ex-wife saying good-bye to a townhouse in N16: her baby-fever must have been near fatal.

I rang the bell and waited, making little kissing noises at the cat (who ignored me, of course—stuck-up Stokey cat). Suddenly, the door was thrown open by a slightly frazzled but kind-faced middle-aged woman.

"You must be Lauren! Come in, come in! I've heard lots about you," she said, bundling me into the hallway. I was rendered mute with confusion. Was this his ex-wife? Maybe they weren't actually divorced . . . Maybe they were swingers, and this was how they lured in their conquests. "Well," I thought to myself, "if they think they're getting another threesome out of me this month, they've got another thing coming."

In the background, I heard the sound of cartoons and a small child softly singing to herself, and started to panic. Holy fuck: did he actually have a kid with her? What sort of fucked-up world had I entered?

"That's just Poppy," the middle-aged lady said. "Don't mind her! I'm Jane, by the way, though I expect you know that already. I'll just run up and get him." I hoped desperately that she meant Bike Guy and not another rogue child.

I tried to calm myself down. Surely there was a rational explanation for all this. I had just managed to get my breathing back to normal when I felt a tap on my shoulder. I turned, readying myself to ask Bike Guy a lot of pertinent questions, and was faced instead with another frazzled but kind-faced middle-aged person, this time a man.

"Lauren!" he said, pulling me in for an awkward embrace. "We've been so looking forward to meeting you! I'm Oliver. I'm sure you know all about me—probably more than I care to think! We've had some adventures in our time, that's for sure. Well, he'll be down in just a tick. Do you fancy a cup of tea? I've just opened a lovely bottle of Rioja if you'd like something a bit stronger . . . ?" Oliver looked at me hopefully.

"No thanks," I managed to stutter. What in the name of all that is holy was going on here? A FOURSOME? I was all for expanding my horizons, but this was pushing it.

I heard footsteps bounding down the stairs and said a silent prayer that it wasn't a fifth player in this bizarre tableau.

"Hey, babe!" I almost passed out with relief when I saw Bike Guy's beaming face charging around the corner toward me. "I see you've met the whole gang! Shall we go upstairs?"

It was a little forward, but I was so desperate to extricate myself from the situation that I nodded mutely. I just hoped Oliver and Jane weren't going to follow.

"Pop down later for a glass of wine if you fancy!" Oliver called as we headed up the stairs.

I heard Jane whisper, "Leave them be!" and the sound of the two of them giggling. Weird. At least we were going to be alone.

Bike Guy pulled on a little rope dangling from the ceiling at the top of the stairs and a metal ladder came tumbling out.

"Watch your head!" he said as he started climbing. "It gets a bit narrow at the top."

I climbed up after him, part of me wondering why I was entering a crawl space and another, larger part of me too confused by recent events to probe any further. Following him seemed the easiest option.

When he reached the top of the ladder, he hopped onto the landing and spun around to give me a helping hand. "Up you get!"

I was pulled up into the crawl space and deposited on the floor.

"Are we in the attic?" I asked, peering through the darkness.

"Technically it's a loft, but yeah, this is my place." He flicked on the light. "Pretty choice, right?"

It was something, all right. You could only stand fully upright in the center of the room—it sloped away into nothingness on either side. There was a tiny kitchen in one corner—well, a sink, fridge and microwave—with a bed tucked under the opposite eave. A bare bulb dangled above an orange velour couch and bike parts were stacked against every available surface. A *Reservoir Dogs* poster was tacked up above the bed, one of the corners curled and flapping.

"It's . . . sweet," I said, ducking to avoid hitting my head as I made my way to the kitchen. I pulled out the nice bottle of red I'd picked up on the way over. "I brought this, for dinner."

He grabbed it out of my hand and gave me a quick kiss on the cheek. "You're the best. I knew I'd forgotten something." I started to panic—was that the only bottle he had up here? We might need to venture downstairs after all; I didn't think I could take all this in while sober.

"So, they seem nice," I said, fiddling with my hair as I huddled by the fridge. I felt unbelievably awkward.

Bike Guy poured us wine into two tin mugs and handed one to me. "Ollie and Janey? Yeah, they're ace."

"Is your place being renovated or something?" I asked. He raised a quizzical eyebrow. "I mean, are you going to be here for long?"

He shrugged. "Dunno. I've been here for a couple of years now—since Beth and I split—and I'm not planning on leaving any time soon. I mean—" he gestured around the room—"why would I, right? Got everything I need right here, and my best mates are right downstairs. Plus little Poppy—she's just the *best*."

I nodded. It was weird, for sure, but his enthusiasm was actually pretty sweet. Who was I to judge him? I live in an ex-council flat with an S&M enthusiast.

"Right, I'm going to get cracking on dinner. You sit yourself on the sofa and make yourself at home. Put the telly on, if you like. I tapped in to Ollie's Sky dish so the choices are endless!" He started rustling through his messenger bag and turned to me with a winning grin. "Lamb bhuna or chicken kiev?" he asked, waggling two M&S ready meals in the air.

After dinner (complete with dessert that involved something called an Arctic roll, which was surprisingly delicious in spite of its appearance) had been cleared away, Bike Guy reached underneath the couch and pulled out a ziplock freezer bag containing a truly astonishing amount of weed. He gave me a little grin before rolling one of the most perfect joints I'd ever seen. The man was a pro.

He lit the end of it and took a long, deep drag before handing it to me with a nod. I took the joint and considered it thoughtfully; I wasn't a big partaker of illegal substances, regardless of their class, but maybe this should be the exception.

I tried to remember Belle's feelings toward drugs and hazily recalled her warning against them on early dates as they're likely to impair judgment. (Obviously, the quality of my sober judgment had already been called into question considering I was sitting in someone else's attic with an overgrown—but deeply attractive—teenager.) I thought briefly of my previously held fear of being chopped up and stored in a meat locker and decided I should probably hold on to as many of my wits as were left. I handed the joint back to him with a "No thanks" and he shrugged and took another pull.

Bike Guy was philosophical when stoned, and we proceeded to have a long, aimless discussion about what life would be like if the wheel hadn't been invented.

"It would be ace!" he enthused. "No one would have to go to work. There'd be no capitalism, no globalization, no carbon shit fucking up the ozone. Everyone would just sit home and, like, be at one. Just exist."

I explained that people definitely still had to work before the wheel was invented, usually in the form of running endlessly while trying to stab a wild animal in the head so you could eat it for dinner, but he was having none of it.

I drained the rest of the bottle of wine and then started pawing through his cupboards, hoping for whisky but settling for a half-empty bottle of sherry that had turned decidedly vinegary. Bike Guy started in on a second joint and I lit up another cigarette.

There was a moment, when he was racing around the room trying to find his Stone Roses LP, the fug of smoke hanging in the air and the buzz from the cheap sherry and secondhand weed exhalations swimming around my brain, when I was convinced I was at a party in the Sigma Chi basement in my sophomore year in college.

But then, far below us in the heart of the house, I heard it. "Is that the baby crying?" I asked Bike Guy.

He was still for a minute, and then nodded. "Yeah, that's little Poppy all right. No worries, she'll settle in a bit!" And with that, he turned up the Stone Roses a little louder, peeled off his shirt and led me over to the bed.

September 29

I've had a lot of walks of shame in my time, but nothing topped this morning. I left as soon as I woke up, carefully trying to extract myself from the tangled sheets without waking Bike Guy, dressed as quietly as possible and wrote him a little note before slipping through the door. It was 7 a.m., so I hoped I could creep away before the rest of the house was awake, but of course I ran smack into Oliver as I made my way down the stairs.

"Morning!" he called. "Fancy a coffee? I've just plunged the cafetière!"

"No thanks," I stuttered. I peered past him into the kitchen and spied Jane spooning oatmeal into Poppy's mouth. She gave me a smile and a cheery wave.

"Did you sleep well?" she called. "Poppy was a bit of a grump last night—I hope she didn't wake you."

"Slept like a log," I lied. In actuality, I'd woken up every hour on the hour to Poppy's howls. "Anyway, I've got to get going. Nice to meet you both! And, uh, have a good Sunday!"

I hightailed it out the door before they could invite me to sit down with the newspaper and some baked goods. They were a very nice couple, but their domestic bliss made me all the more aware of the stink of weed and sex clinging to my skin.

I got home and immediately put on my workout clothes: I figured a quick run would clear my head. I was still trying to process the night before.

It turns out that sex with a forty-one-year-old isn't all that different from sex with a twenty-four-year-old, particularly a forty-one-year-old who's as fit as Bike Guy. He had the lean body of a swimmer and had obviously picked up a few tips from his ex-wife, as he knew his way around a woman's body. But the whole living situation was too weird: if I was going to see him again, it would have to be on my turf. I felt like my very presence was corrupting poor little Poppy.

I grabbed my iPod and was about to set off when I spotted an envelope addressed to me sticking through the letter slot in the front door. I slid it out and glanced at it, my stomach dropping to my knees as soon as I saw the handwriting. Dylan. I tucked the letter under a pile of magazines on the coffee table: I'd face it later.

September 30

Well, my month as an honorary call girl has come to an end. It hasn't quite turned out like *Pretty Woman*, but it hasn't turned out like *Requiem for a Dream* either, so I guess it's been a success.

Belle de Jour's Guide to Men in Conclusion

Belle's attitude toward sex has been liberating: she's very open about women wanting sex just as much as men, and she sees no shame in going after someone for purely carnal reasons. The open attitude she encourages exposed me to things I normally wouldn't have tried, and while I'm pretty sure I won't be able to look at a novelty Uncle Sam hat without feeling mortified for a long time, on the whole I think it was good for me. Did I mention I got laid?

Works best on . . .

Any man with a hard-on, though don't necessarily expect him to call the next day. Any man who's nervous about sexually aggressive women will probably run a mile. But it will almost certainly get you your man, even if it's for a limited time only.

To be used by . . .

Women who want to broaden their horizons, sexually or otherwise . . . and who aren't inclined toward jealousy.

BOOK SEVEN
MANNERS FOR WOMEN

by Mrs. Humphry

October 1

"About time you learned some," the bookseller grumbled when he looked at the cover of this month's book.

I'd interrupted him stacking leather-bound sets of Charles Dickens on a display table. I was interested to spot a surprisingly toned forearm peeking out of a rolled-up shirtsleeve in the process: so he *didn't* just sit at his desk and make snide remarks all day, after all. Though it was definitely how he spent the majority of his time.

I gave him a smirk and shoved my ten pounds at him. "The customer service in here is excellent, as always."

"I aim to please," he said with a bow.

"Well, your aim is terrible," I said.

He held my change in his hand for a minute as though he was weighing it up. "Look, sorry if I was a bit . . . forthright in my opinion the last time you were in," he said finally, running a hand through his unruly hair.

"More like rude," I muttered. "Whatever, it's fine. I know you think what I'm doing is stupid and you have a right to your opinion. Even if that opinion is wrong and pig-headed." I lifted my chin in the air in what I hoped was a lofty and superior manner.

"I was out of order. I just get so fucked off by all this sexual game-playing nonsense. Why can't women behave like normal humans and cut out the bollocks? You know: boy likes girl, girl likes boy, they give it a go . . . just *normal*."

I rolled my eyes. "That never works. Take it from an expert: no one ever gets laid by being normal."

He raised a suggestive eyebrow. "You'd be surprised."

"Ha! Please, you're not capable of behaving normally."

An old lady browsing the erotica section gave me an admiring look. "Quite right, dear," she said. "I was just telling him the other day—"

"Stay out of it, Doris!" the bookseller bellowed. The old lady scuttled quickly out the door. He turned back to me. "Look, men are simple creatures. Women don't need to cook up these elaborate plans or pretend to be something they're not. We're just happy when a woman turns up and doesn't recoil in horror at the sight of us." I took in his slim, straight nose and sharp cheekbones and rolled my eyes: I couldn't imagine many women recoiling at the sight of him. At the sound of him, on the other hand . . .

"Ha!" I scoffed. "Simple creatures? The next time I meet a man who says what he really feels and does what he says he's going to, I'll let you know, though we'll all be too busy being encased in ice because hell will have frozen over. Until then, I'll keep on with my research." I held out my hand for the change.

He dropped the coins onto my palm. "What utter, utter shite," he muttered, shaking his head.

"Well, thanks very much for your *concern*," I said in what I hoped was my most withering voice, "but I'm very capable of looking after myself without your help or advice. I have everything under control!"

He opened his mouth as if to speak, and then closed it again, firmly.

I grabbed Mrs. Humphry out of his hand and turned on my heel. "And another thing," I called from over my shoulder. "Apology not accepted!" I slammed the door behind me, the bell jangling in my wake.

A great start to the month, right? Now, without further ado, let's get Victorian.

Manners for Women was written in 1897 by a Mrs. Humphry, or "Madge of Truth" as she apparently liked to be known. It's a guide to all things etiquette, and was indispensable for young middle-class ladies looking to break into aristocratic society.

The idea of following a Victorian dating guide was daunting at first. Let's face it, the Victorians weren't exactly known as party animals, and I figured most of the advice would be about how to avoid any flirtation or sexual contact with the opposite sex.

But Mrs. Humphry is much more concerned with a young lady's development into a well-rounded and socially acceptable person than she is with finding her a husband. I mean, obviously there's a bit of that, but mainly she just wants to make sure that a woman doesn't go around embarrassing herself by putting the family crest on her notepaper or showing too much shoulder at supper.

Her attitude toward women is actually pretty benevolent, unlike some of the authors I've dealt with so far. "Can anything in the world be nicer than a really nice girl?" she asks in the opening line. When I saw that, I worried I was in for some more 1950s-style appeasement, but the rest of the paragraph put me at ease: "She is full of contradictions and often 'set with wilful thorns', but where would her charm be if she were plainly to be read by all comers?"

So it looks like she doesn't want a bunch of cookie-cutter nicey-nice girls, either. In fact, Mrs. Humphry is happy for me to live a freewheeling, physically active, professionally ambitious, socially exciting life. There's a whole chapter on bicycling, for God's sake! At least Bike Guy would approve of that much . . .

Comforted by the thought that I could continue living a normal life, wilful thorns and all, I went back to the office and started Googling business card printers. Because a Victorian woman is nothing without her stationery.

October 3

Calling cards arrived today! I ordered them online on Tuesday and had them express delivered. The modern age is surprisingly convenient for the Victorian way of life.

Mrs. Humphry has very specific requirements when it comes to a proper card. It must be a plain white piece of cardboard with one's name in the center in copperplate italic characters, and it must be exactly 3.5 inches by 2.5 inches. That was it: no address, no phone number, no email (well, it was 1897).

"Ta-dah!" I sang as I opened the box of 100 cards (I might have gone a little overboard on the ordering). I slid one across the desk to Cathryn. "What do you think?"

Cathryn cast her discerning eye over the card and nodded her approval. "My granny used something very similar."

I felt a glow of achievement. I was well on my way to societal nirvana, but there was still work to be done.

October 5

Lucy and I spent the morning lazing around on the couch. Tristan was on business in Hong Kong for ten days, which meant she was actually living in the flat for once. It was nice: having the flat to myself had its perks, but I missed her company.

We were discussing what I should do for Bike Guy's upcoming birthday. He'd slipped it into conversation when I saw him last week, and while forty-two wasn't exactly a milestone, I still wanted to do something nice for him.

I read out the list of acceptable parties from *Manners for Women*. "Ascot, Lord's, ball—Christ, who has room for a ball?—formal dinner party, boating . . ."

"Oooh, boating! That sounds romantic!" Lucy purred.

I thought about it for a minute. I wasn't great in boats—my last experience resulted in capsizing a small sailboat in the middle of a still-polluted Charles River in Boston—but I did love the Thames, and the idea of gliding over it in a little boat sounded pretty great.

I started Googling boat rentals in London and quickly realized that I couldn't even afford a dinghy.

"Well, that's that idea nixed," I said, tapping out a cigarette.

Suddenly, Lucy's eyes lit up. "Hang on! My cousin's got a boat!"

"I didn't know you had a rich cousin!"

"Well, it's not quite a yacht . . ."

"Oh? Is it, like, a speedboat?" I imagined myself careening under Westminster Bridge, wind whipping through my hair as we waved to Big Ben.

"It's more of a . . . canoe. You won't be able to take it out on the Thames, though. Just Regent's Canal."

I doubted a canoeing party was what Mrs. Humphry had in

mind, and Regent's Canal was best known for being filled with trash and the occasional dead body, but I had to make do with what I had.

"Do you think he'd let me borrow it?"

October 6

Floating vessel secured, it was time to invite Bike Guy to his birthday boating party for two. Normally, I would have just texted something like, "Yo, me, you and a canoe next Saturday," but my newfound manners demanded something a little more ceremonial.

The instructions were clear: only a formal invitation, printed on plain white or cream card with embossed lettering, would do. I couldn't stretch to another order with the printers, so I typed it up on the computer, printed it out and stuck it on some cardboard with a glue stick I'd found in the junk drawer. I thought it looked pretty good.

> *Miss Lauren Cunningham*
> *requests the pleasure of*
> *Bike Guy's company to boat on Regent's Canal*
> *on October 12th*
> *R.S.V.P.*

I slipped it into the fanciest envelope that Ryman's had, tucked it in my bag to mail tomorrow and poured myself a glass of wine the size of a watermelon.

I poked my head into the living room, where Lucy was watching *Real Housewives of Beverly Hills* and painting her toenails. "Want a glass of wine?"

"Ooh, yes please!" Her eyes were glued to the television, where a terrifyingly thin blond woman was screaming at a bizarre-world version of Demi Moore. "God, Kyle is such a cow!"

I poured her a glass and handed it to her.

"Thanks, babe. Oh, shit! I keep forgetting: I found something for you the other day when I was tidying up." She started digging around underneath the couch cushions (Lucy had an interesting cleaning style). "Here you are!"

I felt a little shock as I realized what it was. Dylan's letter. It's not that I'd forgotten about it, more that I'd hoped I could keep burying the knowledge of its existence in my consciousness long enough that eventually it would just disintegrate beneath the pile of magazines and cease to exist. But there it was, as clear as day: my name and address in Dylan's strong, angular hand. "Fuck," I said.

"Who's it from?" Lucy asked, eyes bright with excitement. "Someone exciting?"

"Not exactly," I said. "It's from my ex."

"Oooh. Even better! How could you have misplaced that? I'd have torn it open as soon as I'd got it if it was from *my* ex." She flopped back on the couch. "He's probably writing to say he loves you desperately and that he was a complete prat to lose you and he can't sleep without you."

"I doubt that."

"Go on, open it! The suspense is terrible!"

I slipped off to my room and lay down on the bed, glass of wine perched on my stomach in one hand and Dylan's letter in the other. I couldn't bear to read it under Lucy's watchful gaze, though she made me pinky swear that I'd tell her all the juicy (or gory) details later.

Lauren,

So I've been doing this bike tour across the States (Meg probably told you). It's strange out here—all the miles, all the

asphalt, all the little middle-of-nowhere towns passing by—it's
like some version of heaven, or maybe hell.

  Most nights I lie out here under the stars and think about you
and I try to tell myself, "Remember her leaving. Remember what
her face looked like when she told you she wasn't going to try
anymore. Remember her walking out the door and not turning
back to look at you as your heart broke. Remember that."

  But the truth is, when I think about you, I remember the first
time we kissed, in the rain, on the porch of that shitty
apartment in Breckenridge. I remember how the rain was
catching on your eyelashes. I remember the first time I realized I
was in love with you, on our third date, when you tried to make
tuna casserole because I told you it was my favorite food, and it
was so terrible, but you laughed as you scraped it into the sink.

  I try to remember your face when you told me you didn't love
me anymore, but all I can see is you on our wedding day. All I
can see is you reciting that excerpt from the Velveteen Rabbit
about how love makes us real.

  You made me real, Lauren. And I am resigned to the truth: I
don't want to remember you leaving. All is forgiven.

  I'll love you forever.

  Dylan

I let the letter fall on the bed and sat up. I needed a cigarette.

October 8

This morning, I found a postcard that had slipped under the
doormat. On the front, a bunch of topless NYC firefighters posed in
Times Square. I flipped it over and read the following message:

Cunningham!

I've been doing a good deal of research on the ground over the past few weeks and can confirm that you remain the sexiest American. Certainly the filthiest.

Adrian xxxxx

When it rains, it fucking pours, huh? I stuck the postcard to the fridge with the sombrero magnet Lucy had brought back from Mexico last year. I wasn't sure which one was worse, Adrian's rude little note or Dylan's bleeding-heart letter. Both had left me feeling decidedly off-kilter.

And no, I still haven't thought about how I'm going to respond to Dylan's letter, so don't ask me. I can't think about it yet. I just can't.

So what I've been thinking about instead is what to get Bike Guy for his birthday. We haven't been seeing each other long, so I don't want to go crazy, but the other day he gave me a bike that was lying spare in his shop—all polished and looking brand new—so I figured I should probably give him something for his trouble.

Guys are always hard to buy presents for. Even though every man on earth goes around saying how easy he is to buy for ("You could get me anything and I'd love it!"), everyone knows that this is a big fat lie. Men are impossible to buy for: if you get them an item of clothing, they won't like it or they'll stain/rip it immediately; if you get them a book, they won't read it; if you get them anything technological, it will be the wrong kind; and if you get them anything grooming related, they'll be offended. It's seriously a giant pain in the ass.

Women, on the other hand, are incredibly easy to buy for: just go to the nearest Boots, swipe every nice-smelling lotion/serum on the beauty shelf into a basket, throw in a loofah and go to the checkout counter. It literally could not be simpler.

Anyway, I was in a jam about what to get Bike Guy, so I turned to the book for some advice. Helpfully, there was a whole chapter on gift giving, with Mrs. Humphry agreeing that choosing a gift for a man is a near-Sisyphean task. "Men are very troublesome about presents," she says. "One is often at a loss about what to get them, especially if they do not smoke."

Luckily, it was already well established that Bike Guy was a smoker, though probably not the type of smoker Mrs. Humphry was referring to. Her list of suggestions is as follows: custom-made smoking table (don't think it would fit in the attic), a cigar box of precious metals (above my pay grade), cigarette case with a jeweled monogram (don't think he's meant to be carrying joints around with him), or matchbox. Bingo! I found a sweet little Victorian matchbox on eBay and managed to win the auction with a last-minute stealth bid. It was dark wood with a little frieze of wood nymphs inlaid in ivory on the back, and on the front was a copper-plate photograph of a woman who appeared to be in a sailor's uniform, complete with little hat. It was weirdly fitting for the up-coming boating party.

Bike Guy had replied to my invitation by text, which wasn't exactly the level of formality I was hoping for, but at least I knew he'd show up. He mentioned that he was a little afraid of water, but I'm sure that won't be too much of a problem; after all, we'll be on the water, not in it.

So invitation accepted and gift acquired, the only thing left to sort out was the menu. The book lays out a very specific (and, for my culinary aptitude, very ambitious) three-course meal, each course made up of four scary-sounding French dishes consisting, if my translation is right, almost entirely of cream and ice in various itera-tions (Victorians must have been busting out of their corsets left, right and center eating all this stuff). I think I need to scale it back a little before Saturday. And I probably need to invest in a cooler.

October 10

I told Lucy about the letter. I'd been avoiding her for days but she finally trapped me on the balcony and wouldn't let me inside until I told her.

"You were *married*?!" I thought her head was going to pop off her neck and fly over the railing.

"Well, technically, I'm *still* married. But we're separated. Obviously."

"Hang on, when the hell did you get married? How old were you—ten? I knew that sort of thing happened in the South, but I wasn't expecting it from someone from Maine. That's near New York!"

I brushed Lucy's hazy knowledge of geography aside for the minute. "We were twenty-three, only a couple years out of college. Babies, basically. We'd been together in high school, split up for a while and then got back together when we both moved back to Portland."

"High school sweethearts! That sounds so romantic! How did he propose?"

I really didn't want to talk about this, but I figured I owed Lucy an explanation considering I'd been lying to her for a year. "He hid it in a doughnut."

Lucy wrinkled her nose. "A doughnut? God, I haven't eaten one of those since the nineties."

"Yeah, we had this Saturday-morning tradition of going for a run together and then getting doughnuts from this amazing little bakery on the waterfront. He hid the ring in my doughnut one morning. I nearly swallowed it, but my sensitive gag reflex came in handy for once."

"Not quite as romantic as I'd pictured, but it's still sweet." She paused and I watched the whole thing sink in afresh. "Fuck. I *cannot* picture you in a wedding dress."

"Well, it happened, and there are pictures to prove it somewhere in my parents' living room."

"Lo, this is major! I can't believe you didn't tell me! And here I was thinking we were best friends and all."

"Look, I'm sorry I didn't tell you earlier—I just couldn't deal with it. I still can't, really."

"So what happened between the two of you? I mean, he seems pretty perfect from the sounds of that letter."

I shrugged. "It just didn't work." I could feel myself welling up and pressed my fingernails into my palms to stop myself from crying. "Can we not talk about this right now?"

Lucy handed me another cigarette and gave me a little squeeze. "Of course, babe. Sorry. Let me get you a whisky."

So the cat's out of the bag now, officially. I guess that means I'm going to have to deal with things: write him back, find a lawyer, the whole nine yards, but just not yet. I felt drained at the thought of it.

I took my whisky to bed with me and watched reruns of *Gilmore Girls*, wishing I was safe in the arms of Stars Hollow.

October 12

Bike Guy's Birthday Boating Party was today! It went moderately to plan.

I spent yesterday evening hauling the canoe out of Lucy's cousin's garage in Walthamstow, strapping it to the top of a Zipcar, and driving—terrified—through east London before storing the canoe on the balcony next to my new bike.

I then spent five hours cooking the various dishes I was bringing to this boating party.

As previously mentioned, Mrs. Humphry's menu involved a truly unbelievable amount of food for a day on a boat. For lunch alone, her menu consisted of lobster with mayonnaise, salmon with tartar sauce, quail stuffed with truffles, roasted chickens (plural!), beef tongues, lamb, and strawberries and cream. Who were these Victorians and how were they rich enough to afford lobster, salmon and truffles all in one meal? And how the hell did they digest all that? On a boat, no less! They must have been impermeable to seasickness.

Anyway, my scaled-down menu was as follows:

Lunch at 1:00

ROAST CHICKEN *(one, slightly charred)*

STRAWBERRIES AND CREAM

Tea at 4:00

CAKES AND BISCUITS

(well, some Jaffa cakes, which I figured covered both categories)

TEA

ICED COFFEE

Dinner at 8:00

BOEUF ÉPICÉ

*(spicy beef to you and me—basically I just stir-fried some steak
with a shit-ton of Sriracha sauce)*

SALADE FRANÇAISE

(some salad leaves in a bag)

GELÉES AUX FRUITS

*(Remember those Jello molds with the pieces
of canned fruit floating in it? That.)*

Mrs. Humphry doesn't mention booze anywhere in her menu (an oversight, surely) so I added a few six-packs of Carlsberg and a bottle of cheap cava.

Bike Guy arrived at my flat at exactly the moment I was trying to wrestle the canoe back on top of the Zipcar.

"Hello!" he called as he cycled up next to me. "Let me give you a hand with that."

"Stupid fucking—arrrghh!" I shouted as we hoisted the canoe onto the roof. I tied it up quickly with a piece of bungee cord I'd found in the hall closet. "Happy birthday!" I yelled, throwing my arms around him.

"Bloody hell!" he said, eyeing up the canoe now balancing perilously on top of the tiny car. "You weren't joking about this boating party, were you?"

I gave him a peck on the lips. "Would I joke about something as serious as a boating party? Come on, let's get this baby onto the canal in time for lunch."

I handed him the keys and climbed into the passenger seat; after my perilous journey yesterday (where I clipped three wing mirrors and nearly de-limbed a cyclist), I was very happy to leave the driving to him. Besides, Victorian women couldn't even vote; I was pretty sure they weren't meant to drive.

We zoomed through the City, down Commercial Street and out to Limehouse. We parked up by the basin and pulled the canoe off the roof.

"Can you give me a hand with these bags?" I asked, pulling the seat forward and folding myself into the back seat.

Bike Guy peered in and saw the two overstuffed Sainsbury's bags. "How the hell are we going to get all that onto the boat? Mate, we'll bloody capsize the thing!"

A little spark of worry shot through me: I hadn't fully thought out the logistics of this, but it was too late now and I was damned if

I was going to throw away a single morsel. I'd slaved for hours over that luncheon and, by God, we were going to eat every bite.

"It'll be fine!" I said, tugging one of the bags out and handing it to him. "We can drag the beer along beside the boat. Anyway, we're both pretty small—there'll be plenty of room once we're in."

The two of us hauled the canoe and the two grocery bags down to the edge of the river and set them down.

I looked at the canoe skeptically. I'd never actually set foot in one before, so had no real idea how we were meant to go from dry land to sailing on the open seas. Were we meant to just climb in while the boat was still docked on the sand? Or were we meant to—God help me—leap in once it was afloat?

Bike Guy was outdoorsy, so I figured he'd know. I looked at him expectantly before remembering that he was afraid of water, and probably wasn't quite as expert as I'd hoped.

"How the fuck are we meant to get in then?" he asked, giving the canoe a little shove with his foot.

Ah, shit. Well, I might as well pretend I knew what I was doing. I cleared my throat and spoke in what I hoped was an authoritative manner. "First, we have to get all the stuff in the boat so that the weight is evenly distributed."

We got to work unloading the food, tucking Tupperware containers in every available crevice and squeezing the aluminum-foil-wrapped chicken into the bow. We attached the two six-packs to the boat with a long piece of string; they could trail peacefully behind us, chilling nicely in the river while we rowed away. I couldn't find space for the cava so I opened it, took a swig and passed it to Bike Guy. "Bottoms up!"

We drank half the bottle while circling the canoe and discussing the physics of buoyancy, until—emboldened by the aforementioned cava—I gave the canoe a little shove into the water and hurled myself in, hitting my pubic bone on the yoke on the way.

"Fuuuuuuuuck!" I yelled. I pulled myself upright and squeezed myself into the bow, curling my feet around the chicken. I looked back to see a panicked-looking Bike Guy running along the sand, trying desperately to keep up with the rapidly receding boat. I found the paddles and started rowing furiously back to shore. "Get in!" I hollered as the boat bobbed close.

"How?!" he hollered back.

"Make a jump for it!"

Bike Guy backed up a little and then took a running leap at the canoe. He sailed toward me and then flopped sideways across the boat, his arms clutching the sides while his legs thrashed furiously in the water.

"Gaaaaaah!" he yelled. "Help me on! I'm going to fucking drown!"

I peered over the side and saw silt. "It's shallow! Just stand up!"

"Oh." He stopped thrashing and stood up. The water was only knee height. "Eurgh, it's all seaweedy!"

"I thought you were meant to be outdoorsy and shit!" I gave him a hand and pulled him into the boat, the two of us collapsing with laughter.

He pulled off his soaked shoes and placed them on the lapboard to dry in the sun. "Fuck me, that was all a bit dramatic! I need a drink."

I spotted the half-drunk bottle of cava lying sadly on its side on the shore. "Beer it is!" I pulled two cans out of the river and handed one to him. We clinked. "To the high seas!"

We started paddling lazily toward Shoreditch, whacking floating debris and the occasional tin of baked beans out of the way. Now that we had set out, I took a minute to survey our surroundings: it was a beautiful day, sunny but with a hint of autumnal crispness in the air.

By the time we made our way to the Towpath Cafe, it was one o'clock: time for luncheon. Bike Guy was eyeing the cafe's chalkboard menu beadily, but I was determined to carry on with my Victorian feast. I reached down to my feet and pulled out the chicken. "Hungry?" I asked, unwrapping the foil and offering it up for him to see.

He looked confused at first—I assumed it was the first time anyone had ever offered him a whole roast chicken while in a canoe—but after a moment's pause he picked a bit of skin off and popped it in his mouth with a grin.

I hadn't packed any cutlery (I knew I was forgetting something) so we had to pull it apart with our hands, which was fun in an animalistic sort of way. It felt briefly like we were on one of those survival shows. I could see the tagline now: LOST AT SEA WITH CHICKEN.

The morning's exertions had obviously taken their toll—we demolished that chicken in seconds. I looked at the picked-over carcass lying limply in the foil. "Do you think I should just throw it overboard?"

Bike Guy had given up all pretense of paddling and was lying back with his head tipped to the sun. "Why not? Feed the ducks and all that."

"Isn't that, like, cannibalism? Ducks eating chickens?"

He considered this, then shook his head. "Nah. Different species."

"Really?" I looked down at the chicken remains and over at a flock of ducks floating peacefully nearby. "It still feels sort of sick. Like a human eating a monkey: you're basically eating family."

Bike Guy sat up and started rolling a joint, shielding it carefully with his hand to prevent the bud from blowing away. "Pigs are closer to humans than monkeys and we eat them all the time."

"That's fucked up," I said, throwing the chicken bones into the river and tucking the ball of used foil back into the bow.

We sailed along, letting the tide pull us where it wanted us to go. We floated into Islington and then King's Cross, where we

waved at the customers sitting outside the Rotunda. Bike Guy finished his first joint and rolled another while I polished off my fourth
beer. We picked at the strawberries (the cream had curdled in the
sun). Occasionally, one of us would stick an oar into the water and
make a halfhearted attempt to propel us in a direction, but mainly
we just meandered.

Bike Guy was in his element, skin turning pink in the sun,
blond hair all tousled in the breeze, the laugh lines from his forty-
two years seeming to deepen in the light. By Camden, I was feeling
mellow and happy and leaned across to kiss him. We nearly cap-
sized.

By teatime, we'd reached Regent's Park. I found the Thermos
languishing under the bag full of salad leaves and poured us each a
cup of tea. We threw most of the Jaffa cakes to the ducks floating
lazily alongside us.

In short, it was a glorious, glorious day. And it almost stayed
that way.

"Do you ever think about your ex-wife?" I asked as I licked the
chocolate off the top of a Jaffa Cake. I was lying back in the canoe,
six beers down, staring at the clouds as they floated past.

Bike Guy picked his head up slightly and looked at me. "Sort of.
Not really, though. I know she's set, which is all that matters. Got
her fella and the house and all. Happier all around, I suppose." He
lay back in the boat and took a long drag.

I sat up, reeled in another beer and lit a cigarette. "I have a
husband."

He sat up. "Sorry?"

"I mean, I had a husband. We're separated."

He lay back down. "Oh. Right." There was a long pause, in
which I could tell he was trying to determine just how much he was
obliged to ask about it. But he was a decent guy, so after a few
minutes he said, "Want to talk about it?"

"Not particularly."

"Cool. That cloud looks like an octopus."

I stared up at the multitendriled cloud. Two things were clear: it *did* look like an octopus and I *didn't* want to talk about my ex-husband. I really fucking didn't. But since I'd got Dylan's letter, it was like something had opened up in me. Like when you pee for the first time when drinking keg beer: the seal had been broken. I didn't want to talk about it, but suddenly I wanted very badly to acknowledge it, and I wanted other people to acknowledge it, too. "I was married!" I wanted to scream. "I took fucking VOWS."

Instead, I took a sip of the new beer and lay back down, watching my cigarette burn to a perfect column of ash. I stared at the sky and thought of Dylan sleeping under the same sky. The song from *An American Tail* started playing in a loop in my head— you know, the one the mouse sings on the rooftop? And, to my horror, I felt a tear leak out of the corner of my eye and fall into the hollow of my ear. "Fuck," I said softly.

"You all right?" Bike Guy was propped up on his elbows and was looking at me worriedly.

I scrubbed my cheek and smiled. "Just some ash in my eye. Let's dock this baby and go to the pub." We'd reached Little Venice and a place called the Summerhouse was winking promisingly at me. "I'll bring dinner and we can eat it at one of the picnic tables."

Bike Guy peered at the gray-looking steak stir-fry that had been moldering away in the Tupperware container beneath him and grimaced. "Tell you what: I'll buy us some dinner."

We rowed to shore and hauled the boat onto the bank. I felt sticky and dehydrated from all the cans of beer I'd drunk, and my clothes were embedded with Jaffa Cake crumbs and bits of cigarette ash. Bike Guy didn't look so hot, either: the weed had caught up with him, and his face—which had been a rosy pink in the sunlight—was a disturbing yellow color in the shade of the trees.

We looked at each other for a minute and seemed to come to the same unspoken decision: forget the pub, let's just go home. We nodded in agreement.

"Right, how are we getting back then?" he asked, looking around to see if I'd hidden a car or a jetpack somewhere in the shrubs.

My heart sank: in all of my frantic menu preparing, I'd forgotten about the whole "getting back" thing.

Bike Guy read the look on my face. "Fuck the canoe: I'll buy the bloke a new one." He grabbed my hand and started pulling me up the embankment. "Let's find a cab and get home." I had to hand it to him: for a pothead, he could be remarkably clear-sighted.

October 13

I woke up covered in a fine layer of silt, with a godawful hangover and a sudden acute awareness that we'd left Lucy's cousin's canoe in Paddington Basin, where it had presumably now been commandeered by a bunch of tramps.

I pressed my face into the pillow and then took a peek at Bike Guy, who was starfished across the majority of the bed. I had a quick look around and saw an ashtray heaped with cigarette butts and half-finished joints, and a bottle of Jack Daniel's propped up against a framed photo of Bike Guy with little Poppy balanced on his shoulders.

This definitely wasn't what Mrs. Humphry had in mind.

I pulled on my still-damp clothes and crept out of the flat. Thankfully it was early enough that Poppy and parents had yet to stir. I slipped out the front door, closed it as quietly as I could behind me and hurried down the street to the bus stop.

It was strange: I was dating someone well over a decade older than me, and yet I'd never lived like more of a teenager. As fun as Bike Guy was, I wasn't sure how much more my liver could handle. And I definitely wasn't keen on doing another walk of shame through middle-class bliss.

I got back to my flat by 7:30 and went immediately back to bed. I woke up to the sound of Lucy shutting the door behind her as she left and heaved a sigh of relief; at least I wouldn't have to explain the canoe yet.

I checked the time on my phone—11:34 a.m.—and saw I had six missed calls, all from Meghan. I sat up and hit redial. It was still incredibly early in Maine, so it must have been an emergency.

She picked up on the first ring. "Kid? That you?" Her voice was thick and choked.

"What's going on? Are you okay?"

"It's Sue. She's gone."

My heart dropped. "What do you mean?" An image of a car crash flashed through my head.

"I mean she's *gone*." I heard her stifle a sob on the end of the line. "She left." I felt a little twinge of relief knowing she wasn't dead. "We had a huge fight and she packed her stuff and left and now she's *gone*." Meghan broke down and started to quietly cry. "What am I gonna do, bub?"

"Oh, Meg. Don't worry, she'll come back! She's probably just gone somewhere to cool off for the day. It's you guys! You guys are solid."

Meghan made a noise that sounded like a wounded animal. "We're not solid, though. She's been working super long hours at the hospital, so we never see each other anymore, and when we do, we just argue. And last night, I found all these texts between her and some nurse and when I confronted her about it, she said she'd been having a *flirtation* or some bullshit. She promised me nothing had happened but how am I supposed to believe that when she's never fucking home? We had this huge blowout, and we said all these awful things to each other and now she's fucking *gone*."

It sounded like she'd started to hyperventilate. "Meg, you've got to calm down. Deep breaths. It's going to be okay, I promise."

I listened to her cry and felt a helplessness I had never experienced before. What the fuck was I doing here, in this shitty flat in this godforsaken rainy city, while my sister had her heart stamped on? Why wasn't I there to give her a hug? I was useless here: a disembodied voice murmuring platitudes down a piece of plastic. I made my mind up immediately.

"I'm coming home. I'll tell work on Monday and I'll book the first flight I can get. I haven't had a vacation yet this year so they can't get pissed off about it."

"You don't have to do that, kid. I'll be okay."

"No. I want to. It's been too long and I miss your Meghan-face."

Meghan sniffed and took a deep breath. "Really?"

"Really. Now, go to bed—it's too fucking early where you are—and when you wake up, take a hot shower and go for a run. And call me. Call me whenever you want and as much as you want. It's going to be okay, I promise."

I hung up the phone and hoped to God that what I'd said would be true.

Home meant a whole lot of shit I wasn't sure I was ready to deal with. But home also meant my sister, and that's where I had to be.

October 25

I packed a bag this morning. My flight wasn't until late afternoon, so I went for a run, wandered around the empty flat, drank too much coffee, smoked too many cigarettes and, when I had checked and double-checked that I had my passport, locked the door behind me and set out.

I'd booked a return flight for two weeks later, but something heavy inside me suggested that date could be stretched and stretched. It scared me.

I'd spoken to Meghan every night, just letting her cry on the phone and murmuring what I hoped were comforting words. She still hadn't heard from Sue, and I found that the little seed of hatred I'd felt toward her the moment Meghan told me she'd left had now blossomed into a full-blown arboretum. Sue was now Public Enemy Number One.

Work had been totally fine about me taking time off—Cathryn gave me a hug (our first) and practically pushed me out the door, chattering about how pale and exhausted I looked and how a break would do me good. I wasn't proving to be much use at work under the circumstances, anyway. Yesterday, I'd completely forgotten about the group of twenty-five fourteen-year-olds coming in for a tour of the Large Hadron Collider exhibition and it fell to Cathryn to lead them around. Apparently she'd found two of them doing some heavy petting in one of the detector caverns. I'd bought her a bottle of wine to say thank you, but I think she was still a little shaken by the experience.

Lucy had been great about it, too. After reading Dylan's letter, she seemed convinced that my destiny was to get back together with him, so she could hardly contain her glee when I told her that I was going home for a few weeks. When I went to get the milk this morning, I found a note from her taped to the fridge: an enormous GOOD LUCK surrounded by little hearts. I tore it off and stuck it in my wallet: I figured I needed all the luck I could get.

Bike Guy and I had our final date last night: a long cycle along Regent's Canal and a pint at the Palm in Victoria Park. I told him I was going home for a few weeks, and when I talked about meeting up when I got back he started getting all hazy-eyed and evasive.

"Let's not make any promises," he'd said. "Two weeks is a long time."

I'd rolled my eyes and explained that I wasn't looking for a betrothal, just a pint or two when I was back in London, but it was too late: he'd been infected with The Fear.

"I think you're ace," he'd said, "but I'm not looking for anything serious."

So apparently neither prostitution nor Victoriana put him off, but the thought of making a vague plan two weeks in advance was enough to send him running for the hills. I cut my losses and mentally detached, though I still took him back to my place for a goodbye roll in the hay. He didn't spend the night. I told him I had to pack (which was true) but, really, I just wanted the bed to myself.

I got off the tube at South Ken and made a pit stop at the bookshop to buy something to read on the plane.

It had been sunny when I left the flat, but by the time I surfaced onto Onslow Square, the skies had darkened and fat raindrops had started attacking the earth. I ran into the bookshop, closing the door behind me just before the hail began.

The young bookseller was sitting, as ever, at his little desk in the back of the shop, engrossed in a tattered old paperback. He was wearing an enormous gray knit cardigan and baggy reddish corduroys, a pair of tortoiseshell reading glasses balanced carefully on his nose. I paused in the doorway and watched as he pushed his hair out of his eyes. Looking at him like this, I could almost forget all his withering comments and grumpy demeanor. In fact, from where I stood, he looked sort of . . . adorable. My mind started wandering. Take off the glasses and maybe . . . I leaned on a stack of Penguin Classics and sent them flying to the ground. He started out of his chair and scowled at me. The spell was abruptly broken and I felt myself blush deeply.

"You're dripping all over my floor!"

I looked down at my sodden jacket. "It's not exactly like I can help it."

He tutted to himself and got up. "Let me get you a towel. But stay where you are and don't touch anything! You'll make everything damp."

I followed his orders, turning only slightly to the left so I could look at the first edition of *Black Beauty* that was under glass. One day, I thought, you will be mine. Even if I have to steal you.

The bookseller emerged from the back of the shop carrying a surprisingly fluffy towel. "Here, sort yourself out."

"Thanks," I said, toweling myself dry.

"So what tome from the literary canon are you after today? *Bastards and the Women Who Love Them? Barbara Cartland's Twenty Rules for Love?*"

"Actually, I'm looking for a novel that was written in 1897."

"Oh?" he said, softening slightly. "Can you remember the title? The author?"

"Oh, no. I don't care what it is—I just want any novel that was written in 1897." I knew it was unlikely I'd be able to continue following Mrs. Humphry's advice when I was in Maine, but I figured I could at least maintain the Victorian spirit through my literature choices.

He furrowed his brow. "How very specific of you. Let me see what I've got." He moved toward the classics section, running a hand through his unruly hair and tutting again. "Right. Well, there's this . . . and this . . . and this." He collected three books in his arms and shoved them toward me. "*The Invisible Man's* quite good, though I do think Wells can be a bit silly at times. *Dracula* is fairly self-explanatory. And then there's *What Maisie Knew*, which is what I'd recommend. James is an expert at dysfunction, and poor little Maisie's parents are truly loathsome. It's good fun."

"I'm just impressed that you knew three books that had been published in 1897 off the top of your head like that."

"I do own this bookshop, you know. I'm not a total philistine."

I took his advice and chose the Henry James. I was fishing around in my bag for my wallet when he spotted my suitcase.

"Going somewhere?"

I nodded. "I'm going home. To Maine." The word "home" slightly stuck in my throat.

He looked at me sharply. "For good?"

"I don't think so. My sister is going through—" To my horror, I started to tear up. "My sister is—" I began again, only to find my throat tightening. It had been a terrible ten days. It was nearly impossible to find a flight home at such short notice, and the few seats that were available had been astronomical. I'd finally grabbed a place on a Delta flight after a last-minute cancellation, but it had been a nail-biting wait. Every night, I'd listened to Meg cry on the phone, knowing it would still be days before I got to her. I've never felt so helpless in my life. And now it appeared that all of the strain of the past week and a half was about to be unleashed in the most awkward place possible. A tear slipped down my cheek and my shoulders started to shake.

"Oh God. Oh dear." The bookseller was looking at me like I might spontaneously combust. I expected him to phone in the bomb squad at any minute.

"Sorry, it's just . . ." I tried to pull myself together, but something had been shaken loose and it was proving hard to push back down into place. Stupid, traitorous tears: there was no stopping them now. Oh God. Oh gross.

The bookseller stood stock-still for a minute, looking as if he'd been mildly electrocuted, and then took me by the elbow and guided me into a chair. "Right. I'll get you a cup of tea," he said, hurrying to the back of the shop. He returned a few minutes later holding a chipped enamel mug and a few tissues.

"Here you are," he said, gingerly handing me the cup of tea. He patted me awkwardly on the shoulder as my sobs grew louder. I couldn't tell who was more mortified in that moment, him or me.

He kneeled down in front of my chair. "Now, what's all this about your sister? She's not ill, is she?" There was genuine concern etched on his face, which only made me cry harder.

After a few excruciating minutes, I took a deep breath and pulled myself together. "Her wife left her," I said. "And I wasn't there to help her and it took me forever to get a flight and she's been all on her own and now I'm going home and everyone there hates me and I'm probably going to have to see my ex-husband and he probably hates me the most but he's being all nice about everything, which makes it a million times worse and my parents . . . my parents . . ." I started up again and the bookseller silently passed me a tissue.

Eventually I managed to calm myself down. "Sorry, this definitely doesn't come under your purview," I said with a weak smile.

"Nonsense. Every good bookseller is always armed with tea and tissues. These shops are hotbeds of emotional activity, you know," he said with a wry smile.

I laughed. "Well, thanks. Sorry I'm kind of a mess."

He shook his head. "It's no wonder you're a bit overwhelmed. I'm sure it will be all right. Surely no one could really hate you?" He placed his hand gently on my shoulder. Our eyes met and a jolt passed through me; I could tell by his eyes that he'd felt it, too. He pulled his hand away and jumped to his feet. "Well," he said, staring firmly at the floor, "you'd better be off or you'll miss your flight."

I wiped the errant mascara from under my eyes and got to my feet. "Of course. Sorry, I shouldn't have kept you so long."

He shook his head. "Please, don't mention it. The foliage is meant to be lovely at this time of year."

"It is." I'd forgotten about the leaves turning color, and suddenly felt a deep longing to be in my parents' backyard beneath the multi-colored maples. "Well, thanks again for . . . everything."

The mortification had crept back in and the two of us started backing away slowly, nodding and smiling at each other like a pair of bobblehead dolls.

I was nearly out the door when I heard him shout out. "Hang on!" he called. "Just one moment!" I turned back and he pressed a book into my hands. "I think you might like this," he said.

I stared dumbly at the cover, my feet glued in place. *The Age of Innocence* by Edith Wharton.

I looked at him blankly but he just shooed me out the door. "Off you go!" he called, waving me away.

I lugged my suitcase down the stairs of the tube station, turning over our conversation in my mind. I had no idea what the hell had just happened in there, but I did know that I had two industrial-strength sleeping pills for the plane that would ensure I wouldn't think about it until I was far, far away.

An hour-long tube journey, seven-hour plane ride and forty-five-minute wait at customs later, I was charging through the arrivals gate toward a waving Meghan. I vaulted over a baggage trolley and enveloped her in a hug.

"I am so sorry it's taken me so long to get here," I said, squeezing her tightly. "Everything's going to be okay. I know it's still raw, but believe me when I say that one day you'll look back on this and be thankful that she left. I never liked Sue, anyway—always going on and on about saving lives and boring us all to death with—"

"Lauren, stop." Meghan pulled away from me and I noticed that she wasn't nearly as pale or puffy-eyed as I'd expected. She looked almost . . . happy. "A lot has happened in the last nine hours," she said.

"What do you mean?"

"I mean . . . Sue came back this morning."

I was indignant. "Oh, come on! You mean I just flew 3,500 miles into the belly of my emotional past and you guys are all hunky-dory now? What about the big blowout? She thinks she can disappear for *ten days* and then just waltz back in like nothing happened?"

"She didn't just waltz back in!" Meghan put her arm around me and started guiding me toward the parking lot. "Look, I'll explain on the drive home."

I shook her off. "This wasn't just some elaborate scheme to get me to come home, was it?"

Meghan rolled her eyes. "No, you narcissist. I promise you that my emotional distress was completely genuine at the time." She pulled me in for a hug. "I'm so glad you're home, and I can't tell you how much it means to me that you came. It's just—" she started to laugh—"your timing is a little off."

I tried to remain indignant, but the sound of Meghan laughing was such a relief that I felt my anger melting away.

"Timing has never been my specialty," I said. "I'm still pissed at Sue, though. Just for the record."

"Duly noted. Now let's get you home," she said, taking my suitcase in one hand and me in the other.

October 26

I woke up to the sight of the Beatles poster hanging on the wall next to my bed. An alarm clock in the shape of a cartoon rabbit was perched on the nightstand: 6:56 a.m.

I could hear my parents talking downstairs. As they got older, they'd become more and more like wombats, napping by day and waking in the early hours, usually before dawn. I knew from years of experience that it was pointless trying to go back to sleep: once they were up, you were up, and you might as well go down and enjoy the coffee.

I pulled on a pair of track pants and a T-shirt from my high school soccer days and padded downstairs.

My dad spotted me first. "Good morning, sunshine. What time did you get in last night? We tried to stay up but both of us fell asleep."

I gave him a kiss on the cheek. "I got in around one thirty. Didn't want to wake you so I just snuck in and went straight to bed. Hi, Mom."

My mom got up from the kitchen table and gave me a hug. I sank into her familiar warmth and realized suddenly how much I'd missed them.

"Lulu! I'm so glad you're home. Look at you, you're so thin! What have they been feeding you in England? I thought it was all fish and chips and—what do you call it—spotted dick over there!"

"It's not all that bad, Mom. And I have never once seen a spotted dick, if that's any consolation."

I heard my dad stifle a laugh behind me. My mom swatted him with a dish towel.

"Well, let me get you some breakfast. What do you want? I've got pancakes, eggs, toast, English muffins . . . and I sent your father out to get doughnuts earlier on, so there's a half-dozen in the pantry."

I poured myself a cup of coffee and looked at the clock on the microwave: 7:13 a.m. "What the hell time does the doughnut place open?"

"Language, Lulu. And it's one of those twenty-four-hour ones in the Market Basket."

Market Basket. I made a silent promise to myself to visit an

American grocery store when I was home. Aisle upon aisle of snack-food nirvana, heaps of produce buffed and waxed to a high shine: a consumerist promised land, and very different from the three limp lettuce leaves and half a loaf of thin-sliced white bread to be found in my local Co-op back in London.

I sat down with my coffee and my parents sat opposite me, the pages of the *Portland Daily Sun* spread out between us. My dad put his hand over mine and gave me a sad smile.

"We missed you."

"I missed you, too. Both of you. I'm sorry it's been so long."

My dad shook his head. "No need to explain, sunshine."

"Has Meghan told you about Sue?"

He nodded. "They came around yesterday. I have to say, Sue looked like hell."

"Good. She should look like hell after what she put Meghan through." She and I had had a long conversation on the drive home last night, and while I could see that Meghan was determined to take Sue back and to work on their marriage, I couldn't bring myself to forgive Sue for what she'd done. To me, she was still dead meat.

My dad shrugged. "Marriage is tough, Lu. You never know what happens behind closed doors. And your sister . . . well, she can be stubborn as an old mule."

"How can you say that? Sue was the one who left!"

My mother piped up. "Your father is right, Lauren. It's none of our beeswax what happened between those two. I was as mad as anyone when I heard that Sue had left, and Lord knows Meggy was heartbroken, poor thing, but if she wants to take her back, that's her decision."

"I still think Sue sucks," I said sullenly. Seven hours at home and I was already reverting to my teenaged self.

My dad patted me on the hand. "You're gonna have to buck up, buckaroo, because they're both coming over for dinner tonight."

The rest of the day was spent unpacking, doing laundry and catching up on American television. My mom and I got sucked into a *Property Wars* marathon and, before I knew it, Meghan was pulling up in the drive, a pale-looking Sue sitting in the passenger seat.

"Oh, shoot!" my mom exclaimed, leaping off the couch and running toward the kitchen. "I forgot to defrost the chicken!"

My dad opened the door for them and enveloped them both in a bear hug. "C'mere, Lu!" he called to me. "I want to get all my girls together in one hug!"

I skulked over to them and allowed myself to be wrapped up in the embrace. Once released from my dad's vice-grip, Meghan gave me a hug and pointed me toward Sue, who was looking suitably nervous. "Say hi to Sue," she said, giving me a shove.

"Hey," I mumbled.

"Hi, Lauren! Great to see you!" She tried to pull me in for a hug but I kept my arms tucked neatly by my sides. Meghan gave me a sharp poke in the back.

My mom returned from the kitchen looking slightly harried. She wrapped her arms around Meghan and Sue in another double hug. "Hello, girls. Now, what would you like to drink? The chicken is still frozen solid so dinner might be a while."

My dad shuffled off toward the kitchen. "I'll get the menu for the Chinese place!" he called.

Dinner was a slightly stilted affair. I sat as far away from Sue as I could get, and every time she reached out for another spring roll, I dove across the table and snatched it before her fork could get there. I ate all of the Kung Pao chicken because I knew it was her favorite. Meghan continually kicked me under the table and my mom kept whispering to me sharply about manners, but I was filled with righteous indignation. I didn't care if this bunch of saps were going to sit around and pretend like nothing happened. For me, this was war. And by the end of it, I would be the bloated, MSG-laden victor.

I was polishing off the last of the crab rangoons when Sue grabbed me by the elbow and steered me toward the study. "Can I talk to you for a sec?" she said. "Alone?" I looked at her properly for the first time that evening and was pleased to see that Dad was right: she did look like hell.

I shrugged. "I guess," I said. I looked over at Meg, who was glaring at me and mouthing BE NICE. I stuck my tongue out at her and reluctantly followed Sue into the study.

Sue shut the door behind us. "Look, I know you're pissed at me, but I love your sister."

I made a spluttering noise that surprised both of us. "I know all about your little *flirtation*," I spat. "How can you call that love? And you go and fucking *disappear* without so much as a word for a week and a half and expect you can just walk back into her life and pretend it never happened? Do you have any idea how hurt she was? How scared?"

"Lauren, I know that what I did was shitty, and I've apologized a thousand times and will continue to apologize until I make things right but . . . Christ, you know better than most that marriage can be hard."

"Don't you dare bring my shit into this," I hissed.

She put her hands up. "I'm not trying to compare us. I'm just saying . . . sometimes things break, and sometimes they can be fixed. I promise you, I am going to fix this."

I studied her for a minute. Her eyes were rubbed red and raw, her blond hair was shot through with white strands and there were fine lines around her mouth. She looked like she'd aged ten years. I knew that look. I understood it.

I stood up and hugged her. "Okay, okay. I believe you." I pulled back and looked her in the eyes. "But I promise you this: if you ever hurt her again, I will beat you up. Like, for real. I will go Schwarzenegger on your ass."

She smiled and I could see the relief in her eyes. "Deal."

"*And* I get dibs on the last spring roll. You're not out of the dog-house yet."

October 29

I spent my days splitting my time between Meghan and Sue's place and my parents', living off a steady diet of inventive snack foods (M&Ms *and* pretzels, you say?), cable television and *US Weekly*.

It was nice to be back in the comforting bosom of family. My mom fussed over me, plying me with grilled cheeses and straw-berry milk and giving me long, searching looks. I knew what she wanted to ask—*What happened with Dylan?*—but she never did, and I loved her all the more for it.

Some nights, when Sue was on a late shift at the hospital, Meg came over for dinner and my dad would come in from working in the yard, open a couple of beers and silently hand one to each of us with a nod before retreating to his den to watch the Red Sox. After dinner, Meghan and I went on Facebook to look at photos of people we went to high school with, checking who'd got fat, who'd had kids, who'd been to jail.

Last night, after we inspected the former prom queen's terrible dye job, I showed Meg my Victorian calling cards. I was on the verge of throwing them out; there were only a few days left with Mrs. Humphry, and it looked unlikely that I'd be able to road test my Victorian wiles at home. The project, like an unsuccessful sitcom, was temporarily on hiatus.

"These are awesome!" she said, holding one of the cards up to the light, the gold embossed lettering glinting. "You can't chuck these away. They might come in handy some day!"

"In what possible way could a hundred cards with just my name come in handy?"

She shrugged. "You never know." A wicked little grin appeared on her face. "You should leave one at Dylan's house."

I shoved her away. "Are you insane?"

"Come on, you can't hide from him forever! When are you going to see him?"

I threw a tortilla chip at her. "Never, if I can help it. Besides, I thought he was off on his cycling quest."

Meghan had the good grace to look sheepish. "I think he's back in town."

"What?!" I stood up, sending the bowl of Doritos nestled between us flying. "Have you seen him? Does he know I'm here?"

"Calm down! I haven't seen him, but I ran into his cousin the other day and he said he just got back."

"And when the hell were you going to share this little gem of knowledge with me? Jesus, Meg."

"Uh, have you forgotten about my recent extreme emotional turmoil? Sorry if I've been a little distracted from yours." She tugged on my arm and I sat back down next to her. "Look, if you don't want to see him, don't see him. There's no law saying you have to make your presence known when you're in the New England area, and considering you've spent most of your time here so far on my couch or this one, I think you're safe." She shifted so she was facing me and looked at me evenly. "But I think you should see him. It'll be good for you. He's not an asshole—he's not going to make a big scene or anything. But you guys should talk it out."

"He sent me a letter."

"I thought he might. What did it say?"

"All is forgiven," I said in a fake-menacing voice.

"Do you believe him?"

I shrugged. "How can I?" I could barely forgive myself.

The thought of seeing him again, or digging up all those old bones and laying them out for the two of us to examine and discard . . .

Meghan frowned at me. "He deserves at least a phone call."

I knew she was right. I had hurt him, badly. The least I could do was allow him the opportunity to tell me as much. But still, the idea of facing him felt impossible.

Meghan, as if sensing my thoughts, said, "I'm not saying you have to wear a hair shirt around town and beg forgiveness or anything. It's just—you were *married* to the guy. And I think a little closure would be good for you, too."

I put my head on her shoulder. "I'll think about it."

"Whatever you decide, I'm behind you. Now, have you seen how fat Greg Bellows is these days? Seriously, he looks like he swallowed an inner tube."

October 31

I woke up this morning to discover that I'd gotten my period.

I jumped in my mom's car, not bothering to shower or put on matching socks, and headed straight for the drugstore. I fought my way through a horde of harried moms buying last-minute bags of candy and crêpe-paper skeletons. I picked a jumbo-sized bag of mini-Snickers out of a display bin, ostensibly for tonight's trick-or-treaters but more accurately for the car ride home.

Anyway, I think we can guess how this goes: me, looking bloodless and miserable, in sweatpants in the tampon aisle. And as I stood there, wielding a box of Tampax like a really useless weapon, I heard it.

"Lauren?"

I knew it was him immediately. He approached me with quiet

caution, as though if he moved too quickly I might dematerialize, which was a fair point. He looked good. Tanned and blond, like a G.I. JOE action figure. He was wearing a pair of battered gray trousers and a navy-blue University of Maine sweatshirt I used to steal from him all the time. I'd wear it on weekend afternoons on the dock. I felt sick.

"Dylan!" I trilled, like this was a pleasant surprise. "I thought you were pedaling through Wyoming!" My voice was a full octave higher than usual. "What are you doing here?"

"I think that's my line in this case," he said. There was an edge to his voice, but he looked like he was trying to swallow it.

"Meghan and Sue broke up."

"Shit." His eyes did that crinkly concerned thing I loved and a fresh wave of nausea swept over me. "Poor Meg. How is she?"

"Fine now. They got back together while I was on the plane."

He laughed. "I see your timing hasn't gotten any better. They okay now?"

"Yeah, I think so. They're solid."

A stretch of empty silence yawned before us. We were each the deer and the headlights.

He cracked first. "How long have you been in town?"

"About a week," I said.

"Were you gonna call me?" he asked, quietly. He sounded wounded and—oh God—maybe a little hopeful.

I thought about lying, but I knew he'd see through me. "No."

"Oh." Another endless pause.

"Look, Dylan, I know I owe you a—"

"Lo. I can't do this here," he said, gesturing around him. "Whatever you're gonna say, I don't want to hear it while standing in front of a bunch of fucking tampons and adult diapers. Let's go for a drink before you go. Talk things out."

"I . . . I don't think that's such a good idea."

Dylan gave me a long, steady look. "C'mon, Lauren. One drink. One hour."

I met his gaze. "Okay," I said. "But not Sangillo's." I couldn't face the idea of sitting in our old haunt, rehashing all this shit while some drunks downed Jäeger meister shots at the table next to us.

"Deal. Should I just call your folks' place?"

"No!" I yelped. The thought of him calling my parents' house for a long, emotional, not-particularly-flattering-to-me conversation with my mom filled me with horror. "I—I'll give you my mobile number. International fees for texting aren't bad."

He raised an eyebrow. "*Mobile*, eh? Whatever happened to your plain old cell phone?"

"Sorry, force of habit." I dug around in my bag and could only come up with an eyeliner and one of my Victorian calling cards. I scribbled my number on the back and handed it to him. "Watch out, it might smudge. It's kohl."

He looked at the number and then flipped it over to see my name embossed in gold. "Shit, you're *fancy* now, huh?"

"They're for work," I said quickly, hands flapping toward the card in his hands. "I'm just as un-fancy as ever."

"I don't know about that," he said with a slight smile. "It was good to see you, Lauren." He nodded toward the box of tampons and his smile widened. "I'm glad you were—uh—unprepared."

I smacked him on the arm. "This is a dangerous time to tease a girl, you know."

We looked at each other and, for a split second, it all came back to us. *We* came back to us. And then I felt a tap on my shoulder.

"Excuse me." I turned to find a minuscule elderly woman clutching a handbag. She beckoned me to come closer and whispered, "Would you help me get one of those down from up there?" She pointed discreetly to a bumper pack of adult diapers balanced precariously on the top shelf. She peered around me and saw Dylan lurking in the background. She pressed her finger to her lips. "Sshhh!" she said, nodding toward him.

I heard Dylan chuckle quietly behind me and turned back to see him walking away. "See you later," he called from over his shoulder. "Tell your folks I said hello. I'll call you in the next couple of days!"

I handed the old lady her Depends and immediately high-tailed it over to the health and beauty section, where I pulled every face mask, hot roller, body lotion, epilator, loofah, salt scrub and volumizing mousse into the basket alongside the tampons. If I was going to have to see him again, I was going to make damn well sure I looked good this time.

Which is why I'm now locked in my parents' bathroom, covered in Nair.

As I've got some time on my hands and as it's the last day of the month, I guess it's time for a little round-up of *Manners for Women*, even though it's been a sort of truncated experiment. Still, I think I managed to squeeze a lot in: there was a canoe, embossed stationery, a full roast chicken . . .

Manners for Women in Conclusion

Mrs. Humphry wasn't nearly as restrictive as I thought she'd be, and basically didn't seem to care what I got up to as long as I did it with excellent manners. And I think we can all agree that I have an innate knowledge of proper social etiquette.

Works best on . . .

Bike Guy seemed completely nonplussed by my Victorian ways, though that might have been due to all the weed he smokes. I'm pretty sure I could have revealed myself as some sort of shape-shifting dragon, or a Republican, and he wouldn't have batted an eyelid. I can't see it working particularly well on the more skittish man—I can imagine Adrian getting the hell out of Dodge if I presented him with a formal invitation to a boating party. Still, I think the enforced propriety—and the general sense that I was doing things correctly in the eyes of society, albeit outmoded society—was strangely reassuring. Plus, I got all that nice stationery.

To be used by . . .

Women who love customized stationery.

BOOK EIGHT
FIND a HUSBAND AFTER 35

by Rachel Greenwald

November 1

I spent the morning browsing my favorite used bookstore in Portland, hoping to find a guide for this month. I was determined not to let the project stall despite my brief American adventure; at this point, it was the only thing keeping me sane.

After discarding countless *Rules* copycats and weird cosmic ordering books, I finally found it: *Find a Husband After 35 (Using What I Learned at Harvard Business School)* by Rachel Greenwald, MBA. How could I *not* try this book?

I bought it immediately, jumped in my car and drove home, where I locked myself in the study with the book and a jumbo-sized box of Junior Mints. According to the introduction, I was about to embark on something called "The Program," which was "a combination job search and strict diet: there are commitments, sacrifices and rules involved." I groaned. I missed the Victorians already.

The more I read, the more terrifying the prospect of being single at thirty-six became. Because, apparently, even if you're the most successful, attractive, socially engaged thirty-five-year-old around, once you hit thirty-six, the party is officially over.

You're on the shelf. Like, way up on the shelf. The top shelf, where it's dusty and only reachable using one of those wobbly little step stools. The vast majority of men have been fished out of the sea and those still obliviously swimming along will only be caught by the cleverest of women, women who have made finding a husband their *number-one priority*. Have a fulfilling career? If there aren't enough men at your workplace, you should probably quit. Own your own home? If your neighborhood isn't teeming with eligible bachelors, sell and get out!

What I'm saying is, you're probably fucked. At least, that's what Rachel Greenwald, MBA, is saying.

I decided to take a Diet Coke break and walked into the kitchen to find my parents giggling like a couple of teens who'd just huffed a whole lot of glue. I stopped in the doorway for a second and watched him pinch her on the ass, watched her swat him away and collapse into another fit of giggles, and I thought: this is nice. Marriage is nice. Stability is nice. Home is nice.

I was going to be twenty-nine soon. Most of the people I went to high school with were on their first child by now, spreading softly and contentedly into domestication.

I had the domestic dream once—a handsome, handy husband and a little clapboard house. According to Rachel Greenwald, I'd achieved the ultimate goal. If her book was any indication, there were lots of women who were desperate to fill my former wifely shoes. They were willing to consider leaving their jobs and moving to a different city in the hopes of finding a stable, committed relationship. They wanted exactly what I'd thrown away.

The truth was, each day that passed here, I started to wonder more and more why I'd left Portland and everything that came with it. It was a sweet little town, comforting and kind, and filled with people who I loved. People who loved me. What was so wrong with that? Maybe London, Adrian and this whole ridiculous dating project had just been a fevered dream I was destined to wake up from.

Tonight, just as I was about to go to bed, my phone flashed with a text message from Bike Guy.

Did I ever tell you that you give great head?

I threw the phone across the room. It was flattering, sure, in a really weird way, but it also made me feel kind of gross. What was I doing with my life that a forty-two-year-old almost-homeless man was texting me about my blowjob prowess while I sat in my childhood bedroom, trying to figure out what I was going to say to my ex-husband when I saw him?

I picked up the book and studied its cover. Maybe the idea of finding a husband wasn't so bad, after all. Particularly as I already had a perfectly good one lying around here somewhere.

November 2

After a slightly stilted breakfast with my mom, who I was both desperate to tell that I'd seen Dylan and also desperate not to in case it set off a deluge of hopeful questioning, I threw on my running gear and headed over to Meg and Sue's. I let myself in and helped myself to a banana from the fruit bowl while Harold noisily sniffed at my shins. I knelt down and gave him a good scratch behind the ears.

I heard Meghan moving around upstairs. "That you, kid? Be down in a sec!" she called. "Just putting my running stuff on!"

Meghan came crashing down the stairs, holding her sneakers in one hand and Harold's dog leash in the other.

"You ready?" she said, pulling on a sneaker.

I filled Meghan in on the tampon encounter during our run, Harold yapping at our heels. It was a beautiful day: blue-skied, autumn crisp and unseasonably warm. We looped around the Eastern Parkway and finished up at Back Cove. Meg let the dog off his leash and we watched him chase after flocks of seagulls, stretching our legs out under trees with branches still heavy with leaves in brilliant reds and yellows.

I lay down on my back and stared up at the sky through the canopy.

"What are you going to do about Dylan?" Meghan asked.

"I don't know," I said, picking nervously at a clump of dirt. "I'm starting to think I made a mistake."

"What do you mean?" she said, turning toward me and propping herself up on her elbow.

"I wonder if I should . . . if we should get back together."

Meghan sat up and looked at me like I'd gone crazy. "Why the hell would you want to do that?"

"It's just—I feel like I had what everyone wants and then ran away from it. What's wrong with me that I don't want what everyone else wants?"

"A more pertinent question would be: why do you think you should want what everyone else wants?"

"I don't know. I'm reading this new guide and it's all about how finding a husband after thirty-six is, like, impossible and—"

"Uh, I'll stop you right there. Why are you taking these guides seriously? You know as well as I do that they're bullshit. Now, what's really going on?"

I shrugged. I could feel my throat constricting with unspent tears. "I feel like I've let everyone down by running away like that. I'm such a fucking wimp."

Meg grabbed my chin. "Hey, look at me. You are the bravest person I know. You were unhappy so you left everything behind and started a completely new life for yourself. Do you know how amazing that is?"

"It sounds pretty chickenshit to me."

"No, it doesn't. So many people in your position would have just stayed where they were and been miserable forever. But you had the courage to walk away from it."

"But look at you and Sue! You guys went through a rough patch, but you're working through it. Maybe I left too soon. Maybe I should have tried harder."

Meghan stroked my hair. "Don't you think the fact that you weren't willing to stick it out is proof that it wasn't right between you and Dylan?" She sat up and faced me. "Sue and I are willing to work on things because we both know that we want to spend the rest of our lives together. Can you honestly say that's how you felt about Dylan?"

I thought for a minute, remembering Dylan's kind eyes and the way he used to kiss the tip of my nose before bed every night. "I loved him, Meg."

"I know you did, kid. But I don't think you loved him completely. That's not a criticism—it's just a fact. You did the right thing by leaving. Just because you had something that other people want doesn't mean it has to make you happy. You've got to make your own happiness."

I nodded. I knew she was right, but I couldn't let go of the fear that had set into my bones since coming home. "But . . . what if I end up alone?"

She put her arm around me and squeezed. "There are worse things to be than alone."

I thought of my last weeks with Dylan: the stilted suppers, the endless bickering, the simmering resentment, the cold freeze in the bedroom . . . she had a point.

"So, what are you going to say to him?"

"Fucked if I know," I said, plucking a handful of grass and tossing it in the air. "Meet him for a drink, let him tell me what an asshole I am for an hour, come over to yours and get shitfaced. That's the current plan at least."

"He's not going to tell you you're an asshole, kid. Well, at least not for a whole hour. He's a good guy. He just wants to know what the hell happened."

I heard from Dylan later that afternoon: drinks on Tuesday at the Old Trawlerman, 7 o'clock.

November 3

I was wandering around the aisles of the closest twenty-four-hour grocery superstore, mindlessly chucking a pack of peanut-butter Oreo cookies into the cart and still mulling over yesterday's conversation with Meghan when my phone rang: it was Lucy.

She started speaking as soon as I picked up. "Lo, I have some *shocking* news." Her voice was high and breathy, like she'd taken a break from a panic attack to give me a call.

"Have we been robbed?" I asked. I'd been waiting for us to get robbed since the day I moved in. It wasn't exactly the most salubrious apartment building in the area.

"No!" she said. "Nothing like that. It's . . . well . . . oh my God, I can't believe I'm about to say this, but . . ." Her voice was getting higher and higher.

"Lucy, for chrissakes, spit it out!"

"Lo, I'm getting *married*!"

"What the fuck?!" I screamed. A woman with two toddlers

tucked in the front of a shopping cart stopped to give me a dirty look.

"What do you mean, you're getting married?" I hissed.

"Tristan proposed last night! Oh, Lo, it was amazing! He took me to the top of the Shard and there was champagne and roses and he was like, 'Look across the river,' and when I did, that funny looking building, what's it called . . ."

"The Gherkin?" I offered.

"No, the other one. You know—the funny trianglish one that melted cars."

"The Cheese Grater."

"Yes! The Cheese Grater was all lit up and the windows spelled 'Marry Me Lucy!' Can you believe it? I felt my legs go and when I turned around, Tristan was on one knee and holding out the most *enormous* diamond you have *ever* seen! I'll send you a photo—it's on my Instagram. Isn't it incredible?"

It was incredible, all right. I was happy for Lucy, I really was, but there was something faintly depressing about hearing of a friend's engagement spectacular when one has just run into one's own ex-husband buying tampons. It really takes the shine off one's perception of one's life, particularly when one has recently been ruminating on one's future of loneliness and desperation.

Still, I rallied. It wasn't Lucy's fault that Dylan had found me in the tampon aisle, and Tristan was a great guy and I was sure he'd treat her well (especially if she put him in Aunt Dorothy's Cupboard regularly). They would be happy together, and that's all that mattered.

"I'm really happy for you, Luce. I can't wait to see a photo of the ring."

"Wait till you see it in person—it's a stonker! Speaking of, when are you coming home, babe? I miss you! We're going to have a little engagement do on the sixteenth so you *have* to be back for that."

"I wouldn't miss it for the world."

So Lucy was getting married to a gazillionaire and would soon be moving from our little flat into an enormous penthouse in West London, where she would spend her life flogging him into their happily ever after.

And here I was, contemplating a bag of chocolate-covered pretzel pieces while wearing my dad's old tracksuit, mentally preparing myself for meeting my ex-husband.

November 5

I tried to slip out of the house unnoticed, but my mom heard me rummaging around in her purse, looking for the car keys.

"Are you going over to Meg and Sue's?" she asked, bustling into the kitchen.

I gave her a kiss on the cheek. "Nope."

"You girls going out for dinner then? Maybe to Sangillo's? See who you run into?" Her voice sounded innocent, but she was eyeing me shrewdly. The game was up.

I sighed. "I'm going for a drink with Dylan, Mom." She let out an involuntary squeak. "I ran into him at the drugstore the other day and I said I'd have a drink with him. I didn't tell you earlier because I didn't want to get you excited."

"I'm not saying anything!" she said, even though her eyes had gone all misty and hopeful. She gave my arm a squeeze. "Just tell him we said 'hi' and that he's always welcome here."

I rolled my eyes. "I'm not sure how helpful that would be."

I drove down to the docks, parked behind the railroad museum and walked over to the Old Trawlerman. I hadn't been there since high school—it was the only place in town that didn't check ID—but it hadn't changed a bit. The same weather-beaten locals were lined up at the bar. It wasn't Sangillo's, but this place had its own ghosts. I scanned the room for Dylan and, when I didn't see him, I ordered myself a bottle of Bud and sat down at a table in the corner. I had successfully peeled off three-quarters of the label when I saw him walk in.

He looked good. Better than in the drugstore. He was wearing a thin gray T-shirt and loose Levi's, and had obviously made some effort to tame the mess of blond curls on top of his head. An involuntary little rush of comfort washed over me when he spotted me, and for an instant I thought: maybe I could. I waved, but instead of coming over he nodded and headed to the bar, where he greeted the bartender with an elaborate handshake and started talking to him enthusiastically.

So it was going to be like that.

Finally, after six solid minutes of bar chat, two elaborate handshakes and one apparently free bottle of beer, Dylan sat down across from me. His face was a blank—he must have been preparing for this since the tampon encounter.

He took a swig of his beer and finally looked at me. "How's your family?"

"Okay. Mom's heading up some campaign to save the Grasshopper Sparrow and my dad has basically retired to focus full-time on yard work. You know, the usual."

"Good to hear." He took another sip and looked at me squarely. "So I guess you'll be heading back to London in a few days?"

My flight was booked for Friday, but the idea of actually boarding it seemed sort of inconceivable. I shrugged and said, "I guess."

We were silent for a moment. I fiddled with my hair and wondered if my eyeliner had drifted up to my eyebrows; I couldn't remember ever being this nervous in front of Dylan, not even when I passed him our first note back in junior year of high school. I lifted my beer to my lips and took a drink, spilling at least a third of it down my shirt in the process. We both cracked up.

"Smooth move, Ex-lax," he laughed, handing me a wad of napkins from the plastic dispenser on the table. "I thought you were meant to be some European sophisticate now."

I laughed. "Yeah, my elocution lessons are going fucking swimmingly. Can I have a cigarette?"

We headed outside and leaned against the brick wall of the Old Trawlerman, shielding our cigarettes from the sea breeze with our hands and talking about old times. The bartender kept coming out onto the patio and silently placing more beers on the table. When the sun went in, Dylan ran and got two sweatshirts from his car: one for him and one for me. I put it on and inhaled: it smelled like our old house. Like home.

Finally, after we'd smoked all our cigarettes and the bartender started clearing away the empty bottles at our feet, he grabbed my hand and pulled me toward him.

"Where'd you go, Lauren? Where'd you go?"

The truth was, I still didn't know. We'd been happy. High school sweethearts, college years spent apart in different cities, each of us sowing our wild oats before we both ended up back in Portland and back together. When he proposed, it seemed like the most obvious thing in the world to say yes. Even my dad shed a little dad-tear of happiness when we told him we were engaged. The wedding was a big DIY drunken party in an old barn outside of town: candles stuck in jam jars, paper chains strewn all over the place, me in a white slip dress I'd bought off eBay for $14. Dylan had even made our wedding rings in his workshop. Seriously, if it hadn't been my own wedding, I would have thrown up from the Etsy-ness of it all. But it had been mine, and I'd loved every minute of it.

We moved into our little house and settled into our little life together, and at first it was great. Happy. Comfortable. But after a few years, I started to feel like it was just that: little. The same morning routines, the same good-bye kiss, the same beers drunk at the same bar with the same people at the same end of the day. I was twenty-six and I could predict the tenor of every day that stretched out in front of me. I started to get scared.

One morning, after another night in Sangillo's, I woke up and realized that, if I didn't do something, I'd end up hating him. So when an old professor got in touch with me about a job opening at the Science Museum in London, I realized I'd found my escape route. London would save me. Before I knew it I was boarding a plane and leaving my life behind. It had happened so suddenly, it was almost like violence. And throughout it all, Dylan had remained silent, watching me disassemble our life together with military precision without so much as raising his voice.

The moment came when I'd packed up the last of my things and was waiting for my dad to come over with the truck to haul the boxes—and me—away. The little house looked so empty without my stuff everywhere. Dylan sat in the middle of the room, marooned in a sea of packing tape and cardboard, and slowly lifted his gaze to meet mine.

"You coming back?" he'd said, his voice low and gravelly.

"I don't think so," I'd said, trying desperately to hold on to the idea of the new life I'd so vividly imagined for myself. "I think I'm gone for good."

I looked at Dylan now, felt his calloused hand sure in mine, and every part of me wanted to let go. To fall into his arms and say, let's just forget the past year. To hell with London. To hell with being single. To hell with the project, with the job, with being independent. Let's just go home.

But instead of falling, I stayed on my own two feet. There was a reason I'd left and I couldn't turn back now. If I did, I'd end up ruining both of our lives.

I took a deep breath. "Dylan, I love you—you know that—and I always will. But I had to get out of here. We were too young for all that—we were like a couple of kids playing fucking house! We're in our twenties—we should be out getting shitfaced and propositioning the bartender, not picking out furniture and worrying about putting a new roof on the house. It was too much."

He grasped my hand a little more tightly. "But what about me? I wanted a life with you."

I pulled away. "I know, and I thought I wanted that, too. But we tried and it wasn't enough. I love you, but it's just not enough."

He dropped my hand like a match that had burned to the tip and, in an instant, he was angry. "Nothing's ever enough for you. I tried so fucking hard to make you happy, to make a good life for us, but it was never enough."

"Dylan, it has nothing to do with you—"

"Don't give me that bullshit: it has everything to do with me. I wasn't enough for you. Our life wasn't enough for you. It was like, as soon as we got married, you had one foot out the door. Why do you think I didn't fight it when you said you were leaving?"

"I don't know," I said quietly. I'd wondered that a lot over the past year. For someone who proclaimed to love me so much, he'd sure made it easy for me to leave him.

He smiled sadly. "It's because I was waiting for you to go."

I looked at Dylan's face, and I knew I'd never be able to make up for what I'd done. But I also knew that I needed to do it, and there was no going back now.

I took his hands in mine and looked him in the eyes. "I'm sorry. I'm so, so sorry. You're an amazing man, and you didn't deserve the way I treated you. I hope you find someone who makes you deliriously happy. And I hope she's blond and her boobs are, like, twice as big as mine." I thought for a second. "Not Kelly Leibler, though. Any other big-boobed blond but her."

"Not Kelly Leibler," he said. "Got it." He pulled me in for a hug. "I just hope you find what you're looking for someday," he said into my hair.

With that, he let me go. And when he walked away, he didn't look back.

November 6

When I came down for breakfast, my dad was already in his workshop and my mom was clearing away the detritus from breakfast. She looked up from wiping down the countertop as I came in.

"Morning, Lu. There's still some coffee left if you want it."

"Thanks." I poured myself a mug of coffee and sat down at the kitchen table and watched the birds busily swooping in and out of the feeder in the backyard.

Mom sat down opposite me. "So," she said, "how was last night?"

I was still trying to absorb it myself, so I tried to be as noncommittal as possible. "Okay," I said, turning back to the birds.

"How's Dylan?"

"Good, I guess."

She sighed. "Lauren, work with me here. Please?"

I looked at her. She looked older than she had a year ago. Smaller, somehow. My heart hurt thinking about it. I put my hand over hers. "Sorry, Mom."

"I just wish you'd tell me what happened."

"I don't know what to say. I turned up, we had a drink and he told me that I was a terrible, selfish person. Is that what you want to hear?"

"You are *not* a terrible, selfish person."

"I'm not so sure." I felt the abyss open up in me.

"Lu, I'd be lying if I said I understood every decision you've made over the years. Sometimes I feel like I must have done something wrong to make you want to run so far away from this family. But you are certainly not a terrible person."

"Mom, you didn't do anything wrong! My leaving had nothing to do with you." I couldn't bear the thought of her feeling in any way responsible. "I left because I wanted to see what else was out there for me."

"I know you think we're just a boring couple of old farts, but your father and I have made each other very happy over the years. And Meg and Sue . . . I just want that same happiness for you, that's all. Dylan is such a nice boy."

"You're right, Dylan is a great guy. But I didn't love him, Mom. Not really. And I made him miserable."

"I'm sure that's not true," she said. "You could never make anyone miserable."

"Well, I did."

There was a long pause and Dylan's angry face came rushing back to me. I turned to the birds and tried hard not to cry.

She scooted her chair closer to mine and put her arm around me. "I just want you to be happy, sweetheart."

"I know, Mom. I am happy. I'm happy on my own."

She smiled sadly. "You always were adventurous. Remember when you stuck your finger in that light socket?"

I laughed at the memory. "I was, like, two."

"Blew yourself straight across the room. By the time your father and I got to you, you'd already picked yourself up and were headed back to the socket to do it all again!"

I shook my head. "I've always been a stubborn pain in the ass, huh?"

She pulled me close and kissed the top of my head. "I wouldn't have it any other way."

"I miss you," I whispered.

"I miss you, too, Lu. Every single day. But just because you're far away doesn't mean we love each other any less, right?"

I smiled and leaned in to her. "Right."

"You do whatever you need to do. We'll always be here for you."

"Thanks, Mom." I felt the hole inside me close a little.

November 8

I flew back today, leaving at an ungodly hour of the morning.

Yesterday, I'd said good-bye to my parents in the morning before heading to Meghan's for my last night in Portland. I'd promised them that I'd call more often, and that I'd come back for Christmas in a couple of months, but they still looked unspeakably sad and small when I hauled my suitcase down the stairs.

Sue went to bed early after a long shift, so Meghan and I stayed up way too late getting unfeasibly drunk on boxed red wine. My last memory was us laughing hysterically about the time she fell through the set of our junior high musical revue; when I came to, Sue was shoving a granola bar and a Thermos of black coffee in my hands, Harold running circles around us and barking hysterically while Meg, red-eyed and disheveled, held out my bag.

"Do you think that means he's going to miss me?" I asked, touched by Harold's enthusiasm.

"Nah, he's just scared of men," Meghan said, nodding toward the cabbie waiting in the driveway. "I'm going to miss you, though."

I hugged her tightly. "Me too. I love you."

"I love you." She pulled back and looked at me. "You can always come home, you know. You don't have to make life so hard for yourself."

"I know, but it's what I want," I said, with more confidence than I felt at that moment. "I want to be in London." As soon as I said it, I knew it was true. London felt like home now.

"You are a stubborn piece of work," she said, shaking her head and smiling.

"You know me too well." I turned to Sue. "You look after this one," I said.

"I'll do my best," she said, putting her arm around Meghan. "I promise."

"You better," I said. "I wasn't kidding about Schwarzenegger."

The cabbie honked his horn. I gave Meg and Sue another hug and Harold another scratch. I looked around for Maud, but she was hiding in some remote corner of the house, the excitement of the morning too much for her.

I got in the cab and gave them all a final wave, and from there it was just a short cab drive, Greyhound bus, plane ride and tube journey before I was unlocking the front door of the Old Street flat that evening. I set my bags down and kicked the door shut behind me, heading immediately for the balcony.

As I smoked, I looked out over the courtyard below and, beyond that, at the view of the London skyline. I leaned far out over the railing and craned my neck to see the lights of the Eye in the distance sweeping up in a great arc. I took a long drag and exhaled: I was home. And, this time, I was sure of it.

November 9

I woke up at 6 a.m. with the mother of all jet lags, but I forced myself out of bed and around a mug of instant espresso before lacing my sneakers and heading out for a run. I'd already wasted a third of my month with Rachel Greenwald, MBA, and I needed to be fighting fit to tackle the Program in the remaining weeks.

After five and a half unpleasant miles, I took a bracingly cold shower (one thing I hadn't missed about London was the plumbing) before settling down on the couch with my notebook. I felt a surge of energy: I was back where I needed to be and doing what made me happy.

The first order of business was to develop my "personal brand." I drew three columns down the length of the page and labeled them Physical, Personality and Other, as per Rachel Greenwald's instructions. Under each heading, I listed a load of adjectives and phrases I felt applied to me.

I sat back and looked at my chart. Man, I was one hell of a catch.

The next step was to choose one phrase from each column to create my ultimate "personal brand," the one I'd be sending out to everyone I'd ever met in the hope of getting a date.

I tried out a few combinations. "High alcohol tolerance," "open-minded" and "apparently gives great head" made me sound like I was really into underground sex clubs, while "mildly unkempt," "sardonic" and "enjoys cheese" painted a perhaps too-realistic portrait. I finally settled on "long-legged," "independent" and "American." I thought it made me sound like a sexy flight attendant from the seventies, which should help cover the maximum spread when it came to possible suitors.

Personal brand solidified, I wandered into the kitchen and started rummaging around for something to eat for breakfast. I had found some peanut butter and a piece of stale malt loaf when a note tacked to the cupboard door caught my eye.

> *Welcome home, lovely! Hope you had a fab time in America! Tristan's meeting my parents (eek!) so we're in Surrey for the weekend. Have left you some milk and some choccies! See you soon!*
>   *Lucy xxxxxx*
>   *PS This came for you—what a nutter! Xx*

Taped to the back of her note was a postcard featuring a nearly naked man in a cowboy hat standing in the middle of Times Square. I flipped it over, though I already knew who it was from.

> *Dearest filthiest American (out of what is now a very large pool of experience),*
>   *Still having a marvelous time under the bright lights of this big city, though I do miss my grimy old London and my grimy little Cunningham. Hope you're thinking depraved thoughts about me, as ever.*
>   *Adrian xxxx*

I stuck the postcard on the fridge next to the NYC firefighters and padded back to the living room with Lucy's chocolates. I curled up on the couch and fell promptly asleep.

November 11

My first day back at work was filled with deleting as many emails from my inbox as possible, excitedly discussing Lucy and Tristan's engagement, and avoiding Cathryn's questions about Dylan.

I'd told her about my ill-fated marriage before I'd left and, like Lucy, I think she'd convinced herself that my trip back home was going to end in the happy reunion of two souls instead of the return of a mildly disturbed one. She was understandably disappointed, but I didn't have time to explain the affairs of the heart to her: I had a huge backlog of emails to deal with and a tour group full of nine-year-olds to lead through the exhibition on the human genome project. Before I knew it, it was 7 p.m. Cathryn and I were the only two left in the office, so I took the opportunity to ask her opinion on the holiday cards I'd ordered.

Rachel Greenwald, MBA, being the marketing wiz that she claims to be, thinks the best way to find a man is by direct mail advertising. Specifically, by printing up a load of cards saying you're looking to find someone and sending them out to every person you've ever met. I decided to send out Thanksgiving cards. Not a traditional Hallmark holiday in Britain, admittedly, but Halloween and Arbor Day had already passed.

I called her over to my desk and showed her one of the cards, which involved a photo of my face superimposed onto a turkey and the words "Gobble Gobble!" written above it. Inside, a generic "Happy Thanksgiving" message was followed by a personal appeal:

*This is the year I would like to find someone to have sex with and
I need your help. If you know anyone suitable, please fill out the
enclosed card and return it to me. Thank you!*
   Lauren xx

Cathryn stared at the card. "This year I would like to find
someone to have sex with?" she read. She looked up at me, aghast.
"Have you gone completely mad?"

"Well, according to the book I'm meant to say I'd like to find a
husband, but I've already got a redundant one of those, so I figured
I should be more precise."

"You can't possibly send these out."

"I can, too! C'mon, don't you remember from Marketing 101?
It's direct mail advertising! The most effective advertising there is."

She rolled her eyes. "Maybe in 1983 it was, but not anymore.
And anyway, you're just going to attract a bunch of mad people
with these!"

"Well, that's what I attract already; at least with this I can get
someone else to do the legwork for me."

Over lunch the next day, I signed and addressed cards to every
single person I knew in London—Lucy and Cathryn, obviously, but
also my landlord, cleaner, local liquor store clerk, and everyone I'd
ever been on a date with. I even sent one to the angry bookseller,
imagining with glee the look of disgust on his face when he opened
the card. I briefly considered giving one to my boss, but Cathryn
talked me out of it.

I tucked a few extras in my desk in case inspiration struck and
put the rest in the mailbox when I left work. I wished them luck as
they slipped through the slot: surely *someone* knew a suitable man
for me to sleep with.

November 15

Lucy and I took the day off in order to run around a posh part of London and spend someone else's money. It was GREAT. Don't ever let anyone tell you that having money is a terrible burden, because it's not. It's awesome and it makes life super easy. Rich people only pretend that it's a burden because they don't want poor people getting ideas above their station and staging a Bolshevik-style revolution.

Anyway, Tristan had given Lucy a stack of money so she could buy a fancy dress for the engagement party on Saturday, but she'd been paralyzed by the thought of going into one of those terrifying designer shops on her own, so she left it until the last minute.

When she tearfully confessed that she didn't have a dress and—worse—had been sitting on a pile of unspent cash, I bundled her on to the tube and off to Bond Street we went.

Now, I had zero experience in dealing with scary designer shops. Growing up, my mom bought all of our clothes from a store called "Slightly Irregular," and Meghan and I spent our youth in "GAK" sweatshirts and "Lewi" jeans. Any item of clothing costing more than $20 was considered a travesty, and I've carried this thrifty tradition into my adulthood. Some of my proudest moments have been when people have complimented me on an item of clothing I'm wearing and I've been able to say, "Thanks, it cost three pounds," or "Thanks, I found it in a Dumpster."

Still, I was determined that we wouldn't be cowed by surly shop assistants. And in order to do this, I figured it was best to pretend to be someone else.

"Okay," I said to Lucy, pulling her toward Balmain. "Here's the plan: we're going to pretend to be rich people, so let's choose our identities now. I'm going to be Lucia, an Argentinian soybean heiress with a checkered past. Now, who are you?"

She looked at me skeptically. "Can you do an Argentinian accent?"

"*Sí*, of course!" I said, rolling my "r" with abandon. "Come on, who are you? Maybe a French countess? Or the daughter of a Neapolitan mobster?"

"Lauren, this is bonkers! I can't pretend to be some rich foreigner!"

"Okay, how about a posh Brit? Like, an aristocrat or an Ecclestone or something. Seriously, Luce, it will make it way more fun and way less scary."

She rolled her eyes, but I could tell she was getting into the idea. "Okay," she said, "I'll be Tara Palmer-Tomkinson's niece, Clara."

"Nice. Give me more."

"Um . . ."

"Okay, I'll do it for you. You were once photographed as one of *Tatler*'s 'tweens to watch' but fell from grace after you were caught selling diet pills at Channing School."

"Love it."

"And now you're marrying a sheikh and moving to Dubai."

"Yes!" she said, eyes lighting up.

"And you're going to live in an exact replica of Versailles. We're ready!"

We sailed into Balmain, giving the saleswoman a frosty nod.

I made a beeline for the cocktail dresses, pulling out a little black number. "*Ay! Dios mío!* Clara, you will look so beaooootiful in this dress!"

Lucy took the dress from me and inspected it with impressive disdain. "Darling," she trilled, "this is just too *gauche* for the sheikh!

He is a very elegant man, you know." Her accent was Patsy Kensit meets the queen—I don't think she actually moved her lips once—but it seemed to work. I saw the saleswoman's sharply defined eyebrows raise slightly.

I thrust the dress back on the rack. "*Ay*, I know! He is a very—how do you say?—discerning man! And rich! Very rich!"

Suddenly, the saleswoman appeared at her side, birdlike little arms flapping in her perfectly tailored sleeves. "Can I be of any assistance, ladies?"

"*Ay! Si, por favor!* My friend here, she is marrying a very important man, and she needs a dress for the—how do you say?—engagement party?"

"Lovely," she said, eyes glinting. "I'd be very happy to pull a few things for you. Please do follow me into the dressing room. Could I tempt either of you with a glass of champagne while you wait?"

"That would be divine," Lucy said frostily.

Three hours, five shops and six free glasses of champagne later, Lucy had a gorgeous new Saint Laurent dress, a pair of Nicholas Kirkwood heels and a Prada bag to make grown women weep. We were triumphant (and very drunk) so we went home and ordered a celebratory curry, which we ate while shouting abuse at *I'm a Celebrity* in Lucia's and Clara's accents.

Eventually, the downstairs neighbor started banging on the ceiling with a broomstick, but it was good while it lasted.

November 17

Last night was Lucy's engagement party and it was one hell of an event. Let's put it like this: I'm writing this on the morning after from my bed, I'm still drunk off my tree on extremely expensive champagne, I'm completely covered in glitter and I'm currently pressing a pack of frozen peas to the welt on my ass from where a man in a gimp mask whacked me with a leather-bound table tennis paddle.

But that's not how the evening began.

The party started promptly at seven, when the great and the good of England's wealthy elite poured through the gilded doors of the Garrick. It was a nice-enough party: unending canapés, silent tuxedoed waiters topping everyone's glasses with Krug and Châteauneuf-du-Pape, and polite conversation among landed gentry. Cathryn and Michael were there, thank God, so I spent most of the evening huddled near them, prodding her for gossip about the other guests and avoiding the roaming hands of several distinguished gentlemen. You'd be surprised how handsy some of those old aristocrats can be.

I still had buckets of cards left over from my Victorian days, so I recycled them into Program cards by writing my phone number and personal brand message on the back of all of them (Rachel Greenwald, MBA, being a lot more direct than Mrs. Humphry). I figured I could give them out at the party in the hopes of getting some more suitable candidates. I managed to give a few cards away, mainly to some of the younger partners at Tristan's firm and a few dear old biddies keen to set me up with their grandsons (presumably they thought I was Upper East Side rather than suburban Portland).

Tristan made a very sweet speech about Lucy being the love of his life and keeping him young, and I only clocked a few raised eyebrows and disapproving clucks among the old hens.

And then, at the stroke of eleven, carriages were called and lots of wealthy dowagers and similar posh old people sailed out in a whiff of Penhaligon's and salmon vol-au-vents, and Tristan climbed on top of a table. "And now, ladies and gentlemen," he yelled to the remaining few, "our evening can begin! If you'll please make your way outside, taxis are ready to whisk us away to Vauxhall!"

A cheer went through the crowd and I started to worry slightly. I caught Lucy by the elbow as she tottered past.

"What's going on?" I asked.

"We're going to Toppers!" she said, beaming with pleasure.

"What the hell is Toppers?"

"Uh, it's only London's premier BDSM club! Tristan's rented out the whole place for the night!" She caught the look of horror on my face. "See, I knew you'd go all funny and squeamish if I told you beforehand! But don't worry, love: I've brought you an outfit." She held up a cloth shoulder bag brimming with black PVC. She grabbed my hand and pulled me toward the exit. "Come on, you'll be absolutely *fine*."

And so began the second party. Lucy and I changed in the taxi, taking turns screening each other from the driver's very curious gaze (though why we felt the need to be modest considering where we were headed, I'll never know). First, Lucy peeled off her extremely expensive dress to reveal the corset I'd helped hoist her boobs into earlier and pulled on a pair of custom-made, black patent leather, lace-up, thigh-high boots that made me wince just looking at them.

"You're not going to wear any bottoms?" I asked, looking at her be-pantied ass for all to see.

"No," she said, "and neither are you." Out of the bag she pulled a black playsuit made almost entirely of mesh, except for a few key solid patches, and a pair of lipstick-red spike-heeled ankle boots.

"What the fuck is wrong with you?" I said, aghast. I tried to disentangle the various scraps of material so I could hold it up to myself, but eventually gave up and hurled it at her head. "There is no way I'm wearing that. It's not even structurally sound!"

Lucy plucked the playsuit off of her head and smoothed it out on her lap. She'd managed to make it resemble a wearable garment, though it was still a garment I had no intention of wearing.

She looked at me with her big blue eyes. "But, babe, it's my night! And this is my nicest outfit—apart from the one I'm wearing, of course—and it will totally suit you!" She shoved the playsuit at me. "C'mon, lovely. Please? For me?"

I knew I was beaten. "Fine, fine. But I reserve the right to keep my coat on all night if I want to."

"Deal," she said, scrambling to cover me as I wriggled out of my dress and (eventually, with much huffing and swearing and one brief panic attack when I thought I was trapped) managed to put on the playsuit. Thankfully, there was no full-length mirror in the car, so I couldn't really see what I looked like, but I was definitely surprised to look down and see so very much of myself on display.

"You look fabulous!" Lucy said, gazing at my huddled, crumpled, mesh-strewn form.

"After tonight, we can never speak of this again," I said as I wedged my feet into the ankle boots and hastily wrapped myself up in my coat like an unloved Christmas present.

The cab pulled up outside an old railway arch and Lucy let out a little squeal of glee as she pulled me out the door. "We're here! Come on, let's get you in there and show you off! The boys are going to eat you up!"

"That's what I'm afraid of," I muttered, clutching my coat closed and struggling to remain upright on the cobblestones.

The bouncers greeted Lucy by name and assured her that "Mr. T" was already inside.

"Mr. T?" I said, collapsing in a fit of giggles. "Was the *A-Team* not aired over here?"

Lucy rolled her eyes and dragged me through the heavy red velvet curtains. We walked into a huge, cavernous space lit by bare red light bulbs. Hard house thumped out of the speakers. It was incredibly dark, but through the gloom I could make out forms in various strange and often complicated positions. A man was chained to a plinth in the center of the room and a trio of near-naked women were hitting him with what appeared to be brooms. A man walking another man on a lead strolled by us, stopping to give Lucy a kiss on the cheek.

Tristan was waiting for us in a side room. He was wearing a dog collar and something that looked like a black leather diaper. "Ladies, welcome. I live to serve," he said, gesturing toward a bottle of Dom chilling in an ice bucket and two champagne flutes. And, with that, he got down on his hands and knees. Lucy poured us each a glass, returned the bottle to the ice bucket, placed the ice bucket atop Tristan's bare back and placed her stilettoed foot on the top of his head, pushing it down to the ground.

I heard him mumble, "Thank you," and watched her give him a little prod with her heel.

"No talking," she said to his slumped form. She turned to me. "It's showtime!" she sang as she tried to wrestle my coat off.

I struggled against her. "Leave me alone! I don't want to end up getting whacked with a broom!" But Lucy was stronger than she looked and soon I was standing in the middle of the room in a mesh playsuit, wishing for death.

"Babe, you look hot! Doesn't she look hot, Mr. T?"

A tiny voice rose up from the floor. "Permission to speak?"

"Granted."

Tristan twisted his head around and looked up at me. "You look wonderful! Just like Diana Rigg!"

"That's enough, Tristan," Lucy barked. She turned to me, thigh-high boots glinting dangerously under the lights. "Come on then!" She grabbed my hand and tugged me into the main room. She was definitely in her element here and seemed to dominate the entire room as soon as she walked in. I was impressed, but also a little sad: she'd really moved on from our old life.

At first, I was mortified. I didn't think of myself as a prude (I had a threesome and everything, remember?) but the idea of parading in front of a bunch of sexual deviants wearing only a brief suggestion of clothing was a little beyond my limits. My days of following a prostitute's advice were behind me—I was meant to be a Harvard woman now!

After a few minutes, I started to chill out. "I wear less than this on the beach," I told myself, "and the sun is way less forgiving than a few red lightbulbs." Besides, it rapidly became clear that everyone there had far better things to do than scrutinize me, i.e., get their mother-loving freak on. It was like some crazy sex carnival, with people whacking each other with things and pouring hot things on sensitive parts and getting themselves tied to various objects. I'd never seen so much polyvinyl in my life.

When the first person approached me, I was scared. She was a leggy Amazonian type and was wearing a red pointed bra and cape. She looked like Elizabeth Hurley in *Bedazzled*. I made a mental note to add that movie to my Netflix list while trying to slip away from her grasp unharmed.

But instead of poking me with one of her stilettos, she just pointed to my shoes and said, "Nice boots, doll face."

"Thanks," I said, "they're hers," pointing my thumb at Lucy.

"I should have known," she said, giving Lucy a friendly little goose. "Spill it: where did you get them? Because I need them in my life."

Turns out, everyone in there was just normal, apart from the sex stuff. Sure, a couple of guys tried to tie me to things and one woman accidentally poured hot wax in my hair, but on the whole it was very much like a normal party. I met a pair of accountants who told me all about their trip to the Maldives while one of them spanked the other one with the UK tax manual; an overworked solicitor who professed his love of Chelsea FC through a gimp mask; a stripper-turned-make-up artist wearing a snakeskin catsuit who told me how to contour my cheekbones; and two very sweet gay men who took turns attaching clamps to each other's nipples while telling me about the renovation work on their house in France.

By the end of the night, I'd given out almost all of my cards. They were all so nice and so open: I figured if anyone was going to know a suitable partner, it would be them, though I wrote "No Weird Shit" on the card every time I gave one out, just as a precaution.

I left the party just at the moment the future bride and groom were climbing into the sex swing suspended above the room as the crowd cheered them on.

There are certain things you just don't want to share with a roommate.

November 19

Something has occurred. I am suddenly very popular.

My phone hasn't stopped ringing for the past two days, with various unknown numbers lighting up my screen. Eighteen have left messages, six of which consisted of more than heavy breathing. I've had eight RSVP cards so far, each stating that they know someone perfect for me, and I've had three notes scrawled in dubious hand-writing shoved under my door. Every time I go to the shop, the clerk tries to tell me about his brother-in-law in Malawi who's apparently my soul mate. The plumber came around to fix the toilet and hung about for an hour and a half, eking out his surely cold tea sip by sip until I finally made up a fake appointment to get him out of the flat. After he left, I went to the shop for more cigarettes, only to be ac-costed by the shopkeeper *again*, this time brandishing a photo of a thin, melancholy man sitting atop a pile of gourds.

Apparently everyone knows someone who would like to have sex with me.

In a way, I guess that's heartening. It would be way more mortifying if all of my direct mail marketing had been met with a stony silence. But it was also a little daunting: how the hell was I supposed to choose? I didn't know any of these guys, and it wasn't like online dating, where at least you could see a photo and check if they were literate. With this, I was relying solely on some vague acquaintance's opinion of my attractiveness level and sexual preferences. Yikes.

I sat down and consulted my Program Expansion Grid, which I'd completed earlier in the week. Rachel Greenwald, MBA, thinks I'm being too picky. She thinks I should forget I ever had a type, and just settle for someone who ticks only a couple of boxes. And those boxes should be pretty general, as in, "Is he breathing? TICK! Marry the man, you desperate spinster!" In order to open yourself up to the greatest potential, you have to identify what you consider to be attractive in a man and then broaden that opinion to extend to more men. Ideally all single, living men on the face of the earth.

Anyway, I drew up my Program Expansion Grid (or, as I like to call it, where dreams go to die) on Sunday while still recovering from Lucy's engagement party. Sure, every woman has an image in her head of Prince Charming, but maybe we should be looking for Prince Acceptable instead. For example, my perfect man would be slim and muscular, my slightly less perfect man would have let himself go to seed a little, and Prince Acceptable would be able to find pants that fit him without going to a specialist shop. See? Just like every little girl dreams about.

Taking all this into account, theoretically all of my potential suitors could fit into the net, being male vertebrates. I decided that, in order to really commit myself to the Program, the best course of action would be to date all of them and, in the spirit of Harvard-level industriousness and because I was running out of time this month, I would date all of them on the same day.

I screened out the guys who had left me creepy heavy-breathing messages (they hadn't left their numbers, anyway) and threw out a couple of the RSVP cards because I knew that, despite my clear instructions, the applicants were married and looking to swing.

In the end, I was left with fourteen possibilities. I got out my notebook and set about calling each of them back: the guys who answered the phone would get a date (a very short date, but a date nonetheless). After an hour and a half of at times excruciatingly awkward phone conversations, I had ten dates lined up over ten hours for next Saturday.

Ladies and gentlemen, start your engines.

November 20

Uh, I just got a little *too* popular.

"It's for you," Cathryn said, pointing to the telephone. "I'll transfer the call."

I picked up, expecting it to be one of the caterers for the upcoming corporate sponsors gala. "Lauren Cunningham speaking."

"Hello, Lauren," said a deep male voice. "I'm so glad we've finally connected."

"Me too," I said. It wasn't uncommon for people who I'd never actually spoken to before to phone the office—such is the beauty of the email age. I figured it was one of the geneticists I'd been writing to about the "Forever Young" exhibition we were putting together. I put on my cheeriest phone voice. "How are you?"

"I'm a damn sight better now that I'm talking to you," he said with a laugh. "Now, when can I take you for a drink? Or shall we skip the formalities and go straight to a hotel?"

Uh, this definitely didn't sound like any geneticist I'd ever met. "Excuse me?" I said. "Who is this?"

"Don't play coy with me, you little minx. I know you want me."

Minx? I only allowed a handful of people to call me that, and certainly not in the workplace. "Who is this?" I asked, trying to keep my voice steady.

"You know very well who this is. I must say, I was a bit surprised as you hadn't seemed the type, but I was very glad indeed. Now, how will we sneak around without the boss finding out? Wouldn't want to get the sack for getting *in* the sack, if you know what I mean."

Boss? Oh God. The white heat of panic had fully enveloped me. I channeled my inner Cathryn. "I have to insist that you tell me your name," I said in my most officious voice. "And I don't know what you're talking about, but I can promise you that no one is getting in the sack." Across the desk, Cathryn raised a concerned eyebrow at me and I waved her away.

There was a pause on the end of the line. "This is Charles. Charles Eastwood," he said in a slightly faltering voice. "The accounts director at Grange Petroleum? We met at the museum's summer party?"

I had a vague recollection of a tall, balding man with a paunch. I still had no idea why he was calling me a minx, but I did know that he was in charge of one of our most important corporate sponsors. "Oh," I said. "Yes, of course. But I don't . . ." I let the words drift into the dead air between us.

"You did send me that card, didn't you? I mean, it had your name on it and it came with the conference invitation, so I assumed . . ."

Oh no. I pulled open my desk drawer and saw a slightly diminished pile of Thanksgiving Day cards. I must have accidentally mailed one (God, please let it be only one) to this poor man when I was stuffing the invitation envelopes last week.

"I'm so sorry," I said, whispering into the phone in the hope that Cathryn wouldn't overhear. "I think there's been a terrible mix-up. That card . . . it wasn't meant for you."

"Oh God," he said, now sounding very shaken. "Oh dear. I'm going to be fired, aren't I? Please, whatever you do, don't sue."

"I'm the one who should be apologizing! I'm following this stupid dating guide and—oh, forget it. I can assure you that I won't be suing anyone. I just hope we can be . . . discreet about all this?"

"Consider it forgotten," he said.

Relief washed over me. "Thank you so much!" I said.

"Of course, if you ever change your mind . . . you know, we could still be very discreet. And I do love an American accent."

I let out a high, nervous laugh and Cathryn looked up at me, alarmed. "No!" I babbled. "That's okay! I think we're all set!"

He let out a small sigh. "It was worth a try."

I hung up and put my head in my hands.

"Everything all right?" Cathryn asked, her face a picture of worry. "Not bad news, I hope."

I shook my head. "Just a little misunderstanding. Nothing to worry about."

But I was starting to worry. Sure, Rachel Greenwald, MBA, suggested I give up my job for the project, but I wasn't so keen on getting fired.

November 21

Adrian's back.

I left work this evening to find him standing on the pavement, holding a One Direction pinwheel. I saw him before he saw me, so I had time to compose myself. I lit a cigarette and affected my most nonchalant air.

"Adrian?" I called. "Is that you?"

He turned the full wattage of his smile on me, the black frames of his glasses glinting in the sun. He was wearing a white button-down with a navy-blue knitted tie, trousers rolled up to the ankle to showcase some very yellow socks and a pair of newly shined brown leather oxfords. He looked like he'd fallen out of *Vice*. "It is indeed, Cunningham!" He bowed deeply and held out the pinwheel as I approached. "For my favorite American."

I gave the pinwheel a spin and kissed him on the cheek. "What the hell are you doing here?"

"I'm back!" he announced. "I left New York on Tuesday—for good. It's a lovely town and all, but so overrated. All that hustle and bustle, all that macho bravado . . . all anyone talks about is how amazing New York is! They all act as though it's the center of the bloody universe!"

"Well, I mean, it is one of the major cities in the world . . ."

"I had to get out of there, Cunningham. It was suffocating me. It's good to be back on the shores of Albion, enfolded in the comforting embrace of Mother London. Now, let's get you a drink and you can tell me how desperately you've missed me."

We went to the Hoop & Toy and settled at a table at the back with a couple of pints.

I plucked a chip out of the open packet and popped it in my mouth, studying him intently from across the table. He was the same old Adrian, but there was something different about him. He looked a little smaller, somehow. A little deflated. "Okay, spill it," I said, pushing the chips toward him. "What really happened in New York?"

He waved me away. "I told you, New York is dead! It's an anachronism! A fool's paradise!"

I folded my arms in front of me and narrowed my eyes.

"All right, all right. Jesus, you're like the bloody KGB! There was this little thing about me shagging the intern . . ."

I rolled my eyes. "I knew it."

"It was just a dalliance, but you know how Americans are: so uptight. No fun at all. So I had a little fling with the intern—so what? It was nothing and I can assure you that she enjoyed herself very much—but then some little brown-noser grassed me up to the boss and suddenly it was all 'misconduct in the workplace' and 'constructive dismissal.'" He shrugged his shoulders. "Apparently it was a problem that she was eighteen, though that is technically over the age of consent so I don't see what all the fuss was about." He picked up a coaster and flicked it across the table. "It's all water under the bridge. Now, let's talk about more important things, like what color underwear you're wearing."

I brushed his wandering hand aside. "So what are you going to do now that you're back in London?"

He shrugged and took a long sip from his pint. "Something will turn up, I expect. I've had this screenplay in mind for a while, so I might give that a run. My mate has a pub in Peckham, so I can pick up a few shifts there. You know me, Cunningham: I always land on my feet."

I nodded, but felt a little stab of pity for him. "Where are you staying?"

Adrian slumped down in his chair and started flicking another coaster around the table with his thumb and forefinger. "I'm at the old familial home in Wandsworth for now, but that's only temporary. My mate has a place in Brixton, so I might crash with him for a bit." He flicked the coaster off the table. "Something will turn up." For a minute, he looked like a lost little boy, but he recovered quickly and put on his most charming grin. "Now, enough questions about logistics and finances from you, Cunningham. I want you to tell me, in detail, the last filthy dream you had about me."

I rolled my eyes. Normally, this sort of talk would have rendered me near-unconscious with pent-up sexual energy, but so far I was unmoved. "They all merge into one at some point."

"I'm sure they do, you filthy thing. Now, what are you doing tomorrow?"

"Working," I said, slightly exasperated. "Remember, I've got a job?"

"Not anymore you're not. We're going to spend the day together. I'll plan everything: just leave it to me." He reached out and gave my knee a squeeze. "It'll be a scream."

I considered for a moment. Work was pretty quiet, and that little card mix-up the other day proved that my head wasn't entirely in the game; I could probably do with a day off. But was spending an entire day with Adrian really the respite I needed?

Adrian saw my hesitation and pulled my hand to his lips. "Come along, Cunningham. Be a good sport. I really have missed you."

He looked so earnest in that moment that I almost didn't recognize him. I nodded my head in assent. "Deal. But we'll have to keep clear of South Ken so I don't get caught out."

He kissed my hand again and I felt a little flurry in my stomach. Maybe I wasn't so unmoved after all.

November 22

After I sent the requisite email to work (migraine, didn't sleep, will check emails later if I can), I started the day with Lucy bouncing up and down on my bed, making sweeping proclamations about true love. Obviously, I'd told her about Adrian's return.

"Oh, Lo, this is it! He's come back because he's finally realized that you're meant to be together!" She collapsed on the bed with a sigh. "It's so romantic."

I threw a balled-up pair of socks at her. "He has not. Besides, I thought you hated Adrian! I thought you were convinced that Dylan was my destiny."

She waved away the thought. "No, no, I was all wrong about that. I *did* think Adrian was a bit of a knobber, but that was because he was always disappointing you! But now he's come all the way back from America to tell you that he was a fool before and that he loves you deeply and that he wants to spend the rest of his life with you." She sat up suddenly, eyes widening. "We could have a double wedding!" She lay back down and twisted around on her stomach, propping herself up on her elbows. "No, I want to have my own day. Sorry, babe. But you can get married straight after."

I got out of bed and pulled my yellow robe over the oversized T-shirt I'd slept in. "Lucy, get a grip, will you? He's not back because he realized that he's in love with me, he's back because he fucked a teenage intern and got fired."

She rolled her eyes. "Everything happens for a reason. Anyway, he's back now and the first thing he did was to come and find you, and he's spending the whole day with you! If that's not love, I don't know what is. And now you can stop following all these silly guides and just be with him!"

I flung another pair of socks at her and went off to the shower.

As I applied a conditioning mask to my hair, shaved my overgrown bikini line (there was no time for a wax) and buffed my entire body to a high shine with a fancy salt scrub, I thought about what Lucy had said. It was a little weird that he'd turned up like that. What if New York *had* changed him? What if he'd realized . . .

No. The whole thing was ridiculous. I dried myself off and slipped on the fancy underwear from my *Belle de Jour* month. Lucy caught me agonizing over what to wear as she passed my open bedroom door on her way out.

"See?" she called as she ran out the door. "You think he loves you, too!"

"Fuck off!" I shouted down the hall. The door shut and I turned back to inspecting my wardrobe. Well, it didn't hurt to be prepared.

Adrian turned up at my door at eleven twenty-five, a full hour earlier than he was meant to. I was still in the process of getting ready and my hair was only half-dried. I accepted the lurid-green carnation he'd brought and sat him down on the couch while I finished drying my hair.

"You know, Cunningham," he called from the living room, "this place isn't half bad after all." Adrian had always mocked the Old Street flat (I think he referred to it as a dosshouse on several occasions) so this was a surprise. "I might crash here for a few weeks."

I poked my head around the corner and found Adrian sprawled across the couch and flicking through the channels on the TV. "Uh, I think Lucy might object to that," I said, grabbing my bag and pulling on my coat. "C'mon, let's go."

He didn't budge. "Can't we watch telly for a bit?"

I glanced at the screen and saw Dickinson trying to get a Real Deal out of someone. "What do you want to sit around watching this for?"

He shrugged. "Dunno. Just might be nice to chill out here for a bit."

"Fine," I said, sitting next to him with a huff. I wasn't exactly thrilled with the idea of spending my day off watching terrible daytime television, but it *was* with Adrian—he'd probably start ripping my clothes off soon.

"I'd kill for a cup of tea," he said, looking at me expectantly.

I rolled my eyes and got up. "I'll put the kettle on. Anything else you want while I'm up?"

"Have you got any Jammie Dodger biscuits?" he said, spreading back out across the length of the couch. "That'd be lovely."

And so, for the next seven hours, we sat on the couch together watching property shows and old episodes of *Nash Bridges*. At some point, Adrian ordered a curry, which I had to pay for. ("Sorry, Cunningham, a bit skint at the minute.")

When six o'clock came around, I suggested we go to the pub, but he was reluctant.

"Why go all the way outside when we could just stay in?" he asked, holding out his mug for a refill.

"I don't have any booze in the flat," I pointed out.

He dug around in his pocket and placed a pile of loose change on the table. "I could go to the shop?" he said, though he didn't make any move to get up.

I was desperate for an airing at that point, so I jumped at the chance. "I'll go," I said, grabbing my coat. "What do you want?"

"A bottle of Sancerre would do me nicely," he said, flicking over to *Wipeout*. "And maybe something for tea?"

He finally left at a quarter to midnight. I'd thrown together a spaghetti dinner, which we ate on plates balanced on knees while watching a Cassavetes movie marathon. We finished the two bottles of Sancerre I'd bought at great expense from the wine shop around the corner, and at some point during *She's So Lovely*, Adrian fell asleep and started snoring. When I woke him up and told him I was going to bed, he briefly started fumbling with my bra clasp.

I pushed away from him, suddenly angry. "Do you really think it's that easy? You turn up here, expect me to wait on you hand and foot, do precisely *nothing* that could be construed as attractive or endearing, and then expect me to sleep with you? Who do you think I am, exactly? Am I meant to be your girlfriend? Your mom? Or your little piece of ass?"

He reared back as if he'd been slapped, but quickly arranged his face in what he clearly thought was a charming manner. "Darling," he said, reaching for my hand, "I would never want to put a label on what we have."

I snatched my hand away. "You know what, Adrian? Go fuck yourself." I stood up and handed him his coat. "For some stupid reason, I thought you were actually going to make an effort this time. Why did you send me those postcards? Why did you turn up at my work like that?"

"Because you're my filthy little Cunningham," he said, "and I thought we understood each other."

"No, we don't understand each other. It's pretty clear that we never have."

He reached out and tried to pull me toward him. "Come on, let's not argue."

I pushed him away. "Good-bye, Adrian."

"Don't be a little spoilsport." He made another grab for me.

I opened the door and waved him out. "Get out."

He gave me a withering look as he walked out. "I thought you were cool, Cunningham," he said, shaking his head.

"Out!"

After he left, I went out onto the balcony for a smoke.

I wasn't sure what had changed with Adrian, and why he'd sent me over the edge this time. It was like the man behind the curtain in the *Wizard of Oz*; behind all the smoke and mirrors, he was really just a sad lost soul looking for someone to make him tea and clean up after him. A maid who he could occasionally fuck. I'd spent almost a year chasing an illusion, and now that the illusion had solidified in front of me, the magic had worn off.

I shook my head and took another drag. There was more to it than that. I hadn't really wanted Adrian to declare his undying love to me, because I didn't want to be with him. Not really. Deep down, I'd always known that Adrian was more trouble than he was worth: he was selfish, unreliable, immature . . . He was charming, sure, but he wasn't exactly someone you'd want to be responsible for.

I realized suddenly—and with intense clarity—that I'd fallen victim to that age-old dating guide principle: it's all about the chase. Adrian had, completely obliviously (or at least I assumed as much), been using *The Rules* on me all this time. And *The Game*. And the 1920s guide. Hell, all of them. I'd fallen for it hook, line and sinker. And, it turns out, they were right: there's nothing more attractive than someone who's elusive . . . particularly when that someone is never going to remind you of the quiet, kind man back in Portland whose heart you broke.

I heard Lucy's key in the door and called out to say I was on the balcony. She joined me after a minute, cigarette already in hand.

"So?" she said expectantly. "How did it go? Is it true love?"

"He grossed me out," I said. "We ended up having a huge fight and I made him leave." I explained the details of the day to her while we smoked.

"Ugh, that's the worst," she said, stubbing the butt out on an empty flowerpot. "Sounds like he's a bit of a sad sack now. And no one wants to fuck a sad sack."

Truer words were never spoken.

I turned my focus to next Saturday. Surely *one* of the ten candidates would be decent? At least I hoped that would be the case: I was starting to lose faith in the project again, and I needed something to bolster my belief.

November 28

Adrian left three messages on my mobile today, one asking if I'd seen his sock, one asking if he could come around to mine to watch football next week as his mom wouldn't let him, and one to see if I wanted to get a drink after work. I deleted all three.

It was also Thanksgiving. Obviously I was only home a short time ago, but it's my favorite holiday (as it's about eating ridiculous amounts of food and falling asleep in front of the television) so I was pretty bummed to miss out.

I called Meghan at 3:30 her time, as I figured it would be after the big meal but before the Patriots' kick-off. She sounded sleepy and a little drunk when she picked up: classic turkey coma symptoms. I was so jealous.

"Is everyone playing nicely?" I asked. "Any tears over the mashed potatoes?"

"Harold made a grab for the turkey—which is Cajun-style this year, by the way—but Dad managed to wrangle him away and we only lost a drumstick."

"No one likes those anyway. How's the Cajun turkey going down?"

"Pretty much as well as you'd expect."

"Any other excitement?"

"Mom and Sue got into a long, protracted debate about the merits of second-wave versus third-wave feminism and ended it by arguing who would win in a fight: Betty Friedan or Naomi Wolf."

"Oh, Friedan all the way. She's not fucking around."

"That's what I said! So what's new?"

"Adrian's history."

"Thank fuck that's over—that guy sounded like a jerk. Never forget the wise words of TLC. You definitely don't want any scrubs."

"Amen, sister."

November 30

Today I met a random sample of the world's male population and I've got to be honest: the results were not encouraging for the species. I might be doing my best to follow TLC's advice, but it was proving very difficult to avoid scrubs. It seems they're everywhere.

I had scheduled my ten dates with military precision. Every hour, on the hour, I had to move on to a new location and a new man: there was a brunch, a lunch, three coffees, two dinners and three drinks. It was a Herculean task and, by the end of it, I was a drunk, caffeine-rattled maniac, stuffed to the gills with food and despair.

I can't bear to go into details about each date, because each was more tedious and bizarre than the rest, so I'll just tell you the moment I knew that each one wasn't going to work out.

Brunch with a middle-aged toxicologist: "It's amazing how easy it is to poison someone undetected. I'm surprised more people don't top their spouses with a bit of strychnine in the old morning cuppa."

Lunch with a systems analyst: "When I first saw you, I thought you were my mum. It was a lovely surprise."

Coffee with a cameraman: "Call me old-fashioned, but I think a lady should always be told she's beautiful. Saying 'Show us your tits,' is just another way of saying that."

Coffee with a sweaty man in a too-tight Dungeons and Dragons T-shirt: "My tongue is stuck."

Coffee with a tidy-looking computer software engineer (before taking my outstretched hand on meeting me): "When did you last wash your hands?"

Dinner with an extremely well-dressed businessman: "What I'm always telling the Jewish guy I work with is, say what you like about the Holocaust, it *did* get them to the promised land one way or another, eh?"

Second dinner with an electrical engineer: "Right, so an engineer and a mathematician were locked in their rooms for a day with a can of food but without an opener. At the end of the day, the engineer is sitting on the floor of his room and eating from the open can—he threw it against the walls until it cracked open. In the mathematician's room, the can is still closed but the mathematician has disappeared. There are strange noises coming from inside the can . . . When it's opened, the mathematician crawls out saying, 'Damn! I got a sign wrong . . .'" Several beats pass. "Get it?"

Drink with an underfed milk-float driver (setting a bag down on the table when he arrives and gesturing toward it as he sits down): "Sorry, it's just a few frozen rats for my snake."

Drink with a junior advertising executive wearing a bowler hat: "I mean, culture should just be, like, META, you know? Like, we should just be taking existing archetypes and smashing them up! Like, BAM! You know? . . . Fuck, what were we talking about again?"

Drink with a ponytailed aromatherapist (as he pushed an iPhone filled with photos of Japanese bondage across the table toward me): "I think I could really help you explore your sensual boundaries."

Good Lord. What a ragtag bunch of weirdos and creeps. What did people think of me, sending them my way? Did they really think I was that desperate? Or did they lump me in with the rest of the weirdos and creeps? Fuck: was I a weirdo or a creep? If I had to choose, I guess I'd go for weirdo, but neither category particularly appealed. I'd rather take option three: a nice quiet night in with a vibrator.

To make matters worse, my phone was still ringing constantly and my voicemail was reaching its full capacity, overflowing with messages from mouthbreathers describing increasingly disturbing sexual fantasies. It turns out that I'm only two degrees of separation away from a bunch of very perverted souls. Thankfully, I hadn't had any more callers at work, but it seemed like only a matter of time. I was starting to think I might have to change my number.

I climbed into bed with a glass of whisky as soon as I got through the door, determined to sleep off the memory of the day.

December 1

Thank the Lord above, November is finally over. I spent much of the day nursing my trauma-and-whisky-induced hangover and only started to feel human again after a long run and a hot shower. Oof.

Find a Husband After 35 in Conclusion

This whole book really fucking depressed me: it's all about low-ering your standards, swallowing your pride and rearranging your entire life in the hope that it might snag you a man. The whole thing felt forced and decidedly un-fun. Sure, there was no shortage of prospective partners, but only weirdos and creeps respond to this level of desperation. If this is what it takes to find a partner after a certain age, well—give me spinsterhood any day.

Works best on . . .

Weirdos and creeps. Seriously, if you want to maintain any dignity, avoid this book. If you want to put yourself at serious risk of finding a stalker, be my guest.

To be used by . . .

I wouldn't wish this on anyone, but I guess if you're looking for quantity over quality (and don't mind sacrificing your dignity in the process) this book could be for you.

———

I closed my notebook and lit a cigarette. I felt jaded. Deeply jaded. What exactly was I doing to myself? What was I trying to accomplish by offering my sex life up like a sacrifice on the altar of gurus, misogynists and lunatics?

The whole point of the project had been to find new, interesting, non-psychopathic people to have sex with on the regular, but the results didn't add up. Sure, I managed to meet a few decent guys in the process, but I didn't feel like I was any closer to unlocking the mystery of the male mind, and I definitely wasn't getting laid very often.

I couldn't stomach one more ridiculous piece of advice, one more awkward dinner or one more moment of deflation at the end of an evening. I couldn't stomach the emotional ride anymore: the anticipation on the way up, the hope and excitement during, and then the inevitable plummet back to earth. If going on all these dates and following all this crazy advice wasn't fun anymore, what was the point?

I started the project because I thought I was terrible at dating. Eight months on, I didn't know that I was any wiser about men, but I knew I was fed up trying to mold myself into something or someone I thought they might like. I was a free agent now—and it was time I started living in my own reality, even if the idea of it was still scary as all hell. I didn't need a crutch: it was time to stand on my own two feet.

I stubbed out my cigarette. I'd made a decision.

As of tomorrow, no more dating guides. In fact, no more dating. Instead, I'd do all the things I'd been wanting to do—should have been doing—during the time I spent going on terrible dates. I'd go for long runs, make myself decent dinners, read books I actually wanted to read, focus on building my career, spend evenings in the bath with a bottle of wine and a pack of Marlboro Lights—anything I wanted to do, I'd do.

Fuck this shit: I was going to date myself for a while.

December 2

I woke up this morning full of determination. Time to clear house.

Before I left for work, I got together all of my dating guides and stuck them outside on the curb, where hopefully they'd be used as toilet paper by a tramp.

Lucy was moving in with Tristan in a month, so I had to sort out my living situation. I'd been planning on getting another roommate to replace her, but my newfound burst of independence made me think about finding a studio to rent instead; I'd never lived on my own and it felt like something I should do. I made a few calculations and, if I stopped buying lunch, cycled everywhere and never allowed myself to set foot in Zara again, I could just about afford a shoebox in South Tottenham. I sent a few emails to real estate agents on my lunch break and felt a swell of excitement at the prospect of having my own shitty little bolthole.

I worked late that night, trying to clear the backlog from the past few distracted weeks. When I told Cathryn that I was quitting the project, she looked at me with a mixture of pride and relief that almost alone justified my decision.

By the time I got to the bookstore, I found a drawn shade and a locked door. I checked my watch: three minutes after closing. "Ah, fuck," I muttered to myself. It had begun to drizzle and I was digging around my bag for an umbrella when the shade flew up and the bookseller's face appeared in the window.

"Jesus!" I yelled, leaping back in surprise. He looked at me for a long moment and then held up a finger and started fumbling with the lock. The door opened and he ushered me inside.

I was confused—and a little scared—by this act of kindness, and immediately started apologizing profusely.

"Sorry! Sorry! I know, I always turn up at closing time and you're about to shut and it's really annoying—you don't have to tell me. I promise I'll be super fast!"

I turned to see the bookshop owner still standing by the door, staring at me as if seeing an apparition. "You've come back," he said. He was wearing a white button-down shirt and what appeared to be a completely intact cardigan. I'd forgotten how handsome he was when he wasn't scowling.

"Yep!" I said, charging past him to the literature section.

"I didn't think you'd come back," he muttered.

I couldn't tell if this had been a hope of his or a fear; after all, I was probably helping to keep him afloat with all my guide-buying, even if I did so obviously insult his delicate literary sensibilities and occasionally have emotional breakdowns in the middle of his shop.

"I bet you missed me something terrible, huh?" I said as I searched through the stacks. I glanced back to find he'd turned a slightly pink color. His hair had grown longer and was now curling wildly in pretty much every direction. He looked different, somehow. Happier, maybe.

"How was your trip home? Did you get everything sorted out?"

"Yep, all fine now, thanks. And thanks for . . . uh . . . looking after me. Sorry about that."

"My pleasure," he said. I searched his face for any hint of mockery or sarcasm, but couldn't find any. It was unsettling.

"I got your card," he said with a grin. "Happy belated Thanksgiving to you, too. I would have replied, but my plumber is a big old bugger and I didn't think you'd fancy him." Ah, there was the mockery!

I waved my hands in the air, hoping it would somehow dispel my mortification. "Oh God, that. Yeah, sorry about that. I was following this crazy Harvard business school guide and the author made me do it. Anyway, that's done now, so you can throw it out. Actually, the whole project is done."

He raised his eyebrows. "But what about your devotion to science?"

"I decided that I'm more devoted to myself, so now I'm just doing whatever I want. Speaking of which, I've come with a list: can you help?"

I held out the piece of paper I'd torn from my notebook earlier.

"*Persuasion, Lady Chatterley's Lover, Moll Flanders* . . ." A smile spread across his face as he read out the titles. "Excellent choices." He started rocketing around the store, collecting books from various shelves and balancing them in his arms. When he'd finished, he placed the towering stack on the desk and nodded at it. "That's everything."

I was stunned by his helpfulness, but knew better than to comment. Instead, I walked over to the glass case and pointed at *Black Beauty*. "Any chance you're willing to let this one go yet?" I figured I'd be saving a bundle on dinners, drinks and depilation now that I was dating myself exclusively, so might as well treat myself.

He glanced at the case and shook his head. "Afraid not."

"Ah well," I said, "a girl's got to try. I'll just pay for these and get out of your hair. I read your book, by the way. *The Age of Innocence*."

He kept his eyes focused on the counter as he wrapped my purchases up in brown paper. "Oh, yes?" he said. "And what did you think?"

"I loved it. Ellen is such a great character—so vibrant and full of life."

"I agree," he murmured. "I think she's quite wonderful." He held my gaze for a minute before we both looked away, suddenly embarrassed.

"Well, I should be going. Thanks again!" I grabbed the package of books off the counter and hustled toward the door, hoping he wouldn't notice how furiously I was now blushing.

"I'm glad you came back," he said quietly, following me to the door. He was about to close it behind me when he pulled it back open and stuck his head around. "Don't leave it so long next time."

I smiled. "I won't. I've got plenty of free time now."

I walked toward the tube, clutching my bag of books to my chest and feeling as liberated as a little bird. I had an empty flat that night, a couple of box sets to break in to, a bunch of new books and a fridge full of chocolate mousse and gin. Being unattached definitely had its perks.

December 7

Ah, my first dating-free Saturday. I went for a long run before taking myself to Ironmonger Row for a steam and a sauna. After being pummeled by a large Turkish woman for three-quarters of an hour, I got back to the flat and had a coffee and a slice of cake before cocooning myself in a nest of books and magazines, Ani DiFranco blaring on the stereo. So far, this dating myself thing was amazing.

I was about to make myself another cup of coffee when the doorbell rang. It was a bike courier, holding out a parcel wrapped in brown paper addressed to me. I retreated to the couch to open it. Inside was a first-edition copy of *Black Beauty*. I ran my fingers over the purple embossing, admiring the softness of the brown leather cover beneath my hands. Tucked between the pages was one of my Program RSVP cards, a note scrawled on the back:

Something to add to your reading pile. Xx

Something clicked inside of me. I wanted to run straight out the door, hail a cab and throw myself into his arms, but if there was one thing I'd learned over the past year, it was that it was important not to rush things. The real beauty in life came from savoring the in-between bits, the anticipation and uncertainty and suspense. The important things would wait: this moment was all mine.

I settled down in my couch cocoon and read the book from cover to cover, savoring every word and only pausing to make more coffee or smoke the occasional cigarette. It was just as good as I'd remembered.

It was dark by the time I'd finished. I slipped the book in my bag and set off into the London night.

When I got to the shop, the door was locked but I could see a dim light coming from the back room. I knocked once, softly, and felt the nerves flutter up inside me.

No answer.

I knocked again, louder this time. I knew I could always come back tomorrow, but I was gripped by a sense of urgency. I had to see him.

On the third knock, I heard footsteps, and then the bookseller's face appeared in the window. We smiled shyly at each other through the glass, and then he opened the door.

"Hello," I said.

"Hello."

We stood there for a moment, both on the threshold, neither of us certain where to begin.

"I . . . I wanted to thank you for the book," I said. "It meant a lot to me. I know you were attached to it."

He shook his head. "It shouldn't be kept under glass like that—it should be loved. It belongs with you."

"Well, I promise I'll take good care of it. And you can have visitation rights—we can share partial custody."

He smiled. "I like the sound of that." He paused as if searching for the right words. "I . . . I know this might sound a bit mad, but . . . he reminds me of you."

I was confused. "Him who?"

"The horse," he said. "Black Beauty."

"I remind you of a *horse*?" I said incredulously. This wasn't working out the way I'd planned.

"Sorry, I know that sounds weird, and it probably came out all wrong, but . . . yes. Not just any horse. That *particular* horse."

"Gee, thanks," I said. "I should probably be going now . . ."

"No, wait!" he said, pulling me inside. "It's just—Black Beauty is so full of life, so brave, so . . . so fearless. That's why I always loved the book so much—it represented everything I admired. And you . . ." He placed his hands gently on my arms. "You're it. You're fearless."

"I don't know about that," I said, laughing awkwardly. "I've done some pretty cowardly things in my time."

His eyes locked onto mine and I felt my breath catch in my throat. "I think you're extraordinary," he said. He slid his hands onto my waist and I felt a shiver run through me. "What do you say—how would you like a lifetime supply of free books?" he asked, waggling his eyebrows suggestively.

"Well, when you put it like that . . ." I said, wrapping my arms around him.

And there, among the stacks of dusty old books, he kissed me and the world fell away.

Three Months Later

(Journal forgotten due to sexual bliss)

Name: Callum (i.e., The Angry Bookseller)
Age: 32
Occupation: See above
Nationality: Scottish
Description: Auburn-haired, green-eyed, cardigan-wearing, very
    handsome when he smiles
Method: Rancor, sarcasm and capriciousness
Result: Unmitigated success

AUTHOR'S NOTE

Dear Reader (or person who flips to the back of a book before finishing it, in which case, Hello, Kindred Spirit!),

Far back in the annals of time (2009), I made the decision to turn my love life into a sociological experiment. I can't remember where the idea came from; I just woke up one morning and there it was, lying fully formed on my pillow, waiting for me. Like Lauren, I was fed up with men assuming that I was desperate to settle down and bear their children just because I'd spent a couple of nights in their company, so that certainly influenced my decision to start the project. I'd spent so much time running around London bleating about how noncommittal I was that it was starting to feel like a bit of a . . . commitment. So when the idea of following the experts' advice on dating came to mind, I figured it would be a good way to find out if it was me from which men were fleeing, or just my approach. To make things more interesting (and perhaps to legitimize what might be construed as a sign of mental illness), I decided to write a blog about it, too. I went out and bought my first dating guide (*The Rules*) the next day.

Four months on and four books down, I'd written forty-two posts, gone on twenty-three dates, drank God only knows how many drinks and alienated approximately half of London's single male population. I'd signed up to two different dating sites—Match and My Single Friend, the inspiration for the fictional Castaways and YoDate—and been on several blind or almost-blind setups. I also somehow managed to meet the love of my life. All in all, not a bad way to spend a summer.

But the meeting-the-love-of-my-life thing, while nice, is sort of beside the point. The real objective of my little dating project—and, I hope, this book—was to show that dating can and should be really, really fun. Sure, there are terrible kisses with garlicky men, and moments of crippling shame the mornings after the nights before, but even those bits end up being fun in that slightly manic, gossipy, breathless way. Dating is surely one of the weirdest human behaviors we engage in—two relative strangers spending a few hours together in order to determine whether or not they want to see each other naked—so we might as well have fun while doing it.

Anyway, all of this is a long-winded way of saying that I hope you enjoyed the book, and I hope it inspires you to go out there and be brave in the big bad dating world. And, as I'd wished for myself and for Lauren, I hope you get to have lots of sex with attractive, non-psychopathic men while doing it. If you happen to meet the love of your life along the way, even better.

Melissa x

ACKNOWLEDGMENTS

I would never have even attempted to write a book if it wasn't for the patience and encouragement of my editor at Penguin UK, Hana Osman, so she gets the top billing—Hana, I can't thank you enough for taking me out for that pint all those years ago. Sorry it took me so long. Enormous thanks to the incredible Felicity Blunt, who I've long been proud to call a friend and am now equally proud to call my agent, and to my wonderful U.S. editor, Tara Singh Carlson, whose insight and energy have been truly remarkable. Thanks to everyone at Penguin (on both sides of the Atlantic), with special thanks to the translation rights team led by Chantel Noel: you guys are awesome. Thanks to my foreign editors, particularly Andrea Best at Goldmann Verlag and Quezia Ceto at Companhia das Letras.

An unfillable debt of gratitude to Katie Cunningham, who fielded countless panicked emails and read countless half-formed sentences and never once lost her patience (or at least hid it well), and who has also been the best friend a girl could ever ask for these twenty-two years: I'd be lost without you. Endless thanks to Simon Robertson, who put up with lots of furrowed brows in the pub and weekends of me staring at my computer screen or into the middle distance: you make me feel lucky every day and I love you a stupid amount. Thanks, too, to Carly Peters, my partner in crime and exercise, who has supported and at times enabled my lunacy from the very beginning. Thanks to everyone at Curtis Brown, a lovely place to work and an even lovelier place to be represented by, with particular thanks to my office-mate Helen Manders, who answered lots of hypothetical questions about a book she hadn't read and always offered excellent advice, and to Emma Herdman, for her help and good cheer.

Mom and Dad, I know this book has probably mortified you (sorry about that) but your constant love and support has been the making of me, and I can never say thank you enough. Chad and Meighan, I love you both and trust that you will ensure that my two favorite girls will never be allowed to read this book, at least not until I'm dead. To the lovely Robertson clan, thank you for being the best second family I could have imagined. And to both the Pimentels and the Robertsons: remember, it's heavily fictionalized.

BIBLIOGRAPHY

Duvall, Evelyn Millis. *The Art of Dating*. New York, NY: Association, 1958.

Fein, Ellen, and Sherrie Schneider. *The Rules: Time-tested Secrets for Capturing the Heart of Mr. Right*. New York, NY: Warner, 1995.

Greenwald, Rachel. *Find a Husband After 35 (Using What I Learned at Harvard Business School): A Simple 15-step Action Program*. New York, NY: Ballantine, 2003.

Humphry, C. E. *Manners for Women*. 1897. Whitstable, UK: Pryor Publications, 1993.

Jour, Belle de. *Belle de Jour's Guide to Men*. London, UK: Orion, 2009.

Moore, Doris Langley, and Norrie Epstein. *The Technique of the Love Affair*. 1928. New York, NY: Pantheon, 1999.

Strauss, Neil. *The Rules of the Game: The Stylelife Challenges and the Style Diaries*. Edinburgh, Scotland: Canongate, 2007.

Taylor, Kate. *Not Tonight, Mr. Right: Why Good Men Come to Girls Who Wait*. London, UK: Michael Joseph, 2007.